IN OR OUT . . .

Libby entered the control room. "What happened?"

Lazarus said regretfully, "Had to vector, Andy."

"Yes, I know. But why?" Libby was already strapping himself against the copilot's couch while studying the astrogational situation.

"Red lights on the screen." Lazarus described the display, giving coordinates and relative vectors.

Libby nodded thoughtfully. "Naval craft. No commercial vessels would be in such trajectories. A minelaying bracket." Libby looked worried. "I thought we were free of any possible Naval interference."

"They're not ours," put in Slayton Ford. They must be Venerian craft."

Libby was hardly listening. He was examining data and processing it through the calculator inside his skull. "Lazarus . . . this new orbit isn't too good."

"I know," Lazarus agreed. "I had to duck in the only direction they left open to me—closer to the Sun."

"Too close, perhaps."

It was hot in the control room. On the great stellarium screen an enormous circle of blackness marked where the Sun's disc should have been; the receptors had cut out automatically at such a ridiculous demand.

"It looks to me, son, about time to try out your gadget." He poked a thumb at Libby's "space drive."

"Of course I don't really know that it will work," Libby admitted. "There is no way to test it. But if my hypotheses are correct, we will recede from the Sun at a speed just under that of light.

Lazarus eyed the gadget and wiped sweat from his shoulders. "It's getting hotter, Andy. Hook it up."

BAEN BOOKS by ROBERT A. HEINLEIN

REVOLT IN 2100

&

METHUSELAH'S CHILDREN

Robert A. HEINLEIN

BAEN

REVOLT IN 2100 & METHUSELAH'S CHILDREN

A Baen Book.

Baen Publishing Enterprises
P.O. Box 1403
Riverdale, NY 10471

ISBN: 0-671-57780-8

Cover art by Patrick Turner

First printing, January 1999

Distributed by Simon & Schuster
1230 Avenue of the Americas
New York, NY 10020

Typeset by Windhaven Press, Auburn, NH
Printed in the United States of America

Contents

The Heinlein

Note: stories in brackets never written. See Postscript to *Revolt in 2100*.

DATES STORIES	CHARACTERS		TECHNICAL
A.D.			
Life Line	Pinero		
"Let There Be Light"	Martin	Blekinsop	
[Word Edgewise]	Douglas		
The Roads Must Roll			
Blowups Happen			
The Man Who Sold the Moon			
Delilah & the Space Rigger	Wingate	King / Lentz / Harriman	
Space Jockey			
Requiem	Rhysling / Gaines	Harper / Erickson	
The Long Watch			
Gentlemen, Be Seated	Sam Jones / Satchel	McIntyre / Cummings	Mechanized roads
The Black Pits of Luna—			Douglas-Martin sun-power screens
It's Great To Be Back		Nehemiah Scudder	
"—We Also Walk Dogs"			
Searchlight			
2000			
Ordeal in Space			Commercial rocket travel
The Green Hills of Earth			Helicopters
[Fire Down Below]		Lazarus Long	Interplanetary travel
Logic of Empire			
The Menace from Earth			
[The Sound of His Wings]	Novak	Master Peter	
[Eclipse]			Hiatus
[The Stone Pillow]	Zeb Jones		
"If This Goes On—"			
Coventry			
2100			
Misfit	John Lyle		resumed
Universe (prologue only)		Ford / Magelene / MacKinnon / "Fader" Randall / Persephone / "The Doctor" / Libby / McCoy / Rhodes / Doyle	Developments in psychometrics and psychodynamics
Methuselah's Children			
Universe			Limited use of telepathy
Commonsense			
[Da Capo]			

Timeline

	DATA	SOCIOLOGICAL	REMARKS
Growth of submolar mechanics, atomic cont., artificial radioactives - Uranium 235 - Static submolar engineering	Transatlantic rocket flight Antipodes rocker service	THE "CRAZY YEARS" Strike of '76 The "FALSE DAWN" First rocket to the moon	Considerable technical advance during this period, accompanied by a gradual deterioration of mores, orientation and social institutions, terminating in mass psychoses in the sixth decade, and the Interregnum.
	Bacteriophage	Luna City founded Space Precautionary Act Harriman's Lunar Corporations PERIOD OF IMPERIAL EXPLORATION Revolution in Little America Interplanetary exploration and exploitation American–Australasian anschluss	The Interregnum was followed by a period of reconstruction in which the Voorhis financial proposals gave a temporary economic stability and chance for re-orientation. This was ended by the opening of new frontiers and a return to nineteenth-century economy. Three revolutions ended the period of interplanetary imperialism: Antarctica, U.S., and Venus. Space travel ceased until 2072. Little research and only minor technical advances during this period. Extreme puritanism.
	The Travel Unit and the Fighting Unit Commercial stereoptics Booster guns Synthetic foods Weather control Wave mechanics The "Barrier"	Rise of religious fanaticism The "New Crusade" Rebellion and independence of Venusian colonists Religous dictatorship in U.S. THE FIRST HUMAN CIVILIZATION	Certain aspects of psychodynamics and psychometrics, mass psychology and social control developed by the priest class. Re-establishment of civil liberty. Renaissance of scientific research. Resumption of space travel. Luna city refounded. Science of social relations, based on the negative statements of semantics. Rigor of epistemology. The Covenant.
	Atomic "tailoring" Elements 98–416 Parastatic engineering Rigor of colloids Symbiotic research Longevity		Beginning of the consolidation of the Solar System. First attempt at interstellar exploration. Civil disorder, followed by the end of human adolescence, and beginning of first mature culture.

Revolt In 2100

For Stan and Sophia Mullen

The Innocent Eye:
An Introduction

ROBERT A. HEINLEIN is probably the best story-teller in the science-fiction field today. If I were backed into a corner and forced to tell why in one sentence, I'd say, "Heinlein's got a sense of proportion." Well, how does one get a sense of proportion? By experience, I think. And there is only one kind of experience that counts as necessary to a competent writer: experience of mankind.

Literary and scientific techniques are very useful to a writer, but I don't think the study of them is necessary. They are intellectual concepts. Man is also an emotional animal. And a good story must be about man—not man after a lobotomy, but about the irrational part of him as well as the rational. Sentimentality is no substitute; it degrades man instead of treating him with the respect that, God knows, he deserves. Unfortunately, too many science-fiction stories might have been written by robots or spirits.

Now Heinlein does something that is vitally necessary to good writing: he perceives people. He knows how they feel. He has felt that way himself. He has even bridged

*the difficult gap of realizing that people feel much the
same way everywhere, allowing for constitutional differences.*

He has accepted membership in the human race.

*I don't think you can be a good writer unless you
do that. I'm biased, I know; I like good writing, and I
have a great deal of respect for it. Good writing is well
proportioned. Basically, it treats a man in his environment, and both of those elements must have verisimilitude. That's where Heinlein's sense of proportion comes
in. He's eclectic. He follows the principles but not the
rules. His stories have verisimilitude because they are
about people, and he uses other materials only insofar
as they affect those people. And here is the precise point
where his sense of proportion appears. The story-ele-
ments he uses, technological, sociological, psychological,
are chosen according to their natural relation to the
center of interest: man. These elements are symbolic of
man's values. But it is man, realistically handled, who
is the nucleus of each Heinlein story.*

*If I had to pin a label on Heinlein, I'd call him a
romantic humanist. He deals with the relation of man
to science. His attitude to science is to my mind a
rational one: neither idolatry nor panic, and this may
be because he knows something of the social sciences,
the link between man and machine.*

*Man as a dynamic part of a dynamic society is a con-
cept rarely treated in science-fiction. Large faceless
masses surge in the background, in an outrageously
homogeneous fashion, and against this scene unquali-
fied protagonists perform incredible and unmotivated
deeds, through logical processes slightly beyond the
utmost bound of human thought. No society has ever
been homogeneous, even in Sparta. There will always
be Coventries. Heinlein knows this, and is perhaps the
only science-fiction writer who has seen the real purpose of creating a temporal frame for stories which by
definition deal with the movement of man and society*

through time. The use of this method of dynamic continuity is one of Heinlein's major contributions to the field of science-fiction.

Imaginative literature ideally reflects and interprets reality. Future "realities" have often been handled by means of what is actually symbolism. That is, of course, one way to do it. It is not the only way; an integrated mirror of a future reality which can be accepted as three-dimensional rather than as a background of "flats" may be achieved by Heinlein's method of dynamic continuity. Once that is achieved, the writer is free to tell a story about the values of men and women which is significant to the men and women who read the story. Since the future societies which Heinlein postulates are workable societies, he can concentrate upon the important problems of human beings in relation to their culture. Those problems may affect the society, but their importance rests in how they affect the individual. And Heinlein understands that the personality is as complex as the society. The same man who wrote Coventry wrote They.

All this, however, does not entirely explain why Heinlein is such an excellent story-teller. C. L. Moore calls Heinlein's work the result of "the innocent eye and the sophisticated mind," which seems to me an accurate analysis. The term, "a sense of wonder," has been too often profaned for me to profane it, but I will go so far as to say that nobody who knows Heinlein could call him blasé. Since I have known him, his attitude has always been, "If this goes on—." And from that, it's only a step to "Once upon a time—."

Henry Kuttner
Los Angeles, California

"If This Goes On—"

1

It was cold on the rampart. I slapped my numbed hands together, then stopped hastily for fear of disturbing the Prophet. My post that night was just outside his personal apartments—a post that I had won by taking more than usual care to be neat and smart at guard mount . . . but I had no wish to call attention to myself now.

I was young then and not too bright—a legate fresh out of West Point, and a guardsman in the Angels of the Lord, the personal guard of the Prophet Incarnate. At birth my mother had consecrated me to the Church and at eighteen my Uncle Absolom, a senior lay censor, had prayed an appointment to the Military Academy for me from the Council of Elders.

West Point had suited me. Oh, I had joined in the usual griping among classmates, the almost ritualistic complaining common to all military life, but truthfully I enjoyed the monastic routine—up at five, two hours of prayers and meditation, then classes and lectures in the endless subjects of a military education, strategy and tactics, theology, mob psychology, basic miracles. In the afternoons we practiced with vortex guns and blasters, drilled with tanks, and hardened our bodies with exercise.

I did not stand very high on graduation and had not really expected to be assigned to the Angels of the Lord, even though I had put in for it. But I had always gotten top marks in piety and stood well enough in most of the practical subjects; I was chosen. It made me almost sinfully proud—the holiest regiment of the Prophet's hosts, even the privates of which were commissioned officers and whose Colonel-in-Chief was the Prophet's Sword Triumphant, marshal of all the hosts. The day I was invested in the shining buckler and spear worn only by the Angels I vowed to petition to study for the priesthood as soon as promotion to captain made me eligible.

But this night, months later, though my buckler was still shining bright, there was a spot of tarnish in my heart. Somehow, life at New Jerusalem was not as I had imagined it while at West Point. The Palace and Temple were shot through with intrigue and politics; priests and deacons, ministers of state, and Palace functionaries all seemed engaged in a scramble for power and favor at the hand of the Prophet. Even the officers of my own corps seemed corrupted by it. Our proud motto *"Non Sibi, Sed Dei"* now had a wry flavor in my mouth.

Not that I was without sin myself. While I had not joined in the struggle for worldly preference, I had done something which I knew in my heart to be worse: I had looked with longing on a consecrated female.

Please understand me better than I understood myself. I was a grown man in body, an infant in experience. My own mother was the only woman I had ever known well. As a kid in junior seminary before going to the Point I was almost afraid of girls; my interests were divided between my lessons, my mother, and our parish's troop of Cherubim, in which I was a patrol leader and an assiduous winner of merit badges in everything from woodcraft to memorizing scripture. If there had been a merit badge to be won in the subject of girls—but of course there was not.

At the Military Academy I simply saw no females, nor did I have much to confess in the way of evil thoughts. My human feelings were pretty much still in freeze, and my occasional uneasy dreams I regarded as temptations sent by Old Nick. But New Jerusalem is not West Point and the Angels were neither forbidden to marry nor were we forbidden proper and sedate association with women. True, most of my fellows did not ask permission to marry, as it would have meant transferring to one of the regular regiments and many of them cherished ambitions for the military priesthood—but it was not forbidden.

Nor were the lay deaconesses who kept house around the Temple and the Palace forbidden to marry. But most of them were dowdy old creatures who reminded me of my aunts, hardly subjects for romantic thoughts. I used to chat with them occasionally around the corridors, no harm in that. Nor was I attracted especially by any of the few younger sisters—until I met Sister Judith.

I had been on watch in this very spot more than a month earlier. It was the first time I had stood guard outside the Prophet's apartments and, while I was nervous when first posted, at that moment I had been no more than alert against the possibility of the warden-of-the-watch making his rounds.

That night a light had shone briefly far down the inner corridor opposite my post and I had heard a sound of people moving; I had glanced at my wrist chrono— yes, that would be the Virgins ministering to the Prophet . . . no business of mine. Each night at ten o'clock their watch changed—their "guard mount" I called it, though I had never seen the ceremony and never would. All that I actually knew about it was that those coming on duty for the next twenty-four hours drew lots at that time for the privilege of personal attendance in the sacred presence of the Prophet Incarnate.

I had listened briefly and had turned away. Perhaps a quarter of an hour later a slight form engulfed in a dark cloak had slipped past me to the parapet, there to stand and look at the stars. I had had my blaster out at once, then had returned it sheepishly, seeing that it was a deaconess.

I had assumed that she was a lay deaconess; I swear that it did not occur to me that she might be a holy deaconess. There was no rule in my order book telling me to forbid them to come outside, but I had never heard of one doing so.

I do not think that she had seen me before I spoke to her. "Peace be unto you, sister."

She had jumped and suppressed a squeal, then had gathered her dignity to answer, "And to you, *little brother.*"

It was then that I had seen on her forehead the Seal of Solomon, the mark of the personal family of the Prophet. "Your pardon, Elder Sister. I did not see."

"I am not annoyed." It had seemed to me that she invited conversation. I knew that it was not proper for us to converse privately; her mortal being was dedicated to the Prophet just as her soul was the Lord's, but I was young and lonely—and she was young and very pretty.

"Do you attend the Holy One this night, Elder Sister?"

She had shaken her head at that. "No, the honor passed me by. My lot was not drawn."

"It must be a great and wonderful privilege to serve him directly."

"No doubt, though I cannot say of my own knowledge. My lot has never yet been drawn." She had added impulsively, "I'm a little nervous about it. You see, I haven't been here long."

Even though she was my senior in rank, her display of feminine weakness had touched me. "I am sure that you will deport yourself with credit."

"Thank you."

We had gone on chatting. She had been in New Jerusalem, it developed, even less time than had I. She had been reared on a farm in upper New York State and there she had been sealed to the Prophet at the Albany Seminary. In turn I had told her that I had been born in the middle west, not fifty miles from the Well of Truth, where the First Prophet was incarnated. I then told her that my name was John Lyle and she had answered that she was called Sister Judith.

I had forgotten all about the warden-of-the-watch and his pesky rounds and was ready to chat all night, when my chrono had chimed the quarter hour. "Oh, dear!" Sister Judith had exclaimed. "I should have gone straight back to my cell." She had started to hurry away, then had checked herself. "You wouldn't tell on me. . . . John Lyle?"

"Me? Oh, never!"

I had continued to think about her the rest of the watch. When the warden did make rounds I was a shade less than alert.

A mighty little on which to found a course of folly, eh? A single drink is a great amount to a teetotaler; I was not able to get Sister Judith out of my mind. In the month that followed I saw her half a dozen times. Once I passed her on an escalator; she was going down as I was going up. We did not even speak, but she had recognized me and smiled. I rode that escalator all night that night in my dreams, but I could never get off and speak to her. The other encounters were just as trivial. Another time I heard her voice call out to me quietly, "Hello, John Lyle," and I turned just in time to see a hooded figure go past my elbow through a door. Once I watched her feeding the swans in the moat; I did not dare approach her but I think that she saw me.

The *Temple Herald* printed the duty lists of both my

service and hers. I was standing a watch in five; the Virgins drew lots once a week. So it was just over a month later that our watches again matched. I saw her name—and vowed that I would win the guard mount that evening and again be posted at the post of honor before the Prophet's own apartments. I had no reason to think that Judith would seek me out on the rampart—but I was sure in my heart that she would. Never at West Point had I ever expended more spit-and-polish; I could have used my buckler for a shaving mirror.

But here it was nearly half past ten and no sign of Judith, although I had heard the Virgins gather down the corridor promptly at ten. All I had to show for my efforts was the poor privilege of standing watch at the coldest post in the Palace.

Probably, I thought glumly, she comes out to flirt with the guardsmen on watch everytime she has a chance. I recalled bitterly that all women were vessels of iniquity and had always been so since the Fall of Man. Who was I to think that she had singled me out for special friendship? She had probably considered the night too cold to bother.

I heard a footstep and my heart leaped with joy. But it was only the warden making his rounds. I brought my pistol to the ready and challenged him; his voice came back, "Watchman, what of the night?"

I answered mechanically, "Peace on Earth," and added, "It is cold, Elder Brother."

"Autumn in the air," he agreed. "Chilly even in the Temple." He passed on by with his pistol and his bandolier of paralysis bombs slapping his armor to his steps. He was a nice old duffer and usually stopped for a few friendly words; tonight he was probably eager to get back to the warmth of the guardroom. I went back to my sour thoughts.

"Good evening, John Lyle."

I almost jumped out of my boots. Standing in the darkness just inside the archway was Sister Judith. I managed to splutter, "Good evening, Sister Judith," as she moved toward me.

"Sssh!" she cautioned me. "Someone might hear us. John . . . John Lyle—it finally happened. My lot was drawn!"

I said, "Huh?" then added lamely, "Felicitations, Elder Sister. May God make his face to shine on your holy service."

"Yes, yes, thanks," she answered quickly, "but John . . . I had intended to steal a few moments to chat with you. Now I can't—I must be at the robing room for indoctrination and prayer almost at once. I must run."

"You'd better hurry," I agreed. I was disappointed that she could not stay, happy for her that she was honored, and exultant that she had not forgotten me. "God go with you."

"But I just had to tell you that I had been chosen." Her eyes were shining with what I took to be holy joy; her next words startled me. "I'm scared, John Lyle."

"Eh? Frightened?" I suddenly recalled how I had felt, how my voice had cracked, the first time I ever drilled a platoon. "Do not be. You will be sustained."

"Oh, I hope so! Pray for me, John." And she was gone, lost in the dark corridor.

I did pray for her and I tried to imagine where she was, what she was doing. But since I knew as little about what went on inside the Prophet's private chambers as a cow knows about courts-martial, I soon gave it up and simply thought about Judith. Later, an hour or more, my revery was broken by a high scream inside the Palace, followed by a commotion, and running footsteps. I dashed down the inner corridor and found a knot of women gathered around the portal to the Prophet's apartments. Two or three others were carrying someone out the portal; they stopped when they reached the corridor and eased their burden to the floor.

"What's the trouble?" I demanded and drew my side arm clear.

An elderly Sister stepped in front of me. "It is nothing. Return to your post, legate."

"I heard a scream."

"No business of yours. One of the Sisters fainted when the Holy One required service of her."

"Who was it?"

"You are rather nosy, little brother." She shrugged. "Sister Judith, if it matters."

I did not stop to think but snapped, "Let me help her!" and started forward. She barred my way.

"Are you out of your mind? Her sisters will return her to her cell. Since when do the Angels minister to nervous Virgins?"

I could easily have pushed her aside with one finger, but she was right. I backed down and went unwillingly back to my post.

For the next few days I could not get Sister Judith out of my mind. Off watch, I prowled the parts of the Palace I was free to visit, hoping to catch sight of her. She might be ill, or she might be confined to her cell for what must certainly have been a major breach of discipline. But I never saw her.

My roommate, Zebadiah Jones, noticed my moodiness and tried to rouse me out of it. Zeb was three classes senior to me and I had been one of his plebes at the Point; now he was my closest friend and my only confidant. "Johnnie old son, you look like a corpse at your own wake. What's eating on you?"

"Huh? Nothing at all. Touch of indigestion, maybe."

"So? Come on, let's go for a walk. The air will do you good."

I let him herd me outside. He said nothing but banalities until we were on the broad terrace surrounding the south turret and free of the danger of eye and ear devices. When we were well away from anyone else he said softly, "Come on. Spill it."

"Shucks, Zeb, I can't burden anybody else with it."

"Why not? What's a friend for?"

"Uh, you'd be shocked."

"I doubt it. The last time I was shocked was when I drew four of a kind to an ace kicker. It restored my faith in miracles and I've been relatively immune ever since. Come on—we'll call this a privileged communication—elder adviser and all that sort of rot."

I let him persuade me. To my surprise Zeb was not shocked to find that I let myself become interested in a holy deaconess. So I told him the whole story and added to it my doubts and troubles, the misgivings that had been growing in me since the day I reported for duty at New Jerusalem.

He nodded casually. "I can see how it would affect you that way, knowing you. See here, you haven't admitted any of this at confession, have you?"

"No," I admitted with embarrassment.

"Then don't. Nurse your own fox. Major Bagby is broadminded, you wouldn't shock him—but he might find it necessary to pass it on to his superiors. You wouldn't want to face Inquisition even if you were alabaster innocent. In fact, especially since you are innocent—and you *are*, you know; everybody has impious thoughts at times. But the Inquisitor expects to find sin; if he doesn't find it, he keeps on digging."

At the suggestion that I might be put to the Question my stomach almost turned over. I tried not to show it for Zeb went on calmly, "Johnnie my lad, I admire your piety and your innocence, but I don't envy it. Sometimes too much piety is more of a handicap than too little. You find yourself shocked at the idea that it takes politics as well as psalm singing to run a big country. Now take me; I noticed the same things when I was new here, but I hadn't expected anything different and wasn't shocked."

"But—" I shut up. His remarks sounded painfully like heresy; I changed the subject. "Zeb, what do you suppose it could have been that upset Judith so and caused her to faint the night she served the Prophet?"

"Eh? How should I know?" He glanced at me and looked away.

"Well, I just thought you might. You generally have all the gossip around the Palace."

"Well . . . oh, forget it, old son. It's really not important."

"Then you *do* know?"

"I didn't say that. Maybe I could make a close guess, but you don't want guesses. So forget it."

I stopped strolling, stepped in front of him and faced him. "Zeb, anything you know about it—or can guess—I want to hear. It's important to me."

"Easy now! You were afraid of shocking me; it could be that I don't want to shock you."

"What do you mean? Tell me!"

"Easy, I said. We're out strolling, remember, without a care in the world, talking about our butterfly collections and wondering if we'll have stewed beef again for dinner tonight."

Still fuming, I let him take me along with him. He went on more quietly, "John, you obviously aren't the type to learn things just by keeping your ear to the ground—and you've not yet studied any of the Inner Mysteries, now have you?"

"You know I haven't. The psych classification officer hasn't cleared me for the course. I don't know why."

"I should have let you read some of the installments while I was boning it. No, that was before you graduated. Too bad, for they explain things in much more delicate language than I know how to use—and justify every bit of it thoroughly, if you care for the dialectics of religious theory. John, what is your notion of the duties of the Virgins?"

Why, they wait on him, and cook his food, and so forth."

"They surely do. And so forth. This Sister Judith—an innocent little country girl the way you describe her. Pretty devout, do you think?"

I answered somewhat stiffly that her devoutness had first attracted me to her. Perhaps I believed it.

"Well, it could be that she simply became shocked at overhearing a rather worldly and cynical discussion between the Holy One and, oh, say the High Bursar—taxes and tithes and the best way to squeeze them out of the peasants. It might be something like that, although the scribe for such a conference would hardly be a grass-green Virgin on her first service. No, it was almost certainly the 'And so forth.'"

"Huh? I don't follow you."

Zeb sighed. "You really are one of God's innocents, aren't you? Holy Name, I thought you knew and were just too stubbornly straight-laced to admit it. Why, even the Angels carry on with the Virgins at times, after the Prophet is through with them. Not to mention the priests and the deacons. I remember a time when—" He broke off suddenly, catching sight of my face. "Wipe that look off your face! Do you want somebody to notice us?"

I tried to do so, with terrible thoughts jangling around inside my head. Zeb went on quietly, "It's my guess, if it matters that much to you, that your friend Judith still merits the title 'Virgin' in the purely physical sense as well as the spiritual. She might even stay that way, if the Holy One is as angry with her as he probably was. She is probably as dense as you are and failed to understand the symbolic explanations given her—then blew her top when it came to the point where she couldn't fail to understand, so he kicked her out. Small wonder!"

I stopped again, muttering to myself biblical expressions I hardly thought I knew. Zeb stopped, too, and stood looking at me with a smile of cynical tolerance "Zeb," I said, almost pleading with him, "these are terrible things. Terrible! Don't tell me that you approve?"

"Approve? Man, it's all part of the Plan. I'm sorry you haven't been cleared for higher study. See here, I'll give you a rough briefing. God wastes not. Right?"

"That's sound doctrine."

"God requires nothing of man beyond his strength. Right?"

"Yes, but—"

"Shut up. God commands man to be fruitful. The Prophet Incarnate, being especially holy, is required to be especially fruitful. That's the gist of it; you can pick up the fine points when you study it. In the meantime, if the Prophet can humble himself to the flesh in order to do his plain duty, who are you to raise a ruction? Answer me that."

I could not answer, of course, and we continued our walk in silence. I had to admit the logic of what he had said and that the conclusions were built up from the revealed doctrines. The trouble was that I wanted to eject the conclusions, throw them up as if they had been something poisonous I had swallowed. Presently I was consoling myself with the thought that Zeb felt sure that Judith had not been harmed. I began to feel better, telling myself that Zeb was right, that it was not my place, most decidedly not my place, to sit in moral judgment on the Holy Prophet Incarnate.

My mind was just getting around to worrying the thought that my relief over Judith arose solely from the fact that I had looked on her sinfully, that there could not possibly be one rule for one holy deaconess, another rule for all the rest, and I was beginning to be unhappy again—when Zeb stopped suddenly. "What was that?"

We hurried to the parapet of the terrace and looked down the wall. The south wall lies close to the city proper. A crowd of fifty or sixty people was charging up the slope that led to the Palace walls. Ahead of them, running with head averted, was a man dressed in a long gabardine. He was headed for the Sanctuary gate.

Zebediah looked down and answered himself. "That's what the racket is—some of the rabble stoning a pariah. He probably was careless enough to be caught outside the ghetto after five." He stared down and shook his head. "I don't think he is going to make it."

Zeb's prediction was realized at once; a large rock caught the man between the shoulder blades, he stumbled and went down. They were on him at once. He struggled to his knees, was struck by a dozen stones, went down in a heap. He gave a broken high-pitched wail, then drew a fold of the gabardine across his dark eyes and strong Roman nose.

A moment later there was nothing to be seen but a pile of rocks and a protruding slippered foot. It jerked and was still.

I turned away, nauseated. Zebadiah caught my expression.

"Why," I said defensively, "do these pariahs persist in their heresy? They seem such harmless fellows otherwise."

He cocked a brow at me. "Perhaps it's not heresy to them. Didn't you see that fellow resign himself to his God?"

"But that is not the true God."

"He must have thought otherwise."

"But they all know better; we've told them often enough."

He smiled in so irritating a fashion that I blurted out, "I don't understand you, Zeb—blessed if I do! Ten minutes ago you were instructing me in correct doctrine; now you seem to be defending heresy. Reconcile that."

He shrugged. "Oh, I can play the Devil's advocate. I made the debate team at the Point, remember? I'll be a famous theologian someday—if the Grand Inquisitor doesn't get me first."

"Well . . . Look—you *do* think it's right to stone the ungodly? Don't you?"

He changed the subject abruptly. "Did you notice who cast the first stone?" I hadn't and told him so; all I remembered was that it was a man in country clothes, rather than a woman or a child.

"It was Snotty Fassett." Zeb's lip curled.

I recalled Fassett too well; he was two classes senior to me and had made my plebe year something I want to forget. "So that's how it was," I answered slowly. "Zeb, I don't think I could stomach intelligence work."

"Certainly not as an *agent provocateur*," he agreed. "Still, I suppose the Council needs these incidents occasionally. These rumors about the Cabal and all. . . ."

I caught up this last remark. "Zeb, do you really think there is anything to this Cabal? I can't believe that there is any organized disloyalty to the Prophet."

"Well—there has certainly been some trouble out on the West Coast. Oh, forget it; our job is to keep the watch here."

2

But we were not allowed to forget it; two days later the inner guard was doubled. I did not see how there could be any real danger, as the Palace was as strong a fortress as ever was built, with its lower recesses immune even to fission bombs. Besides that, a person entering the Palace, even from the Temple grounds, would be challenged and identified a dozen times before he reached the Angel on guard outside the Prophet's own quarters. Nevertheless people in high places were getting jumpy; there must be something to it. But I was delighted to find that I had been assigned as Zebadiah's partner. Standing twice as many hours of guard was almost offset by having him to talk with—for me at least. As for poor Zeb, I banged his ear endlessly through the long night watches, talking about Judith and how unhappy I was with the way things were at New Jerusalem. Finally he turned on me.

"See here, Mr. Dumbjohn," he snapped, reverting to my plebe year designation, "are you in love with her?"

I tried to hedge. I had not yet admitted to myself that my interest was more than in her welfare. He cut me short.

"You do or you don't. Make up your mind. If you do, we'll talk practical matters. If you don't, then shut up about her."

I took a deep breath and took the plunge. "I guess I do, Zeb. It seems impossible and I know it's a sin, but there it is."

"All of that and folly, too. But there is no talking sense to you. Okay, so you are in love with her. What next?"

"Eh?"

"What do you want to do? Marry her?"

I thought about it with such distress that I covered my face with my hands. "Of course I do," I admitted. "But how can I?"

"Precisely. You can't. You can't marry without transferring away from here; her service can't marry at all. Nor is there any way for her to break her vows, since she is already sealed. But if you can face up to bare facts without blushing, there is plenty you can do. You two could be very cozy—if you could get over being such an infernal bluenose."

A week earlier I would not have understood what he was driving at. But now I knew. I could not even really be angry with him at making such a dishonorable and sinful suggestion; he meant well—and some of the tarnish was now in my own soul. I shook my head. "You shouldn't have said that, Zeb. Judith is not that sort of a woman."

"Okay. Then forget it. And her. And shut up about her."

I sighed wearily. "Don't be rough on me, Zeb. This is more than I know how to manage." I glanced up and down, then took a chance and sat down on the parapet. We were not on watch near the Holy One's quarters but at the east wall; our warden, Captain Peter van

Eyck, was too fat to get that far oftener than once a watch, so I took a chance. I was bone tired from not having slept much lately.

"Sorry."

"Don't be angry, Zeb. That sort of thing isn't for me and it certainly isn't for Judith—for Sister Judith." I knew what I wanted for us: a little farm, about a hundred and sixty acres, like the one I had been born on. Pigs and chickens and bare-footed kids with happy dirty faces and Judith to have her face light up when I came in from the fields and then wipe the perspiration from her face with her apron so that I could kiss her . . . no more connection with the Church and the Prophet than Sunday meeting and tithes.

But it could not be, it could never be. I put it out of my mind. "Zeb," I went on, just as a matter of curiosity—You have intimated that these things go on all the time. How? We live in a goldfish bowl here. It doesn't seem possible."

He grinned at me so cynically that I wanted to slap him, but his voice had no leer in it. "Well, just for example, take your own case—"

"Out of the question!"

"Just for example, I said. Sister Judith isn't available right now; she is confined to her cell. But—"

"Huh? She's been *arrested?*" I thought wildly of the Question and what Zeb had said about the inquisitors.

"No, no, no! She isn't even locked in. She's been told to stay there, that's all, with prayer and bread-and-water as company. They are purifying her heart and instructing her in her spiritual duties. When she sees things in their true light, her lot will be drawn again—and this time she won't faint and make an adolescent fool of herself."

I pushed back my first reaction and tried to think about it calmly. "No," I said. "Judith will never do it. Not if she stays in her cell forever."

"So? I wouldn't be too sure. They can be very persuasive. How would you like to be prayed over in relays? But assume that she does see the light, just so that I can finish my story."

"Zeb, how do you know about this?"

"Sheol, man! I've been here going on three years. Do you think I wouldn't be hooked into the grapevine? You were worried about her—and making yourself a tiresome nuisance if I may say so. So I asked the birdies. But to continue. She sees the light, her lot is drawn, she performs her holy service to the Prophet. After that she is called once a week like the rest and her lot is drawn maybe once a month or less. Inside of a year—unless the Prophet finds some very exceptional beauty in her soul—they stop putting her name among the lots entirely. But it isn't necessary to wait that long, although it is more discreet."

"The whole thing is shameful!"

"Really? I imagine King Solomon had to use some such system; he had even more women on his neck than the Holy One has. Thereafter, if you can come to some mutual understanding with the Virgin involved, it is just a case of following well known customs. There is a present to be made to the Eldest Sister, and to be renewed as circumstances dictate. There are some palms to be brushed—I can tell you which ones. And this great pile of masonry has lots of dark back stairs in it. With all customs duly observed, there is no reason why, almost any night I have the watch and you don't, you should not find something warm and cuddly in your bed."

I was about to explode at the calloused way he put it when my mind went off at a tangent. "Zeb—now I know you are telling an untruth. You were just pulling my leg, admit it. There is an eye and an ear somewhere in our room. Why, even if I tried to find them and cut them out, I'd simply have the security watch banging on the door in three minutes."

"So what? There is an eye and an ear in every room in the place. You ignore them."

I simply let my mouth sag open.

"Ignore them," he went on. "Look, John, a little casual fornication is no threat to the Church—treason and heresy are. It will simply be entered in your dossier and nothing will be said about it—unless they catch you in something really important later, in which case they might use it to hang you instead of preferring the real charges. Old son, they *like* to have such peccadilloes in the files; it increases security. They are probably uneasy about you; you are too perfect; such men are dangerous. Which is probably why you've never been cleared for higher study."

I tried to straighten out in my mind the implied cross purposes, the wheels within wheels, and gave up. "I just don't get it. Look, Zeb, all this doesn't have anything to do with me . . . or with Judith. But I know what I've got to do. Somehow I've *got* to get her out of here."

"Hmm . . . a mighty strait gate, old son."

"I've got to."

"Well . . . I'd like to help you. I suppose I could get a message to her," he added doubtfully.

I caught his arm. "Would you, Zeb?"

He sighed. "I wish you would wait. No, that wouldn't help, seeing the romantic notions in your mind. But it is risky now. Plenty risky, seeing that she is under discipline by order of the Prophet. You'd look funny staring down the table of a court-martial board, looking at your own spear.

"I'll risk even that. Or even the Question."

He did not remind me that he himself was taking even more of a risk than I was; he simply said, "Very well, what is the message?"

I thought for a moment. It would have to be short. "Tell her that the legate she talked to the night her lot was drawn is worried about her."

"Anything else?"

"Yes! Tell her that I am hers to command!"

It seems flamboyant in recollection. No doubt it was—but it was exactly the way I felt.

At luncheon the next day I found a scrap of paper folded into my napkin. I hurried through the meal and slipped out to read it.

I need your help, it read, *and am so very grateful. Will you meet me tonight?* It was unsigned and had been typed in the script of a common voicewriter, used anywhere in the Palace, or out. When Zeb returned to our room, I showed it to him; he glanced at it and remarked in idle tones:

"Let's get some air. I ate too much. I'm about to fall asleep."

Once we hit the open terrace and were free of the hazard of eye and ear he cursed me out in low, dispassionate tones. "You'll never make a conspirator. Half the mess must know that you found something in your napkin. Why in God's name did you gulp your food and rush off? Then to top it off you handed it to me upstairs. For all you know the eye read it and photostated it for evidence. Where in the world were you when they were passing out brains?"

I protested but he cut me off. "Forget it! I know you didn't mean to put both of our necks in a bight—but good intentions are no good when the trial judge-advocate reads the charges. Now get this through your head: the first principle of intrigue is never to be seen doing anything unusual, no matter how harmless it may seem. You wouldn't believe how small a deviation from pattern looks significant to a trained analyst. You should have stayed in the refectory the usual time, hung around and gossiped as usual afterwards, then waited until you were safe to read it. Now where is it?"

"In the pocket of my corselet," I answered humbly. "Don't worry, I'll chew it up and swallow it."

"Not so fast. Wait here." Zeb left and was back in a few minutes. "I have a piece of paper the same size and shape; I'll pass it to you quietly. Swap the two, and then you can eat the real note—but don't be seen making the swap or chewing up the real one."

"All right. But what is the second sheet of paper?"

"Some notes on a system for winning at dice."

"Huh? But that's non-reg, too!"

"Of course, you hammer head. If they catch you with evidence of gambling, they won't suspect you of a much more serious sin. At worst, the skipper will eat you out and fine you a few days pay and a few hours contrition. Get this, John: if you are ever suspected of something, try to make the evidence point to a lesser offense. Never try to prove lily-white innocence. Human nature being what it is, your chances are better."

I guess Zeb was right; my pockets must have been searched and the evidence photographed right after I changed uniforms for parade, for half an hour afterwards I was called into the Executive Officer's office. He asked me to keep my eyes open for indications of gambling among the junior officers. It was a sin, he said, that he hated to have his younger officers fall into. He clapped me on the shoulder as I was leaving. "You're a good boy, John Lyle. A word to the wise, eh?"

Zeb and I had the midwatch at the south Palace portal that night. Half the watch passed with no sign of Judith and I was as nervous as a cat in a strange house, although Zeb tried to keep me calmed down by keeping me strictly to routine. At long last there were soft footfalls in the inner corridor and a shape appeared in the doorway. Zebadiah motioned me to remain on tour and went to check. He returned almost at once and motioned me to join him, while putting a finger to his lips. Trembling, I went in. It was not Judith but some woman strange to me who waited there in the darkness. I started to speak but Zeb put his hand over my mouth.

The woman took my arm and urged me down the corridor. I glanced back and saw Zeb silhouetted in the portal, covering our rear. My guide paused and pushed me into an almost pitchblack alcove, then she took from the folds of her robes a small object which I took to be a pocket ferretscope, from the small dial that glowed faintly on its side. She ran it up and down and around, snapped it off and returned it to her person. "Now you can talk," she said softly. "It's safe." She slipped away.

I felt a gentle touch at my sleeve. "Judith?" I whispered.

"Yes," she answered, so softly that I could hardly hear her.

Then my arms were around her. She gave a little startled cry, then her own arms went around my neck and I could feel her breath against my face. We kissed clumsily but with almost frantic eagerness.

It is no one's business what we talked about then, nor could I give a coherent account if I tried. Call our behavior romantic nonsense, call it delayed puppy love touched off by ignorance and unnatural lives—do puppies hurt less than grown dogs? Call it what you like and laugh at us, but at that moment we were engulfed in that dear madness more precious than rubies and fine gold, more to be desired than sanity. If you have never experienced it and do not know what I am talking about, I am sorry for you.

Presently we quieted down somewhat and talked more reasonably. When she tried to tell me about the night her lot had been drawn she began to cry. I shook her and said, "Stop it, my darling. You don't have to tell me about it. I know."

She gulped and said, "But you don't know. You can't know. I . . . he . . ."

I shook her again. "Stop it. Stop it at once. No more tears. I do know, exactly. And I know what you are in for still—unless we get you out of here. So there is no time for tears or nerves; we have to make plans."

She was dead silent for a long moment, then she said slowly, "You mean for me to . . . desert? I've thought of that. Merciful God, how I've thought about it! But how can I?"

"I don't know—yet. But we will figure out a way. We've *got* to." We discussed possibilities. Canada was a bare three hundred miles away and she knew the upstate New York country; in fact it was the only area she did know. But the border there was more tightly closed than it was anywhere else, patrol boats and radar walls by water, barbed wire and sentries by land . . . and sentry dogs. I had trained with such dogs; I wouldn't urge my worst enemy to go up against them.

But Mexico was simply impossibly far away. If she headed south she would probably be arrested in twenty-four hours. No one would knowingly give shelter to an unveiled Virgin; under the inexorable rule of associative guilt any such good Samaritan would be as guilty as she of the same personal treason against the Prophet and would die the same death. Going north would be shorter at least, though it meant the same business of traveling by night, hiding by day, stealing food or going hungry. Near Albany lived an aunt of Judith's; she felt sure that her aunt would risk hiding her until some way could be worked out to cross the border. "She'll keep us safe. I know it."

"Us?" I must have sounded stupid. Until she spoke I had had my nose so close to the single problem of how she was to escape that it had not yet occurred to me that she would expect both of us to go.

"Did you mean to send me *alone?*"

"Why . . . I guess I hadn't thought about it any other way."

"No!"

"But—look, Judith, the urgent thing, the thing that must be done at once, is to get you out of here. Two people trying to travel and hide are many times more likely to be spotted than one. It just doesn't make sense to—"

"No! I won't go!"

I thought about it, hurriedly. I still hadn't realized that "A" implies "B" and that I myself in urging her to desert her service was as much a deserter in my heart as she was. I said, "We'll get you out first, that's the important thing. You tell me where your aunt lives— then wait for me."

"Not without you."

"But you *must*. The Prophet—"

"Better that than to lose you now!"

I did not then understand women—and I still don't. Two minutes before she had been quietly planning to risk death by ordeal rather than submit her body to the Holy One. Now she was almost casually willing to accept it rather than put up with even a temporary separation. I don't understand women; I sometimes think that there is no logic in them at all.

I said, "Look, my dear one, we have not yet even figured out how we are to get you out of the Palace. It's likely to be utterly impossible for us both to escape the same instant. You see that, don't you?"

She answered stubbornly, "Maybe. But I don't like it. Well, how do I get out? And when?"

I had to admit again that I did not know. I intended to consult Zeb as soon as possible, but I had no other notion.

But Judith had a suggestion. "John, you know the Virgin who guided you here? No? Sister Magdalene. I know it is safe to tell her and she *might* be willing to help us. She's very clever."

I started to comment doubtfully but we were interrupted by Sister Magdalene herself. "Quick!" she snapped at me as she slipped in beside us. "Back to the rampart!"

I rushed out and was barely in time to avoid being caught by the warden, making his rounds. He exchanged challenges with Zeb and myself—and then the old fool wanted to chat. He settled himself down on the steps of the portal and started recalling boastfully a picayune fencing victory of the week before. I tried dismally to help Zeb with chit-chat in a fashion normal for a man bored by a night watch.

At last he got to his feet. "I'm past forty and getting a little heavier, maybe. I'll admit frankly it warms me to know that I still have a wrist and eye as fast as you young blades." He straightened his scabbard and added, "I suppose I had better take a turn through the Palace. Can't take too many precautions these days. They do say the Cabal has been active again." He took out his torch light and flashed it down the corridor.

I froze solid. If he inspected that corridor, it was beyond hope that he would miss two women crouching in an alcove.

But Zebadiah spoke up calmly, casually. "Just a moment, Elder Brother. Would you show me that time riposte you used to win that last match? It was too fast for me to follow it."

He took the bait. "Why, glad to, son!" He moved off the steps, came out to where there was room. "Draw your sword. En garde! Cross blades in line of sixte. Disengage and attack me. There! Hold the lunge and I'll demonstrate it slowly. As your point approaches my chest—" (Chest indeed! Captain van Eyck was as pot-bellied as a kangaroo!) "—I catch it with the forte of my blade and force it over yours in riposte seconde. Just like the book, so far. But I do not complete the riposte. Strong as it is, you might parry or counter. Instead, as my point comes down, I beat your blade out of line—" He illustrated and the steel sang. "—and attack you anywhere, from chin to ankle. Come now, try it on me."

Zeb did so and they ran through the phrase; the warden retreated a step. Zeb asked to do it again to get it down pat. They ran through it repeatedly, faster each time, with the warden retreating each time to avoid by a hair Zeb's unbated point. It was strictly against regulations to fence with real swords and without mask and plastron, but the warden really was good . . . . a swordsman so precise that he was confident of his own skill not to blind one of Zeb's eyes, not to let Zeb hurt him. In spite of my own galloping jitters I watched it closely; it was a beautiful demonstration of a once-useful military art. Zeb pressed him hard.

They finished up fifty yards away from the portal and that much closer to the guardroom. I could hear the warden puffing from the exercise. "That was fine, Jones," he gasped. "You caught on handsomely." He puffed again and added, "Lucky for me a real bout does not go on as long. I think I'll let you inspect the corridor." He turned away toward the guardroom, adding cheerfully, "God keep you."

"God go with you, sir," Zeb responded properly and brought his hilt to his chin in salute.

As soon as the warden turned the corner Zeb stood by again and I hurried back to the alcove. The women were still there, making themselves small against the back wall. "He's gone," I reassured them. "Nothing to fear for a while."

Judith had told Sister Magdalene of our dilemma and we discussed it in whispers. She advised us strongly not to try to reach any decisions just then. "I'm in charge of Judith's purification; I can stretch it out for another week, perhaps, before she has to draw lots again."

I said, "We've got to act before then!"

Judith seemed over her fears, now that she had laid her troubles in Sister Magdalene's lap. "Don't worry, John," she said softly, "the chances are my lot won't be drawn soon again in any case. We must do what she advises."

Sister Magdalene sniffed contemptuously. "You're wrong about that, Judy. When you are returned to duty, your lot will be drawn, you can be sure ahead of time. Not," she added, "but what you could live through it— the rest of us have. If it seems safer to—" She stopped suddenly and listened. "Sssh! Quiet as death." She slipped silently out of our circle.

A thin pencil of light flashed out and splashed on a figure crouching outside the alcove. I dived and was on him before he could get to his feet. Fast as I had been, Sister Magdalene was just as fast; she landed on his shoulders as he went down. He jerked and was still.

Zebadiah came running in, checked himself at our sides. "John! Maggie!" came his tense whisper. "What is it?"

"We've caught a spy, Zeb," I answered hurriedly. "What'll we do with him?"

Zeb flashed his light. "You've knocked him out?"

"He won't come to," answered Magdalene's calm voice out of the darkness. "I slipped a vibroblade in his ribs."

"Sheol!"

"Zeb, I had to do it. Be glad I didn't use steel and mess up the floor with blood. But what do we do now?"

Zeb cursed her softly, she took it. "Turn him over, John. Let's take a look." I did so and his light flashed again. "Hey, Johnnie—it's Snotty Fassett." He paused and I could almost hear him think. "Well, we'll waste no tears on *him*. John!"

"Yeah, Zeb?"

"Keep the watch outside. If anyone comes, I am inspecting the corridor. I've got to dump this carcass somewhere."

Judith broke the silence. "There's an incinerator chute on the floor above. I'll help you."

"Stout girl. Get going, John."

I wanted to object that it was no work for a woman, but I shut up and turned away. Zeb took his shoulders, the women a leg apiece and managed well enough. They were back in minutes, though it seemed endless to me. No doubt Snotty's body was reduced to atoms before they were back—we might get away with it. It did not seem like murder to me then, and still does not; we did what we had to do, rushed along by events.

Zeb was curt. "This tears it. Our reliefs will be along in ten minutes; we've got to figure this out in less time than that. Well?"

Our suggestions were all impractical to the point of being ridiculous, but Zeb let us make them—then spoke straight to the point. "Listen to me, it's no longer just a case of trying to help Judith and you out of your predicament. As soon as Snotty is missed, we—all four of us—are in mortal danger of the Question. Right?"

"Right," I agreed unwillingly.

"But nobody has a plan?"

None of us answered. Zeb went on. "Then we've got to have help . . . and there is only one place we can get it. The Cabal."

3

"The Cabal?" I repeated stupidly. Judith gave a horrified gasp.

"Why . . . why, that would mean our immortal souls! They worship Satan!"

Zeb turned to her. "I don't believe so."

She stared at him. "Are *you* a Cabalist?"

"No."

"Then how do you know?"

"And how," I insisted, "can *you* ask them for help?"

Magdalene answered. "I am a member—as Zebadiah knows."

Judith shrank away from her, but Magadalene pressed her with words. "Listen to me, Judith. I know how you feel—and once I was as horrified as you are at the idea of anyone opposing the Church. Then I learned—as you are learning—what really lies behind this sham we were brought up to believe in." She put an arm around the younger girl. "We aren't devil worshipers, dear, nor do we fight against God. We fight only against this self-styled Prophet who pretends to be the voice of God. Come with us, help us fight him—and we will help you. Otherwise we can't risk it."

Judith searched her face by the faint light from the portal. "You swear that this is true? The Cabal fights only against the Prophet and not against the Lord Himself?"

"I swear, Judith."

Judith took a deep shuddering breath. "God guide me," she whispered. "I go with the Cabal."

Magdalene kissed her quickly, then faced us men. "Well?"

I answered at once, "I'm in it if Judith is," then whispered to myself, "Dear Lord, forgive me my oath—I must!"

Magdalene was staring at Zeb. He shifted uneasily and said angrily, "I suggested it, didn't I? But we are all damned fools and the Inquisitor will break our bones."

There was no more chance to talk until the next day. I woke from bad dreams of the Question and worse, and heard Zeb's shaver buzzing merrily in the bath. He came in and pulled the covers off me, all the while running off at the mouth with cheerful nonsense. I hate having bed clothes dragged off me even when feeling well and I can't stand cheerfulness before breakfast; I dragged them back and tried to ignore him, but he grabbed my wrist. "Up you come, old son! God's sunshine is wasting. It's a beautiful day. How about two fast laps around the Palace and in for a cold shower?"

I tried to shake his hand loose and called him something that would lower my mark in piety if the ear picked it up. He still hung on and his forefinger was twitching against my wrist in a nervous fashion; I began to wonder if Zeb were cracking under the strain. Then I realized that he was tapping out code.

"B-E—N-A-T-U-R-A-L," the dots and dashes said, "S-H-O-W—N-O—S-U-R-P-R-I-S-E—W-E—W-I-L-L—B-E—C-A-L-L-E-D—F-O-R—E-X-A-M-I-N-A-T-I-O-N—D-U-R-I-N-G—T-H-E—R-E-C-R-E-A-T-I-O-N—P-E-R-I-O-D—T-H-I-S—A-F-T-E-R-N-O-O-N"

I hope I showed no surprise. I made surly answers to the stream of silly chatter he had kept up all through it, and got up and went about the mournful tasks of putting the body back in shape for another day. After a bit I found excuse to lay a hand on his shoulder and twitched out an answer: "O-K—I—U-N-D-E-R-S-T-A-N-D"

The day was a misery of nervous monotony. I made a mistake at dress parade, a thing I haven't done since beast barracks. When the day's duty was finally over I went back to our room and found Zeb there with his feet on the air conditioner, working an acrostic in the New York *Times*. "Johnnie my lamb," he asked, looking up, "What is a six-letter word meaning 'Pure in Heart'?"

"You'll never need to know," I grunted and sat down to remove my armor.

"Why, John, don't you think I will reach the Heavenly City?"

"Maybe—after ten thousand years penance."

There came a brisk knock at our door, it was shoved open, and Timothy Klyce, senior legate in the mess and brevet captain, stuck his head in. He sniffed and said in nasal Cape Cod accents, "Hello, you chaps want to take a walk?"

It seemed to me that he could not have picked a worse time. Tim was a hard man to shake and the most punctiliously devout man in the corps. I was still trying to think of an excuse when Zeb spoke up. "Don't mind if we do, provided we walk toward town. I've got some shopping to do."

I was confused by Zeb's answer and still tried to hang back, pleading paper work to do, but Zeb cut me short. "Pfui with paper work. I'll help you with it tonight.

Come on." So I went, wondering if he had gotten cold
feet about going through with it.

We went out through the lower tunnels. I walked
along silently, wondering if possibly Zeb meant to try
to shake Klyce in town and then hurry back. We had
just entered a little jog in the passageway when Tim
raised his hand in a gesture to emphasize some point
in what he was saying to Zeb. His hand passed near
my face, I felt a slight spray on my eyes—and I was
blind.

Before I could cry out, even as I suppressed the
impulse to do so, he grasped my upper arm hard, while
continuing his sentence without a break. His grip on
my arm guided me to the left, whereas my memory of
the jog convinced me that the turn should have been
to the right. But we did not bump into the wall and
after a few moments the blindness wore off. We seemed
to be walking in the same tunnel with Tim in the middle
and holding each of us by an arm. He did not say anything and neither did we; presently he stopped us in
front of a door. Klyce knocked once, then listened.

I could not make out an answer but he replied, "Two
pilgrims, duly guided."

The door opened. He led us in, it closed silently
behind us, and we were facing a masked and armored
guard, with his blast pistol leveled on us. Reaching
behind him, he rapped once on an inner door; immediately another man, armed and masked like the first,
came out and faced us. He asked Zeb and myself separately:

"Do you seriously declare, upon your honor, that,
unbiased by friends and uninfluenced by mercenary
motives, you freely and voluntarily offer yourself to the
service of this order?"

We each answered, "I do."

"Hoodwink and prepare them."

Leather helmets that covered everything but our
mouths and noses were slipped over our heads and

fastened under our chins. Then we were ordered to strip
off all our clothing. I did so while the goose bumps
popped out on me. I was losing my enthusiasm rapidly—
there is nothing that makes a man feel as helpless as
taking his pants away from him. Then I felt the sharp
prick of a hypodermic in my forearm and shortly, though
I was awake, things got dreamy and I was no longer
jittery. Something cold was pressed against my ribs on
the left side of my back and I realized that it was almost
certainly the hilt of a vibroblade, needing only the touch
of the stud to make me as dead as Snotty Fassett—but
it did not alarm me. Then there were questions, many
questions, which I answered automatically, unable to lie
or hedge if I had wanted to. I remember them in
snatches:

"—of your own free will and accord?" "—conform
to the ancient established usages—" "—a man, free born,
of good repute, and well recommended."

Then, for a long time I stood shivering on the cold
tile floor while a spirited discussion went on around me;
it had to do with my motives in seeking admission. I
could hear it all and I knew that my life hung on it,
with only a word needed to cause a blade of cold energy
to spring into my heart. And I knew that the argument
was going against me.

Then a contralto voice joined the debate. I recognized
Sister Magdalene and knew that she was vouching for
me, but doped as I was I did not care; I simply welcomed her voice as a friendly sound. But presently the
hilt relaxed from my ribs and I again felt the prick of
a hypodermic. It brought me quickly out of my dazed
state and I heard a strong bass voice intoning a prayer:

"Vouchsafe thine aid, Almighty Father of the Universe. . . . love, relief, and truth to the honor of Thy
Holy Name. Amen."

And the answering chorus, "So mote it be!"

Then I was conducted around the room, still hoodwinked, while questions were again put to me. They

were symbolic in nature and were answered for me by
my guide. Then I was stopped and was asked if I were
willing to take a solemn oath pertaining to this degree,
being assured that it would in no material way interfere with duty that I owed to God, myself, family,
country, or neighbor.

I answered, "I am."

I was then required to kneel on my left knee, with
my left hand supporting the Book, my right hand steadying certain instruments thereon.

The oath and charge was enough to freeze the blood
of anyone foolish enough to take it under false pretenses.
Then I was asked what, in my present condition, I most
desired. I answered as I had been coached to answer:
"Light!"

And the hoodwink was stripped from my head.

It is not necessary and not proper to record the rest
of my instruction as a newly entered brother. It was long
and of solemn beauty and there was nowhere in it any
trace of the blasphemy or devil worship that common
gossip attributed to us; quite the contrary it was filled
with reverence for God, brotherly love, and uprightness,
and it included instruction in the principles of an ancient
and honorable profession and the symbolic meaning of
the working tools thereof.

But I must mention one detail that surprised me
almost out of the shoes I was not wearing. When they
took the hoodwink off me, the first man I saw, standing in front of me dressed in the symbols of his office
and wearing an expression of almost inhuman dignity,
was Captain Peter van Eyck, the fat ubiquitous warden
of my watch—*Master* of this lodge!

The ritual was long and time was short. When the
lodge was closed we gathered in a council of war. I was
told that the senior brethren had already decided not
to admit Judith to the sister order of our lodge at this
time even though the lodge would reach out to protect
her. She was to be spirited away to Mexico and it was

better, that being the case, for her not to know any secrets she did not need to know. But Zeb and I, being of the Palace guard, could be of real use; therefore we were admitted.

Judith had already been given hypnotic instructions which—it was hoped—would enable her to keep from telling what little she already knew if she should be put to the Question. I was told to wait and not to worry; the senior brothers would arrange to get Judith out of danger before she next was required to draw lots. I had to be satisfied with that.

For three days running Zebadiah and I reported during the afternoon recreation period for instruction, each time being taken by a different route and with different precautions. It was clear that the architect who had designed the Palace had been one of us; the enormous building had hidden in it traps and passages and doors which certainly did not appear in the official plans.

At the end of the third day we were fully accredited senior brethren, qualified with a speed possible only in time of crisis. The effort almost sprained my brain; I had to bone harder than I ever had needed to in school. Utter letter-perfection was required and there was an amazing lot to memorize—which was perhaps just as well, for it helped to keep me from worrying. We had not heard so much as a rumor of a kickback from the disappearance of Snotty Fassett, a fact much more ominous than would have been a formal investigation.

A security officer can't just drop out of sight without his passing being noticed. It was remotely possible that Snotty had been on a roving assignment and was not expected to check in daily with his boss, but it was much more likely that he had been where we had found him and killed him because some one of us was suspected and he had been ordered to shadow. If that was the case, the calm silence could only mean that the chief security officer was letting us have more rope, while his psychotechnicians analyzed our behavior—in which case

the absence of Zeb and myself from any known location during our free time for several days running was
almost certainly a datum entered on a chart. If the entire
regiment started out equally suspect, then our personal
indices each gained a fractional point each of those days.

I never boned savvy in such matters and would
undoubtedly have simply felt relieved as the days
passed with no overt trouble had it not been that the
matter was discussed and worried over in the lodge
room. I did not even know the name of the Guardian of Morals, nor even the location of his security
office—we weren't supposed to know. I knew that he
existed and that he reported to the Grand Inquisitor
and perhaps to the Prophet himself, but that was all.
I discovered that my lodge brothers, despite the almost
incredible penetration of the Cabal throughout the
Temple and Palace, knew hardly more than I did—
for the reason that we had no brothers, not one, in
the staff of the Guardian of Morals. The reason was
simple; the Cabal was every bit as careful in evalu-
ating the character, *persona,* and psychological poten-
tialities of a prospective brother as the service was in
measuring a prospective intelligence officer—and the
two types were as unlike as geese and goats. The
Guardian would never accept the type of personality
who would be attracted by the ideals of the Cabal;
my brothers would never pass a—well, a man like
Fassett.

I understand that, in the days before psychological
measurement had become a mathematical science, an
espionage apparatus could break down through a change
in heart on the part of a key man—well, the Guardian of Morals had no such worry; his men *never* suffered a change in heart. I understand, too, that our own
fraternity, in the early days when it was being purged
and tempered for the ordeal to come, many times had
blood on the floors of lodge rooms—I don't know; such
records were destroyed.

On the fourth day we were not scheduled to go to the lodge room, having been told to show our faces where they would be noticed to offset our unwonted absences. I was spending my free time in the lounge off the mess room, leafing through magazines, when Timothy Klyce came in. He glanced at me, nodded, then started thumbing through a stack of magazines himself. Presently he said, "These antiques belong in a dentist's office. Have any of you chaps seen this week's TIME?"

His complaint was addressed to the room as a whole; no one answered. But he turned to me. "Jack, I think you are sitting on it. Raise up a minute."

I grunted and did so. As he reached for the magazine his head came close to mine and he whispered, "Report to the Master."

I had learned a little at least so I went on reading. After a bit I put my magazine aside, stretched and yawned, then got up and ambled out toward the washroom. But I walked on past and a few minutes later entered the lodge room. I found that Zeb was already there, as were several other brothers; they were gathered around Master Peter and Magdalene. I could feel the tension in the room.

I said, "You sent for me, Worshipful Master?"

He glanced at me, looked back at Magdalene. She said slowly, "Judith has been arrested."

I felt my knees go soft and I had trouble standing. I am not unusually timid and physical bravery is certainly commonplace, but if you hit a man through his family or his loved ones you almost always get him where he is unprotected. "The Inquisition?" I managed to gasp.

Her eyes were soft with pity. "We think so. They took her away this morning and she has been incommunicado ever since."

"Has any charge been filed?" asked Zeb.

"Not publicly."

"Hm-m-m— That looks bad."

"And good as well," Master Peter disagreed. "If it is the matter we think it is—Fassett, I mean—and had they had any evidence pointing to the rest of you, all four of you would have been arrested at once. At least, that is in accordance with their methods."

"But what can we *do*?" I demanded.

Van Eyck did not answer. Magdalene said soothingly, "There is nothing for you to do, John. You couldn't get within several guarded doors of her."

"But we can't just do nothing!"

The lodge Master said, "Easy, son. Maggie is the only one of us with access to that part of the inner Palace. We must leave it in her hands."

I turned again to her; she sighed and said, "Yes, but there is probably little I can do." Then she left.

We waited. Zeb suggested that he and I should leave the lodge room and continue with being seen in our usual haunts; to my relief van Eyck vetoed it. "No. We can't be sure that Sister Judith's hypnotic protection is enough to see her through the ordeal. Fortunately you two and Sister Magdalene are the only ones she can jeopardize—but I want you here, safe, until Magdalene finds out what she can. Or fails to return," he added thoughtfully.

I blurted out, "Oh, Judith will never betray us!"

He shook his head sadly. "Son, *anyone* will betray *anything* under the Question—unless adequately guarded by hypno compulsion. We'll see."

I had paid no attention to Zeb, being busy with my own very self-centered thoughts. He now surprised me by saying angrily, "Master, you are keeping us here like pet hens—but you have just sent Maggie back to stick her head in a trap. Suppose Judith *has* cracked? They'll grab Maggie at once."

Van Eyck nodded. "Of course. That is the chance we must take since she is the only spy we have. But don't you worry about her. They'll never arrest her—she'll suicide first."

The statement did not shock me; I was too numbed

by the danger to Judith. But Zeb burst out with, "The swine! Master, you shouldn't have sent her."

Van Eyck answered mildly, "Discipline, son. Control yourself. This is war and she is a soldier." He turned away.

So we waited. . . and waited. . . and waited. It is hard to tell anyone who has not lived in the shadow of the Inquisition how we felt about it. We knew no details but we sometimes saw those unlucky enough to live through it. Even if the inquisitors did not require the auto da fé, the mind of the victim was usually damaged, often shattered.

Presently Master Peter mercifully ordered the Junior Warden to examine both of us as to our progress in memorizing ritual. Zeb and I sullenly did as we were told and were forced with relentless kindness to concentrate on the intricate rhetoric. Somehow nearly two hours passed.

At last came three raps at the door and the Tyler admitted Magdalene. I jumped out of my chair and rushed to her. "Well?" I demanded. "Well?"

"Peace, John," she answered wearily. "I've seen her."

"How is she? Is she all right?"

"Better than we have any right to expect. Her mind is still intact and she hasn't betrayed us, apparently. As for the rest, she may keep a scar or two—but she's young and healthy; she'll recover.

I started to demand more facts but the Master cut me off. "Then they've already put her to the Question. In that case, how did you get in to see her?"

"Oh, that!" Magdalene shrugged it off as something hardly worth mentioning. "The inquisitor prosecuting her case proved to be an old acquaintance of mine; we arranged an exchange of favors."

Zeb started to interrupt; the Master snapped, "Quiet!" then added sharply, "The Grand Inquisitor isn't handling it himself? In that case I take it they don't suspect that it could be a Cabal matter?"

Maggie frowned. "I don't know. Apparently Judith
fainted rather early in the proceedings; they may not
have had time to dig into that possibility. In any case
I begged a respite for her until tomorrow. The excuse
is to let her recover strength for more questioning, of
course. They will start in on her again early tomorrow
morning."

Van Eyck pounded a fist into a palm. "They must not
start again—we can't risk it! Senior Warden, attend me!
The rest of you get out! Except you, Maggie."

I left with something unsaid. I had wanted to tell
Maggie that she could have my hide for a door mat any
time she lifted her finger.

Dinner that night was a trial. After the chaplain
droned through his blessing I tried to eat and join in
the chatter but there seemed to be a hard ring in my
throat that kept me from swallowing. Seated next to me
was Grace-of-God Bearpaw, half Scottish, half Chero-
kee. Grace was a classmate but no friend of mine; we
hardly ever talked and tonight he was as taciturn as ever.

During the meal he rested his boot on mine; I impatiently moved my foot away. But shortly his foot was
touching mine again and he started to tap against my boot:
"—hold still, you idiot—" he spelled out. "You have
been chosen—it will be on your watch tonight—details
later—eat and start talking—take a strip of adhesive tape
on watch with you—six inches by a foot—repeat message back."

I managed somehow to tap out my confirmation while
continuing to pretend to eat.

4

We relieved the watch at midnight. As soon as the
watch section had marched away from our post I told

Zeb what Grace had passed on to me at chow and asked him if he had the rest of my instructions. He had not. I wanted to talk but he cut me short; he seemed even more edgy than I was.

So I walked my post and tried to look alert. We were posted that night at the north end of the west rampart; our tour covered one of the Palace entrances. About an hour had passed when I heard a hiss from the dark doorway. I approached cautiously and made out a female form. She was too short to be Magdalene and I never knew who she was, for she shoved a piece of paper into my hand and faded back into the dark corridor.

I rejoined Zeb. "What shall I do? Read it with my flash? That seems risky."

"Open it up."

I did and found that it was covered with fine script that glowed in the darkness. I could read it but it was too dim to be picked up by any electronic eye. I read it:

At the middle of the watch exactly on the bell you will enter the Palace by the door where you received this. Forty paces inside, take the stair on your left; climb two flights. Proceed north fifty paces. The lighted doorway on your right leads to the Virgins' quarters; there will be a guard at this door. He will not resist you but you must use a paralysis bomb on him to give him an alibi. The cell you seek is at the far end of the central east & west corridor of the quarters. There will be a light over the door and a Virgin on guard. She is not one of us. You must disable her completely but you are forbidden to injure or kill her. Use the adhesive tape as gag and blindfold and tie her up with her clothes. Take her keys, enter the cell, and remove Sister Judith. She will probably be unconscious. Bring her to your post and hand her over to the warden of your watch.

You must make all haste from the time you paralyze the guard, as an eye may see you when you pass the lighted doorway and the alarm may sound at once.

Do not swallow this note; the ink is poisonous. Drop it in the incinerator chute at the head of the stairs. Go with God.

Zeb read it over my shoulder. "All you need," he said grimly, "is the ability to pass miracles at will. Scared?"

"Yes."

"Want me to go along?"

"No. I guess we had better carry out the orders as given."

"Yes, we had—if I know the Lodge Master. Besides, it just might happen that I might need to kill somebody rather suddenly while you are gone. I'll be covering your rear."

"I suppose so."

"Now let's shut up and bone military." We went back to walking our post.

At the two muted strokes of the middle of the watch I propped my spear against the wall, took off my sword and corselet and helmet and the rest of the ceremonial junk we were required to carry but which would hamper me on this job. Zeb shoved a gauntleted hand in mine and squeezed. Then I was off.

Two—four—six—forty paces. I groped in the dark along the left wall and found the opening, felt around with my foot. Ah, there were the steps! I was already in a part of the Palace I had never been in; I moved by dead reckoning in the dark and hoped the person who had written my orders understood that. One flight, two flights—I almost fell on my face when I stepped on a top step that wasn't there.

Where was the refuse chute? It should be at hand level and the instructions said "head of the stairs." I was debating frantically whether to show a light or chance keeping it when my left hand touched its latch; with a sigh of relief I chucked away the evidence that could have incriminated so many others. I started to turn away, then was immediately filled with panic. Was that really an incinerator chute?

Could it have been the panel for a delivery lift instead? I groped for it in the dark again, opened it and shoved my hand in.

My hand was scorched even through my gauntlet; I jerked it back with relief and decided to trust my instructions, have no more doubts. But forty paces north the passageway jogged and that was not mentioned in my orders; I stopped and reconnoitered very cautiously, peering around the jog at floor level.

Twenty-five feet away was the guard and the doorway. He was supposed to be one of us but I took no chances. I slipped a bomb from my belt, set it by touch to minimum intensity, pulled the primer and counted off five seconds to allow for point blank range. Then I threw it and ducked back into the jog to protect myself from the rays.

I waited another five seconds and stuck my head around. The guard was slumped down on the floor, with his forehead bleeding slightly where it had struck a fragment of the bomb case. I hurried out and stepped over him, trying to run and keep quiet at the same time. The central passage of the Virgins' quarters was dim, with only blue night lights burning, but I could see and I reached the end of the passage quickly—then jammed on the brakes. The female guard at the cell there, instead of walking a post, was seated on the floor with her back to the door.

Probably she was dozing, for she did not look up at once. Then she did so, saw me, and I had no time to make plans; I dove for her. My left hand muffled her scream; with the edge of my left hand I chopped the side of her neck—not a killing stroke but I had no time to be gentle; she went limp.

Half the tape across her mouth first, then the other half across her eyes, then tear clothing from her to bind her—and hurry, hurry, hurry all the way, for a security man might already have monitored the eye that was certainly at the main doorway and have seen the unconscious guard. I found her keys on a chain around her waist and straightened up with a silent apology for what I had done to her. Her little body was almost childlike; she seemed even more helpless than Judith.

But I had no time for soft misgivings; I found the right key, got the door open—and then my darling was in my arms.

She was deep in a troubled sleep and probably drugged. She moaned as I picked her up but did not wake. But her gown slipped and I saw some of what they had done to her—I made a life vow, even as I ran, to pay it back seven times, if the man who did it could live that long.

The guard was still where I had left him. I thought I had gotten away with it without being monitored or waking anyone and was just stepping over him, when I heard a gasp from the corridor behind me. Why are women restless at night? If this woman hadn't gotten out of bed, no doubt to attend to something she should have taken care of before retiring, I might never have been seen at all.

It was too late to silence her, I simply ran. Once around the jog I was in welcome darkness but I overran the stair head, had to come back, and feel for it—then had to grope my way down step by step. I could hear shouts and high-pitched voices somewhere behind me.

Just as I reached ground level, turned and saw the portal outlined against the night sky before me, all the lights came on and the alarms began to clang. I ran the last few paces headlong and almost fell in the arms of Captain van Eyck. He scooped her out of my arms without a word to me and trotted away toward the corner of the building.

I stood staring after them half-wittedly when Zeb brought me to my senses by picking up my corselet and shoving it out for me to put in my arms. "Snap out of it, man!" he hissed. "That general alarm is for *us*. You're supposed to be on guard duty."

He strapped on my sword as I buckled the corselet,

then slapped my helmet on my head and shoved my spear into my left hand. Then we stood back to back in front of the portal, pistols drawn, safeties off, in drill-manual full alert. Pending further orders, we were not expected nor permitted to do anything else, since the alarm had not taken place on our post.

We stood like statues for several minutes. We could hear sounds of running feet and of challenges. The Officer of the Day ran past us into the Palace, buckling his corselet over his night clothes as he ran. I almost blasted him out of existence before he answered my challenge. Then the relief watch section swung past at double time with the relief warden at its head.

Gradually the excitement died away; the lights remained on but someone thought to shut off the alarm. Zeb ventured a whisper. "What in Sheol happened? Did you muff it?"

"Yes and no." I told him about the restless Sister.

"Hmmmph! Well, son, this ought to teach you not to fool around with women when you are on duty."

"Confound it, I wasn't fooling with her. She just popped out of her cell."

"I didn't mean tonight," he said bleakly.

I shut up.

About half an hour later, long before the end of the watch, the relief section tramped back. Their warden halted them, and our two reliefs fell out and we fell in the empty places. We marched back to the guard-room, stopping twice more on the way to drop reliefs and pick up men from our own section.

5

We were halted in the inner parade facing the guard-room door and left at attention. There we stood for fifty mortal minutes while the Officer of the Day strolled around and looked us over. Once a man in the rear rank shifted his weight. It would have gone unnoticed at dress parade, even in the presence of the Prophet, but tonight the Officer of the Day bawled him out at once and Captain van Eyck noted down his name.

Master Peter looked just as angry as his superior undoubtedly was. He passed out several more gigs, even stopped in front of me and told the guardroom orderly to put me down for "boots not properly shined"—which was a libel, unless I had scuffed them in my efforts. I dared not look down to see but stared him in the eye and said nothing, while he stared back coldly.

But his manner recalled to me Zeb's lecture about intrigue. Van Eyck's manner was perfectly that of a subordinate officer let down and shamed by his own men; how should I feel if I were in fact new-born innocent?

Angry, I decided—angry and self-righteous. Interested and stimulated by the excitement at first, then angry at being kept standing at attention like a plebe. They were trying to soften us up by the strained wait; how would I have felt about it, say two months ago? Smugly sure of my own virtue, it would have offended me and humiliated me—to be kept standing like a pariah waiting to whine for the privilege of a ration card—to be placed on the report like a cadet with soup on his jacket.

By the time the Commander of the Guard arrived almost an hour later I was white-lipped with anger. The process was synthetic but the emotion was real. I had never really liked our Commander anyway. He was a short, supercilious little man with a cold eye and a way of looking through his junior officers instead of looking at them. Now he stood in front of us with his priest's robes thrown back over his shoulders and his thumbs caught in his sword belt.

He glared at us. "Heaven help me, Angels of the

Lord indeed," he said softly into the dead silence—then barked, "Well?"

No one answered.

"Speak up!" he shouted. "Some one of you knows about this. Answer me! Or would you all rather face the Question?"

A murmur ran down our ranks—but no one spoke.

He ran his eyes over us again. His eye caught mine and I stared back truculently. "Lyle!"

"Yes, reverend sir?"

"What do you know of this?"

"I know that I would like to sit down, reverend sir!"

He scowled at me, then his eye got a gleam of cold amusement. "Better to stand before me, my son, than to sit before the Inquisitor." But he passed on and heckled the man next to me.

He badgered us endlessly, but Zeb and I seemed to receive neither more nor less attention than the others. At last he seemed to give up and directed the Officer of the Day to dismiss us. I was not fooled; it was a certainty that every word spoken had been recorded, every expression cinemographed, and that analysts were plotting the data against each of our past behavior patterns before we reached our quarters.

But Zeb is a wonder. He was gossiping about the night's events, speculating innocently about what could have caused the hurrah, even before we reached our room. I tried to answer in what I had decided was my own "proper" reaction and groused about the way we had been treated. "We're officers and gentlemen," I complained. "If he thinks we are guilty of something, he should prefer formal charges."

I went to bed still griping, then lay awake and worried. I tried to tell myself that Judith must have reached a safe place, or else the brass would not be in the dark about it. But I dropped off to sleep still fretting.

I felt someone touch me and I woke instantly. Then I relaxed when I realized that my hand was being gripped in the recognition grip of the lodge. "Quiet," a voice I did not recognize whispered in my ear. "I must give you certain treatment to protect you." I felt the bite of a hypodermic in my arm; in a few seconds I was relaxed and dreamy. The voice whispered, "You saw nothing unusual on watch tonight. Until the alarm was sounded your watch was quite without incident—" I don't know how long the voice droned on.

I was awakened a second time by someone shaking me roughly. I burrowed into my pillow and said, "Go 'way! I'm going to skip breakfast."

Somebody struck me between my shoulder blades; I turned and sat up, blinking. There were four armed men in the room, blasters drawn and pointed at me. "Come along!" ordered the one nearest to me.

They were wearing the uniform of Angels but without unit insignia. Each head was covered by a black mask that exposed only the eyes—and by these masks I knew them: proctors of the Grand Inquisitor.

I hadn't really believed it could happen to me. Not to *me* . . . not to Johnnie Lyle who had always behaved himself, been a credit to his parish and a pride to his mother. No! The Inquisition was a bogieman, but a bogieman for sinners—not for John Lyle.

But I knew with sick horror when I saw those masks that I was already a dead man, that my time had come and here at last was the nightmare that I could not wake up from.

But I was not dead yet. From somewhere I got the courage to pretend anger. "What are *you* doing here?"

"Come along," the faceless voice repeated.

"Show me your order. You can't just drag an officer out of his bed any time you feel—"

The leader gestured with his pistol; two of them grabbed my arms and hustled me toward the door, while the fourth fell in behind. But I am fairly strong; I made it hard for them while protesting. "You've got to let me get dressed, at least. You've no right to haul me away half naked, no matter what the emergency is. I've a right to appear in the uniform of my rank."

Surprisingly the appeal worked. The leader stopped. "Okay. But snap into it!"

I stalled as much as I dared while going through the motions of hurrying—jamming a zipper on my boot, fumbling clumsily with all my dressing. How could I leave some sort of a message for Zeb? Any sort of a sign that would show the brethren what had happened to me?

At last I got a notion, not a good one but the best I could manage. I dragged clothing out of my wardrobe, some that I would need, some that I did not, and with the bunch a sweater. In the course of picking out what I must wear I managed to arrange the sleeves of the sweater in the position taken by a lodge brother in giving the Grand Hailing Sign of Distress. Then I picked up loose clothing and started to put some of it back in the wardrobe; the leader immediately shoved his blaster in my ribs and said, "Never mind that. You're dressed."

I gave in, dropping the meaningless clothing on the floor. The sweater remained spread out as a symbol to him who could read it. As they led me away I prayed that our room servant would not arrive and "tidy" it out of meaning before Zeb spotted it.

They blindfolded me as soon as we reached the inner Palace. We went down six flights, four below ground level as I figured it, and reached a compartment filled with the breathless silence of a vault. The hoodwink was stripped from my eyes. I blinked.

"Sit down, my boy, sit down and make yourself comfortable." I found myself looking into the face of the Grand Inquisitor himself, saw his warm friendly smile and his collie-dog eyes.

His gentle voice continued, "I'm sorry to get you so rudely out of a warm bed, but there is certain information needed by our Holy Church. Tell me, my son, do you fear the Lord? Oh, of course you do; your piety is well known. So you won't mind helping me with this little matter even though it makes you late for breakfast. It's to the greater glory of God." He turned to his masked and black-robed assistant questioner, hovering behind him. "Make him ready—and pray be gentle."

I was handled quickly and roughly, but not painfully. They touched me as if they regarded me as so much lifeless matter to be manipulated as impersonally as machinery. They stripped me to the waist and fastened things to me, a rubber bandage tight around my right arm, electrodes in my fists which they taped closed, another pair of electrodes to my wrists, a third pair at the temples, a tiny mirror to the pulse in my throat. At a control board on the left wall one of them made some adjustments, then threw a switch and on the opposite wall a shadow show of my inner workings sprang into being.

A little light danced to my heart beat, a wiggly line on an iconoscope display showed my blood pressure's rise and fall, another like it moved with my breathing, and there were several others that I did not understand. I turned my head away and concentrated on remembering the natural logarithms from one to ten.

"You see our methods, son. Efficiency and kindness, those are our watch words. Now tell me— *Where did you put her?*"

I broke off with the logarithm of eight. "Put who?"

"Why did you do it?"

"I am sorry, Most Reverend Sir. I don't know what it is I am supposed to have done."

Someone slapped me hard, from behind. The lights on the wall jiggled and the Inquisitor studied them thoughtfully, then spoke to an assistant. "Inject him."

Again my skin was pricked by a hypodermic. They let me rest while the drug took hold; I spent the time continuing with the effort of recalling logarithms. But that soon became too difficult; I grew drowsy and lackadaisical, nothing seemed to matter. I felt a mild and childish curiosity about my surroundings but no fear. Then the soft voice of the Inquisitor broke into my reverie with a question. I can't remember what it was but I am sure I answered with the first thing that came into my head.

I have no way of telling how long this went on. In time they brought me back to sharp reality with another injection. The Inquisitor was examining a slight bruise and a little purple dot on my right forearm. He glanced up. "What caused this, my boy?"

"I don't know, Most Reverend Sir." At the instant it was truth.

He shook his head regretfully. "Don't be naive, my son—and don't assume that I am. Let me explain something to you. What you sinners never realize is that the Lord always prevails. Always. Our methods are based in loving-kindness but they proceed with the absolute certainty of a falling stone, and with the result equally preordained.

"First we ask the sinner to surrender himself to the Lord and answer from the goodness that remains in his heart. When that loving appeal fails—as it did with you—then we use the skills God has given us to open the unconscious mind. That is usually as far as the Question need go—unless some agent of Satan has been there before us and has tampered with the sacred tabernacle of the mind.

"Now, my son, I have just returned from a walk through your mind. I found much there that was commendable, but I found also, in murky darkness, a wall that had been erected by some other sinner, and what I want—what the Church needs—is behind that wall."

Perhaps I showed a trace of satisfaction or perhaps the lights gave me away, for he smiled sadly and added, "No wall of Satan can stop the Lord. When we find such an obstacle, there are two things to do: given time enough I could remove that wall gently, delicately, stone by stone, without any damage to your mind. I wish I had time to, I really do, for you are a good boy at heart, John Lyle, and you do not belong with the sinners.

"But while eternity is long, time is short; there is the second way. We can disregard the false barrier in the unconscious mind and make a straightforward assault on the conscious mind, with the Lord's banners leading us." He glanced away from me. "Prepare him."

His faceless crew strapped a metal helmet on my head, some other arrangements were made at the control board. "Now look here, John Lyle." He pointed to a diagram on the wall. "No doubt you know that the human nervous system is partly electrical in nature. There is a schematic representation of a brain, that lower part is the thalamus; covering it is the cortex. Each of the sensory centers is marked as you can see. Your own electrodynamic characteristics have been analyzed; I am sorry to say that it will now be necessary to heterodyne your normal senses."

He started to turn away, turned back. "By the way, John Lyle, I have taken the trouble to minister to you myself because, at this stage, my assistants through less experience in the Lord's work than my humble self sometimes mistake zeal for skill and transport the sinner unexpectedly to his reward. I don't want that to happen to you. You are merely a strayed lamb and I purpose saving you."

I said, "Thank you, Most Reverend Sir."

"Don't thank me, thank the Lord I serve. However," he went on, frowning slightly, "this frontal assault on the mind, while necessary, is unavoidably painful. You will forgive me?"

I hesitated only an instant. "I forgive you, holy sir."

He glanced at the lights and said wryly, "A falsehood. But you are forgiven that falsehood; it was well intended." He nodded at his silent helpers. "Commence."

A light blinded me, an explosion crashed in my ears.

My right leg jerked with pain, then knotted in an endless cramp. My throat contracted; I choked and tried to throw up. Something struck me in the solar plexus; I doubled up and could not catch my breath. "Where did you put her?" A noise started low and soft, climbed higher and higher, increasing in pitch and decibels, until it was a thousand dull saws, a million squeaking slate pencils, then wavered in a screeching ululation that tore at the thin wall of reason. "Who helped you?" Agonizing heat was at my crotch; I could not get away from it. "Why did you do it?" I itched all over, intolerably, and tried to tear at my skin—but my arms would not work. The itching was worse than pain; I would have welcomed pain in lieu of scratching. "Where is she?"

Light . . . sound . . . pain . . . heat . . . convulsions . . . cold . . . falling . . . light and pain . . . cold and falling . . . nausea and sound. "Do you love the Lord?" Searing heat and shocking cold . . . pain and a pounding in my head that made me scream— "Where did you take her? Who else was in it? Give up and save your immortal soul." Pain and an endless nakedness to the outer darkness.

I suppose I fainted.

Some one was slapping me across the mouth. "Wake up, John Lyle, and confess! Zebadiah Jones has given you away."

I blinked and said nothing. It was not necessary to simulate a dazed condition, nor could I have managed it. But the words had been a tremendous shock and my brain was racing, trying to get into gear. Zeb? Old Zeb? Poor old Zeb! Hadn't they had time to give him hypnotic treatment, too? It did not occur to me even then to suspect that Zeb had broken under torture alone; I simply assumed that they had been able to tap his unconscious mind. I wondered if he were already dead and remembered that I had gotten him into this, against his good sense. I prayed for his soul and prayed that he would forgive me.

My head jerked to another roundhouse slap. "Wake up! You can hear me—Jones has revealed your sins."

"Revealed what?" I mumbled.

The Grand Inquisitor motioned his assistants aside and leaned over me, his kindly face full of concern. "Please, my son, do this for the Lord—and for me. You have been brave in trying to protect your fellow sinners from the fruits of their folly, but they failed you and your stiff-necked courage no longer means anything. But don't go to judgment with this on your soul. Confess, and let death come with your sins forgiven."

"So you mean to kill me?"

He looked faintly annoyed. "I did not say that. I know that you do not fear death. What you should fear is to meet your Maker with your sins still on your soul. Open your heart and confess."

"Most Reverend Sir, I have nothing to confess."

He turned away from me and gave orders in low, gentle tones. "Continue. The mechanicals this time; I don't wish to burn out his brain."

There is no point in describing what he meant by "the mechanicals" and no sense in making this account needlessly grisly. His methods differed in no important way from torture techniques used in the Middle Ages and even more recently—except that his knowledge of the human nervous system was incomparably greater and his knowledge of behavior psychology made his operations more adroit. In addition, he and his assistants behaved as if they were completely free of any sadistic pleasure in their work; it made them coolly efficient.

But let's skip the details.

I have no notion of how long it took. I must have passed out repeatedly, for my clearest memory is of catching a bucket of ice water in the face not once but over and over again, like a repeating nightmare—each time followed by the inevitable hypo. I don't think I told them anything of any importance while I was awake and the hypno instructions to my unconscious may have protected me while I was out of my head. I seem to remember trying to make up a lie about sins I had never committed; I don't remember what came of it.

I recall vaguely coming semi-awake once and hearing a voice say, "He can take more. His heart is strong."

I was pleasantly dead for a long time, but finally woke up as if from a long sleep. I was stiff and when I tried to shift in bed my side hurt me. I opened my eyes and looked around; I was in bed in a small, windowless but cheerful room. A sweet-faced young woman in a nurse's uniform came quickly to my side and felt my pulse.

"Hello."

"Hello," she answered. "How are we now? Better?"

"What happened?" I asked. "Is it over? Or is this just a rest?"

"Quiet," she admonished. "You are still too weak to talk. But it's over—you are safe among the brethren."

"I was rescued?"

"Yes. Now be quiet." She held up my head and gave me something to drink. I went back to sleep.

It took me days to convalesce and catch up with events. The infirmary in which I woke up was part of a series of subbasements under the basement proper of a department store in New Jerusalem; there was some sort of underground connections between it and the lodge room under the Palace—just where and how I could not say; I was never in it. While conscious, I mean.

Zeb came to see me as soon as I was allowed to have visitors. I tried to raise up in bed. "Zeb! Zeb boy—I thought you were dead!"

"Who? Me?" He came over and shook my left hand. "What made you think that?"

I told him about the dodge the Inquisitor had tried to pull on me. He shook his head. "I wasn't even arrested. Thanks to you, pal. Johnnie, I'll never call you stupid again. If you hadn't had that flash of genius to rig your sweater so that I could read the sign in it, they might have pulled us both in and neither one of us have gotten out of it alive. As it was, I went straight to Captain van Eyck. He told me to lie doggo in the lodge room and then planned your rescue."

I wanted to ask how that had been pulled off but my mind jumped to a more important subject. "Zeb, where is Judith? Can't you find her and bring her to see me? My nurse just smiles and tells me to rest."

He looked surprised. "Didn't they tell you?"

"Tell me what? No, I haven't seen anybody but the nurse and the doctor and they treat me like an idiot. Don't keep me in suspense, Zeb. Did anything go wrong? She's all right—*isn't she?*"

"Oh, sure! But she's in Mexico by now—we got a report by sensitive circuit two days ago."

In my physical weakness I almost wept. "Gone! Why what a dirty, scabby trick! Why couldn't they have waited until I was well enough to tell her good-by?"

Zeb said quickly, "Hey, look, stupid—no, forget that 'stupid'; you aren't. Look, old man, your calendar is mixed up. She was on her way before you were rescued, before we were even sure you could be rescued. You don't think the brethren could bring her back just to let you two bill and coo, do you?"

I thought about it and calmed down. It made sense, even though I was bitterly disappointed. He changed the subject. "How do you feel?"

"Oh, pretty good."

"They tell me you get that cast off your leg tomorrow."

"So? They haven't told me." I twisted, trying to get comfortable. "I'm almost more anxious to get out of this corset, but the doc says I'll have to wear it for several weeks yet."

"How about your hand? Can you bend your fingers?"

I tried it. "Fairly well. I may have to write left-handed for a while."

"All in all, it looks like you're too mean to die, old

son. By the way, if it's any consolation to you, the laddy boy who worked on Judith got slightly dead in the raid in which you were rescued."

"He was? Well, I'm sorry. I had planned to save him for myself."

"No doubt, but you would have had to take your place in line, if he had lived. Lots of people wanted him. Me, for example."

"But I had thought of something special for him— I was going to make him bite his nails."

"Bite his nails?" Zeb looked puzzled.

"Until he reached his elbows. Follow me?"

"Oh." Zeb grinned sourly. "Not nearly imaginative enough, boy. But he's dead, we can't touch him."

"He's infernally lucky. Zeb, why didn't you arrange to get him yourself? Or did you, and things were just too hurried to let you do a proper job?"

"Me? Why, I wasn't on the rescue raid. I haven't been back in the Palace at all."

"Huh?"

"You didn't think I was still on duty, did you?"

"I haven't had time to think about it."

"Well, naturally I couldn't go back after I ducked out to avoid arrest; I was through. No, my fine fellow, you and I are both deserters from the United States Army— with every cop and every postmaster in the country anxious to earn a deserter's reward by turning us in."

I whistled softly and let the implications of his remark sink in.

6

I had joined the Cabal on impulse. Certainly, under the stress of falling in love with Judith and in the excitement of the events that had come rushing over me as a result of meeting her, I had no time for calm consideration. I had not broken with the Church as a result of philosophical decision.

Of course I had known logically that to join the Cabal was to break with all my past ties, but it had not yet hit me emotionally. What was it going to be like never again to wear the uniform of an officer and a gentleman? I had been proud to walk down the street, to enter a public place, aware that all eyes were on me.

I put it out of my mind. The share was in the furrow, my hand was on the plow; there could be no turning back. I was in this until we won or until we were burned for treason.

I found Zeb looking at me quizzically. "Cold feet, Johnnie?"

"No. But I'm still getting adjusted. Things have moved fast."

"I know. Well, we can forget about retired pay, and our class numbers at the Point no longer matter." He took off his Academy ring, chucked it in the air, caught it and shoved it into his pocket. "But there is work to be done, old lad, and you will find that this is a military outfit, too—a real one. Personally, I've had my fill of spit-and-polish and I don't care if I never again hear that 'Sound off' and 'Officers, center!' and 'Watchman, what of the night?' manure again. The brethren will make full use of our best talents—and the fight really matters."

Master Peter van Eyck came to see me a couple of days later. He sat on the edge of my bed and folded his hands over his paunch and looked at me. "Feeling better, son?"

"I could get up if the doctor would let me."

"Good. We're shorthanded; the less time a trained officer spends on the sick list the better." He paused and chewed his lip. "But, son, I don't know just what to do with you."

"Eh? Sir?"

"Frankly, you should never have been admitted to the Order in the first place—a military command should not mess around with affairs of the heart. It confuses motivations, causes false decisions. Twice, because we took you in, we have had to show our strength in sorties that—from a strictly military standpoint—should never have happened."

I did not answer, there was no answer—he was right. My face was hot with embarrassment.

"Don't blush about it," he added kindly. "Contrariwise, it is good for the morale of the brethren to strike back occasionally. The point is, what to do with you? You are a stout fellow, you stood up well— but do you really understand the ideals of freedom and human dignity we are fighting for?"

I barely hesitated. "Master—I may not be much of a brain, and the Lord knows it's true that I've never thought much about politics. But I know which side I'm on!"

He nodded. "That's enough. We can't expect each man to be his own Tom Paine."

"His own what?"

"Thomas Paine. But then you've never heard of him, of course. Look him up in our library when you get a chance. Very inspiring stuff. Now about your assignment. It would be easy enough to put you on a desk job here—your friend Zebadiah has been working sixteen hours a day trying to straighten out our filing system. But I can't waste you two on clerical jobs. What is your savvy subject, your specialty?"

"Why, I haven't had any P.G. work yet, sir."

"I know. But what did you stand high in? How were you in applied miracles, and mob psychology?"

"I was fairly good in miracles, but I guess I'm too wooden for psychodynamics. Ballistics was my best subject."

"Well, we can't have everything. I could use a technician in morale and propaganda, but if you can't, you can't."

"Zeb stood one in his class in mob psychology, Master. The Commandant urged him to aim for the priesthood."

"I know and we'll use him, but not here. He is too much interested in Sister Magdalene; I don't believe in letting couples work together. It might distort their judgments in a pinch. Now about you. I wonder if you wouldn't make a good assassin?"

He asked the question seriously but almost casually; I had trouble believing it. I had been taught—I had always taken it for granted that assassination was one of the unspeakable sins, like incest, or blasphemy. I blurted out, "The brethren use *assassination*?"

"Eh? Why not?" Van Eyck studied my face. "I keep forgetting. John, would you kill the Grand Inquisitor if you got a chance?"

"Well—yes, of course. But I'd want to do it in a fair fight."

"Do you think you will ever be given that chance? Now let's suppose we are back at the day Sister Judith was arrested by him. Suppose you could stop him by killing him—but only by poisoning him, or knifing him in the back. What would you do?"

I answered savagely, "I would have killed him!"

"Would you have felt any shame, any guilt?"

"None!"

"So. But he is only one of many in this foulness. The man who eats meat cannot sneer at the butcher—and every bishop, every minister of state, every man who benefits from this tyranny, right up to the Prophet himself, is an accomplice before the fact in every murder committed by the inquisitors. The man who condones a sin because he enjoys the results of the sin is equally guilty of the sin. Do you see that?"

Oddly enough, I did see it, for it was orthodox doctrine as I had learned it. I had choked over its new application. But Master Peter was still talking: "But we don't indulge in vengeance—vengeance still belongs to the Lord. I would never send *you* against the Inquisitor because you might be tempted to exult in it personally. We don't tempt a man with sin as a bait. What we do do, what we are doing, is engaging in a calculated military operation in a war already commenced. One key man is often worth a regiment; we pick out that key man and kill him. The bishop in one diocese may be such a man; the bishop in the next state may be just a bungler, propped up by the system. We kill the first, let the second stay where he is. Gradually we are eliminating their best brains. Now—" He leaned toward me. "—do you want a job picking off those key men? It's very important work."

It seemed to me that, in this business, someone was continually making me face up to facts, instead of letting me dodge unpleasant facts the way most people manage to do throughout their lives. Could I stomach such an assignment? Could I refuse it—since Master Peter had implied at least that assassins were volunteers—refuse it and try to ignore in my heart that it was going on and that I was condoning it?

Master Peter was right; the man who buys the meat is brother to the butcher. It was squeamishness, not morals . . . like the man who favors capital punishment but is himself too "good" to fit the noose or swing the axe. Like the person who regards war as inevitable and in some circumstances moral, but who avoids military service because he doesn't like the thought of killing.

Emotional infants, ethical morons—the left hand *must* know what the right hand doeth, and the heart is responsible for both. I answered almost at once, "Master Peter, I am ready to serve . . . that way or whatever the brethren decide I can do best."

"Good man!" He relaxed a bit and went on, "Between ourselves, it's the job I offer to every new recruit when I'm not sure that he understands that this is not a ball game, but a cause to which he must commit himself without any reservation—his life, his fortune, his sacred

honor. We have no place for the man who wants to give
orders but who won't clean the privy."

I felt relieved. "Then you weren't seriously picking
me out for assassination work?"

"Eh? Usually I am not; few men are fitted for it. But
in your case I am quite serious, because we already
know that you have an indispensable and not very
common qualification."

I tried to think what was so special about me and
could not. "Sir?"

"Well, you'll get caught eventually, of course. Three
point seven accomplished missions per assassin is what
we are running now—a good score, but we ought to
do better as suitable men are so scarce. But with you
we know already that when they do catch you and put
you to the Question, you won't crack."

My face must have shown my feelings. The Question? Again? I was still half dead from the first time.
Master Peter said kindly, "Of course you won't have to
go up against it again to the fullest. We always protect
assassins; we fix it so that they can suicide easily. You
don't need to worry."

Believe me, having once suffered the Question, his
assurance to me did not seem calloused; it was a real
comfort. "How, sir?"

"Eh? A dozen different ways. Our surgeons can
booby-trap you so that you can die at will in the tightest
bonds anyone can put on you. There is the old hollow
tooth, of course, with cyanide or such—but the proctors are getting wise to that; sometimes they gag a man's
mouth open. But there are many ways. For example—"
He stretched his arms wide and bent them back, but
not far. "—if I were to cramp my arms backward in a
position a man never assumes without very considerable
conscious effort, a little capsule would rupture and I
would make my last report. Yet you could pound me
on the back all day and never break it."

"Uh . . . were you an assassin, sir?"

"Me? How could I be, in my job? But all of our people in positions of maximum exposure are loaded— it's the least we can do for them. Besides that, I've got a bomb in my belly—" He patted his paunch. "—that will take a roomful of people with me if it seems desirable."

"I could have used one of those last week," I said emphatically.

"You're here, aren't you? Don't despise your luck. If you need one, you'll have one." He stood up and prepared to leave. "In the meantime, don't give any special thought to being selected as an executioner. The psychological evaluation group will still have to pass on you and they are hard men to convince."

Despite his words, I did think about it, of course, though it ceased to worry me. I was put on light duty shortly thereafter and spent several days reading proof on the *Iconoclast*, a smug, mildly critical, little reform-from-within paper which the Cabal used to pave the way for its field missionaries. It was a "Yes, but—" paper, overtly loyal to the Prophet but just the sort of thing to arouse doubt in the minds of the stiff-necked and intolerant. Its acid lay in how a thing was said, not what was said. I had even seen copies of it around the Palace.

I also got acquainted with some of the ramifications of the amazing underground headquarters at New Jerusalem. The department store above us was owned by a Past Grand Master and was an extremely important means of liaison with the outside world. The shelves of the store fed us and clothed us; through taps into the visiphone circuits serving the store commercially we had connection with the outside and could even put in transcontinental calls if the message could be phrased or coded to allow for the likelihood that it would be monitored. The owner's delivery trucks could be used to spirit fugitives to or from our clandestine quarters— I learned that Judith started her flight that way, with a bill of lading that described her as gum boots. The store's manifold commercial operations were a complete and plausible blind for our extensive operations.

Successful revolution is Big Business—make no mistake about that. In a modern, complex, and highly industrialized state, revolution is not accomplished by a handful of conspirators whispering around a guttering candle in a deserted ruin. It requires countless personnel, supplies, modern machinery and modern weapons. And to handle these factors successfully there must be loyalty, secrecy, and superlative staff organization.

I was kept busy but my work was fill-in work, since I was awaiting assignment. I had time to dig into the library and I looked up Tom Paine, which led me to Patrick Henry and Thomas Jefferson and others—a whole new world was opened up to me. I had trouble at first in admitting the possibility of what I read; I think perhaps of all the things a police state can do to its citizens, distorting history is possibly the most pernicious. For example, I learned for the first time that the United States had not been ruled by a bloodthirsty emissary of Satan before the First Prophet arose in his wrath and cast him out—but had been a community of free men, deciding their own affairs by peaceful consent. I don't mean that the first republic had been a scriptural paradise, but it hadn't been anything like what I had learned in school.

For the first time in my life I was reading things which had not been approved by the Prophet's censors, and the impact on my mind was devastating. Sometimes I would glance over my shoulder to see who was watching me, frightened in spite of myself. I began to sense faintly that secrecy is the keystone of all tyranny. Not force, but secrecy . . . censorship. When any government, or any church for that matter, undertakes to say to its subjects, "This you may not read, this you must not see, this you are forbidden to know," the end result is tyranny and oppression, no matter how holy the motives. Mighty little force is needed to control a man whose mind has been hoodwinked; contrariwise, no

amount of force can control a free man, a man whose
mind is free. No, not the rack, not fission bombs, not
anything—you can't conquer a free man; the most you
can do is kill him.

My thoughts did not then fall into syllogisms; my
head was filled with an inchoate spate of new ideas, each
more exciting than the last. I discovered that travel
between the planets, almost a myth in my world, had
not stopped because the First Prophet had forbidden
it as a sin against the omnipotence of God; it had ceased
because it had gone into the red financially and the
Prophet's government would not subsidize it. There was
even an implied statement that the "infidels" (I still used
that word in my mind) still sent out an occasional
research ship and that there were human beings even
now on Mars and Venus.

I grew so excited at that notion that I almost forgot the plight we were all in. If I had not been chosen for the Angels of the Lord, I would probably have
gone into rocketry. I was good at anything of that sort,
the things that called for quick reflexes combined with
knowledge of the mathematical and mechanical arts.
Maybe someday the United States would have space
ships again. Perhaps I . . .

But the thought was crowded out by a dozen new
ones. Foreign newspapers—why, I had not even been
sure the infidels could read and write. The London
Times made unbelievable and exciting reading. I gradually got it through my head that the Britishers apparently did not now eat human flesh, if indeed they ever
had. They seemed remarkably like us, except that they
were shockingly prone to do as they pleased—there were
even letters in the *Times* criticizing the government. And
there was another letter signed by a bishop of their
infidel church, criticizing the people for not attending
services. I don't know which one puzzled me the more;
both of them seemed to indicate a situation of open
anarchy.

Master Peter informed me that the psych board had turned me down for assassination duty. I found myself both relieved and indignant. What was wrong with me that they would not trust me with the job? It seemed like a slur on my character—by then.

"Take it easy," van Eyck advised dryly. "They made a dummy run based on your personality profile and it figured almost an even chance that you would be caught your first time out. We don't like to expend men that fast."

"But—"

"Peace, lad. I'm sending you out to General Headquarters for assignment."

"General Headquarters? Where is that?"

"You'll know when you get there. Report to the staff metamorphist."

Dr. Mueller was the staff face-changer; I asked him what he had in mind for me. "How do I know until I find out what you are?" He had me measured and photographed, recorded my voice, analyzed my walk, and had a punched card made up of my physical characteristics. "Now we'll find your twin brother." I watched the card sorter go through several thousand cards and I was beginning to think I was a unique individual, resembling no one else sufficiently to permit me to be disguised successfully, when two cards popped out almost together. Before the machine whirred to a stop there were five cards in the basket.

"A nice assortment," Dr. Mueller mused as he looked them over, "one synthetic, two live ones, a deader, and one female. We can't use the woman for this job, but we'll keep it in mind; it might come in very handy someday to know that there is a female citizen you could impersonate successfully."

"What's a synthetic?" I enquired.

"Eh? Oh, it's a composite personality, very carefully built from faked records and faked backgrounds. A risky business—it involves tampering with the national archives. I don't like to use a synthetic, for there really isn't any way to fill in completely the background of a man who doesn't exist. I'd much rather patch into the real background of a real person."

"Then why use synthetics at all?"

"Sometimes we have to. When we have to move a refugee in a hurry, for example, and there is no real person we can match him with. So we try to keep a fairly broad assortment of synthetics built up. Now let me see," he added, shuffling the cards, "we have two to choose from—"

"Just a second, Doctor," I interrupted, "why do you keep dead men in the file?"

"Oh, they aren't legally dead. When one of the brethren dies and it is possible to conceal the fact, we maintain his public personality for possible future use. Now then," he continued, "can you sing?"

"Not very well."

"This one is out, then. He's a concert baritone. I can make a lot of changes in you, but I can't make a trained singer of you. It's Hobson's choice. How would you like to be Adam Reeves, commercial traveler in textiles?" He held up a card.

"Do you think I could get away with it?"

"Certainly—when I get through with you."

A fortnight later my own mother wouldn't have known me. Nor, I believe, could Reeves' mother have told me from her son. The second week Reeves himself was available to work with me. I grew to like him very much while I was studying him. He was a mild, quiet man with a retiring disposition, which always made me think of him as small although he was, of course, my height, weight, and bone structure. We resembled each other only superficially in the face.

At first, that is. A simple operation made my ears stand out a little more than nature intended; at the same time they trimmed my ear lobes. Reeves' nose was slightly aquiline; a little wax under the skin at the bridge caused mine to match. It was necessary to cap several of my teeth to make mine match his dental repair work; that was the only part I really minded. My complexion had to be bleached a shade or two; Reeves' work did not take him out into the sun much.

But the most difficult part of the physical match was artificial fingerprints. An opaque, flesh-colored flexible plastic was painted on my finger pads, then my fingers were sealed into molds made from Reeves' fingertips. It was touchy work; one finger was done over seven times before Dr. Mueller would pass it.

That was only the beginning; now I had to learn to act like Reeves—his walk, his gestures, the way he laughed, his table manners. I doubt if I could ever make a living as an actor—my coach certainly agreed and said so.

"Confound it, Lyle, won't you ever get it? Your life will depend on it. You've *got* to learn!"

"But I thought I was acting just like Reeves," I objected feebly.

"Acting! That's just the trouble—you were *acting* like Reeves. And it was as phony as a false leg. You've got to *be* Reeves. Try it. Worry about your sales record, think about your last trip, think about commissions and discounts and quotas. Go on. Try it."

Every spare minute I studied the current details of Reeves' business affairs, for I would actually have to sell textiles in his place. I had to learn a whole trade and I discovered that there was more to it than carrying around samples and letting a retailer make his choice—and I didn't know a denier from a continuous fibre. Before I finished I acquired a new respect for business men. I had always thought that buying and selling was simple; I was wrong again. I had to use the old phonographic tutor stunt and wear earphones to bed. I never sleep well that way and would

wake up each morning with a splitting head and with
my ears, still tender from the operations, sore as two
boils.

But it worked, all of it. In two short weeks I *was*
Adam Reeves, commercial traveler, right down to my
thoughts.

7

"Lyle," Master Peter van Eyck said to me, "Reeves
is due to catch the *Comet* for Cincinnati this afternoon.
Are you ready?"

"Yes, sir."

"Good. Repeat your orders."

"Sir, I am to carry out my—I mean his—selling
schedule from here to the coast. I check in at the San
Francisco office of United Textiles, then proceed on his
vacation. In Phoenix, Arizona, I am to attend church
services at the South Side Tabernacle. I am to hang
around afterwards and thank the priest for the inspi-
ration of his sermon; in the course of which I am to
reveal myself to him by means of the accustomed usages
of our order. He will enable me to reach General Headquarters."

"All correct. In addition to transferring you for duty,
I am going to make use of you as a messenger. Report
to the psychodynamics laboratory at once. The chief
technician will instruct you."

"Very well, sir."

The lodge Master got up and came around his desk
to me. "Good-by, John. Watch yourself, and may the
Great Architect help you."

"Thank you, sir. Uh, is this message I am to carry
important?"

"Quite important."

He let it go at that and I was a bit irked; it seemed silly to be mysterious about it when I would find out just what it was in a few minutes. But I was mistaken. At the laboratory I was told to sit down, relax, and prepare myself for hypnosis.

I came out of it with the pleasant glow that usually follows hypnosis. "That's all," I was told. "Carry out your orders."

"But how about the message I was to carry?"

"You have it."

"Hypnotically? But if I'm arrested, I'll be at the mercy of any psycho-investigator who examines me!"

"No, you won't. It's keyed to a pair of signal words; you can't possibly remember until they are spoken to you. The chance that an examiner would hit on both words and in the right order is negligible. You can't give the message away, awake or asleep."

I had rather expected to be "loaded" for suicide, if I was to carry an important message—though I hadn't seen how they could do it at the last minute, other than supplying me with a pill, I mean, a method almost useless if the policeman knows his business. But if I couldn't give away the message I carried, then I preferred to take my chances; I didn't ask for poison. I'm not the suiciding type anyhow—when Satan comes for me, he'll have to drag me . . .

The rocket port serving New Jerusalem is easier to get to than is the case at most of the older cities. There was a tube station right across from the department store that hid our headquarters. I simply walked out of the store, took the bridge across the street, found the tube stall marked "Rocket Port," waited for an empty cartridge, and strapped myself and my luggage in. The attendant sealed me and almost at once I was at the port.

I bought my ticket and took my place at the end of the queue outside the port police station. I'll admit I was nervous; while I didn't anticipate having any trouble getting my travel pass validated, the police officers who must handle it were no doubt on the lookout for John Lyle, renegade army officer. But they were always looking for someone and I hoped the list of wanted faces was too long to make the search for me anything other than routine.

The line moved slowly; and that looked like a bad sign—especially so when I noticed that several people had been thumbed out of line and sent to wait behind the station railing. I got downright jittery. But the wait itself gave me time to get myself in hand. I shoved my papers at the sergeant, glanced at my chrono, up at the station clock, and back at my wrist.

The sergeant had been going through my papers in a leisurely, thorough manner. He looked up. "Don't worry about catching your ship," he said not unkindly. "They can't leave until we clear their passenger list." He pushed a pad across the counter. "Your fingerprints, please."

I gave them without comment. He compared them with the prints on my travel pass and then with the prints Reeves had left there on his arrival a week earlier. "That's all, Mr. Reeves. A pleasant trip."

I thanked him and left.

The *Comet* was not too crowded. I picked a seat by a window, well forward, and had just settled down and was unfolding a late-afternoon copy of the *Holy City*, when I felt a touch on my arm.

It was a policeman.

"Will you step outside, please?"

I was herded outside with four other male passengers. The sergeant was quite decent about it. "I'm afraid I'll have to ask you four to return to the station for further identification. I'll order your baggage removed and have the passenger list changed. Your tickets will be honored on the next flight."

I let out a yelp. "But I've got to be in Cincinnati tonight!"

"I'm sorry." He turned to me. "You're Reeves, aren't you? Hmm . . . you are the right size and build. Still . . . let me see your pass again. Didn't you arrive in town just last week?"

"That's right."

He went through my papers again. "Uh, yes, I remember now; you came in Tuesday morning on the *Pilgrim*. Well, you can't be in two places at once, so I guess that clears you." He handed my papers back to me. "Go aboard again. Sorry we bothered you. The rest of you come along."

I returned to my seat and picked up my newspaper. A few minutes later the first heavy surge of the rockets threw us to the west. I continued reading the paper to cover up my agitation and relief, but soon got interested. I had been reading a Toronto paper only that morning, underground; the contrast was startling. I was back in a world for which the outside world hardly existed; the "foreign affairs" news, if you could call it that, consisted of glowing reports of our foreign missions and some accounts of atrocities among the infidels. I began to wonder where all that money went that was contributed each year for missionary work; the rest of the world, if you could believe *their* newspapers, didn't seem much aware that our missions existed.

Then I began going through the paper, picking out items that I knew to be false. By the time I was through we were down out of the ionosphere and gliding into Cincy. We had overtaken the sun and had sunset all over again.

There must be a peddler's pack in my family tree. I not only covered Reeves' territory in Cincinnati, but bettered his quota. I found that I got as much pleasure out of persuading some hard-boiled retailer that he should increase his line of yard goods as I ever had from military work. I stopped worrying about my disguise and thought only about textiles. Selling isn't just a way to eat; it's a game, it's fun.

I left for Kansas City on schedule and had no trouble with the police in getting a visa for my travel pass. I decided that New Jerusalem had been the only ticklish check point; from here west nobody would expect to pick up John Lyle, formerly officer and gentleman; he would be one of thousands of wanted men, lost in the files.

The rocket to K.C. was well filled; I had to sit beside another passenger, a well-built chap in his middle thirties. We looked each other over as I sat down, then each busied himself with his own affairs. I called for a lap table and started straightening out the order blanks and other papers I had accumulated during busy, useful days in Cincinnati. He lounged back and watched the news broadcast in the TV tank at the forward end of the car.

I felt a nudge about ten minutes later and looked around. My seatmate flicked a thumb toward the television tank; in it there was displayed a large public square filled with a mob. It was surging toward the steps of a massive temple, over which floated the Prophet's gold-and-crimson banner and the pennant of a bishopric. As I watched, the first wave of the crowd broke against the temple steps.

A squad of temple guards trotted out a side door near the giant front doors and set up their tripods on the terrace at the head of the wide stairs. The scene cut to another viewpoint; we were looking down right into the faces of the mob hurrying toward us—apparently from a telephoto pick-up somewhere on the temple roof.

What followed made me ashamed of the uniform I had once worn. Instead of killing them quickly, the guards aimed low and burned off their legs. One instant the first wave was running toward me up the steps—then they fell, the cauterized stumps of their legs jerking convulsively. I had been watching a youngish couple right in the center of the pick-up; they had been running hand in hand. As the beam swept across them they went down together.

She stayed down. He managed to lift himself on what had been his knees, took two awkward dying steps toward her and fell across her. He pulled her head to his, then the scene cut away from them to the wide view of the square.

I snatched the earphones hanging on the back of the seat in front of me and listened: "—apolis, Minnesota. The situation is well in hand and no additional troops will be needed. Bishop Jennings has declared martial law while the agents of Satan are rounded up and order restored. A period of prayer and fasting will commence at once.

"The Minnesota ghettos have been closed and all local pariahs will be relocated in the reservations in Wyoming and Montana in order to prevent future outbreaks. Let this be a warning to the ungodly everywhere who might presume to dispute the divine rule of the Prophet Incarnate.

"This on-the-spot cast by the No-Sparrow-Shall-Fall News Service is coming to you under the sponsorship of the Associated Merchants of the Kingdom, dealers in the finest of household aids toward grace. Be the first in your parish to possess a statuette of the Prophet that miraculously *glows in the dark!* Send one dollar, care of this station—"

I switched off the phones and hung them up. Why blame the pariahs? That mob wasn't made up of pariahs. But I kept my lip zipped and let my companion speak first—which he did, with vehemence. "Serves them right, the bloody fools! Imagine charging against a fortified position with your bare hands." He kept his voice down and spoke almost in my ear.

"I wonder why they rioted?" was all that I answered.

"Eh? No accounting for the actions of an heretic. They aren't sane."

"You can sing that in church," I agreed firmly. "Besides, even a sane heretic—if there could be such a thing, I mean—could see that the government is doing

a good job of running the country. Business is good."
I patted my brief case happily. "For me, at least, praise
the Lord."

We talked business conditions, and the like for some
time. As we talked I looked him over. He seemed to
be the usual leading-citizen type, conventional and con-
servative, yet something about him made me uneasy.
Was it just my guilty nerves? Or some sixth sense of
the hunted?

My eyes came back to his hands and I had a vague
feeling that I should be noticing something. But there
was nothing unusual about them. Then I finally noticed
a very minor thing, a calloused ridge on the bottom joint
of the third finger of his left hand, the sort of a mark
left by wearing a heavy ring for years and just the sort
I carried myself from wearing my West Point class ring.
It meant nothing, of course, since lots of men wear
heavy seal rings on that finger. I was wearing one
myself—not my West Point ring naturally, but one
belonging to Reeves.

But why would this conventional-minded oaf wear
such a ring habitually, then stop? A trifling thing, but it
worried me; a hunted animal lives by noticing trifles. At
the Point I had never been considered bright in psychology; I had missed cadet chevrons on that issue alone. But
now seemed a good time to use what little I had learned
. . . so I ran over in my mind all I had noticed about him.

The first thing he had noticed, the one thing he had
commented on, was the foolhardiness of charging into
a fortified position. That smacked of military orientation in his thinking. But that did not prove he was a
Pointer. On the contrary, an Academy man wears his
ring at all times, even into his grave, even on leave and
wearing mufti . . . unless for some good reason he does
not wish to be recognized.

We were still chatting sociably and I was worrying
over how to evaluate insufficient data when the stew-
ardess served tea. The ship was just beginning to bite

air as we came down out of the fringes of space and
entered the long glide into Kansas City; it was somewhat bumpy and she slopped a little hot tea on his
thigh. He yelped and uttered an expletive under his
breath. I doubt if she caught what he said.

But I did catch it—and I thought about it furiously
while I dabbed at him with a handkerchief. "B. J. idiot!"
was the term he used and it was strictly West Point
slang.

Ergo, the ring callous was no coincidence; he was
a West Pointer, an army officer, pretending to be a
civilian. Corollary: he was almost certainly on a secret
service assignment. Was I his assignment?

Oh, come now, John! His ring might be at a
jeweller's, being repaired; he might be going home on
thirty days. But in the course of a long talk he had let
me think that he was a business man. No, he was an
undercover agent.

But even if he was not after *me*, he had made two
bad breaks in my presence. But even the clumsiest tyro
(like myself, say) does not make two such slips in
maintaining an assumed identity—and the army secret
service was not clumsy; it was run by some of the most
subtle brains in the country. Very well, then—they were
not accidental slips but calculated acts; I was intended
to notice them and *think* that they were accidents.
Why?

It could not be simply that he was not sure I was
the man he wanted. In such case, after the old and
tested principle that a man was sinful until proved
innocent, he would simply have arrested me and I would
have been put to the Question.

Then *why?*

It could only be that they wanted me to run free for
a while yet—but to be scared out of my wits and run
for cover . . . and thereby lead them to my fellow conspirators. It was a far-fetched hypothesis, but the only
one that seemed to cover all the facts.

When I first concluded that my companion must be an agent on my trail I was filled with that cold, stomach-twisting fear that can be compared only with seasickness. But when I thought I had figured out their motives I calmed down. What would Zebadiah do? "The first principle of intrigue is not to be stampeded into any unusual act—" Sit tight and play dumb. If this cop wanted to follow me, I'd lead him into every department store in K.C.—and let him watch while I peddled yard goods.

Nevertheless my stomach felt tight as we got off the ship in Kansas City. I expected that gentle touch on the shoulder which is more frightening than a fist in the face. But nothing happened. He tossed me a perfunctory God-keep-you, pushed ahead of me, and headed for the lift to the taxicab platform while I was still getting my pass stamped. It did not reassure me, as he could have pointed me out half a dozen ways to a relief. But I went on over to the New Muehlbach by tube as casually as I could manage.

I had a fair week in K.C., met my quota and picked up one new account of pretty good size. I tried to spot any shadow that might have been placed on me, but I don't know to this day whether or not I was being trailed. If I was, somebody spent an awfully dull week. But, although I had about concluded that the incident had been nothing but imagination and my jumpy nerves, I was happy at last to be aboard the ship for Denver and to note that my companion of the week before was not a passenger.

We landed at the new field just east of Aurora, many miles from downtown Denver. The police checked my papers and fingerprinted me in the routine fashion and I was about to shove my wallet back into my pocket when the desk sergeant said, "Bare your left arm, please, Mr. Reeves."

I rolled up my sleeve while trying to show the right amount of fretful annoyance. A white-coated orderly took a blood sample. "Just a normal precaution," the sergeant

explained. "The Department of Public Health is trying
to stamp out spotted fever."

It was a thin excuse, as I knew from my own training in P.H.—but Reeves, textiles salesman, might not
realize it. But the excuse got thinner yet when I was
asked to wait in a side room of the station while my
blood sample was run. I sat there fretting, trying to
figure out what harm they could do me with ten c.c.
of my blood—and what I could do about it even if I
did know.

I had plenty of time to think. The situation looked
anything but bright. My time was probably running out
as I sat there—yet the excuse on which they were holding me was just plausible enough that I didn't dare cut
and run; that might be what they wanted. So I sat tight
and sweated.

The building was a temporary structure and the wall
between me and the sergeant's office was a thin lami-
nate; I could hear voices through it without being able
to make out the words. I did not dare press my ear
to it for fear of being caught doing so. On the other
hand I felt that I just had to do it. So I moved my
chair over to the wall, sat down again, leaned back
on two legs of the chair so that my shoulders and the
back of my neck were against the wall. Then I held
a newspaper I had found there up in front of my face
and pressed my ear against the wall.

I could hear every word then. The sergeant told a
story to his clerk which would have fetched him a
month's penance if a morals proctor had been listening—still, I had heard the same story, only slightly
cleaned up, right in the Palace, so I wasn't really
shocked, nor was I in any mood to worry about other
people's morals. I listened to several routine reports
and an inquiry from some semi-moron who couldn't
find the men's washroom, but not a word about myself.
I got a crick in my neck from the position.

Just opposite me was an open window looking out

over the rocket field. A small ship appeared in the sky, braked with nose units, and came in to a beautiful landing about a quarter of a mile away. The pilot taxied toward the administration building and parked outside the window, not twenty-five yards away.

It was the courier version of the *Sparrow Hawk,* ram jet with rocket take-off and booster, as sweet a little ship as was ever built. I knew her well; I had pushed one just like her, playing number-two position for Army in sky polo—that was the year we had licked both Navy and Princeton.

The pilot got out and walked away. I eyed the distance to the ship. If the ignition were not locked— Sheol! what if it was? Maybe I could short around it, I looked at the open window. It might be equipped with vibrobolts; if so, I would never know what hit me. But I could not spot any power leads or trigger connections and the flimsy construction of the building would make it hard to hide them. Probably there was nothing but contact alarms; there might not be so much as a selenium circuit.

While I was thinking about it I again heard voices next door; I flattened my ear and strained to listen.

"What's the blood type?"

"Type one, sergeant."

"Does it check?"

"No, Reeves is type three."

"Oho! Phone the main lab. We'll take him into town for a retinal."

I was caught cold and knew it. They knew positively that I wasn't Reeves. Once they photographed the pattern of blood vessels in the retina of either eye they would know just as certainly who I really was, in no longer time than it took to radio the picture to the Bureau of Morals and Investigation—less, if copies had been sent out to Denver and elsewhere with the tab on me.

I dove out the window.

I lit on my hands, rolled over in a ball, was flung to my feet as I unwound. If I set off an alarm I was too busy to hear it. The ship's door was open and the ignition was not locked—there was help indeed for the Son of a Widow! I didn't bother to taxi clear, but blasted at once, not caring if my rocket flame scorched my pursuers. We bounced along the ground, the little darling and I, then I lifted her nose by gyro and scooted away to the west.

8

I let her reach for the sky, seeking altitude and speed where the ram jets would work properly. I felt exalted to have a good ship under me and those cops far behind. But I snapped out of that silly optimism as I leveled off for jet flight.

If a cat escapes up a tree, he must stay there until the dog goes away. That was the fix I was in and in my case the dog would not go away, nor could I stay up indefinitely. The alarm would be out by now; behind me, on all sides of me, police pilots would be raising ship in a matter of minutes, even seconds. I was being tracked, that was sure, and the blip of my craft on several screens was being fed as data into a computer that would vector them in on me no matter where I turned. After that—well, it was land on command or be shot down.

The miracle of my escape began to seem a little less miraculous. Or *too* miraculous, perhaps? Since when were the police so sloppy that they would leave a prisoner in a room with an unguarded window? Wasn't it just a little too much of a coincidence that a ship I knew how to herd should come to that window and be left there—with the ignition unlocked—just as the sergeant said loudly the one thing that would be sure to make me try for it?

Maybe this was a second, and successful, attempt to panic me. Maybe somebody else knew my liking for the *Sparrow Hawk* courier, knew it because he had my dossier spread out in front of him and was as familiar with my sky polo record as I was. In which case they might not shoot me down just yet; they might be counting on me to lead them straight to my comrades.

Or perhaps, just possibly, it was a real escape—if I could exploit it. Either way, I was neither ready to be caught again, nor to lead them to my brethren—nor to die. I had an important message (I told myself); I was too busy to oblige them by dying just now.

I flipped the ship's commer to the police & traffic frequency and listened. There was some argument going on between the Denver port and a transport in the air but no one as yet was shouting for me to ground or get my pants shot off. Later perhaps—I left it switched on and thought.

The dead-reckoner showed me some seventy-five miles from Denver and headed north of west; I was surprised to see that I had been in the air less than ten minutes . . . so hopped up with adrenalin, no doubt, that my time sense was distorted. The ram-jet tanks were nearly full; I had nearly ten hours and six thousand miles at economy cruising—but of course at that speed they could almost throw rocks at me.

A plan, silly and perhaps impossible and certainly born of desperation but even so better than no plan at all, was beginning to form in my brain. I consulted the great-circle indicator and set a course for the Republic of Hawaii; my baby nosed herself slightly south of west. Then I turned to the fuel-speed-distance gnomograph and roughed a problem—3100 miles about, at around 800 mph, ending with dry tanks and depending on rocket juice and the nose units to cushion a cold-jet landing. Risky.

Not that I cared. Somewhere below me, shortly after I set the autopilot on the indicated course and speed, analyzers in the cybernetwork would he telling their human operators that I was attempting to escape to the Free State of Hawaii, on such a course, such an altitude, and at max speed for that range . . . and that I would pass over the Pacific coast between San Francisco and Monterey in sixty-odd minutes unless intercepted. But interception was certain. Even if they were still playing with me, cat and mouse, ground-to-air snarlers would rise up from the Sacramento Valley. If they missed (most unlikely!), manned ships as fast or faster than my baby, with full tanks and no need to conserve radius, would be waiting at altitude at the coast. I had no hope of running that gauntlet.

Nor did I intend to. I *wanted* them to destroy the little honey I was pushing, destroy her completely and in the air—because I had no intention of being aboard when it happened.

Operation Chucklehead, phase two: how to get out of the durn thing! Leaving a jet plane in powered flight has all been figured out by careful engineers; you slap the jettison lever and pray; the rest is done for you. The survival capsule closes down on you and seals, then the capsule with you in it is shot clear of the ship. In due course, at proper pressure and terminal air speed, the drogue is fired; it pulls your chute open, and there you are, floating comfortably toward God's good earth, with your emergency oxygen bottle for company.

There is only one hitch: both the capsule and the abandoned ship start sending out radio signals, dots for the capsule, dashes for the ship, and, for good measure, the capsule has a built-in radar-beacon.

The whole thing is about as inconspicuous as a cow in church.

I sat there chewing my thumb and staring out ahead. It seemed to me that the yonder was looking even wilder and bluer than usual—my own mood, no doubt, for I knew that thirteen ground miles were slipping out from under me each minute and that it was high time for me to find my hat and go home. Of course, there was a door right alongside me; I could strap on a chute and leave. But you can't open a door in a ram-jet plane in powered flight; nor do you jettison it—to do so will cause the plane to behave like a kicked pup. Nor is an eight-hundred-mile-an-hour breeze to be ignored even at 60,000 feet; I'd be sliced like butter on the door frame.

The answer depended on how good an autopilot this buggy had. The better robopilots could do everything but sing hymns; some of the cheaper ones could hold course, speed, and altitude but there their talents ended. In particular I wanted to know whether or not this autopilot had an emergency circuit to deal with a case of "fire out," for I intended to stop the ship, step out, and let the ship continue on in the direction of Hawaii by itself—if it could.

A ram jet won't operate at all except at high speed; that's why ram ships have rocket power as well, else they could never take off. If you drop below the critical speed of your jet engines your fire goes out, then you must start it again, either by rocket power or by diving to gain speed. It is a touchy business and a number of ram-jet pilots have been gathered to their heavenly reward through an unexpected case of "fire out."

My earlier experience with the courier *Sparrow Hawk* told me nothing, as you don't use autopilots in sky polo. Believe me, you don't. So I looked for the instruction manual in the glove compartment, failed to find it, then looked over the pilot itself. The data plate failed to say. No doubt, with a screw driver and plenty of time, I could have opened it, worried out the circuits and determined the fact—say in about a day and a half; those autopilots are a mass of transistors and spaghetti.

So I pulled the personal chute out of its breakaway clips and started shrugging my way into it while sighing, "Pal, I *hope* you have the necessary gimmick built into your circuits." The autopilot didn't answer, though I wouldn't have been much surprised if it had. Then I squeezed back into place and proceeded to override the autopilot manually. I didn't have too much time; I was already over the Deseret basin and I could see the setting sun glinting on the waters of the Great Salt Lake ahead and to the right.

First I took her down some, because 60,000 feet is thin and chilly—too little partial pressure of oxygen for the human lung. Then I started up in a gentle curving climb that would neither tear her wings off nor gee me into a blackout. I had to take her fairly high, because I intended to cut out the rocket motors entirely and force my best girl to light her stovepipes by diving for speed, it being my intention to go into a vertical stall, which would create "fire out"—and get off in a hurry at that point. For obvious reasons I did not want the rocket motors to cut loose just as I was trying to say good-by.

I kept curving her up until I was lying on my back with the earth behind me and sky ahead. I nursed it along, throttling her down, with the intention of stalling with the fire dead at thirty thousand feet—still thin but within jumping distance of breathable air and still high enough to give my lady a chance to go into her dive without cracking up on the Utah plateau. At about 28,000 I got that silly, helpless feeling you get when the controls go mushy and won't bite. Suddenly a light flashed red on the instrument board and both fires were out. It was time to leave.

I almost forgot the seat bottle. I was still stuffing the mouthpiece between my teeth and snapping the nose-piece over my nose while I was trying with the other hand to get the door open—all of this greatly impeded by the fact that the ship and I together were effectively in free fall; the slight air drag at the top of the stall trajectory made me weigh a few ounces, no more.

The door would not open. I finally remembered to slap the spill valve, then it came open and I was almost snatched outside. I hung there for a second or two, while the ground spun crazily overhead, then the door slammed shut and latched—and I shoved myself away from the plane. I didn't jump—we were falling together, I shoved.

I may have banged my head against a wing. In any case there is a short blank in my memory before I found myself sitting on space about twenty-five yards from the ship. She was spinning slowly and earth and sky were revolving lazily around me. There was a thin cold wind as I fell but I was not yet aware of the cold. We stayed pretty well together for a few moments—or hours; time had stopped—then the ship straightened out into a dive and pulled away from me.

I tried to follow her down by eye and became aware of the icy wind of my fall. My eyes hurt and I remembered something I had read about frozen eyeballs; I covered them with both hands. It helped a lot.

Suddenly I became frightened, panicky at the thought that I had delayed the jump too long and was about to smash into the desert floor. I uncovered my eyes and sneaked a look.

No, the ground was still a long way off, two or three miles perhaps. My guess was not worth much as it was already dark down there. I tried to catch sight of the ship, could not see it, then suddenly spotted it as her fires came on. I risked frozen eyes and watched, exaltation in my heart. The autopilot did indeed have built into it the emergency circuit for "fire out" and everything was proceeding according to plan. The little sweetheart leveled off headed west on course, and began to climb for the altitude she had been told to use. I sent a prayer after her that she would win through and end up in the clean Pacific, rather than be shot down.

I watched her glowing tailpipes out of sight while I continued to fall.

The triumph of my little ship had made me forget to be scared. I had known when I bailed out that it would have to be a delayed jump. My own body, in leaving the ship, would make a secondary blip on the screen of anything tracking the ship; my only hope of convincing the trackers that what they had witnessed was a real emergency—"fire out"—lay in getting away from the ship quickly and then in not being spotted on the way down. That meant that I must fall rapidly right out of the picture and not pull the rip cord until I was close to the ground, in visual darkness and in ground radar shadow.

But I had never made a delayed jump before; in fact I had jumped only twice, the two easy practice jumps under a jumpmaster which are required of every cadet in order to graduate. I wasn't especially uncomfortable as long as I kept my eyes closed, but I began to get a truly overpowering urge to pull that rip cord. My hand went to the handle and gripped it. I told myself to let go but I couldn't make myself do it. I was still much too high, dead sure to be spotted if I broke out that great conspicuous bumbershoot and floated down the rest of the way.

I had intended to rip the chute out somewhere between one thousand and five hundred feet above ground, but my nerve played out and I couldn't wait that long. There was a large town almost under me— Provo, Utah, by what I remembered of the situation from higher up. I convinced myself that I had to pull the rip cord to keep from landing right in the city.

I remembered just in time to remove the oxygen face piece, thereby avoiding a mouthful of broken teeth most likely, for I had never gotten around to strapping the bottle to me; I had been holding it in my left hand all the way down. I suppose I could have taken time even then to secure it, but what I did was to throw it in the general direction of a farm, hoping that it would land on plowed ground rather than on some honest citizen's skull. Then I pulled the handle.

For a horrible split second I thought that I had a faultily-packed chute. Then it opened and knocked me out—or I fainted with fright. I came to, hanging in the harness with the ground swinging and turning slowly beneath me. I was still too high up and I seemed to be floating toward the lights of Provo. So I took a deep breath—real air tasted good after the canned stuff—gathered a double handful of shrouds and spilled some wind.

I came down fast then and managed to let go just in time to get full support for the landing. I couldn't see the ground well in the evening darkness but I knew it was close; I gathered up my knees just as it says in the manual, then took it rather unexpectedly, stumbling, falling, and getting tangled in the chute. It is supposed to be equal to a fourteen-foot free jump; all I can say is it seems like more.

Then I was sitting on my tail in a field of sugar beets, and rubbing my left ankle.

Spies always bury their parachutes so I suppose I should have buried mine. But I didn't feel up to it and I didn't have any tools; I stuffed it into a culvert I found running under the road that edged the field, then started slogging that road toward the lights of Provo. My nose and right ear had been bleeding and the blood was dry on my face; I was covered with dirt, I had split my trousers, my hat was the Lord knows where—Denver, maybe, or over Nevada—, my left ankle seemed slightly sprained, my right hand was badly skinned, and I had had a childish accident. I felt swell.

I could hardly keep from whistling as I walked, I felt so good. Sure, I was still hunted, but the Prophet's proctors thought I was still high in the sky and headed for Hawaii. At least I hoped they believed that and, in any case, I was still free, alive, and reasonably intact. If one has to be hunted, Utah was a better place for it than most; it had been a center of heresy and schism ever since the suppression of the Mormon church, back in the days of the First Prophet. If I could keep out of the direct sight of the Prophet's police, it was unlikely that any of the natives would turn me in.

Nevertheless I lay flat in the ditch every time a truck or a ground car came along and I left the road and took to the fields again before it entered the city proper. I swung wide and entered by a dimly lighted side street. It lacked two hours of curfew; I needed to carry out the first part of my plan before the night patrol took to the streets.

I wandered around dark residential streets and avoided any direct encounters with people for most of an hour before finding what I wanted—some sort of a flier I could steal. It turned out to be a Ford family skycar, parked in a vacant lot. The house next to it was dark.

I sneaked up to it, keeping to the shadows, and broke my penknife jimmying the door—but I got it open. The ignition was locked, but I had not expected that sort of luck twice. I had had an extremely practical education at taxpayers expense which included detailed knowledge of I.C. engines, and this time there was no hurry; it took me twenty minutes, working in the dark, to short around the lock.

After a quick reconnoitre of the street I got in and started the electric auxiliary and glided quietly into the street, then rounded a corner before turning on the car's lights. Then I drove away as openly as a farmer returning from prayer meeting in town. Nevertheless I was afraid of running into a police check point at the city limits, so as soon as the houses thinned out I ran the car into the first open field and went on well away from the road—then unexpectedly dropped a front wheel into an irrigation ditch. That determined my take-off point.

The main engine coughed and took hold; the rotor unfolded its airfoils with a loud creak. She was sloppy on the take-off, being canted over into the ditch, but she made it. The ground dropped away.

9

The car I had stolen was a jalopy, old, not properly kept up, a bad valve knock in the engine, and a vibration in the rotor that I didn't like at all. But she would run and she had better than half a tank of fuel, enough to get me to Phoenix. I couldn't complain.

Worst was a complete lack of any navigating equipment other than an old-style uncompensated Sperry robot and a bundle of last year's strip maps of the sort the major oil companies give away. There was radio, but it was out of order.

Well, Columbus got by with less. Phoenix was almost due south and almost five hundred miles away. I estimated my drift by crossing my eyes and praying, set the robot on course and set her to hold real altitude of five hundred feet. Any more might get me into the cybernetwork; any less might get some local constable annoyed with me. I decided that running lights were safer than no running lights, this being no time to pick up a ticket, so I switched them on to "dim." After that I took a look around.

No sign of pursuit to the north—apparently my latest theft had not been noticed as yet. As for my first—well, the sweet darling was either shot down by now or far out over the Pacific. It occurred to me that I was hanging up quite a record for a mother's boy—accessory before and after the fact in murder, perjury before the Grand Inquisitor, treason, impersonation, grand larceny twice. There was still arson, and barratry, whatever that was, and rape. I decided I could avoid rape, but barratry I might manage, if I could find out what it meant. I still felt swell even though my nose was bleeding again.

It occurred to me that marrying a holy deaconess might be considered statutory rape under the law and that made me feel better; by then I didn't want to miss anything.

I stayed at the controls, overriding the pilot and avoiding towns, until we were better than a hundred miles south of Provo. From there south, past the Grand Canyon and almost to the ruins of the old "66" roadcity, people are awfully scarce; I decided that I could risk some sleep. So I set the pilot on eight hundred feet, ground altitude, told it firmly to watch out for trees and bluffs, went back to the after passenger bench and went at once to sleep.

I dreamt that the Grand Inquisitor was trying to break my nerve by eating juicy roast beef in my presence. "Confess!" he said, as he stabbed a bite and chewed. "Make it easy on yourself. Will you have some rare, or the slice off the end?" I was about to confess, too, when I woke up.

It was bright moonlight and we were just approaching the Grand Canyon. I went quickly to the controls and overrode the order about altitude—I was afraid that the simple little robot might have a nervous breakdown and start shedding capacitances in lieu of tears if it tried to hold the ship just eight hundred feet away from that Gargantuan series of ups and downs and pinnacles.

In the meantime I was enjoying the view so much that I forgot that I was starving. If a person hasn't seen the Canyon, there is no point in describing it—but I strongly recommend seeing it by moonlight from the air.

We sliced across it in about twenty minutes and I turned the ship back to automatic and started to forage, rummaging through the instrument panel compartment and the lockers. I turned up a chocolate almond bar and a few peanuts, which was a feast as I was ready for raw skunk. . . . I had eaten last in Kansas City. I polished them off and went back to sleep.

I don't recall setting the pilot alarm but must have done so for it woke me up just before dawn. Dawn over the desert was another high-priced tourist item but I had navigating to do and could not spare it more than a glance. I turned the crate at right angles for a few minutes to check drift and speed made good over ground to south, then figured a bit on the edge of a strip map. With luck and assuming that my guesses about wind were about right, Phoenix should show up in about half an hour.

My luck held. I passed over some mighty rough country, then suddenly, spread out to the right, was a wide flat desert valley, green with irrigated crops and with a large city in it—the Valley of the Sun and Phoenix. I made a poor landing in a boxed-in, little dry arroyo leading into the Salt River Canyon; I tore off one wheel and smashed the rotor but I didn't care—the important thing was that it wasn't likely to be found there very soon, it and my fingerprints . . . Reeves' prints, I mean. Half an hour later, after picking my way around enormous cacti and still bigger red boulders, I came out on the highway that leads down the canyon and into Phoenix.

It was going to be a long walk into Phoenix, especially with one sore ankle, but I decided not to risk hitching a ride. Traffic was light and I managed to get off the road and hide each time for the first hour. Then I was caught on a straight up-and-down piece by a freighter; there was nothing to do but give the driver a casual wave as I flattened myself to the rock wall and pretended to be nonchalant. He brought his heavy vehicle to a quick, smooth stop. "Want a lift, bud?"

I made up my mind in a hurry. "Yes, thanks!"

He swung a dural ladder down over the wide tread

and I climbed into the cab. He looked me over. "Brother!" he said admiringly. "Was it a mountain lion, or a bear?"

I had forgotten how I looked. I glanced down at myself. "Both," I answered solemnly. "Strangled one in each hand."

"I believe it."

"Fact is," I added, "I was riding a unicycle and bounced it off the road. On the high side, luckily, but I wrecked it."

"A unicycle? On *this* road? Not all the way from Globe?"

"Well, I had to get off and push at times. It was the down grade that got me, though."

He shook his head. "Let's go back to the lion-and-bear theory. I like it better." He didn't question me further, which suited me. I was beginning to realize that off-hand fictions led to unsuspected ramifications; I had never been over the road from Globe.

Nor had I ever been inside a big freighter before and I was interested to see how much it resembled, inside, the control room of an Army surface cruiser—the same port and starboard universal oleo speed gears controlling the traction treads, much the same instrument board giving engine speed, port and starboard motor speeds, torque ratios, and so forth. I could have herded it myself.

Instead I played dumb and encouraged him to talk. "I've never been in one of these big babies before. Tell me how it works, will you?"

That set him off and I listened with half an ear while thinking about how I should tackle Phoenix. He demonstrated how he applied both power and steering to the treads simply by tilting the two speed bars, one in each fist, and then discussed the economy of letting the diesel run at constant speed while he fed power as needed to the two sides. I let him talk—my first need was a bath and a shave and a change of clothes, that was sure; else I'd be picked up on sight for suspected vagrancy.

Presently I realized he had asked a question. "I think I see," I answered. "The Waterburies drive the treads."

"Yes and no," he went on. "It's a diesel-electric hook up. The Waterburies just act like a gear system, although there aren't any gears in them; they're hydraulic. Follow me?"

I said I thought so (I could have sketched them)— and filed away in my mind the idea that, if the Cabal should ever need cruiser pilots in a hurry, freighter jacks could be trained for the job in short order.

We were going downhill slightly even after we left the canyon; the miles flowed past. My host pulled off the road and ground to a stop by a roadside restaurant and oil station. "All out," he grunted. "Breakfast for us and go-juice for the go-buggy."

"Sounds good." We each consumed a tall stack with eggs and bacon and big, sweet Arizona grapefruit. He wouldn't let me pay for his and tried to pay for mine. As we went back to the freighter he stopped at the ladder and looked me over.

"The police gate is about three-quarters of a mile on in," he said softly. "I suppose that's as good a spot to check in as any." He looked at me and glanced away.

"Mmm . . ." I said. "I think I could stand to walk the rest of the way, to settle my breakfast. Thanks a lot for the lift."

"Don't mention it. Uh, there's a side road about two hundred yards back. It swings south and then west again, into town. Better for walking. Less traffic."

"Uh, thanks."

I walked back to the side road, wondering if my criminal career was that plain to everyone. One thing sure, I *had* to improve my appearance before tackling the city. The side road led through ranches and I passed several ranch houses without having the nerve to stop. But I came presently to a little house occupied by a

Spanish-Indian family with the usual assortment of
children and dogs. I took a chance; many of these
people were clandestine Catholics, I knew, and probably hated the proctors as much as I did.

The Señora was home. She was fat and kindly and
mostly Indian by her appearance. We couldn't talk much
as my Spanish is strictly classroom quality, but I could
ask for *agua,* and *agua* I got, both to drink and to wash
myself. She sewed up the rip in my trousers while I
stood foolishly in my shorts with the children making
comments; she brushed me off and she even let me use
her husband's razor. She protested over letting me pay
her but I was firm about it. I left there looking passable.

The road swung back into town as the freighter jack
had said—and without benefit of police. Eventually I
found a neighborhood shopping center and in it a little
tailor shop. There I waited while the rest of my transformation back to respectability was completed. With
my clothes freshly pressed, the spots removed, a brand-
new shirt and hat I was then able to walk down the
street and exchange a blessing with any proctor I might
meet while looking him calmly in the eye. A phone book
gave me the address of the South Side Tabernacle; a
map on the wall of the tailor shop got me oriented
without asking questions. It was within walking distance.

I hurried down the street and reached the church
just as eleven o'clock services were starting. Sighing with
relief I slipped into a back pew and actually enjoyed
the services, just as I had as a boy, before I had learned
what was back of them. I felt peaceful and secure; in
spite of everything I had made it safely. I let the familiar
music soak into my soul while I looked forward to
revealing myself to the priest afterwards and then let
him do the worrying for a while.

To tell the truth I went to sleep during the sermon.
But I woke up in time and I doubt if anyone noticed.
Afterwards I hung around, waited for a chance to speak
to the priest, and told him how much I had enjoyed

his sermon. He shook hands and I gave him the recognition grip of the brethren.

But he did not return it. I was so upset by that that
I almost missed what he was saying. "Thank you, my
boy. It's always good news to a new pastor to hear that
his ministrations are appreciated."

I guess my face gave me away. He added, "Something wrong?"

I stammered. "Oh, no, reverend sir. You see, I'm a
stranger myself. Then you aren't the Reverend Baird?"
I was in cold panic. Baird was my only contact with the
brethren short of New Jerusalem; without someone to
hide me I would be picked up in a matter of hours.
Even as I answered I was making wild plans to steal
another ship that night and then try to run the border
patrol into Mexico.

His voice cut into my thoughts as if from a great distance. "No, I'm afraid not, my son. Did you wish to see
the Reverend Baird?"

"Well, it isn't terribly important, sir. He is an old
friend of my uncle. I was to look him up while I was
here and pay my respects." Maybe that nice Indian
woman would hide me until dark?

"That won't be difficult. He's here in town. I'm just
supplying his pulpit while he is laid up."

My heart made a full turn at about twelve gee; I tried
to keep it out of my face. "Perhaps if he is sick I had
better not disturb him."

"Oh, not at all. A broken bone in his foot—he'll enjoy
a bit of company. Here." The priest fumbled under his
robes, found a piece of paper and a pencil and wrote
out the address. "Two streets over and half a block
down. You can't miss it."

Of course I did miss it, but I doubled back and found
it, an old vine-grown house with a suggestion of New
England about it. It was set well back in a large, untidy
garden—eucalyptus, palms, shrubs, and flowers, all in
pleasant confusion. I pressed the announcer and heard

the whine of an old-style scanner; a speaker inquired: "Yes?"

"A visitor to see the Reverend Baird, if he so pleases."

There was a short silence while he looked me over, then: "You'll have to let yourself in. My housekeeper has gone to the market. Straight through and out into the back garden." The door clicked and swung itself open.

I blinked at the darkness, then went down a central hallway and out through the back door. An old man was lying in a swing there, with one foot propped up on pillows. He lowered his book and peered at me over his glasses.

"What do you want of me, son?"

"Light."

An hour later I was washing down the last of some superb enchiladas with cold, sweet milk. As I reached for a cluster of muscatel grapes Father Baird concluded his instructions to me. "Nothing to do until dark, then. Any questions?"

"I don't think so, sir. Sanchez takes me out of town and delivers me to certain others of the brethren who will see to it that I get to General Headquarters. My end of it is simple enough."

"True. You won't be comfortable however."

I left Phoenix concealed in a false bottom of a little vegetable truck. I was stowed like cargo, with my nose pressed against the floor boards. We were stopped at a police gate at the edge of town; I could hear brusque voices with that note of authority, and Sanchez' impassioned Spanish in reply. Someone rummaged around over my head and the cracks in the false bottom gleamed with light.

Finally a voice said, "It's okay, Ezra. That's Father Baird's handyman. Makes a trip out to the Father's ranch every night or so."

"Well, why didn't he say so?"

"He gets excited and loses his English. Okay. Get going, chico. Vaya usted con Dios."

"Gracias, senores. Buenas noches."

At the Reverend Baird's ranch I was transferred to a helicopter, no rickety heap this time, but a new job, silent and well equipped. She was manned by a crew of two, who exchanged pass grips with me but said nothing other than to tell me to get into the passenger compartment and stay there. We took off at once.

The windows of the passenger space had been covered; I don't know which way we went, nor how far. It was a rough ride, as the pilot seemed dead set on clipping daisies the whole way. It was a reasonable precaution to avoid being spotted in a scope, but I hoped he knew what he was doing—I wouldn't want to herd a heli that way in broad daylight. He must have scared a lot of coyotes—I know he frightened me.

At last I heard the squeal of a landing beam. We slid along it, hovered, and bumped gently to a stop. When I got out I found myself staring into the maw of a tripod-mounted blaster backed up by two alert and suspicious men.

But my escort gave the password, each of the guards questioned me separately, and we exchanged recognition signals. I got the impression that they were a little disappointed that they couldn't let me have it; they seemed awfully eager. When they were satisfied, a hoodwink was slipped over my head and I was led away. We went through a door, walked maybe fifty yards, and crowded into a compartment. The floor dropped away.

My stomach caught up with me and I groused to myself because I hadn't been warned that it was an elevator, but I kept my mouth shut. We left the lift, walked a way, and I was nudged onto a platform of some sort, told to sit down and hang on—whereupon we lurched away at breakneck speed. It felt like a rollercoaster—not a good thing to ride blindfolded. Up to then I hadn't really been scared. I began to think that the hazing was intentional, for they could have warned me.

We made another elevator descent, walked several hundred paces, and my hoodwink was removed. I caught my first sight of General Headquarters.

I didn't recognize it as such; I simply let out a gasp. One of my guards smiled. "They all do that," he said dryly.

It was a limestone cavern so big that one felt outdoors rather than underground and so magnificently lavish in its formations as to make one think of fairyland, or the Gnome King's palace. I had assumed that we were underground from the descents we had made, but nothing had prepared me for what I saw.

I have seen photographs of what the Carlsbad Caverns used to be, before the earthquake of '96 destroyed them; General Headquarters was something like that, although I can't believe that the Carlsbad Caverns were as big or half as magnificent. I could not at first grasp the immensity of the room I was in; underground there is nothing to judge size by and the built-in rangefinder of a human's two-eyed vision is worthless beyond about fifty feet without something in the distance to give him scale—a house, a man, a tree, even the horizon itself. Since a natural cave contains nothing at all that is well known, customary, the human eye can't size it.

So, while I realized that the room I stood in was big, I could not guess just how big; my brain scaled it down to fit my prejudices. We were standing higher than the main floor and at one end of the room; the whole thing was softly flood-lighted. I got through craning my neck and *oh*ing and *ah*ing, looked down and saw a toy village some distance away below us. The little buildings seemed to be about a foot high.

Then I saw tiny people walking around among the buildings—and the whole thing suddenly snapped into scale. The toy village was at least a quarter of a mile away; the whole room was not less than a mile long and many hundreds of feet high. Instead of the fear of being shut in that people normally experience in caves I was suddenly hit by the other fear, the fear of open spaces, agoraphobia. I wanted to slink along close to the walls, like a timid mouse.

The guide who had spoken touched my arm. "You'll have plenty of time for rubbernecking later. Let's get going." They led me down a path which meandered between stalagmites, from a baby-finger size to Egyptian pyramids, around black pools of water with lilypads of living stone growing on them, past dark wet domes that were old when man was new, under creamy translucent curtains of onyx and sharp rosy-red and dark green stalactites. My capacity to wonder began to be overloaded and presently I quit trying.

We came out on a fairly level floor of bat droppings and made good time to the village. The buildings, I saw as I got closer, were not buildings in the outdoors sense, but were mere partitions of that honeycomb plastic used for sound-deadening—space separators for efficiency and convenience. Most of them were not roofed. We stopped in front of the largest of these pens; the sign over its door read ADMINISTRATION. We entered and I was taken into the personnel office. This room almost made me homesick, so matter of fact, so professionally military was it in its ugly, efficient appointments. There was even the elderly staff clerk with the nervous sniff who seems to be general issue for such an office since the time of Caesar. The sign on his desk described him as Warrant Officer R. E. Giles and he had quite evidently come back to his office after working hours to check me in.

"Pleased to meet you, Mr. Lyle," he said, shaking hands and exchanging recognition. Then he scratched his nose and sniffed. "You're a week or so early and your quarters aren't ready. Suppose we billet you tonight with a blanket roll in the lounge of B.O.Q. and get you squared away in the morning?"

I said that would be perfectly satisfactory and he seemed relieved.

10

I guess I had been expecting to be treated as some sort of a conquering hero on my arrival—you know, my new comrades hanging breathlessly on every word of my modest account of my adventures and hairbreadth escapes and giving thanks to the Great Architect that I had been allowed to win through with my all-important message.

I was wrong. The personnel adjutant sent for me before I had properly finished breakfast, but I didn't even see him; I saw Mr. Giles. I was a trifle miffed and interrupted him to ask how soon it would be convenient for me to pay my formal call on the commanding officer.

He sniffed. "Oh, yes. Well, Mr. Lyle, the C.G. sends his compliments to you and asks you to consider that courtesy calls have been made, not only on him but on department heads. We're rather pushed for time right now. He'll send for you the first spare moment he has."

I knew quite well that the general had not sent me any such message and that the personnel clerk was simply following a previously established doctrine. It didn't make me feel better.

But there was nothing I could do about it; the system took me in hand. By noon I had been permanently billeted, had had my chest thumped and so forth, and had made my reports. Yes, I got a chance to tell my story—to a recording machine. Flesh-and-blood men did receive the message I carried, but I got no fun out of that; I was under hypnosis at the time, just as I had been when it was given to me.

This was too much for me; I asked the psycho-technician who operated me what the message was I carried. He answered stiffly, "We aren't permitted to tell couriers what they carry." His manner suggested that my question was highly improper.

I lost my temper a bit. I didn't know whether he was senior to me or not as he was not in uniform, but I didn't care. "For pity's sake! What is this? Don't the brethren *trust* me? Here I risk my neck—"

He cut in on me in a much more conciliatory manner. "No, no, it's not that at all. It's for your protection."

"Huh?"

"Doctrine. The less you know that you don't need to know the less you can spill if you are ever captured—and the safer it is for you and for everybody. For example, do you know where you are now? Could you point it out on a map?"

"No."

"Neither do I. We don't need to know so we aren't told. However," he went on, "I don't mind telling you, in a general way, what you were carrying—just routine reports, confirming stuff we already had by sensitive circuits mostly. You were coming this way, so they dumped a lot of such stuff into you. I took three spools from you."

"Just routine stuff? Why, the Lodge Master told me I was carrying a message of vital importance. That fat old joker!"

The technician grudged a smile. "I'm afraid he was pulling—Oh!"

"Eh?"

"I know what he meant. You were carrying a message of vital importance—to you. You carried your own credentials hypnotically. If you had not been, you would never have been allowed to wake up."

I had nothing to say. I left quietly.

My rounds of the medical office, psych office, quartermaster, and so forth had begun to give me a notion of the size of the place. The "toy village" I had first seen was merely the administrative group. The power plant, a packaged pile, was in a separate cavern with many yards of rock wall as secondary shielding. Married couples were quartered where they pleased—about a third of us were female—and usually chose to set up their houses (or pens) well away from the central grouping. The armory and ammo dump were located in a side passage, a safe distance from offices and quarters.

There was fresh water in abundance, though quite hard, and the same passages that carried the underground streams appeared to supply ventilation—at least the air was never stale. It stayed at a temperature of 69.6 Fahrenheit and a relative humidity of 32%, winter and summer, night and day.

By lunchtime I was hooked into the organization, and found myself already hard at work at a temporary job immediately after lunch—in the armory, repairing and adjusting blasters, pistols, squad guns, and assault guns. I could have been annoyed at being asked, or ordered, to do what was really gunnery sergeant work, but the whole place seemed to be run with a minimum of protocol—we cleared our own dishes away at mess, for example. And truthfully it felt good to sit at a bench in the armory, safe and snug, and handle calipers and feather gauges and drifts again—good, useful work.

Just before dinner that first day I wandered into the B.O.Q. lounge and looked around for an unoccupied chair. I heard a familiar baritone voice behind me: "Johnnie! Johnnie Lyle!" I whirled around and there, hurrying toward me, was Zebadiah Jones—good old Zeb, large as life and his ugly face split with a grin.

We pounded each other on the back and swapped insults. "When did you get here?" I finally asked him.

"Oh, about two weeks ago."

"You did? You were still at New Jerusalem when I left. How did you do it?"

"Nothing to it. I was shipped as a corpse—in a deep trance. Sealed up in a coffin and marked 'contagious'."

I told him about my own mixed-up trip and Zeb seemed impressed, which helped my morale. Then I asked him what he was doing.

"I'm in the Psych & Propaganda Bureau," he told me, "under Colonel Novak. Just now I'm writing a series of oh-so-respectful articles about the private life of the Prophet and his acolytes and attending priests, how many servants they have, how much it costs to run the Palace, all about the fancy ceremonies and rituals, and such junk. All of it perfectly true, of course, and told with unctuous approval. But I lay it on a shade too thick. The emphasis is on the jewels and the solid gold trappings and how much it all costs, and I keep telling the yokels what a privilege it is for them to be permitted to pay for such frippery and how flattered they should feel that God's representative on earth lets them take care of him."

"I guess I don't get it," I said, frowning. "People like that circusy stuff. Look at the way the tourists to New Jerusalem scramble for tickets to a Temple ceremony."

"Sure, sure—but we don't peddle this stuff to people on a holiday to New Jerusalem; we syndicate it to little local papers in poor farming communities in the Mississippi Valley, and in the Deep South, and in the back country of New England. That is to say, we spread it among some of the poorest and most puritanical elements of the population, people who are emotionally convinced that poverty and virtue are the same thing. It grates on their nerves; in time it should soften them up and make doubters of them."

"Do you seriously expect to start a rebellion with picayune stuff like that?"

"It's not picayune stuff, because it acts directly on their emotions, below the logical level. You can sway a thousand men by appealing to their prejudices quicker than you can convince one man by logic. It doesn't have to be a prejudice about an important matter either. Johnnie, you savvy how to use connotation indices, don't you?"

"Well, yes and no. I know what they are; they are supposed to measure the emotional effects of words."

"That's true, as far as it goes. But the index of a word isn't fixed like the twelve inches in a foot; it is a complex variable function depending on context, age and sex and occupation of the listener, the locale and a dozen other things. An index is a particular solution of the variable that tells you whether a particular word used in a particular fashion to a particular reader or type of reader will affect that person favorably, unfavorably, or simply leave him cold. Given proper measurements of the group addressed it can be as mathematically exact as any branch of engineering. We never have all the data we need so it remains an art—but a very precise art, especially as we employ 'feedback' through field sampling. Each article I do is a little more annoying than the last—and the reader never knows why."

"It sounds good, but I don't see quite how it's done."

"I'll give you a gross case. Which would you rather have? A nice, thick, juicy, tender steak—or a segment of muscle tissue from the corpse of an immature castrated bull?"

I grinned at him. "You can't upset me. I'll take it by either name . . . not too well done. I wish they would announce chow around here; I'm starved."

"You think you aren't affected because you were braced for it. But how long would a restaurant stay in business if it used that sort of terminology? Take another gross case, the Anglo-Saxon monosyllables that naughty little boys write on fences. You can't use them in polite company without offending, yet there are circumlocutions or synonyms for every one of them which may be used in any company."

I nodded agreement. "I suppose so. I certainly see how it could work on other people. But personally, I guess I'm immune to it. Those taboo words don't mean a thing to me—except that I'm reasonably careful not to offend other people. I'm an educated man, Zeb— 'Sticks and stones may break my bones, et cetera.' But I see how you could work on the ignorant."

Now I should know better than to drop my guard with Zeb. The good Lord knows he's tripped me up enough times. He smiled at me quietly and made a short statement involving some of those taboo words.

"You leave my mother out of this!"

I was the one doing the shouting and I came up out of my chair like a dog charging into battle. Zeb must have anticipated me exactly and shifted his weight before he spoke, for, instead of hanging one on his chin, I found my wrist seized in his fist and his other arm around me, holding me in a clinch that stopped the fight before it started. "Easy, Johnnie," he breathed in my ear. "I apologize. I most humbly apologize and ask your forgiveness. Believe me, I wasn't insulting you."

"So you say!"

"So I say, most humbly. Forgive me?"

As I simmered down I realized that my outbreak had been very conspicuous. Although we had picked a quiet corner to talk, there were already a dozen or more others in the lounge, waiting for dinner to be announced. I could feel the dead silence and sense the question in the minds of others as to whether or not it was going to be necessary to intervene. I started to turn red with embarrassment rather than anger. "Okay. Let me go."

He did so and we sat down again. I was still sore and not at all inclined to forget Zeb's unpardonable breach of good manners, but the crisis was past. But he spoke quietly, "Johnnie, believe me, I was not insulting you nor any member of your family. That was a scientific demonstration of the dynamics of connotational indices, and that is all it was."

"Well—you didn't have to make it so personal."

"Ah, but I did have to. We were speaking of the psychodynamics of emotion . . . and emotions are personal, subjective things which must be experienced to be

understood. You were of the belief that you, as an educated man, were immune to this form of attack—so I
ran a lab test to show you that no one is immune. Now
just what did I say to you?"

"You said— Never mind. Okay, so it was a test. But
I don't care to repeat it. You've made your point: I don't
like it."

"But what did I say? All I said, in fact, was that you
were the legitimate offspring of a legal marriage. Right?
What is insulting about that?"

"But—" I stopped and ran over in my mind the infur-
iating, insulting, and degrading things he had said—and,
do you know, that is absolutely all they added up to. I
grinned sheepishly. "It was the *way* you said it."

"Exactly, exactly! To put it technically, I selected terms
with high negative indices, for this situation and for this
listener. Which is precisely what we do with this propaganda, except that the emotional indices are lesser
quantitatively to avoid arousing suspicion and to evade
the censors—slow poison, rather than a kick in the belly.
The stuff we write is all about the Prophet, lauding him
to the skies . . . so the irritation produced in the reader
is transferred to him. The method cuts below the
reader's conscious thought and acts on the taboos and
fetishes that infest his subconscious."

I remembered sourly my own unreasoned anger. "I'm
convinced. It sounds like heap big medicine."

"It is, chum, it is. There is magic in words, black
magic—if you know how to invoke it."

After dinner Zeb and I went to his cubicle and continued to bat the breeze. I felt warm and comfortable
and very, very contented. The fact that we were part
of a revolutionary plot, a project most unlikely to succeed and which would most probably end with us both
dead in battle or burned for treason, affected me not
at all. Good old Zeb! What if he did get under my guard
and hit me where it hurt? He was my "family"—all the
family that I had. To be with him now made me feel

the way I used to feel when my mother would sit me down in the kitchen and feed me cookies and milk.

We talked about this and that, in the course of which I learned more about the organization and discovered— was very surprised to discover—that not all of our comrades were brethren. Lodge Brothers, I mean. "But isn't that dangerous?"

"What isn't? And what did you expect, old son? Some of our most valuable comrades can't join the Lodge; their own religious faith forbids it. But we don't have any monopoly on hating tyranny and loving freedom and we need all the help we can get. Anybody going our direction is a fellow traveler. Anybody."

I thought it over. The idea was logical, though somehow vaguely distasteful. I decided to gulp it down quickly. "I suppose so. I imagine even the pariahs will be of some use to us, when it comes to the fighting, even if they aren't eligible for membership."

Zeb gave me a look I knew too well. "Oh, for Pete's sake, John! When are you going to give up wearing diapers?"

"Huh?"

"Haven't you gotten it through your head yet that the whole 'pariah' notion is this tyranny's scapegoat mechanism that every tyranny requires?"

"Yes, but—"

"Shut up. Take sex away from people. Make it forbidden, evil, limit it to ritualistic breeding. Force it to back up into suppressed sadism. Then hand the people a scapegoat to hate. Let them kill a scapegoat occasionally for cathartic release. The mechanism is ages old. Tyrants used it centuries before the word 'psychology' was ever invented. It works, too. Look at yourself."

"Look, Zeb, I don't have anything against the pariahs."

"You had better not have. You'll find a few dozen of them in the Grand Lodge here. And by the way, forget that word 'pariah.' It has, shall we say, a very high negative index."

He shut up and so did I; again I needed time to get my thoughts straight. Please understand me—it is easy to be free when you have been brought up in freedom; it is *not* easy otherwise. A zoo tiger, escaped, will often slink back into the peace and security of his bars. If he can't get back, they tell me he will pace back and forth within the limits of bars that are no longer there. I suppose I was still pacing in my conditioned pattern.

The human mind is a tremendously complex thing; it has compartments in it that its owner himself does not suspect. I had thought that I had given my mind a thorough housecleaning already and had rid it of all the dirty superstitions I had been brought up to believe. I was learning that the "housecleaning" had been no more than a matter of sweeping the dirt under the rugs—it would be years before the cleansing would be complete, before the clean air of reason blew through every room.

All right, I told myself, if I meet one of these par— no, "comrades," I'll exchange recognition with him and be polite—as long as he is polite to me! At the time I saw nothing hypocritical in the mental reservation.

Zeb lay back, smoking, and let me stew. I knew that he smoked and he knew that I disapproved. But it was a minor sin and, when we were rooming together in the Palace barracks, I would never have thought of reporting him. I even knew which room servant was his bootlegger. "Who is sneaking your smokes in now?" I asked, wishing to change the subject.

"Eh? Why, you buy them at the P.X., of course." He held the dirty thing out and looked at it. "These Mexican cigarettes are stronger than I like. I suspect that they use real tobacco in them, instead of the bridge sweepings I'm used to. Want one?"

"Huh? Oh, no, thanks!"

He grinned wryly. "Go ahead, give me your usual lecture. It'll make you feel better."

"Now look here, Zeb, I wasn't criticizing. I suppose it's just one of the many things I've been wrong about."

"Oh, no. It's a dirty, filthy habit that ruins my wind and stains my teeth and may eventually kill me off with lung cancer." He took a deep inhalation, let the smoke trickle out of the corners of his mouth, and looked profoundly contented. "But it just happens that I *like* dirty, filthy habits."

He took another puff. "But it's not a sin and my punishment for it is here and now, in the way my mouth tastes each morning. The Great Architect doesn't give a shout in Sheol about it. Catch on, old son? He isn't even watching."

"There is no need to be sacrilegious."

"I wasn't being so."

"You weren't, eh? You were scoffing at one of the most fundamental—perhaps the one fundamental—proposition in religion: the certainty that God is watching!"

"*Who* told *you?*"

For a moment all I could do was to sputter. "Why, it isn't necessary. It's an axiomatic certainty. It's—"

"I repeat, *who* told *you?* See here, I retract what I said. Perhaps the Almighty is watching me smoke. Perhaps it is a mortal sin and I will burn for it for eons. Perhaps. But who told *you?* Johnnie, you've reached the point where you are willing to kick the Prophet out and hang him to a tall, tall tree. Yet you are willing to assert your own religious convictions and to use them as a touchstone to judge my conduct. So I repeat: who told you? What hill were you standing on when the lightning came down from Heaven and illuminated you? Which archangel carried the message?"

I did not answer at once. I could not. When I did it was with a feeling of shock and cold loneliness. "Zeb . . . I think I understand you at last. You are an—atheist. Aren't you?"

Zeb looked at me bleakly. "Don't call me an atheist," he said slowly, "unless you are really looking for trouble."

"Then you aren't one?" I felt a wave of relief, although I still didn't understand him.

"No, I am not. Not that it is any of your business. My religious faith is a private matter between me and my God. What my inner beliefs are you will have to judge by my actions . . . for you are not invited to question me about them. I decline to explain them nor to justify them to you. Nor to anyone . . . not the Lodge Master . . . nor to the Grand Inquisitor, if it comes to that."

"But you do believe in God?"

"I told you so, didn't I? Not that you had any business asking me."

"Then you must believe in other things?"

"Of course I do! I believe that a man has an obligation to be merciful to the weak . . . patient with the stupid . . . generous with the poor. I think he is obliged to lay down his life for his brothers, should it be required of him. But I don't propose to prove any of those things; they are beyond proof. And I don't demand that you believe as I do."

I let out my breath. "I'm satisfied, Zeb."

Instead of looking pleased he answered, "That's mighty kind of you, brother, mighty kind! Sorry—I shouldn't be sarcastic. But I had no intention of asking for your approval. You goaded me—accidentally, I'm sure—into discussing matters that I never intend to discuss." He stopped to light up another of those stinking cigarettes and went on more quietly. "John, I suppose that I am, in my own cantankerous way, a very narrow man myself. I believe very strongly in freedom of religion—but I think that that freedom is best expressed as freedom to keep quiet. From my point of view, a great deal of openly expressed piety is insufferable conceit."

"Huh?"

"Not every case—I've known the good and the humble and the devout. But how about the man who claims to know what the Great Architect is thinking? The man who claims to be privy to His Inner Plans? It strikes me as sacrilegious conceit of the worst sort— this character probably has never been any closer to His Trestle Board than you or I. But it makes him feel good to claim to be on chummy terms with the Almighty, it builds his ego, and lets him lay down the law to you and me. Pfui! Along comes a knothead with a loud voice, an I.Q. around 90, hair in his ears, dirty underwear, and a lot of ambition. He's too lazy to be a farmer, too stupid to be an engineer, too unreliable to be a banker—but, brother, can he pray! After a while he has gathered around him other knotheads who don't have his vivid imagination and self-assurance but like the idea of having a direct line to Omnipotence. Then this character is no longer Nehemiah Scudder but the First Prophet."

I was going along with him, feeling shocked but rather pleasantly so, until he named the First Prophet. Perhaps my own spiritual state at that time could have been described as that of a "primitive" follower of the First Prophet—that is to say, I had decided that the Prophet Incarnate was the devil himself and that all of his works were bad, but that belief did not affect the basics of the faith I had learned from my mother. The thing to do was to purge and reform the Church, not to destroy it. I mention this because my own case paralleled a very serious military problem that was to develop later.

I found that Zeb was studying my face. "Did I get you on the raw again, old fellow? I didn't mean to."

"Not at all," I answered stiffly, and went on to explain that, in my opinion, the sinfulness of the present gang of devils that had taken over the Church in no way invalidated the true faith. "After all, no matter what you think nor how much you may like to show off your cynicism, the doctrines are a matter of logical necessity. The Prophet Incarnate and his cohorts can pervert them, but they can't destroy them—and it doesn't matter whether the real Prophet had dirty underwear or not."

Zeb sighed as if he were very tired. "Johnnie, I certainly did not intend to get into an argument about religion with you. I'm not the aggressive type—you know that. I had to be pushed into the Cabal." He paused. "You say the doctrines are a matter of logic?"

"You've explained the logic to me yourself It's a perfect, consistent structure."

"So it is. Johnnie, the nice thing about citing God as an authority is that you can prove anything you set out to prove. It's just a matter of selecting the proper postulates, then insisting that your postulates are 'inspired.' Then no one can possibly prove that you are wrong."

"You are asserting that the First Prophet was *not* inspired?"

"I am asserting nothing. For all you know, *I* am the First Prophet, come back to kick out the defilers of my temple."

"Don't be—" I was all wound up to kick it around further when there came a knock at Zeb's door. I stopped and he called out, "Come in!"

It was Sister Magdalene.

She nodded at Zeb, smiled sweetly at my open-mouthed surprise and said, "Hello, John Lyle. Welcome." It was the first time I had even seen her other than in the robes of a holy deaconess. She seemed awfully pretty and much younger.

"Sister Magdalene!"

"No. Staff Sergeant Andrews. 'Maggie,' to my friends."

"But what happened? Why are you here?"

"Right at the moment I'm here because I heard at dinner that you had arrived. When I didn't find you in your own quarters I concluded that you would be with Zeb. As for the rest, I couldn't go back, any more than you or Zeb—and our hideout back in New Jerusalem was getting overcrowded, so they transferred me."

"Well, it's good to see you!"

"It's good to see you, John." She patted me on the cheek and smiled again. Then she climbed on Zeb's bed and squatted tailor-fashion, showing a rather immodest amount of limb in the process. Zeb lit another cigarette and handed it to her; she accepted it, drew smoke deep into her lungs, and let it go as if she had been smoking all her life.

I had never seen a woman smoke—never. I could see Zeb watching me, confound him!—and I most carefully ignored it. Instead I grinned and said, "This is a *wonderful* reunion! If only—"

"I know," agreed Maggie. "If only Judith were here. Have you heard from her yet, John?"

"Heard from her? How could I?"

"That's right, you couldn't—not yet. But you can write to her now."

"Huh? How?"

"I don't know the code number off hand, but you can drop it at my desk—I'm in G-2. Don't bother to seal it; all personal mail has to be censored and paraphrased. I wrote to her last week but I haven't had an answer yet."

I thought about excusing myself at once and writing a letter, but I didn't. It was wonderful to be with both of them and I didn't want to cut the evening short. I decided to write before I went to bed—while realizing, with surprise, that I had been so much on the go that, as far as I could remember, I hadn't even had time to think about Judith once . . . well, since Denver, at least.

But I did not get to write to her even later that night. It was past eleven o'clock and Maggie was saying something about reveille coming early when an orderly showed up: "The Commanding General's compliments and will Legate Lyle see him at once, sir."

I gave my hair a quick brush with Zeb's gear and

hurried away, while wishing mightily that I had something fit to report in, rather than a civilian suit much the worse for wear.

The inner sanctum was deserted and dark except for a light that I could see in the far inner office—even Mr. Giles was not at his desk. I found my way in, knocked on the door frame, stepped inside, clicked my heels and saluted. "Legate Lyle reports to the Commanding General as ordered, sir."

An elderly man seated at a big desk with his back to me turned and looked up, and I got another surprise. "Ah, yes, John Lyle," he said gently. He got up and came toward me, with his hand out. "It's been a long time, hasn't it?"

It was Colonel Huxley, head of the Department of Applied Miracles when I was a cadet—and almost my only friend among the officers at that time. Many was the Sunday afternoon that I had relaxed in his quarters, my stock unhooked, free for the moment from the pressure of discipline.

I took his hand. "Colonel—I mean 'General,' sir. . . . I thought you were dead!"

"Dead colonel into live general, eh? No, Lyle, though I was listed as dead when I went underground. They usually do that when an officer disappears; it looks better. You're dead, too—did you know?"

"Uh, no, I didn't, sir. Not that it matters. This is wonderful, sir!"

"Good."

"But—I mean, how did you ever—well—" I shut up.

"How did I land here and in charge at that? I've been a Brother since I was your age, Lyle. But I didn't go underground until I had to—none of us do. In my case the pressure for me to join the priesthood became a bit too strong; the Superintendent was quite restless about having a lay officer know too much about the more abstruse branches of physics and chemistry. So I took a short leave and died. Very sad." He smiled. "But sit down.

I've been meaning to send for you all day, but it's been a busy day. They all are. It wasn't until now that I've had time to listen to the record of your report."

We sat down and chatted, and I felt that my cup runneth over. Huxley I respected more than any officer I had ever served under. His very presence resolved any residual doubts I might have—if the Cabal was right for him, it was right for me, and never mind the subtleties of doctrine.

At last he said, "I didn't call you in at this late hour just to chat, Lyle. I've a job for you."

"Yes, sir?"

"No doubt you've already noticed what a raw militia we have here. This is between ourselves and I'm not criticizing our comrades—every one of them has pledged his life to our cause, a harder thing for them to do than for you and me, and they have all placed themselves under military discipline, a thing still harder. But I haven't enough trained soldiers to handle things properly. They mean well but I am tremendously handicapped in trying to turn the organization into an efficient fighting machine. I'm swamped with administrative details. Will you help me?"

I stood up. "I shall be honored to serve with the General to the best of my ability."

"Fine! We'll call you my personal aide for the time being. That's all for tonight, Captain. I'll see you in the morning."

I was halfway out the door before his parting designation sunk in—then I decided that it was a slip of the tongue.

But it was not. I found my own office the next morning by the fact that a sign had been placed on it reading: "CAPTAIN LYLE." From the standpoint of a professional military man there is one good thing about revolutions: the opportunities for swift promotion are excellent . . . even if the pay is inclined to be irregular.

My office adjoined General Huxley's and from then on I almost lived in it—eventually I had a cot installed back of my desk. The very first day I was still fighting my way down a stack of papers in my incoming basket at ten at night. I had promised myself that I would find the bottom, then write a long letter to Judith. But it turned out to be a very short note, as there was a memorandum addressed to me personally, rather than to the General, at the bottom.

It was addressed to "Legate J. Lyle," then someone had scratched out "Legate" and written "Captain." It went on:

MEMORANDUM FOR ALL PERSONNEL NEWLY REPORTED
SUBJECT: Personal Conversion Report
1. You are requested and directed to write out, as fully as possible, all of the events, thoughts, considerations, and incidents which led up to your decision to join our fight for freedom. This account should be as detailed as possible and as subjective as possible. A report written hastily, too briefly, or too superficially will be returned to be expanded and corrected and may be supplemented by hypno examination.
2. This report will be treated as confidential as a whole and any portion of it may be classified secret by the writer. You may substitute letters or numbers for proper names if this will help you to speak freely, but the report must be complete.
3. No time off from regular duties is allotted for this purpose, but this report must be treated as extra-duty of highest priority. A draft of your report will be expected by *(here some one had written in a date and hour less than forty-eight hours away; I used some profane expressions under my breath.)*
        BY ORDER OF THE COMMANDING GENERAL
            (s) M. NOVAK, Col., F.U.S.A
            Chief of Psychology

I was considerably annoyed by this demand and decided to write to Judith first anyway. The note didn't go well—how can one write a love letter when you know that one or more strangers will read it and that one of them will rephrase your tenderest words? Besides that, while writing to Judith, my thoughts kept coming back to that night on the rampart of the Palace when I had first met her. It seemed to me that my own personal conversion, as the nosy Colonel Novak called it, started then . . . although I had begun to have doubts before then. Finally I finished the note, decided not to go to bed at once but to tackle that blasted report.

After a while I noticed that it was one o'clock in the morning and I still hadn't carried my account up to the point where I was admitted to the Brotherhood. I stopped writing rather reluctantly (I found that I had grown interested) and locked it in my desk.

At breakfast the next morning I got Zebadiah aside, showed him the memorandum, and asked him about it. "What's the big idea?" I asked. "You work for this particular brass. Are they still suspicious of us, even after letting us in here?"

Zeb barely glanced at it. "Oh, that— Shucks, no. Although I might add that a spy, supposing one could get this far, would be bound to be caught when his personal story went through semantic analysis. Nobody can tell a lie that long and that complicated."

"But what's it for?"

"What do you care? Write it out—and be sure you do a thorough job. Then turn it in."

I felt myself grow warm. "I don't know as I will. I rather think I'll ask the General about it first."

"Do so, if you want to make a ruddy fool of yourself. But look, John, the psychomathematicians who will read that mess of bilge you will write won't have the slightest interest in you as an individual. They don't even want to know who you are—a girl goes through your report and deletes all personal names, including your own, if you haven't done so yourself and substitutes numbers . . . all this before an analyst sees it. You're just data, that's all; the Chief has some heap big project on the fire—I don't know what it is myself—and he is trying to gather together a large enough statistical universe to be significant."

I was mollified. "Well, why don't they say so, then? This memo is just a bald order—irritating."

Zeb shrugged. "That is because it was prepared by the semantics division. If the propaganda division had written it, you would have gotten up early and finished the job before breakfast." He added, "By the way, I hear you've been promoted. Congratulations."

"Thanks." I grinned at him slyly. "How does it feel to be junior to me, Zeb?"

"Huh? Did they bump you that far? I thought you were a captain."

"I am."

"Well, excuse me for breathing—but I'm a major."

"Oh. Congratulations."

"Think nothing of it. You have to be at least a colonel around here, or you make your own bed."

I was too busy to make my bed very often. More than half the time I slept on the couch in my office and once I went a week without bathing. It was evident at once that the Cabal was bigger and had more complicated ramifications to it than I had ever dreamed and furthermore that it was building to a crescendo. I was too close to the trees to see the woods, even though everything but the utter top-secret, burn-after-reading items passed across my desk.

I simply endeavored to keep General Huxley from being smothered in pieces of paper—and found myself smothered instead. The idea was to figure out what he would do, if he had time, and then do it for him. A person who has been trained in the principles of staff or doctrinal command can do this; the trick is to make your mind work like your boss's mind in all routine matters, and to be able to recognize what is routine and what he must pass on himself. I made my share of mistakes, but apparently not too many for he didn't fire me, and three months later I was a major with the fancy title of assistant chief of staff. Chalk most of it up to the West Point ring, of course—a professional has a great advantage.

I should add that Zeb was a short-tailed colonel by then and acting chief of propaganda, his section chief having been transferred to a regional headquarters I knew only by the code name JERICHO.

But I am getting ahead of my story. I heard from Judith about two weeks later—a pleasant-enough note but with the juice pressed out of it through rephrasing. I meant to answer her at once but actually delayed a week—it was so pesky hard to know what to say. I could not possibly tell her any news except that I was well and busy. If I had told her I loved her three times in one letter some idiot in cryptography would have examined it for "pattern" and rejected it completely when he failed to find one.

The mail went to Mexico through a long tunnel, partly artificial but mostly natural, which led right under the international border. A little electric railroad of the sort used in mines ran through this tunnel and carried not only my daily headaches in the way of official mail but also a great deal of freight to supply our fair-sized town. There were a dozen other entrances to GHQ on the Arizona side of the border, but I never knew where any of them were—it was not my pidgin. The whole area overlay a deep layer of paleozoic limestone and it may well be honeycombed from California to Texas. The area known as GHQ had been in use for more than twenty years as a hideout for refugee brethren. Nobody knew the extent of the caverns we were in; we simply lighted and used what we needed. It was a favorite sport of us troglodytes—permanent residents were "trogs"; transients were "bats" because they flew by night—we trogs liked to go on "spelling bees," picnics which included a little amateur speleology in the unexplored parts.

It was permitted by regulations, but just barely and subject to stringent safety precautions, for you could break a leg awfully easily in those holes. But the General permitted it because it was necessary; we had only such recreations as we could make ourselves and some of us had not seen daylight in years.

Zeb and Maggie and I went on a number of such outings when I could get away. Maggie always brought another woman along. I protested at first but she pointed out to me that it was necessary in order to avoid gossip . . . mutual chaperonage. She assured me that she was certain that Judith would not mind, under the circumstances. It was a different girl each time and it seemed to work out that Zeb always paid a lot of attention to the other girl while I talked with Maggie. I had thought once that Maggie and Zeb would marry, but now I began to wonder. They seemed to suit each other like ham and eggs, but Maggie did not seem jealous and I can only describe Zeb, in honesty, as shameless—that is, if he thought Maggie would care.

One Saturday morning Zeb stuck his head in my sweat box and said, "Spelling bee. Two o'clock. Bring a towel."

I looked up from a mound of papers. "I doubt if I can make it," I answered. "And why a towel?"

But he was gone. Maggie came through my office later to take the weekly consolidated intelligence report in to the Old Man, but I did not attempt to question her, as Maggie was all business during working hours— the perfect office sergeant. I had lunch at my desk, hoping to finish up, but knowing it was impossible. About a quarter of two I went in to get General Huxley's signature on an item that was to go out that night by hypnoed courier and therefore had to go at once to psycho in order that the courier might be operated. He glanced at it and signed it, then said, "Sergeant Andy tells me you have a date."

"Sergeant Andrews is mistaken," I said stiffly. "There are still the weekly reports from Jericho, Nod, and Egypt to be gone over."

"Place them on my desk and get out. That's an order. I can't have you going stale from overwork."

I did not tell him that he had not even been to lodge himself in more than a month; I got out.

I dropped the message with Colonel Novak and hurried to where we always met near the women's mess. Maggie was there with the other girl—a blonde named Miriam Booth who was a clerk in Quartermaster's stores. I knew her by sight but had never spoken to her. They had our picnic lunch and Zeb arrived while I was being introduced. He was carrying, as usual, the portable flood we would use when we picked out a spot and a blanket to sit on and use as a table. "Where's your towel?" he demanded.

"Were you serious? I forgot it."

"Run get it. We'll start off along Appian Way. You can catch up. Come on, kids."

They started off, which left me with nothing but to do as I was told. After grabbing a towel from my room I dogtrotted until I had them in sight, then slowed to a walk, puffing. Desk work had ruined my wind. They heard me and waited.

We were all dressed alike, with the women in trousers and each with a safety line wrapped around the waist and torch clipped to the belt. I had gotten used to women in men's clothes, much as I disliked it—and, after all, it is impractical and quite immodest to climb around in caves wearing skirts.

We left the lighted area by taking a turn that appeared to lead into a blind wall; instead it led into a completely concealed but easily negotiated tunnel. Zeb tied our labyrinth string and started paying it out as soon as we left permanent and marked paths, as required by

the standing order; Zeb was always careful about things
that mattered.

For perhaps a thousand paces we could see blazes
and other indications that others had been this way
before, such as a place where someone had worked a
narrow squeeze wider with a sledge. Then we left the
obvious path and turned into a blind wall. Zeb put down
the flood and turned it on. "Sling your torches. We
climb this one."

"Where are we going?"

"A place Miriam knows about. Give me a leg up,
Johnnie."

The climb wasn't much. I got Zeb up all right and
the girls could have helped each other up, but we took
them up roped, for safety's sake. We picked up our
gear and Miriam led us away, each of us using his
torch.

We went down the other side and there was another
passage so well hidden that it could have been missed
for ten thousand years. We stopped once while Zeb tied
on another ball of string. Shortly Miriam said, "Slow
up, everybody. I think we're there."

Zeb flashed his torch around, then set up the portable flood and switched it on. He whistled. "Whew!
This is all right!"

Maggie said softly, "It's lovely." Miriam just grinned
triumphantly.

I agreed with them all. It was a perfect small domed
cavern, perhaps eighty feet wide and much longer. How
long, I could not tell, as it curved gently away in a
gloom-filled turn. But the feature of the place was a
quiet, inky-black pool that filled most of the floor. In
front of us was a tiny beach of real sand that might have
been laid down a million years ago for all I know.

Our voices echoed pleasantly and a little bit spook-
ily in the chamber, being broken up and distorted by
stalactites and curtains hanging from the roof. Zeb
walked down to the water's edge, squatted and tested

it with his hand. "Not too cold," he announced. "Well, the last one in is a proctor's nark."

I recognized the old swimming hole call, even though the last time I had heard it, as a boy, it had been "last one in is a dirty pariah." But here I could not believe it.

Zeb was already unbuttoning his shirt. I stepped up to him quickly and said privately, "Zeb! Mixed bathing? You must be joking?"

"Not a bit of it." He searched my face. "Why not? What's the matter with you, boy? Afraid someone will make you do penance? They won't, you know. That's all over with."

"But—"

"But what?"

I could not answer. The only way I could make the words come out would have been in the terms we had been taught in the Church, and I knew that Zeb would laugh at me—in front of the women. Probably they would laugh, too, since they had known and I hadn't. "But Zeb," I insisted, "I *can't*. You didn't tell me . . . and I don't even have a bathing outfit."

"Neither do I. Didn't you ever go in raw as a kid— and get paddled for it?" He turned away without waiting for me to answer this enormity and said, "Are you frail vessels waiting on something?"

"Just for you two to finish your debate," Maggie answered, coming closer. "Zeb, I think Mimi and I will use the other side of that boulder. All right?"

"Okay. But wait a second. No diving, you both understand. And a safety man on the bank at all times—John and I will take turns."

"Pooh!" said Miriam. "I dove the last time I was here."

"You weren't with me, that's sure. No diving—or I'll warm your pants where they are tightest."

She shrugged. "All right, Colonel Crosspatch. Come on, Mag." They went on past us and around a boulder half as big as a house. Miriam stopped, looked right at me, and waggled a finger. "No peeking, now!" I blushed to my ears.

They disappeared and we heard no more of them, except for giggles. I said hurriedly, "Look. You do as you please—and on your own head be it. But I'm not going in. I'll sit here on the bank and be safety man."

"Suit yourself. I was going to match you for first duty, but nobody is twisting your arm. Pay out a line, though, and have it ready for heaving. Not that we'll need it; both the girls are strong swimmers."

I said desperately, "Zeb, I'm sure the General would forbid swimming in these underground pools."

"That's why we didn't mention it. 'Never worry the C.O. unnecessarily'—standing orders in Joshua's Army, circa 1400 B.C." He went right on peeling off his clothes.

I don't know why Miriam warned me not to peek—not that I would!—for when she was undressed she came straight out from behind that boulder, not toward us but toward the water. But the flood light was full on her and she even turned toward us for an instant, then shouted, "Come on, Maggie! Zeb is going to be last if you hurry."

I did not want to look and I could not take my eyes off her. I had never seen anything remotely resembling the sight she was in my life—and only once a picture, one in the possession of a boy in my parish school and on that occasion I had gotten only a glimpse and then had promptly reported him.

But I could not stop looking, burning with shame as I was.

Zeb beat Maggie into the water—I don't think she cared. He went into the water quickly, almost breaking his own injunction against diving. Sort of a surface dive I would call it, running into the water and then breaking into a racing start. His powerful crawl was soon overtaking Miriam, who had started to swim toward the far end.

Then Maggie came out from behind the boulder and went into the water. She did not make a major evolution of it, the way Miriam had, but simply walked quickly and with quiet grace into the water. When she was waist deep, she let herself sink forward and struck out in a strong breast stroke, then shifted to a crawl and followed the others, whom I could hear but hardly see in the distance.

Again I could not take my eyes away if my eternal soul had depended on it. What is it about the body of a human woman that makes it the most terribly beautiful sight on earth? Is it, as some claim, simply a necessary instinct to make sure that we comply with God's will and replenish the earth? Or is it some stranger, more wonderful thing?

I found myself quoting: "How fair and how pleasant art thou, O love, for delights!

"This thy stature is like to a palm tree, and thy breasts to clusters of grapes."

Then I broke off, ashamed, remembering that the Song of Songs which is Solomon's was a chaste and holy allegory having nothing to do with such things.

I sat down on the sand and tried to compose my soul. After a while I felt better and my heart stopped pounding so hard. When they all came swimming back with Zeb in the lead, racing Miriam, I even managed to throw them a smile. It no longer seemed quite so terrible and as long as they stayed in the water the women were not shockingly exposed. Perhaps evil was truly in the eye of the beholder—in which case the idea was to keep it out of mine.

Zeb called out, "Ready to be relieved?"

I answered firmly, "No. Go ahead and have your fun."

"Okay." He turned like a dolphin and started back the other way. Miriam followed him. Maggie came in to where it was shallow, rested her finger tips on the bottom, and held facing me, with just her head and her ivory shoulders out of the inky water, while her waist-length mane of hair floated around her.

"Poor John," she said softly. "I'll come out and spell you."

"Oh, no, really!"

"Are you sure?"

"Quite sure."

"All right." She turned, flipped herself over, and started after the others. For one ghostly, magic instant she was partly out of the water.

Maggie came back to my end of the cavern about ten minutes later. "I'm cold," she said briefly, climbed out and strode quickly to the protection of the boulder. Somehow she was not naked, but merely unclothed, like Mother Eve. There is a difference—Miriam had been naked.

With Maggie out of the water and neither one of us speaking I noticed for the first time that there was no other sound. Now there is nothing so quiet as a cave; anywhere else at all there is noise, but the complete zero decibel which obtains underground if one holds still and says nothing is very different.

The point is that I should have been able to hear Zeb and Miriam swimming. Swimming need not be noisy but it can't be as quiet as a cave. I sat up suddenly and started forward—then stopped with equal suddenness as I did not want to invade Maggie's dressing room, which another dozen steps would have accomplished.

But I was really worried and did not know what to do. Throw a line? Where? Peel down and search for them? If necessary. I called out softly, "Maggie!"

"What is it, John?"

"Maggie, I'm worried."

She came at once from behind the rock. She had already pulled on her trousers, but held her towel so that it covered her from the waist up; I had the impression she had been drying her hair. "Why, John?"

"Keep very quiet and listen."

She did so. "I don't hear anything."

"That's just it. We should. I could hear you all

swimming even when you were down at the far end, out of my sight. Now there isn't a sound, not a splash. Do you suppose they possibly could both have hit their heads on the bottom at the same time?"

"Oh. Stop worrying, John. They're all right."

"But I *am* worried."

"They're just resting, I'm sure. There is another little beach down there, about half as big as this. That's where they are. I climbed up on it with them, then I came back. I was cold."

I made up my mind, realizing that I had let my modesty hold me back from my plain duty. "Turn your back. No, go behind the boulder—I want to undress."

"What? I tell you it's not necessary." She did not budge.

I opened my mouth to shout. Before I got it out Maggie had a hand over my mouth, which caused her towel to be disarranged and flustered us both. "Oh, heavens!" she said sharply. "Keep your big mouth shut." She turned suddenly and flipped the towel; when she turned back she had it about her like a stole, covering her front well enough, I suppose, without the need to hold it.

"John Lyle, come here and sit down. Sit down by me." She sat on the sand and patted the place by her—and such was the firmness with which she spoke that I did as I was told.

"By me," she insisted. "Come closer. I don't want to shout." I inched gingerly closer until my sleeve brushed her bare arm. "That's better," she agreed, keeping her voice low so that it did not resound around the cavern. "Now listen to me. There are two people down there, of their own free will. They are entirely safe— I saw them. And they are both excellent swimmers. The thing for you to do, John Lyle, is to mind your own business and restrain that nasty itch to interfere."

"I'm afraid I don't understand you." Truthfully, I was afraid I did.

"Oh, goodness me! See here, does Miriam mean anything to you?"

"Why, no, not especially."

"I should think not, since you haven't addressed six words to her since we started out. Very well, then—since you have no cause to be jealous, if two people choose to be alone, why should you stick your nose in? Understand me now?"

"Uh, I guess so."

"Then just be quiet."

I was quiet. She didn't move. I was acutely aware of her nakedness—for now she was naked, though covered—and I hoped that she was not aware that I was aware. Besides that I was acutely aware of being almost a participant in—well, I don't know what. I told myself angrily that I had no right to assume the worst, like a morals proctor.

Presently I said, "Maggie . . ."

"Yes, John?"

"I don't understand you."

"Why not, John? Not that it is really needful."

"Uh, you don't seem to give a hoot that Zeb is down there, with Miriam—alone."

"Should I give a hoot?"

Confound the woman! She was deliberately misunderstanding me. "Well . . . look, somehow I had gotten the impression that you and Zeb—I mean . . . well, I suppose I sort of expected that you two meant to get married, when you could."

She laughed a low chuckle that had little mirth in it. "I suppose you could have gotten that impression. But, believe me, the matter is all settled and for the best."

"Huh?"

"Don't misunderstand me. I am very fond of Zebadiah and I know he is equally fond of me. But we are both dominant types psychologically—you should see my profile chart; it looks like the Rocky Mountains! Two such people should not marry. Such marriages are *not* made in Heaven, believe me! Fortunately we found it out in time."

"Oh."

"Oh, indeed."

Now I don't know just how the next thing happened. I was thinking that she seemed rather forlorn—and the next thing I knew I was kissing her. She lay back in my arms and returned the kiss with a fervor I would not have believed possible. As for me, my head was buzzing and my eyeballs were knocking together and I couldn't have told you whether I was a thousand feet underground or on dress parade.

Then it was over. She looked up for a bare moment into my eyes and whispered, "Dear John . . ." Then she got suddenly to her feet, leaned over me, careless of the towel, and patted my cheek. "Judith is a very lucky girl. I wonder if she knows it."

"Maggie!" I said.

She turned away and said, without looking back, "I really must finish dressing. I'm cold."

She had not felt cold to me.

She came out shortly, fully dressed and towelling her hair vigorously. I got my dry towel and helped her. I don't believe I suggested it; the idea just took care of itself. Her hair was thick and lovely and I enjoyed doing it. It sent goose pimples over me.

Zeb and Miriam came back while I was doing so, not racing but swimming slowly; we could hear them laughing long before they were in sight. Miriam climbed out of the water as shamelessly as any harlot of Gomorrah, but I hardly noticed her. Zeb looked me in the eye and said aggressively, "Ready for your swim, chum?"

I started to say that I did not believe that I would bother and was going to make some excuse about my towel already being wet—when I noticed Maggie watching me . . . not saying anything but watching. I answered, "Why, surely! You two took long enough." I called out, "Miriam! Get out from behind that rock! I want to use it."

She squealed and giggled and came out, still arranging her clothes. I went behind it with quiet dignity.

I hope I still had quiet dignity when I came out. In any case I set my teeth, walked out and straight into the water. It was bitingly cold at first, but only for a moment. I was never varsity but I swam on my class team and I've even been in the Hudson on New Year's Day. I liked that black pool, once I was in.

I just had to swim down to the other end. Sure enough, there was a little shelf beach there. I did not go up on it.

On the way back I tried to swim down to the bottom. I could not find it, but it must have been over twenty feet down. I liked it down there—black and utterly still. Had I the breath for it, or gills, it seemed to me that it would have been a good place to stay, away from Prophets, away from Cabals, and paperwork, and worries, and problems too subtle for me.

I came up gasping, then struck out hard for our picnic beach. The girls already had the food laid out and Zeb shouted for me to hurry. Zeb and Maggie did not look up as I got out of the water, but I caught Miriam eyeing me. I don't think I blushed. I never did like blondes anyhow. I think Lilith must have been a blonde.

11

The Supreme Council, consisting of heads of departments, General Huxley, and a few others, met weekly or oftener to advise the General, exchange views, and consider the field reports. About a month after our rather silly escapade in the underground pool they were in session and I was with them, not as a member but as recorder. My own girl was ill and I had borrowed Maggie from G-2 to operate the voicewriter, since she was cleared for top secret. We were always terribly shorthanded of competent personnel. My nominal boss, for example, was Wing General Penoyer, who carried the title of Chief of Staff. But I hardly ever saw him, as he was also Chief of Ordnance. Huxley was his own chief of staff and I was sort of a glorified aide—"midshipmite, and bosun tite, and crew of the captain's gig." I even tried to see to it that Huxley took his stomach medicine regularly.

This meeting was bigger than usual. The regional commanders of Gath, Canaan, Jericho, Babylon, and Egypt were present in person; Nod and Damascus were represented by deputies—every Cabal district of the United States except Eden and we were holding a sensitive hook-up to Louisville for that command, using idea code that the sensitives themselves would not understand. I could feel the pressure of something big coming up, although Huxley had not taken me into his confidence. The place was tyled so that a mouse couldn't have got in.

We droned through the usual routine reports. It was duly recorded that we now had eighty-seven hundred and nine accepted members, either lodge brethren or tested and bound members of the parallel military organization. There were listed as recruited and instructed more than ten times that number of fellow travelers who could be counted on to rise against the Prophet, but who had not been intrusted with knowledge of the actual conspiracy.

The figures themselves were not encouraging. We were always in the jaws of a dilemma; a hundred thousand men was a handful to conquer a continent-wide country whereas the less than nine thousand party to the conspiracy itself were 'way too many to keep a secret. We necessarily relied on the ancient cell system wherein no man knew more than he had to know and could not give away too much no matter what an inquisitor did to him—no, not even if he had been a spy. But we had our weekly losses even at this passive stage.

One entire lodge had been surprised in session and arrested in Seattle four days earlier; it was a serious loss but only three of the chairs had possessed critical knowledge and all three had suicided successfully. Prayers would be said for all of them at a grand session that night, but here it was a routine report. We had lost four hatchet men that week but twenty-three assassinations had been accomplished—one of them the Elder Inquisitor for the entire lower Mississippi Valley.

The Chief of Communications reported that the brethren were prepared to disable 91% (figured on population coverage) of the radio & TV stations in the country, and that with the aid of assault groups we could reasonably hope to account for the rest—with the exception of the Voice of God station at New Jerusalem, which was a special problem.

The Chief of Combat Engineering reported readiness to sabotage the power supply of the forty-six largest cities, again with the exception of New Jerusalem, the supply of which was self-contained with the pile located under the Temple. Even there major interruption could be accomplished at distribution stations if the operation warranted the expenditure of sufficient men. Major surface transportation and freight routes could be sabotaged sufficiently with present plans and personnel to reduce traffic to 12% of normal.

The reports went on and on—newspapers, student action groups, rocket field seizure or sabotage, miracles, rumor propagation, water supply, incident incitement, counter-espionage, long-range weather prediction, weapons distribution. War is a simple matter compared with revolution. War is an applied science, with well-defined principles tested in history; analogous solutions may be found from ballista to H-bomb. But every revolution is a freak, a mutant, a monstrosity, its conditions never to be repeated and its operations carried out by amateurs and individualists.

While Maggie recorded the data I was arranging it and transmitting it to the calculator room for analysis. I was much too busy even to attempt a horse-back evaluation in my head. There was a short wait while the analysts finished programming and let the "brain" have it—then the remote-printer in front of me chattered briefly and stopped. Huxley leaned across me and tore off the tape before I could reach it.

He glanced at it, then cleared his throat and waited for dead silence. "Brethren," he began, "comrades—we agreed long ago on our doctrine of procedure. When every predictable factor, calculated, discounted for probable error, weighted and correlated with all other significant factors, gave a calculated risk of two to one in our favor, we would strike. Today's solution of the probability equation, substituting this week's data for the variables, gives an answer of two point one three. I propose to set the hour of execution. How say you?"

It was a delayed shock; no one said anything. Hope delayed too long makes reality hard to believe—and all of these men had waited for years, some for most of a lifetime. Then they were on their feet, shouting, sobbing, cursing, pounding each others' backs.

Huxley sat still until they quieted, an odd little smile on his face. Then he stood up and said quietly, "I don't think we need poll the sentiment. I will set the hour after I have—"

"General! If you please! I do not agree." It was Zeb's boss, Sector General Novak, Chief of Psych. Huxley stopped speaking and the silence fairly ached. I was as stunned as the rest.

Then Huxley said quietly, "This council usually acts by unanimous consent. We have long since arrived at the method for setting the date . . . but I know that you would not disagree without good reason. We will listen now to Brother Novak."

Novak came slowly forward and faced them. "Brethren," he began, running his eyes over bewildered and hostile faces, "you know me, and you know I want this thing as much as you do. I have devoted the last seventeen years to it—it has cost me my family and my home. But I can't let you go ahead without warning you, when I am sure that the time is not yet. I think—no, I *know* with mathematical certainty that we are not ready for revolution." He had to wait and hold up both hands for silence; they did not want to hear him. "Hear me out! I concede that all military plans are ready. I admit that if we strike now we have a strong probability of being able to seize the country. Nevertheless we are not ready—

"Why not?"

"—because a majority of the people still believe in the established religion, they believe in the Divine authority of the Prophet. We can seize power but we can't hold it!"

"The Devil we won't!"

"*Listen* to me! No people was ever held in subjection long except through their own consent. For three generations the American people have been conditioned from cradle to grave by the cleverest and most thorough psycho-technicians in the world. They *believe!* If you turn them loose now, without adequate psychological preparation, they will go back to their chains . . . like a horse returning to a burning barn. We can win the revolution but it will be followed by a long and bloody civil war—which we will lose!"

He stopped, ran a trembling hand across his eyes, then said to Huxley, "That's all."

Several were on their feet at once. Huxley pounded for order, then recognized Wing General Penoyer.

Penoyer said, "I'd like to ask Brother Novak a few questions."

"Go ahead."

"Can his department tell us what percentage of the population is sincerely devout?"

Zebadiah, present to assist his chief, looked up; Novak nodded and he answered, "Sixty-two per cent, plus-or-minus three per cent."

"And the percentage who secretly oppose the government whether we have enlisted them or not?"

"Twenty-one percent, plus proportional error. The balance can be classed as conformists, not devout but reasonably contented."

"By what means were the data obtained?"

"Surprise hypnosis of representative types."

"Can you state the trend?"

"Yes, sir. The government lost ground rapidly during the first years of the present depression, then the curve flattened out. The new tithing law and to some extent the vagrancy decrees were unpopular and the government again lost ground before the curve again flattened at a lower level. About that time business picked up a little but we simultaneously started our present intensified propaganda campaign; the government has been losing ground slowly but steadily the past fifteen months."

"And what does the first derivative show?"

Zeb hesitated and Novak took over. "You have to figure the second derivative," he answered in a strained voice; "the rate is accelerating."

"Well?"

The Psych Chief answered firmly but reluctantly, "On extrapolation, it will be three years and eight months before we can risk striking."

Penoyer turned back to Huxley. "I have my answer, sir. With deep respect to General Novak and his careful scientific work, I say—win while we can! We may never have another chance."

He had the crowd with him. "Penoyer is right! If we wait, we'll be betrayed."—"You can't hold a thing like this together forever."—"I've been underground ten years; I don't want to be buried here."—"Win . . . and worry about making converts when we control communications."—"Strike now! Strike now!"

Huxley let them carry on, his own face expressionless, until they had it out of their systems. I kept quiet myself, since I was too junior to be entitled to a voice here, but I went along with Penoyer; I couldn't see waiting nearly four years.

I saw Zeb talking earnestly with Novak. They seemed to be arguing about something and were paying no attention to the racket. But when Huxley at last held up a hand for silence Novak left his place and hurried up to Huxley's elbow. The General listened for a moment, seemed almost annoyed, then undecided. Novak crooked a finger at Zeb, who came running up. The three whispered together for several moments while the council waited.

Finally Huxley faced them again. "General Novak has proposed a scheme which may change the whole situation. The Council is recessed until tomorrow."

Novak's plan (or Zeb's, though he never admitted authorship) required a delay of nearly two months, to the date of the annual Miracle of the Incarnation. For what was contemplated was no less than tampering with the Miracle itself. In hindsight it was an obvious and probably essential stratagem; the psych boss was right. In essence, a dictator's strength depends not upon guns but on the faith his people place in him. This had been true of Caesar, of Napoleon, of Hitler, of Stalin. It was necessary to strike first at the foundation of the Prophet's power: the popular belief that he ruled by direct authority of God.

Future generations will undoubtedly find it impossible to believe the importance, the extreme importance both to religious faith and political power, of the Miracle of Incarnation. To comprehend it even intellectually it is necessary to realize that the people literally believed that the First Prophet actually and physically returned from Heaven once each year to judge the stewardship of his Divinely appointed successor and to confirm him in his office. The people *believed* this—the minority of doubters dared not open their faces to dispute it for fear of being torn limb from limb . . . and I am speaking of a rending that leaves blood on the pavement, not some figure of speech. Spitting on the Flag would have been much safer.

I had believed it myself, all my life; it would never have occurred to me to doubt such a basic article of faith—and I was what is called an educated man, one who had been let into the secrets of and trained in the production of lesser miracles. I believed it.

The ensuing two months had all the endless time-stretching tension of the waiting period while coming into range and before "Commence firing!"—yet we were so busy that each day and each hour was too short. In addition to preparing the still-more-miraculous intervention in the Miracle we used the time to whet our usual weapons to greater fineness. Zeb and his boss, Sector General Novak, were detached almost at once. Novak's orders read "—proceed to BEULAHLAND and take charge of OPERATION BEDROCK." I cut the orders myself, not trusting them to a clerk, but no one told me where Beulahland might be found on a map.

Huxley himself left when they did and was gone for more than a week, leaving Penoyer as acting C.-in-C. He did not tell me why he was leaving, of course, nor where he was going, but I could fill in. Operation Bedrock was a psychological maneuver but the means must be physical—and my boss had once been head of the Department of Applied Miracles at the Point. He may have been the best physicist in the entire Cabal; in any case I could guess with certainty that he intended at the very least to see for himself that the means were adequate and the techniques foolproof. For all I know he may actually have used soldering iron and screwdriver and electronic micrometer himself that week—the General did not mind getting his hands dirty.

I missed Huxley personally. Penoyer was inclined to reverse my decisions on minor matters and waste my time and his on details a top C.O. can't and should not cope with. But he was gone part of the time, too. There was much coming and going and more than once I had to chase down the senior department head present, tell him that he was acting, and get him to sign where I had initialed. I took to scrawling "I. M. Dumbjohn, Wing General F.U.S.A., Acting" as indecipherably as possible on all routine internal papers—I don't think anybody ever noticed.

Before Zeb left another thing happened which really has nothing to do with the people of the United States and the struggle to regain their freedoms—but my own personal affairs are so tied into this account that I mention it. Perhaps the personal angle really is important; certainly the order under which this journal was started called for it to be "personal" and "subjective"— however I had retained a copy and added to it because I found it helped me to get my own confused thoughts straight while going through a metamorphosis as drastic as that from caterpillar into moth. I am typical, perhaps, of the vast majority, the sort of person who has to have his nose rubbed in a thing before he recognizes it, while Zeb and Maggie and General Huxley were of the elite minority of naturally free souls . . . the original thinkers, the leaders.

I was at my desk, trying to cope with the usual spate of papers, when I received a call to see Zeb's boss at my earliest convenience. Since he already had his orders, I left word with Huxley's orderly and hurried over.

He cut short the formalities. "Major, I have a letter for you which Communications sent over for analysis to determine whether it should be rephrased or simply destroyed. However, on the urgent recommendation

of one of my division heads I am taking the responsibility of letting you read it without paraphrasing. You
will have to read it here."

I said, "Yes, sir," feeling quite puzzled.

He handed it to me. It was fairly long and I suppose it could have held half a dozen coded messages,
even idea codes that could come through paraphrasing.
I don't remember much of it—just the impact it had
on me. It was from Judith.

"My dear John. . . . I shall always think of you fondly
and I shall never forget what you have done for me . . .
never meant for each other . . . Mr. Mendoza has been
most considerate . . . I know you will forgive me . . . he
needs me; it must have been fate that brought us together
. . . if you ever visit Mexico City, you must think of our
home as yours. . . . I will always think of you as my strong
and wise older brother and I will always be a sister—"
There was more, lots more, all of the same sort—I think
the process is known as "breaking it gently."

Novak reached out and took the letter from me. "I
didn't intend for you to have time to memorize it," he
said dryly, then dropped it at once into his desk incinerator. He glanced back at me. "Maybe you had better sit down, Major. Do you smoke?"

I did not sit down, but I was spinning so fast that
I accepted the cigarette and let him light it for me. Then
I choked on tobacco smoke and the sheer physical discomfort helped to bring me back to reality. I thanked
him and got out—went straight to my room, called my
office and left word where I could be found if the
General really wanted me. But I told my secretary that
I was suddenly quite ill and not to disturb me if it could
possibly be helped.

I may have been there about an hour—I wouldn't
know—lying face down and doing nothing, not even
thinking. There came a gentle tap at the door, then it
was pushed open; it was Zeb. "How do you feel?" he
said.

"Numb," I answered. It did not occur to me to wonder how he knew and at the time I had forgotten the "division head" who had prevailed upon Novak to let me see it in the clear.

He came on in, sprawled in a chair, and looked at me. I rolled over and sat on the edge of the bed. "Don't let it throw you, Johnnie," he said quietly. "'Men have died and worms have eaten them—but not for love.'"

"You don't know!"

"No, I don't," he agreed. "Each man is his own prisoner, in solitary confinement for life. Nevertheless on this particular point the statistics are fairly reliable. Try something for me. Visualize Judith in your mind. See her features. Listen to her voice."

"Huh?"

"Do it."

I tried, I really tried—and, do you know, I couldn't. I had never had a picture of her; her face now eluded me.

Zeb was watching me. "You'll get well," he said firmly. "Now look here, Johnnie. . . . I could have told you. Judith is a very female sort of woman, all gonads and no brain. And she's quite attractive. Turned loose, she was bound to find a man, as sure as nascent oxygen will recombine. But there is no use in talking to a man in love."

He stood up. "Johnnie, I've got to go. I hate like the mischief to walk out and leave you in the shape you are in, but I've already checked out and Grandfather Novak is ready to leave. He'll eat me out as it is, for holding him up this long. But one more word of advice before I go—"

I waited. "I suggest, he continued, "that you see a lot of Maggie while I'm away. She's good medicine."

He started to leave; I said sharply, "Zeb—what happened to you and Maggie? Something like this?"

He looked back at me sharply. "Huh? No. Not at all the same thing. It wasn't . . . well, it wasn't similar."

"I don't understand you—I guess I just don't understand people. You're urging me to see a lot of Maggie—and I thought she was your girl. Uh, wouldn't you be jealous?"

He stared at me, laughed, and clapped me on the shoulder. "She's a free citizen, Johnnie, believe me. If you ever did anything to hurt Maggie, I'd tear off your head and beat you to death with it. Not that you ever would. But jealous of her? No. It doesn't enter the picture. I think she's the greatest gal that ever trod shoe leather—but I would rather marry a mountain lioness."

He left on that, leaving me again with my mouth open. But I took his advice, or Maggie took it for me. Maggie knew all about it—Judith, I mean—and I assumed that Zeb had told her. He hadn't; it seemed that Judith had written to her first. In any case I didn't have to look her up; she looked me up right after dinner that night. I talked with her a while and felt much better, so much so that I went back to my office and made up for time lost that afternoon.

Maggie and I made a habit thereafter of taking a walk together after dinner. We went on no more spelling bees; not only was there no time for such during those last days but also neither one of us felt like trying to work up another foursome with Zeb away. Sometimes I could spare only twenty minutes or even less before I would have to be back at my desk—but it was the high point of the day; I looked forward to it.

Even without leaving the floodlighted main cavern, without leaving the marked paths, there were plenty of wonderfully beautiful walks to take. If I could afford to be away as much as an hour, there was one place in particular we liked to go—north in the big room, a good half mile from the buildings. The path meandered among frozen limestone mushrooms, great columns, domes, and fantastic shapes that have no names and looked equally like souls in torment or great exotic

flowers, depending on the mood one was in. At a spot
nearly a hundred feet higher than the main floor we
had found a place only a few feet off the authorized
path where nature had contrived a natural stone bench.
We could sit there and stare down at the toy village,
talk, and Maggie would smoke. I had taken to lighting
her cigarettes for her, as I had seen Zeb do. It was a
little attention she liked and I had learned to avoid
getting smoke caught in my throat.

About six weeks after Zeb had left and only days
before M-Hour we were doing this and were talking
about what it would be like after the revolution and
what we would do with ourselves. I said that I supposed
I would stay in the regular army, assuming that there
was such and that I was eligible for it. "What will you
do, Maggie?"

She exhaled smoke slowly. "I haven't thought that far,
John. I haven't any profession—that is to say, we are
trying our best to make the one I did have obsolete."
She smiled wryly. "I'm not educated in anything useful. I can cook and I can sew and I can keep house;
I suppose I should try to find a job as a housekeeper—
competent servants are always scarce, they say."

The idea of the courageous and resourceful Sister
Magdalene, so quick with a vibroblade when the need
arose, tramping from one employment bureau to another
in search of menial work to keep her body fed was an
idea at once distasteful to me—"General Housework &
Cooking, live in, Thur. eve. & alternate Sundays off;
references required." Maggie? Maggie who had saved
my own probably worthless life at least twice and never
hesitated nor counted the cost. Not Maggie!

I blurted out, "Look, you don't have to do *that.*"

"It's what I know."

"Yes, but—well, why don't you cook and keep house
for me? I'll be drawing enough to support both of us,
even if I have to go back to my permanent rank. Maybe
it isn't much but—shucks! you're welcome to it."

She looked up. "Why, John, how very generous!" She crushed out the cigarette and threw it aside. "I do appreciate it—but it wouldn't work. I imagine there will be just as many gossips after we have won as before. Your colonel would not like it."

I blushed red and almost shouted, "That wasn't what I meant at all!"

"What? Then what did you mean?"

I had not really known until the words came out. Now I knew but not how to express it. "I meant— Look, Maggie, you seem to like me well enough . . . and we get along well together. That is, why don't we—" I halted, hung up.

She stood up and faced me. "John, are you proposing marriage—to *me?*"

I said gruffly, "Uh, that was the general idea." It bothered me to have her standing in front of me, so I stood up, too.

She looked at me gravely, searching my face, then said humbly, "I'm honored . . . and grateful . . . and I am deeply touched. Bu—*oh, no, John!*" The tears started out of her eyes and she started to bawl. She stopped as quickly, wiping her face with her sleeve, and said brokenly, "Now you've made me cry. I haven't cried in years."

I started to put my arms around her; she pushed me back. "No, John! Listen to me first. I'll accept that job as your housekeeper, but I won't marry you."

"Why not?"

"'Why not?' Oh, my dear, my very dear— Because I am an old, tired woman, that's why."

"Old? You can't be more than a year or two older than I am—three, at the outside. It doesn't matter."

"I'm a thousand years older than you are. Think who I am—where I've been—what I've known. First I was 'bride,' if you care to call it that, to the Prophet."

"Not your fault!"

"Perhaps. Then I was mistress to your friend Zebadiah. You knew that?"

"Well . . . I was pretty sure of it."

"That isn't all. There were other men. Some because it was needful and a woman has few bribes to offer. Some from loneliness, or even boredom. After the Prophet has tired of her, a woman doesn't seem very valuable, even to herself."

"I don't care. I don't care! It doesn't matter!"

"You say that now. Later it would matter to you, dreadfully. I think I know you, my dear."

"Then you don't know me. We'll start fresh."

She sighed deeply. "You think that you love me, John?"

"Uh? Yes, I guess that's it."

"You loved Judith. Now you are hurt—so you think you love me."

"But— Oh, I don't know what love is! I know I want you to marry me and live with me."

"Neither do I know," she said so softly that I almost missed it. Then she moved into my arms as easily and naturally as if she had always lived there.

When we had finished kissing each other I said, "You will marry me, then?"

She threw her head back and stared as if she were frightened. "Oh, no!"

"Huh? But I thought—"

"No, dear, no! I'll keep your house and cook your food and make your bed—and sleep in it, if you want me to. But you don't need to marry me."

"But—Sheol! Maggie, I won't have it that way."

"You won't? Well see." She was out of my arms although I had not let go. "I'll see you tonight. About one—after everyone is asleep. Leave your door unlatched."

"Maggie!" I shouted.

She was headed down the path, running as if she were flying. I tried to catch up, tripped on a stalagmite and fell. When I picked myself up she was out of sight.

Here is an odd thing—I had always thought of

Maggie as quite tall, stately, almost as tall as I was. But when I held her in my arms, she was short. I had to lean way over to kiss her.

12

On the night of the Miracle all that were left of us gathered in the main communications room—my boss and myself, the chief of communications and his technical crew, a few staff officers. A handful of men and a few dozen women, too many to crowd into the comm shack, were in the main messhall where a relay screen had been rigged for them. Our underground city was a ghost town now, with only a skeleton crew to maintain communications for the commanding general; all the rest had gone to battle stations. We few who were left had no combat stations in this phase. Strategy had been settled; the hour of execution was set for us by the Miracle. Tactical decisions for a continent could not be made from headquarters and Huxley was too good a general to try. His troops had been disposed and his subordinate commanders were now on their own; all he could do was wait and pray.

All that we could do, too—I didn't have any finger-nails left to bite.

The main screen in front of us showed, in brilliant color and perfect perspective, the interior of the Temple. The services had been going on all day—processional, hymns, prayers and more prayers, sacrifice, genuflexion, chanting, endless monotony of colorful ritual. My old regiment was drawn up in two frozen ranks, helmets shining, spears aligned like the teeth of a comb. I made out Peter van Eyck, Master of my home lodge, his belly corseted up, motionless before his platoon.

I knew, from having handled the despatch, that

Master Peter had stolen a print of the film we had to have. His presence in the ceremonies was reassuring; had his theft even been suspected our plans could not possibly succeed. But there he was.

Around the other three walls of the comm room were a dozen smaller screens, scenes from as many major cities—crowds in Rittenhouse Square, the Hollywood Bowl jam-packed, throngs in local temples. In each case the eyes of all were riveted on a giant television screen showing the same scene in the Great Temple that we were watching. Throughout all America it would be the same—every mortal soul who could possibly manage it was watching some television screen somewhere—waiting, waiting, waiting for the Miracle of the Incarnation.

Behind us a psychoperator bent over a sensitive who worked under hypnosis. The sensitive, a girl about nineteen, stirred and muttered, the operator bent closer.

Then he turned to Huxley and the communications chief. "The Voice of God Station has been secured, sir."

Huxley merely nodded; I felt like turning handsprings, if my knees had not been so weak. This was the key tactic and one that could not possibly be executed until minutes before the Miracle. Since television moves only on line-of-sight or in its own special cable the only possible way to tamper with this nationwide broadcast was at the station of origin. I felt a wild burst of exaltation at their success—followed by an equally sudden burst of sorrow, knowing that not one of them could hope to live out the night.

Never mind—if they could hold out for a few more minutes their lives would have counted. I commended their souls to the Great Architect. We had men for such jobs where needed, mostly brethren whose wives had faced an inquisitor.

The comm chief touched Huxley's sleeve. "It's coming, sir." The scene panned slowly up to the far end of the Temple, passed over the altar, and settled in closeup on an ivory archway above and behind the altar—

the entrance to the Sanctum Sanctorum. It was closed with heavy cloth-of-gold drapes.

The pick-up camera held steady with the curtained entranceway exactly filling the screen. "They can take over any time now, sir."

Huxley turned his head to the psychoperator. "Is that ours yet? See if you can get a report from the Voice of God."

"Nothing, sir. I'll let you know."

I could not take my eyes off the screen. After an interminable wait, the curtains stirred and slowly parted, drawn up and out on each side—and there, standing before us almost life size and so real that I felt he could step out of the screen, was the Prophet Incarnate!

He turned his head, letting his gaze rove from side to side, then looked right at me, his eyes staring right into mine. I wanted to hide. I gasped and said involuntarily, "You mean we can duplicate *that?*"

The comm chief nodded. "To the millimeter, or I'll eat the difference. Our best impersonator, prepared by our best plastic surgeons. That may be our film already."

"But it's real."

Huxley glanced at me. "A little less talk, please, Lyle." It was the nearest he had ever come to bawling me out; I shut up and studied the screen. That powerful, totally unscrupulous face, that burning gaze—an actor? No! I knew that face; I had seen it too many times in too many ceremonies. Something had gone wrong and this was the Prophet Incarnate himself. I began to sweat that stinking sweat of fear. I very much believe that had he called me by name out of that screen I would have confessed my treasons and thrown myself on his mercy.

Huxley said crossly, "Can't you raise New Jerusalem?"

The psychoperator answered, "No, sir. I'm sorry, sir."

The Prophet started his invocation.

His compelling, organlike voice rolled through magnificent periods. Then he asked the blessings of Eternal God for the people this coming year. He paused, looked at me again, then rolled his eyes up to Heaven, lifted his hands and commenced his petition to the First Prophet, asking him to confer on his people the priceless bounty of seeing and hearing him in the flesh, and offering for that purpose the flesh of the present prophet as an instrument. He waited.

The transformation started—and my hackles stood up. I knew now that we had lost; something had gone wrong . . . and God alone knew how many men had died through the error.

The features of the Prophet began to change; he stretched an inch or two in height; his rich robes darkened—and there standing in his place, dressed in a frock coat of a bygone era, was the Reverend Nehemiah Scudder, First Prophet and founder of the New Crusade. I felt my stomach tighten with fear and dread and I was a little boy again, watching it for the first time in my parish church.

He spoke to us first with his usual yearly greeting of love and concern for his people. Gradually he worked himself up, his face sweating and his hands clutching in the style that had called down the Spirit in a thousand Mississippi Valley camp meetings; my heart began to beat faster. He was preaching against sin in all its forms—the harlot whose mouth is like honey, the sins of the flesh, the sins of the spirit, the money changers.

At the height of his passion he led into a new subject in a fashion that caught me by surprise: "But I did not return to you this day to speak to you of the little sins of little people. No! I come to tell you of a truly hellish thing and to bid you to gird on your armor and fight. Armageddon is upon you! Rise up, mine hosts, and fight you the Battle of the Lord! For Satan is upon you! He is here! Here among you! Here tonight in the flesh! With the guile of the serpent he has come among you, taking on the form of the Vicar of the Lord! Yea! He has disguised himself falsely, taken on the shape of the *Prophet Incarnate!*

"Smite him! Smite his hirelings! In the Name of God destroy them all!"

13

"Bruehler from Voice of God," the psychoperator said quietly. "The station is now off the air and demolition will take place in approximately thirty seconds. An attempt will be made to beat a retreat before the building goes up. Good luck. Message ends."

Huxley muttered something and left the now-dark big screen. The smaller screens, monitoring scenes around the country, were confusing but heartening. There was fighting and rioting everywhere. I watched it, still stunned, and tried to figure out which was friend and which was foe. In the Hollywood Bowl the crowd boiled up over the stage and by sheer numbers overran and trampled the officials and clergy seated there. There were plenty of guards stationed around the edges of the bowl and it should not have happened that way. But instead of the murderous enfilading fire one would have expected, there was one short blast from a tripod mounted on the hillside northeast of the stage, then the guard was shot—apparently by another of the guards.

Apparently the chancy tour de force against the Prophet himself was succeeding beyond all expectations. If government forces were everywhere as disorganized as they were at the Hollywood Bowl, the job would not be one of fighting but of consolidating an accomplished fact.

The monitor from Hollywood went dead and I shifted to another screen, Portland, Oregon. More fighting. I could see men with white armbands, the only uniform we had allowed ourselves for M-Hour—but not all the violence came from our brethren in the armbands. I saw an armed proctor go down before bare fists and not get up.

Testing messages and early reports were beginning to come in, now that it was feasible to use our own radio—now that we had at long, long last shown our hand. I stopped looking and went back to help my boss keep track of them. I was still dazed and could still see in my mind the incredible face of the Prophet—both Prophets. If I had been emotionally battered by it, what did the people think? The devout, the believers?

The first clear-cut report other than contact messages was from Lucas in New Orleans:

HAVE TAKEN CONTROL OF CITY CENTER, POWER AND COMM STATIONS. MOP-UP SQUADS SEIZING WARD POLICE STATIONS. FEDERAL GUARDS HERE DEMORALIZED BY STEREOCAST. SPORADIC FIGHTING BROKE OUT AMONG GUARDS THEMSELVES. LITTLE ORGANIZED RESISTANCE. ESTABLISHING ORDER UNDER MARTIAL LAW. SO MOTE IT BE!—LUCAS.

Then reports started pouring in: Kansas City, Detroit, Philadelphia, Denver, Boston, Minneapolis—all the major cities. They varied but told the same story; our synthetic Prophet's call to arms, followed at once by a cutting of all regular methods of communication, had made of the government forces a body without a head, flopping around and fighting itself. The power of the Prophet was founded on superstition and fraud; we had turned superstition back on him to destroy him.

Lodge that night was the grandest I have ever attended. We tyled the communications room itself, with the comm chief sitting as secretary and passing incoming messages to General Huxley, sitting as Master in the east, as fast as they came in. I was called on to take a chair myself, Junior Warden, an honor I had never had before. The General had to borrow a hat and it was ridiculously too small for him, but it didn't matter—I have never seen ritual so grand, before or since. We all spoke the ancient words from our hearts, as if we were saying them for the first time. If the stately progress was interrupted to hear that Louisville was ours, what better interruption? We were building anew; after an endless time of building in speculation we were at last building operatively.

14

Temporary capital was set up at St. Louis, for its central location. I piloted Huxley there myself. We took over the Prophet's proctor base there, restoring to it its old name of Jefferson Barracks. We took over the buildings of the University, too, and handed back to it the name of Washington. If the people no longer recalled the true significance of those names, they soon would and here was a good place to start. (I learned for the first time that Washington had been one of us.)

However, one of Huxley's first acts as military governor—he would not let himself be called even "Provisional President"—was to divorce all official connection between the Lodge and the Free United States Army. The Brotherhood had served its purpose, had kept alive the hopes of free men; now it was time to go back to its ancient ways and let public affairs be handled publicly. The order was not made public, since the public had no real knowledge of us, always a secret society and for three generations a completely clandestine one. But it was read and recorded in all lodges and, so far as I know, honored.

There was one necessary exception: my home lodge at New Jerusalem and the cooperating sister order there of which Maggie had been a member. For we did not yet hold New Jerusalem although the country as a whole was ours.

This was more serious than it sounds. While we had

the country under military control, with all communication centers in our hands, with the Federal Forces demoralized, routed, and largely dispersed or disarmed and captured, we did not hold the country's heart in our hands. More than half of the population were not with us; they were simply stunned, confused, and unorganized. As long as the Prophet was still alive, as long as the Temple was still a rallying point, it was still conceivably possible for him to snatch back the victory from us.

A fraud, such as we had used, has only a temporary effect; people revert to their old thinking habits. The Prophet and his cohorts were not fools; they included some of the shrewdest applied psychologists this tired planet has ever seen. Our own counterespionage became disturbingly aware that they were rapidly perfecting their own underground, using the still devout and that numerous minority, devout or not, who had waxed fat under the old regime and saw themselves growing leaner under the new. We could not stop this counterrevolution—Sheol! the Prophet had not been able to stop *us* and we had worked under much greater handicaps. The Prophet's spies could work almost openly in the smaller towns and the country; we had barely enough men to guard the television stations—we could not possibly put a snooper under every table.

Soon it was an open secret that we had faked the call to Armageddon. One would think that this fact in itself would show to anyone who knew it that *all* of the Miracles of Incarnation had been frauds—trick television and nothing more. I mentioned this to Zebadiah and got laughed at for being naive. People believe what they want to believe and logic has no bearing on it, he assured me. In this case they wanted to believe in their old time religion as they learned it at their mothers knees; it restored security to their hearts. I could sympathize with that, I understood it.

In any case, New Jerusalem must fall—and time was against us.

While we were worrying over this, a provisional constitutional convention was being held in the great auditorium of the university. Huxley opened it, refused again the title, offered by acclamation, of president—then told them bluntly that all laws since the inauguration of President Nehemiah Scudder were of no force, void, and that the old constitution and bill of rights were effective as of now, subject to the exigencies of temporary military control. Their single purpose, he said, was to work out orderly methods of restoring the old free democratic processes; any permanent changes in the constitution, if needed, would have to wait until after free elections.

Then he turned the gavel over to Novak and left.

I did not have time for politics, but I hid out from work and caught most of one afternoon session because Zebadiah had tipped me off that significant fireworks were coming up. I slipped into a back seat and listened. One of Novak's bright young men was presenting a film. I saw the tail end of it only, but it seemed to be more or less a standard instruction film, reviewing the history of the United States, discussing civil liberty, explaining the duties of a citizen in a free democracy—not the sort of thing ever seen in the Prophet's schools but making use of the same techniques which had long been used in every school in the country. The film ended and the bright young man—I could never remember his name, perhaps because I disliked him. Stokes? Call him Stokes, anyway. Stokes began to speak.

"This reorientation film," he began, "is of course utterly useless in recanalizing an adult. His habits of thought are much too set to be affected by anything as simple as this."

"Then why waste our time with it?" someone called out.

"Please! Nevertheless this film was prepared for

adults—provided the adult has been placed in a receptive frame of mind. Here is the prologue—" the screen lighted up again. It was a simple and beautiful pastoral scene with very restful music. I could not figure what he was getting at, but it was soothing; I remembered that I had not had much sleep the past four nights—come to think about it, I couldn't remember when I had had a good night's sleep. I slouched back and relaxed.

I didn't notice the change from scenery to abstract patterns. I think the music continued but it was joined by a voice, warm, soothing, monotonous. The patterns were going round and around and I was beginning to bore . . . right . . . into . . . the . . . screen. . . .

Then Novak had left his chair and switched off the projector with a curse. I jerked awake with that horrid shocked feeling that makes one almost ready to cry. Novak was speaking sharply but quietly to Stokes—then Novak faced the rest of us. "Up on your feet!" he ordered. "Seventh inning stretch. Take a deep breath. Shake hands with the man next to you. Slap him on the back, hard!"

We did so and I felt foolish. Also irritated. I had felt so good just a moment before and now I was reminded of the mountain of work I must move if I were to have ten minutes with Maggie that evening. I thought about leaving but the b. y. m. had started talking again.

"As Dr. Novak has pointed out," he went on, not sounding quite so sure of himself, "it is not necessary to use the prologue on this audience, since you don't need reorientation. But this film, used with the preparatory technique and possibly in some cases with a light dose of one of the hypnotic drugs, can be depended on to produce an optimum political temperament in 83% of the populace. This has been demonstrated on a satisfactory test group. The film itself represents several years of work analyzing the personal conversion reports of almost everyone—surely everyone in this audience!—who joined our organization while it was still underground. The irrelevant has been eliminated; the essential has been abstracted. What remains will convert a devout follower of the Prophet to free manhood—provided he is in a state receptive to suggestion when he is exposed to it."

So *that* was why we had each been required to bare our souls. It seemed logical to me. God knew that we were sitting on a time bomb, and we couldn't wait for every lunk to fall in love with a holy deaconess and thereby be shocked out of his groove; there wasn't time. But an elderly man whom I did not know was on his feet on the other side of the hall—he looked like the pictures of Mark Twain, an angry Mark Twain. "Mr. Chairman!"

"Yes, comrade? State your name and district."

"You know what my name is, Novak—Winters, from Vermont. Did you okay this scheme?"

"No." It was a simple declarative.

"He's one of your boys."

"He's a free citizen. I supervised the preparation of the film itself and the research which preceded it. The use of null-vol suggestion techniques came from the research group he headed. I disapproved the proposal, but agreed to schedule time to present it. I repeat, he is a free citizen, free to speak, just as you are."

"May I speak now?"

"You have the floor."

The old man drew himself up and seemed to swell up. "I shall! Gentlemen . . . ladies . . . comrades! I have been in this for more than forty years—more years than that young pup has been alive. I have a brother, as good a man as I am, but we haven't spoken in many years—because he is honestly devout in the established faith and he suspects me of heresy. Now this cub, with his bulging forehead and his whirling lights, would 'condition' my brother to make him 'politically reliable.'"

He stopped to gasp asthmatically and went on. "Free

men aren't 'conditioned!' Free men are free because they are ornery and cussed and prefer to arrive at their own prejudices in their own way—not have them spoonfed by a self-appointed mind tinkerer! We haven't fought, our brethren haven't bled and died, just to change bosses, no matter how sweet their motives. I tell you, we got into the mess we are in through the efforts of those same mind tinkerers. They've studied for years how to saddle a man and ride him. They started with advertising and propaganda and things like that, and they perfected it to the point where what used to be simple, honest swindling such as any salesman might use became a mathematical science that left the ordinary man helpless." He pointed his finger at Stokes. "I tell you that the American citizen needs no protection from anything—except the likes of him."

"This is ridiculous," Stokes snapped, his voice rather high. "You wouldn't turn high explosives over to children. That is what the franchise would be now."

"The American people are not children."

"They might as well be!—most of them."

Winters turned his eyes around the hall. "You see what I mean, friends? He's as ready to play God as the Prophet was. I say give 'em their freedom, give 'em their clear rights as free men and women and children under God. If they mess it up again, that's their doing—but we have no right to operate on their minds." He stopped and labored again to catch his breath; Stokes looked contemptuous. "We *can't* make the world safe for children, nor for men either—and God didn't appoint us to do it."

Novak said gently, "Are you through, Mr. Winters?"

"I'm through."

"And you've had *your* say, too, Stokes. Sit down." Then I had to leave, so I slipped out—and missed what must have been a really dramatic event if you care for that sort of thing; I don't. Old Mr. Winters dropped dead about the time I must have been reaching the outer steps.

Novak did not let them recess on that account. They passed two resolutions; that no citizen should be subjected to hypnosis or other psychomanipulative technique without his written consent, and that no religious or political test should be used for franchise in the first elections.

I don't know who was right. It certainly would have made life easier in the next few weeks if we had known that the people were solidly behind us. Temporarily rulers we might be, but we hardly dared go down a street in uniform at night in groups of less than six.

Oh yes, we had uniforms now—almost enough for one for each of us, of the cheapest material possible and in the standard army sizes, either too large or too small. Mine was too tight. They had been stockpiled across the Canadian border and we got our own people into uniform as quickly as possible. A handkerchief tied around the arm is not enough.

Besides our own simple powder-blue dungarees there were several other uniforms around, volunteer brigades from outside the country and some native American outfits. The Mormon Battalions had their own togs and they were all growing beards as well—they went into action singing the long-forbidden "Come, Come, Ye Saints!" Utah was one state we didn't have to worry about, now that the Saints had their beloved temple back. The Catholic Legion had its distinctive uniform, which was just as well since hardly any of them spoke English. The Onward Christian Soldiers dressed differently from us because they were a rival underground and rather resented our coup d'état—we should have waited. Joshua's Army from the pariah reservations in the northwest (plus volunteers from all over the world) had a getup that can only be described as outlandish.

Huxley was in tactical command of them all. But it wasn't an army; it was a rabble.

The only thing that was hopeful about it was that the Prophet's army had not been large, less than two hundred thousand, more of an internal police than an army, and of that number only a few had managed to make their way back to New Jerusalem to augment the Palace garrison. Besides that, since the United States had not had an external war for more than a century, the Prophet could not recruit veteran soldiers from the remaining devout.

Neither could we. Most of our effectives were fit only to guard communication stations and other key installations around the country and we were hard put to find enough of them to do that. Mounting an assault on New Jerusalem called for scraping the bottom of the barrel.

Which we did, while smothering under a load of paperwork that made the days in the old GHQ seem quiet and untroubled. I had thirty clerks under me now and I don't know what half of them did. I spent a lot of my time just keeping Very Important Citizens who Wanted to Help from getting in to see Huxley.

I recall one incident which, while not important, was not exactly routine and was important to me. My chief secretary came in with a very odd look on her face. "Colonel," she said, "your twin brother is out there."

"Eh? I have no brothers."

"A Sergeant Reeves," she amplified.

He came in, we shook hands, and exchanged inanities. I really was glad to see him and told him about all the orders I had sold and then lost for him. I apologized, pled exigency of war and added, "I landed one new account in K.C.—Emery, Bird, Thayer. You might pick it up some day."

"I will. Thanks."

"I didn't know you were a soldier."

"I'm not, really. But I've been practicing at it ever since my travel permit, uh—got itself lost."

"I'm sorry about that."

"Don't be. I've learned to handle a blaster and I'm pretty good with a grenade now. I've been okayed for Operation Strikeout."

"Eh? That code word is supposed to be confo."

"It is? Better tell the boys; they don't seem to real-ize it. Anyhow, I'm in. Are you? Or shouldn't I ask that?"

I changed the subject. "How do you like soldiering? Planning to make a career of it?"

"Oh, it's all right—but not *that* all right. But what I came in to ask you, Colonel, are *you?*"

"Eh?"

"Are you staying in the army afterwards? I suppose you can make a good thing out of it, with your back-ground—whereas they wouldn't let me shine brightwork, once the fun is over. But if by any chance you aren't, what do you think of the textile business?"

I was startled but I answered, "Well, to tell the truth I rather enjoyed it—the selling end, at least."

"Good. I'm out of a job where I was, of course—and I've been seriously considering going in on my own, a jobbing business and manufacturers' representative. I'll need a partner. Eh?"

I thought it over. "I don't know," I said slowly. "I haven't thought ahead any farther than Operation Strikeout. I might stay in the army—though soldiering does not have the appeal for me it once had . . . too many copies to make out and certify. But I don't know. I think what I really want is simply to sit under my own vine and my own fig tree."

"'—and none shall make you afraid,'" he finished. "A good thought. But there is no reason why you shouldn't unroll a few bolts of cloth while you are sit-ting there. The fig crop might fail. Think it over."

"I will. I surely will."

15

Maggie and I were married the day before the assault on New Jerusalem. We had a twenty-minute honeymoon, holding hands on the fire escape outside my office, then I flew Huxley to the jump-off area. I was in the flagship during the attack. I had asked permission to pilot a rocket-jet as my combat assignment but he had turned me down.

"What for, John?" he had asked. "This isn't going to be won in the air; it will be settled on the ground."

He was right, as usual. We had few ships and still fewer pilots who could be trusted. Some of the Prophet's air force had been sabotaged on the ground; a goodly number had escaped to Canada and elsewhere and been interned. With what planes we had we had been bombing the Palace and Temple regularly, just to make them keep their heads down.

But we could not hurt them seriously that way and both sides knew it. The Palace, ornate as it was above ground, was probably the strongest bombproof ever built. It had been designed to stand direct impact of a fission bomb without damage to personnel in its deepest tunnels—and that was where the Prophet was spending his days, one could be sure. Even the part above ground was relatively immune to ordinary HE bombs such as we were using.

We weren't using atomic bombs for three reasons: we didn't have any; the United States was not known to have had any since the Johannesburg Treaty after World War III. We could not get any. We might have negotiated a couple of bombs from the Federation had we been conceded to be the legal government of the United States, but, while Canada had recognized us, Great Britain had not and neither had the North African Confederacy. Brazil was teetering; she had sent a chargé d'affaires to St. Louis. But even if we had actually been admitted to the Federation, it is most unlikely that a mass weapon would have been granted for an internal disorder.

Lastly, we would not have used one if it had been laid in our laps. No, we weren't chicken hearted. But an atom bomb, laid directly on the Palace, would certainly have killed around a hundred thousand or more of our fellow citizens in the surrounding city—and almost as certainly would not have killed the Prophet.

It was going to be necessary to go in and dig him out, like a holed-up badger.

Rendezvous was made on the east shore of the Delaware River. At one minute after midnight we moved east, thirty-four land cruisers, thirteen of them modern battlewagons, the rest light cruisers and obsolescent craft—all that remained of the Prophet's mighty East Mississippi fleet; the rest had been blown up by their former commanders. The heavy ships would be used to breach the walls; the light craft were escort to ten armored transports carrying the shock troops—five thousand fighting men hand-picked from the whole country. Some of them had had some military training in addition to what we had been able to give them in the past few weeks; all of them had taken part in the street fighting.

We could hear the bombing at New Jerusalem as we started out, the dull *Crrump!*, the gooseflesh shiver of the concussion wave, the bass rumble of the ground sonic. The bombing had been continuous the last thirty-six hours; we hoped that no one in the Palace had had any sleep lately, whereas our troops had just finished twelve hours impressed sleep.

None of the battlewagons had been designed as a flagship, so we had improvised a flag plot just abaft the conning tower, tearing out the long-range televisor to make room for the battle tracker and concentration plot. I was sweating over my jury-rigged tracker, hoping to Heaven that the makeshift shock absorbers would be good enough when we opened up. Crowded in behind me was a psychoperator and his crew of sensitives, eight women and a neurotic fourteen-year-old boy. In a pinch, each would have to handle four circuits. I wondered if they could do it. One thin blonde girl had a dry, chronic cough and a big thyroid patch on her throat.

We lumbered along in approach zigzag. Huxley wandered from comm to plot and back again, calm as a snail, looking over my shoulder, reading despatches casually, watching the progress of the approach on the screens.

The pile of despatches at my elbow grew. The *Cherub* had fouled her starboard tread; she had dropped out of formation but would rejoin in thirty minutes. Penoyer reported his columns extended and ready to deploy. Because of the acute shortage of command talent, we were using broad-command organization; Penoyer commanded the left wing and his own battlewagon; Huxley was force commander, right wing commander, and skipper of his own flagship.

At 12:32 the televisors went out. The enemy had analyzed our frequency variation pattern, matched us and blown every tube in the circuits. It is theoretically impossible; they did it. At 12:37 radio went out.

Huxley seemed unperturbed. "Shift to light-phone circuits," was all he said.

The communications officer had anticipated him; our audio circuits were now on infra-red beams, ship to ship. Huxley hung over my shoulder most of the next hour, watching the position plot lines grow. Presently he said, "I think we will deploy now, John. Some of those pilots aren't any too steady; I think we will give them time to settle down in their positions before anything more happens."

I passed the order and cut my tracker out of circuit for fifteen minutes; it wasn't built for so many variables at such high speeds and there was no sense in overloading it. Nineteen minutes later the last transport had checked in by phone, I made a preliminary set up, threw the starting switch and let the correction data feed in. For a couple of minutes I was very busy balancing data, my hands moving among knobs and keys; then the machine was satisfied with its own predictions and I reported, "Tracking, sir."

Huxley leaned over my shoulder. The line was a little ragged but I was proud of them—some of those pilots had been freighter jacks not four weeks earlier.

At three A.M. we made the precautionary signal, "Coming on the range," and our own turret rumbled as they loaded it.

At 3:31 Huxley gave the command, "Concentration Plan III, open fire."

Our own big fellow let go. The first shot shook loose a lot of dust and made my eyes water. The craft rolled back on her treads to the recoil and I nearly fell out of my saddle. I had never ridden one of the big booster guns before and I hadn't expected the long recoil. Our big rifle had secondary firing chambers up the barrel, electronically synchronized with the progress of the shell; it maintained max pressure all the way up and gave a much higher muzzle velocity and striking power. It also gave a bone-shaking recoil. But the second time I was ready for it.

Huxley was at the periscope between shots, trying to observe the effects of our fire. New Jerusalem had answered our fire but did not yet have us ranged. We had the advantage of firing at a stationary target whose range we knew to the meter; on the other hand even a heavy land cruiser could not show the weight of armor that underlay the Palace's gingerbread.

Huxley turned from the scope and remarked, "Smoke, John."

I turned to the communications officer. "Stand by, sensitives; all craft!"

The order never got through. Even as I gave it the comm officer reported loss of contact. But the psychoperator was already busy and I knew the same thing was happening in all the ships; it was normal casualty routine.

Of our nine sensitives, three—the boy and two

women—were wide-awakes; the other six were hypnos. The technician hooked the boy first to one in Penoyer's craft. The kid established rapport almost at once and Penoyer got through a report:

"BLANKETED BY SMOKE. HAVE SHIFTED LEFT WING TO PSYCHO. WHAT HOOK-UP?—PENOYER."

I answered, "Pass down the line." Doctrine permitted two types of telepathic hook-up: relay, in which a message would be passed along until it reached its destination; and command mesh, in which there was direct hook-up from flag to each ship under that flag, plus ship-to-ship for adjacent units. In the first case each sensitive carries just one circuit, that is, is in rapport with just one other telepath; in the second they might have to handle as many as four circuits. I wanted to hold off overloading them as long as possible.

The technician tied the other two wide-awakes into our flanking craft in the battle line, then turned his attention to the hypnos. Four of them required hypodermics; the other two went under in response to suggestion. Shortly we were hooked up with the transports and second-line craft, as well as with the bombers and the rocket-jet spotting the fall of shot. The jet reported visibility zero and complained that he wasn't getting anything intelligible by radar. I told him to stand by; the morning breeze might clear the smoke away presently.

We weren't dependent on him anyway; we knew our positions almost to the inch. We had taken departure from a benchmark and our deadreckoning was checked for the whole battle line every time any skipper identified a map-shown landmark. In addition, the deadreckoners of a tread-driven cruiser are surprisingly accurate; the treads literally measure every yard of ground as they pass over it and a little differential gadget compares the treads and keeps just as careful track of direction. The smoke did not really bother us and we could keep on firing accurately even if radar failed. On

the other hand, if the Palace commander kept us in
smoke he himself was entirely dependent on radar.

His radar was apparently working; shot was falling
all around us. We hadn't been hit yet but we could feel
the concussions when shells struck near us and some
of the reports were not cheerful. Penoyer reported the
Martyr hit; the shell had ruptured her starboard engine
room. The skipper had tried to cross connect and proceed at half speed, but the gear train was jammed; she
was definitely out of action. The *Archangel* had over-
heated her gun. She was in formation but would be
harmless until the turret captain got her straightened
out.

Huxley ordered them to shift to Formation E, a plan
which used changing speeds and apparently random
courses—carefully planned to avoid collision between
ships, however. It was intended to confuse the fire control of the enemy.

At 4:11 Huxley sent the bombers back to base. We
were inside the city now and the walls of the Palace
lay just beyond—too close to target for comfort; we
didn't want to lose ships to our own bombs.

At 4:17 we were struck. The port upper tread cas-
ing was split, the barbette was damaged so that the gun
would no longer train, and the conning tower was
cracked along its after surface. The pilot was killed at
his controls.

I helped the psychoperator get gas helmets over the
heads of the hypnos. Huxley picked himself up off the
floor plates, put on his own helmet, and studied the set-
up on my battle tracker, frozen at the instant the shell
hit us.

"The *Benison* should pass by this point in three minutes, John. Tell them to proceed dead slow, come along
starboard side, and pick us up. Tell Penoyer I am shift-
ing my flag."

We made the transfer without mishap, Huxley,
myself, the psychoperator, and his sensitives. One

sensitive was dead, killed by a flying splinter. One went into a deep trance and we could not rouse her. We left her in the disabled battlewagon; she was as safe there as she could be.

I had torn the current plot from my tracker and brought it along. It had the time-predicted plots for Formation E. We would have to struggle along with those, as the tracker could not be moved and was probably beyond casual repair in any case. Huxley studied the chart.

"Shift to full communication mesh, John. I plan to assault shortly."

I helped the psychoperator get his circuits straightened out. By dropping the *Martyr* out entirely and by using "Pass down the line" on Penoyer's auxiliaries, we made up for the loss of two sensitives. All carried four circuits now, except the boy who had five, and the girl with the cough, who was managing six. The psychoperator was worried but there was nothing to do about it.

I turned back to General Huxley. He had seated himself and at first I thought he was in deep thought; then I saw that he was unconscious. It was not until I tried to rouse him and failed that I saw the blood seeping down the support column of his chair and wetting the floor plates. I moved him gently and found, sticking out from between his ribs near his spine, a steel splinter.

I felt a touch at my elbow, it was the psychoperator. "Penoyer reports that he will be within assault radius in four minutes. Requests permission to change formation and asks time of execution."

Huxley was out. Dead or wounded, he would fight no more this battle. By all rules, command devolved on Penoyer, and I should tell him so at once. But time was pressing hard, it would involve a drastic change of set-up, and we had been forced to send Penoyer into battle with only three sensitives. It was a physical impossibility. What should I do? Turn the flag over to the skipper of the *Benison?* I knew the man, stolid, unimaginative, a gunner by disposition. He was not even in his conning tower but had been fighting his ship from the fire control station in the turret. If I called him down here, he would take many minutes to comprehend the situation—and then give the wrong orders.

With Huxley out I had not an ounce of real authority. I was a brevet short-tailed colonel, only days up from major and a legate by rights; I was what I was as Huxley's flunky. Should I turn command over to Penoyer—and lose the battle with proper military protocol? *What would Huxley have me do, if he could make the decision?*

It seemed to me that I worried that problem for an hour. The chronograph showed thirteen seconds between reception of Penoyer's despatch and my answer:

"Change formation at will. Stand by for execution signal in six minutes." The order given, I sent word to the forward dressing station to attend to the General.

I shifted the right wing to assault echelon, then called the transport *Sweet Chariot:* "Sub-plan D; leave formation and proceed on duty assigned." The psychoperator eyed me but transmitted my orders. Sub-plan D called for five hundred light infantry to enter the Palace through the basement of the department store that was connected with the lodge room. From the lodge room they would split into squads and proceed on assigned tasks. All of our shock troops had all the plans of the Palace graven into their brains; these five hundred had had additional drill as to just where they were to go, what they were to do.

Most of them would be killed, but they should be able to create confusion during the assault. Zeb had trained them and now commanded them.

We were ready. "All units, stand by to assault. Right wing, outer flank of right bastion; left wing, outer flank of left bastion. Zigzag emergency full speed until within assault distance. Deploy for full concentration fire, one salvo, and assault. Stand by to execute. Acknowledge."

The acknowledgments were coming in and I was watching my chronometer preparatory to giving the command of execution when the boy sensitive broke off in the middle of a report and shook himself. The technician grabbed the kid's wrist and felt for his pulse; the boy shook him off.

"Somebody new," he said. "I don't quite get it." Then he commenced in a sing-song, "To commanding general from Lodge Master Peter van Eyck: assault center bastion with full force. I will create a diversion."

"Why the center?" I asked.

"It is much more damaged."

If this were authentic, it was crucially important. But I was suspicious. If Master Peter had been detected, it was a trap. And I didn't see how he, in his position, had been able to set up a sensitive circuit in the midst of battle.

"Give me the word," I said.

"Nay, you give me."

"Nay, I will not."

"I will spell it, or halve it."

"Spell it, then."

We did so. I was satisfied. "Cancel last signal. Heavy cruisers assault center bastion, left wing to left flank, right wing to right flank. Odd numbered auxiliaries make diversion assaults on right and left bastions. Even numbers remain with transports. Acknowledge."

Nineteen seconds later I gave the command to execute, then we were off. It was like riding a rocket plane with a dirty, over-heated firing chamber. We crashed through walls of masonry, lurched sickeningly on turns, almost overturned when we crashed into the basement of some large demolished building and lumbered out again. It was out of my hands now, up to each skipper. As we slewed into firing position, I saw the

psychoperator peeling back the boy's eyelids. "I'm afraid
he's gone," he said tonelessly. "I had to overload him
too much on that last hook-up." Two more of the women
had collapsed.

Our big gun cut loose for the final salvo; we waited
for an interminable period—all of ten seconds. Then
we were moving, gathering speed as we rolled. The
Benison hit the Palace wall with a blow that I thought
would wreck her, but she did not mount. But the pilot
had his forward hydraulic jacks down as soon as we hit;
her bow reared slowly up. We reached an angle so steep
that it seemed she must turn turtle, then the treads took
hold, we ground forward and slid through the breach
in the wall.

Our gun spoke again, at point-blank range, right into
the inner Palace. A thought flashed through my head—
this was the exact spot where I had first laid eyes on
Judith. I had come full circle.

The *Benison* was rampaging around, destroying by
her very weight. I waited until the last cruiser had
had time to enter, then gave the order, "Transports,
assault." That done, I called Penoyer, informed him
that Huxley was wounded and that he was now in
command.

I was all through. I did not even have a job, a battle
station. The battle surged around me, but I was not part
of it—I, who two minutes ago had been in usurped full
command.

I stopped to light a cigarette and wondered what to
do with myself. I put it out after one soul-satisfying drag
and scrambled up into the fire control tower of the turret
and peered out the after slits. A breeze had come up and
the smoke was clearing; the transport *Jacob's Ladder* I
could see just pulling out of the breach. Her sides fell
away and ranks of infantry sprang out, blasters ready. A
sporadic fire met them; some fell but most returned the
fire and charged the inner Palace. The *Jacob's Ladder*
cleared the breach and the *Ark* took her place.

The troops commander in the *Ark* had orders to take the Prophet alive. I hurried down ladders from the turret, ran down the passageway between the engine rooms, and located the escape hatch in the floor plates, clear at the stern of the *Benison*. Somehow I got it unclamped, swung up the hatch cover, and stuck my head down. I could see men running, out beyond the treads. I drew my blaster, dropped to the ground, and tried to catch up with them, running out the stern between the big treads.

They were men from the *Ark*, right enough. I attached myself to a platoon and trotted along with them. We swarmed into the inner Palace.

But the battle was over; we encountered no organized resistance. We went on down and down and down and found the Prophet's bombproof. The door was open and he was there.

But we did not arrest him. The Virgins had gotten to him first; he no longer looked imperious. They had left him barely something to identify at an inquest.

Coventry

"Have you anything to say before sentence is pronounced on you?" The mild eyes of the Senior Judge studied the face of the accused. His question was answered by a sullen silence.

"Very well—the jury has determined that you have violated a basic custom agreed to under the Covenant, and that through this act did damage another free citizen. It is the opinion of the jury and of the court that you did so knowingly, and aware of the probability of damage to a free citizen. Therefore, you are sentenced to choose between the Two Alternatives."

A trained observer might have detected a trace of dismay breaking through the mask of indifference with which the young man had faced his trial. Dismay was unreasonable; in view of his offence, the sentence was inevitable—but reasonable men do not receive the sentence.

After waiting a decent interval, the judge turned to the bailiff. "Take him away."

The prisoner stood up suddenly, knocking over his chair. He glared wildly around at the company assembled and burst into speech.

"Hold on!" he yelled. "I've got something to say first!" In spite of his rough manner there was about him the noble dignity of a wild animal at bay. He stared at those around him, breathing heavily, as if they were dogs waiting to drag him down.

"Well?" he demanded, "Well? Do I get to talk, or don't I? It 'ud be the best joke of this whole comedy, if a condemned man couldn't speak his mind at the last!"

"You may speak," the Senior Judge told him, in the same unhurried tones with which he had pronounced sentence, "David MacKinnon, as long as you like, and in any manner that you like. There is no limit to that freedom, even for those who have broken the Covenant. Please speak into the recorder."

MacKinnon glanced with distaste at the microphone near his face. The knowledge that any word he spoke would be recorded and analyzed inhibited him. "I don't ask for records," he snapped.

"But we must have them," the judge replied patiently, "in order that others may determine whether, or not, we have dealt with you fairly, and according to the Covenant. Oblige us, please."

"Oh—very well!" He ungraciously conceded the requirement and directed his voice toward the instrument. "There's no sense in me talking at all—but, just the same, I'm going to talk and you're going to listen. . . . You talk about your precious 'Covenant' as if it were something holy. I don't agree to it and I don't accept it. You act as if it had been sent down from Heaven in a burst of light. My grandfathers fought in the Second Revolution—but they fought to abolish superstition . . . not to let sheep-minded fools set up new ones.

"There were men in those days!" He looked contemptuously around him. "What is there left today? Cautious, compromising 'safe' weaklings with water in their veins. You've planned your whole world so carefully that you've planned the fun and zest right out of it. Nobody is ever hungry, nobody ever gets hurt. Your ships can't crack up and your crops can't fail. You even have the weather tamed so it rains politely—after midnight. Why wait till midnight, I don't know . . . you all go to bed at nine o'clock!

"If one of you safe little people *should* have an unpleasant emotion—perish the thought!—you'd trot right over to the nearest psychodynamics clinic and get your soft little minds readjusted. Thank God I never succumbed to that dope habit. I'll keep my own feelings, thanks, no matter how bad they taste.

"You won't even make love without consulting a psychotechnician— Is her mind as flat and insipid as mine? Is there any emotional instability in her family? It's enough to make a man gag. As for fighting over a woman—if any one had the guts to do that, he'd find a proctor at his elbow in two minutes, looking for the most convenient place to paralyze him, and inquiring with sickening humility, 'May I do you a service, sir?'"

The bailiff edged closer to MacKinnon. He turned on him. "Stand back, you. I'm not through yet." He turned and added, "You've told me to choose between the Two Alternatives. Well, it's no hard choice for me. Before I'd submit to treatment, before I'd enter one of your neat little, safe little, pleasant little reorientation homes and let my mind be pried into by a lot of soft-fingered doctors—before I did anything like that, I'd choose a nice, clean death. Oh, no—there is just one choice for me, not two. I take the choice of going to Coventry—and glad of it, too . . . I hope I never hear of the United States again!

"But there is just one thing I want to ask you before I go— Why do you bother to live anyhow? I would think that any one of you would welcome an end to your silly, futile lives just from sheer boredom. That's all." He turned back to the bailiff "Come on, you."

"One moment, David MacKinnon." The Senior Judge held up a restraining hand. "We have listened to you. Although custom does not compel it, I am minded to answer some of your statements. Will you listen?"

Unwilling, but less willing to appear loutish in the face of a request so obviously reasonable, the younger man consented.

The judge commenced to speak in gentle, scholarly words appropriate to a lecture room. "David MacKinnon, you have spoken in a fashion that doubtless seems wise to you. Nevertheless, your words were wild, and spoken in haste. I am moved to correct your obvious misstatements of fact. The Covenant is not a superstition, but a simple temporal contract entered into by those same revolutionists for pragmatic reasons. They wished to insure the maximum possible liberty for every person.

"You yourself have enjoyed that liberty. No possible act, nor mode of conduct, was forbidden to you, as long as your action did not damage another. Even an act specifically prohibited by law could not be held against you, unless the state was able to prove that your particular act damaged, or caused evident danger of damage, to a particular individual.

"Even if one should willfully and knowingly damage another—as you have done—the state does not attempt to sit in moral judgment, nor to punish. We have not the wisdom to do that, and the chain of injustices that have always followed such moralistic coercion endanger the liberty of all. Instead, the convicted is given the choice of submitting to psychological readjustment to correct his tendency to wish to damage others, or of having the state withdraw itself from him—of sending him to Coventry.

"You complain that our way of living is dull and unromantic, and imply that we have deprived you of excitement to which you feel entitled. You are free to hold and express your esthetic opinion of our way of living, but you must not expect us to live to suit your tastes. You are free to seek danger and adventure if you wish—there is danger still in experimental laboratories; there is hardship in the mountains of the Moon, and death in the jungles of Venus—but you are not free to expose us to the violence of your nature."

"Why make so much of it?" MacKinnon protested contemptuously. "You talk as if I had committed a murder—I simply punched a man in the nose for offending me outrageously!"

"I agree with your esthetic judgment of that individual," the judge continued calmly, "and am personally rather gratified that you took a punch at him—but your psychometrical tests show that you believe yourself capable of judging morally your fellow citizens and feel justified in personally correcting and punishing their lapses. You are a dangerous individual, David MacKinnon, a danger to all of us, for we can not predict what damage you may do next. From a social standpoint, your delusion makes you as mad as the March Hare.

"You refuse treatment—therefore we withdraw our society from you, we cast you out, we divorce you. To Coventry with you." He turned to the bailiff. "Take him away."

MacKinnon peered out of a forward port of the big transport helicopter with repressed excitement in his heart. There! That must be it—that black band in the distance. The helicopter drew closer, and he became certain that he was seeing the Barrier—the mysterious, impenetrable wall that divided the United States from the reservation known as Coventry.

His guard looked up from the magazine he was reading and followed his gaze. "Nearly there, I see, he said pleasantly. "Well, it won't be long now."

"It can't be any too soon for me!"

The guard looked at him quizzically, but with tolerance. "Pretty anxious to get on with it, eh?"

MacKinnon held his head high. "You've never brought a man to the Gateway who was more anxious to pass through!"

"Mmm-maybe. They all say that, you know. Nobody goes through the Gate against his own will."

"I mean it!"

"They all do. Some of them come back, just the same."

"Say—maybe you can give me some dope as to conditions inside?"

"Sorry," the guard said, shaking his head, "but that is no concern of the United States, nor of any of its employees. You'll know soon enough."

MacKinnon frowned a little. "It seems strange—I tried inquiring, but found no one who would admit that they had any notion about the inside. And yet you say that some come out. Surely some of them must talk. . . ."

"That's simple," smiled the guard, "part of their reorientation is a subconscious compulsion not to discuss their experiences."

"That's a pretty scabby trick. Why should the government deliberately conspire to prevent me, and people like me, from knowing what we are going up against?"

"Listen, buddy," the guard answered, with mild exasperation, "you've told the rest of us to go to the devil. You've told us that you could get along without us. You are being given plenty of living room in some of the best land on this continent, and you are being allowed to take with you everything that you own, or your credit could buy. What the deuce else do you expect?"

MacKinnon's face settled in obstinate lines. "What assurance have I that there will be any land left for me?"

"That's your problem. The government sees to it that there is plenty of land for the population. The divvy-up is something you rugged individualists have to settle among yourselves. You've turned down our type of social cooperation; why should you expect the safeguards of our organization?" The guard turned back to his reading and ignored him.

They landed on a small field which lay close under

the blank black wall. No gate was apparent, but a guard-house was located at the side of the field. MacKinnon was the only passenger. While his escort went over to the guardhouse, he descended from the passenger compartment and went around to the freight hold. Two members of the crew were letting down a ramp from the cargo port. When he appeared, one of them eyed him, and said, "Okay, there's your stuff. Help yourself."

He sized up the job, and said, "It's quite a lot, isn't it? I'll need some help. Will you give me a hand with it?"

The crew member addressed paused to light a cigarette before replying, "It's your stuff. If you want it, get it out. We take off in ten minutes." The two walked around him and reentered the ship.

"Why, you—" MacKinnon shut up and kept the rest of his anger to himself. The surly louts! Gone was the faintest trace of regret at leaving civilization. He'd show them! He could get along without them.

But it was twenty minutes and more before he stood beside his heaped up belongings and watched the ship rise. Fortunately the skipper had not been adamant about the time limit. He turned and commenced loading his steel tortoise. Under the romantic influence of the classic literature of a bygone day he had considered using a string of burros, but had been unable to find a zoo that would sell them to him. It was just as well— he was completely ignorant of the limits, foibles, habits, vices, illnesses, and care of those useful little beasts, and unaware of his own ignorance. Master and servant would have vied in making each other unhappy.

The vehicle he had chosen was not an unreasonable substitute for burros. It was extremely rugged, easy to operate, and almost fool-proof. It drew its power from six square yards of sunpower screens on its low curved roof. These drove a constant-load motor, or, when halted, replenished the storage battery against cloudy weather, or night travel. The bearings were "ever-lasting," and every moving part, other than the caterpillar treads and the controls, were sealed up, secure from inexpert tinkering.

It could maintain a steady six miles per hour on smooth, level pavement. When confronted by hills, or rough terrain, it did not stop, but simply slowed until the task demanded equalled its steady power output.

The steel tortoise gave MacKinnon a feeling of Crusoe-like independence. It did not occur to him his chattel was the end product of the cumulative effort and intelligent co-operation of hundreds of thousands of men, living and dead. He had been used all his life to the unfailing service of much more intricate machinery, and honestly regarded the tortoise as a piece of equipment of the same primitive level as a woodsman's axe, or a hunting knife. His talents had been devoted in the past to literary criticism rather than engineering, but that did not prevent him from believing that his native intelligence and the aid of a few reference books would be all that he would really need to duplicate the tortoise, if necessary.

Metal ores were necessary, he knew, but saw no obstacle in that, his knowledge of the difficulties of prospecting, mining, and metallurgy being as sketchy as his knowledge of burros.

His goods filled every compartment of the compact little freighter. He checked the last item from his inventory and ran a satisfied eye down the list. Any explorer or adventurer of the past might well be pleased with such equipment, he thought. He could imagine showing Jack London his knock-down cabin. See, Jack, he would say, it's proof against any kind of weather—perfectly insulated walls and floor—and can't rust. It's so light that you can set it up in five minutes by yourself, yet it's so strong that you can sleep sound with the biggest grizzly in the world snuffling right outside your door.

And London would scratch his head, and say, Dave, you're a wonder. If I'd had that in the Yukon, it would have been a cinch!

He checked over the list again. Enough concentrated and desiccated food and vitamin concentrates to last six months. That would give him time enough to build hothouses for hydroponics, and get his seeds started. Medical supplies—he did not expect to need those, but foresight was always best. Reference books of all sorts. A light sporting rifle—vintage: last century. His face clouded a little at this. The War Department had positively refused to sell him a portable blaster. When he had claimed the right of common social heritage, they had grudgingly provided him with the plans and specifications, and told him to build his own. Well, he would, the first spare time he got.

Everything else was in order. MacKinnon climbed into the cockpit, grasped the two hand controls, and swung the nose of the tortoise toward the guardhouse. He had been ignored since the ship had landed; he wanted to have the gate opened and to leave.

Several soldiers were gathered around the guardhouse. He picked out a legate by the silver stripe down the side of his kilt and spoke to him. "I'm ready to leave. Will you kindly open the Gate?"

"Okay," the officer answered him, and turned to a soldier who wore the plain grey kilt of a private's field uniform. "Jenkins, tell the power house to dilate—about a number three opening, tell them," he added, sizing up the dimensions of the tortoise.

He turned to MacKinnon. "It is my duty to tell you that you may return to civilization, even now, by agreeing to be hospitalized for your neurosis."

"I have no neurosis!"

"Very well. If you change your mind at any future time, return to the place where you entered. There is an alarm there with which you may signal to the guard that you wish the gate opened."

"I can't imagine needing to know that."

The legate shrugged. "Perhaps not—but we send refugees to quarantine all the time. If I were making

the rules, it might be harder to get out again." He was
cut off by the ringing of an alarm. The soldiers near
them moved smartly away, drawing their blasters from
their belts as they ran. The ugly snout of a fixed blaster
poked out over the top of the guardhouse and pointed
toward the Barrier.

The legate answered the question on MacKinnon's
face. "The power house is ready to open up." He waved
smartly toward that building, then turned back. "Drive
straight through the center of the opening. It takes a
lot of power to suspend the stasis; if you touch the edge,
we'll have to pick up the pieces."

A tiny, bright dot appeared in the foot of the barrier opposite where they waited. It spread into a half
circle across the lampblack nothingness. Now it was large
enough for MacKinnon to see the countryside beyond
through the arch it had formed. He peered eagerly.

The opening grew until it was twenty feet wide, then
stopped. It framed a scene of rugged, barren hills. He
took this in, and turned angrily on the legate. "I've been
tricked!" he exclaimed. "That's not fit land to support
a man."

"Don't be hasty," he told MacKinnon. "There's good
land beyond. Besides—you don't have to enter. But if
you are going, go!"

MacKinnon flushed, and pulled back on both hand
controls. The treads bit in and the tortoise lumbered
away, straight for the Gateway to Coventry.

When he was several yards beyond the Gate, he
glanced back. The Barrier loomed behind him, with
nothing to show where the opening had been. There
was a little sheetmetal shed adjacent to the point where
he had passed through. He supposed that it contained
the alarm the legate had mentioned, but he was not
interested and turned his eyes back to his driving.

Stretching before him, twisting between rocky hills,
was a road of sorts. It was not paved and the surface
had not been repaired recently, but the grade averaged

downhill and the tortoise was able to maintain a respectable speed. He continued down it, not because he fancied it, but because it was the only road which led out of surroundings obviously unsuited to his needs.

The road was untravelled. This suited him; he had no wish to encounter other human beings until he had located desirable land to settle on, and had staked out his claim. But the hills were not devoid of life; several times he caught glimpses of little dark shapes scurrying among the rocks, and occasionally bright, beady eyes stared back into his.

It did not occur to him at first that these timid little animals, streaking for cover at his coming, could replenish his larder—he was simply amused and warmed by their presence. When he did happen to consider that they might be used as food, the thought was at first repugnant to him—the custom of killing for "sport" had ceased to be customary long before his time; and inasmuch as the development of cheap synthetic proteins in the latter half of the preceding century had spelled the economic ruin of the business of breeding animals for slaughter, it is doubtful if he had ever tasted animal tissue in his life.

But once considered, it was logical to act. He expected to live off the country; although he had plenty of food on hand for the immediate future, it would be wise to conserve it by using what the country offered. He suppressed his esthetic distaste and ethical misgivings, and determined to shoot one of the little animals at the first opportunity.

Accordingly, he dug out the rifle, loaded it, and placed it handy. With the usual perversity of the world-as-it-is, no game was evident for the next half hour. He was passing a little shoulder of rocky outcropping when he saw his prey. It peeked at him from behind a small boulder, its sober eyes wary but unperturbed. He stopped the tortoise and took careful aim, resting and steadying the rifle on the side of the cockpit. His quarry accommodated him by hopping out into full view.

He pulled the trigger, involuntarily tensing his muscles and squinting his eyes as he did so. Naturally, the shot went high and to the right.

But he was much too busy just then to be aware of it. It seemed that the whole world had exploded. His right shoulder was numb, his mouth stung as if he had been kicked there, and his ears rang in a strange and unpleasant fashion. He was surprised to find the gun still intact in his hands and apparently none the worse for the incident.

He put it down, clambered out of the car, and rushed up to where the small creature had been. There was no sign of it anywhere. He searched the immediate neighborhood, but did not find it. Mystified, he returned to his conveyance, having decided that the rifle was in some way defective, that he should inspect it carefully before attempting to fire it again.

His recent target watched his actions cautiously from a vantage point yards away, to which it had stampeded at the sound of the shot. It was equally mystified by the startling events, being no more used to firearms than was MacKinnon.

Before he started the tortoise again, MacKinnon had to see to his upper lip, which was swollen and tender and bleeding from a deep scratch. This increased his conviction that the gun was defective. Nowhere in the romantic literature of the nineteenth and twentieth centuries, to which he was addicted, had there been a warning that, when firing a gun heavy enough to drop a man in his tracks, it is well not to hold the right hand in such a manner that the recoil will cause the right thumb and thumb nail to strike the mouth.

He applied an antiseptic and a dressing of sorts, and went on his way, somewhat subdued. The arroyo by which he had entered the hills had widened out, and the hills were greener. He passed around one sharp turn in the road, and found a broad fertile valley spread out before him. It stretched away until it was lost in the warm day's haze.

Much of the valley was cultivated, and he could make out human habitations. He continued toward it with mixed feelings. People meant fewer hardships, but it did not look as if staking out a claim would be as simple as he had hoped. However—Coventry was a big place.

He had reached the point where the road gave onto the floor of the valley, when two men stepped out into his path. They were carrying weapons of some sort at the ready. One of them called out to him:

"Halt!"

MacKinnon did so, and answered him as they came abreast. "What do you want?"

"Customs inspection. Pull over there by the office." He indicated a small building set back a few feet from the road, which MacKinnon had not previously noticed. He looked from it back to the spokesman, and felt a slow, unreasoning heat spread up from his viscera. It rendered his none too stable judgment still more unsound.

"What the deuce are you talking about?" he snapped. "Stand aside and let me pass."

The one who had remained silent raised his weapon and aimed it at MacKinnon's chest. The other grabbed his arm and pulled the weapon out of line. "Don't shoot the dumb fool, Joe," he said testily. "You're always too anxious." Then to MacKinnon, "You're resisting the law. Come on—be quick about it!"

"The law?" MacKinnon gave a bitter laugh and snatched his rifle up from the seat. It never reached his shoulder—the man who had done all the talking fired casually, without apparently taking time to aim. MacKinnon's rifle was smacked from his grasp and flew into the air, landing in the roadside ditch behind the tortoise.

The man who had remained silent followed the flight of the gun with detached interest, and remarked, "Nice shot, Blackie. Never touched him."

"Oh, just luck," the other demurred, but grinned his pleasure at the compliment. "Glad I didn't nick him, though—saves writing out a report." He reassumed an official manner, spoke again to MacKinnon, who had been sitting dumbfounded, rubbing his smarting hands. "Well, tough guy? Do you behave, or do we come up there and get you?"

MacKinnon gave in. He drove the tortoise to the designated spot, and waited sullenly for orders. "Get out and start unloading," he was told.

He obeyed, under compulsion. As he piled his precious possessions on the ground, the one addressed as Blackie separated the things into two piles, while Joe listed them on a printed form. He noticed presently that Joe listed only the items that went into the first pile. He understood this when Blackie told him to reload the tortoise with the items from that pile, and commenced himself to carry goods from the other pile into the building. He started to protest—

Joe punched him in the mouth, coolly and without rancor. MacKinnon went down, but got up again, fighting. He was in such a blind rage that he would have tackled a charging rhino. Joe timed his rush, and clipped him again. This time he could not get up at once.

Blackie stepped over to a washstand in one corner of the office. He came back with a wet towel and chucked it at MacKinnon. "Wipe your face on that, bud, and get back in the buggy. We got to get going."

MacKinnon had time to do a lot of serious thinking as he drove Blackie into town. Beyond a terse answer of "Prize court" to MacKinnon's inquiry as to their destination, Blackie did not converse, nor did MacKinnon press him, anxious as he was to have information. His mouth pained him from repeated punishment, his head ached, and he was no longer tempted to precipitate action by hasty speech.

Evidently Coventry was not quite the frontier anarchy he had expected it to be. There was a government of sorts, apparently, but it resembled nothing that he had ever been used to. He had visualized a land of noble, independent spirits who gave each other wide berth and practiced mutual respect. There would be villains, of course, but they would be treated to summary, and probably lethal, justice as quickly as they demonstrated their ugly natures. He had a strong, though subconscious, assumption that virtue is necessarily triumphant.

But having found government, he expected it to follow the general pattern that he had been used to all his life—honest, conscientious, reasonably efficient, and invariably careful of a citizen's rights and liberties. He was aware that government had not always been like that, but he had never experienced it—the idea was as remote and implausible as cannibalism, or chattel slavery.

Had he stopped to think about it, he might have realized that public servants in Coventry would never have been examined psychologically to determine their temperamental fitness for their duties, and, since every inhabitant of Coventry was there—as he was—for violating a basic custom and refusing treatment thereafter, it was a foregone conclusion that most of them would be erratic and arbitrary.

He pinned his hope on the knowledge that they were going to court. All he asked was a chance to tell his story to the judge.

His dependence on judicial procedure may appear inconsistent in view of how recently he had renounced all reliance on organized government, but while he could renounce government verbally, he could not do away with a lifetime of environmental conditioning. He could curse the court that had humiliated him by condemning him to the Two Alternatives, but he expected courts to dispense justice. He could assert his own rugged independence, but he expected persons he encountered to behave as if they were bound by the Covenant—he had met no other sort. He was no more able to discard his past history than he would have been to discard his accustomed body.

But he did not know it yet.

MacKinnon failed to stand up when the judge entered the court room. Court attendants quickly set him right, but not before he had provoked a glare from the bench. The judge's appearance and manner were not reassuring. He was a well-fed man, of ruddy complexion, whose sadistic temper was evident in face and mien. They waited while he dealt drastically with several petty offenders. It seemed to MacKinnon, as he listened, that almost everything was against the law.

Nevertheless, he was relieved when his name was called. He stepped up and undertook at once to tell his story. The judge's gavel cut him short.

"What is this case?" the judge demanded, his face set in grim lines. "Drunk and disorderly, apparently. I shall put a stop to this slackness among the young if it takes the last ounce of strength in my body!" He turned to the clerk. "Any previous offences?"

The clerk whispered in his ear. The judge threw MacKinnon a look of mixed annoyance and suspicion, then told the customs' guard to come forward. Blackie told a clear, straightforward tale with the ease of a man used to giving testimony. MacKinnon's condition was attributed to resisting an officer in the execution of his duty. He submitted the inventory his colleague had prepared, but failed to mention the large quantity of goods which had been abstracted before the inventory was made.

The judge turned to MacKinnon. "Do you have anything to say for yourself?"

"I certainly have, Doctor," he began eagerly. "There isn't a word of—"

Bang! The gavel cut him short. A court attendant hurried to MacKinnon's side and attempted to explain to him the proper form to use in addressing the court. The explanation confused him. In his experience, "judge" naturally implied a medical man—a psychiatrist skilled in social problems. Nor had he heard of any special speech forms appropriate to a courtroom. But he amended his language as instructed.

"May it please the Honorable Court, this man is lying. He and his companion assaulted and robbed me. I was simply—"

"Smugglers generally think they are being robbed when customs officials catch them," the judge sneered. "Do you deny that you attempted to resist inspection?"

"No, Your Honor, but—"

"That will do. Penalty of fifty percent is added to the established scale of duty. Pay the clerk."

"But, Your Honor, I can't—"

"Can't you pay it?"

"I haven't any money. I have only my possessions."

"So?" He turned to the clerk. "Condemnation proceedings. Impound his goods. Ten days for vagrancy. The community can't have these immigrant paupers roaming at large, and preying on law-abiding citizens. Next case!"

They hustled him away. It took the sound of a key grating in a barred door behind him to make him realize his predicament.

"Hi, pal, how's the weather outside?" The detention cell had a prior inmate, a small, well-knit man who looked up from a game of solitaire to address MacKinnon. He sat astraddle a bench on which he had spread his cards, and studied the newcomer with unworried, bright, beady eyes.

"Clear enough outside—but stormy in the courtroom," MacKinnon answered, trying to adopt the same bantering tone and not succeeding very well. His mouth hurt him and spoiled his grin.

The other swung a leg over the bench and approached him with a light, silent step. "Say, pal, you must 'a' caught that in a gear box," he commented, inspecting MacKinnon's mouth. "Does it hurt?"

"Like the devil," MacKinnon admitted.

"We'll have to do something about that." He went to the cell door and rattled it. "Hey! Lefty! The house is on fire! Come arunnin'!"

The guard sauntered down and stood opposite their cell door. "Wha' d'yuh want, Fader?" he said noncommittally.

"My old school chum has been slapped in the face with a wrench, and the pain is inordinate. Here's a chance for you to get right with Heaven by oozing down to the dispensary, snagging a dressing and about five grains of neoanodyne."

The guard's expression was not encouraging. The prisoner looked grieved. "Why, Lefty," he said, "I thought you would jump at a chance to do a little pure charity like that." He waited for a moment, then added, "Tell you what—you do it, and I'll show you how to work that puzzle about 'How old is Ann?' Is it a go?"

"Show me first."

"It would take too long. I'll write it out and give it to you."

When the guard returned, MacKinnon's cellmate dressed his wounds with gentle deftness, talking the while. "They call me Fader Magee. What's your name, pal?"

"David MacKinnon. I'm sorry, but I didn't quite catch your first name."

"Fader. It isn't," he explained with a grin, "the name my mother gave me. It's more a professional tribute to my shy and unobtrusive nature."

MacKinnon looked puzzled. "Professional tribute? What is your profession?"

Magee looked pained. "Why, Dave," he said, "I didn't ask *you* that. However," he went on, "it's probably the same as yours—self-preservation."

Magee was a sympathetic listener, and MacKinnon welcomed the chance to tell someone about his troubles. He related the story of how he had decided to enter Coventry rather than submit to the sentence of the court, and how he had hardly arrived when he was hijacked and hauled into court. Magee nodded. "I'm not surprised," he observed. "A man has to have larceny in his heart, or he wouldn't be a customs guard."

"But what happens to my belongings?"

"They auction them off to pay the duty."

"I wonder how much there will be left for me?"

Magee stared at him. "Left over? There won't be anything left over. You'll probably have to pay a deficiency judgment."

"Huh? What's that?"

"It's a device whereby the condemned pays for the execution," Magee explained succinctly, if somewhat obscurely. "What it means to you is that when your ten days is up, you'll still be in debt to the court. Then it's the chain gang for you, my lad—you'll work it off at a dollar a day."

"Fader—you're kidding me."

"Wait and see. You've got a lot to learn, Dave."

Coventry was an even more complex place than MacKinnon had gathered up to this time. Magee explained to him that there were actually three sovereign, independent jurisdictions. The jail where they were prisoners lay in the so-called New America. It had the forms of democratic government, but the treatment he had already received was a fair sample of the fashion in which it was administered.

"This place is heaven itself compared with the Free State," Magee maintained. "I've been there—" The Free State was an absolute dictatorship; the head man of the ruling clique was designated the "Liberator." Their watchwords were Duty and Obedience; an arbitrary discipline was enforced with a severity that left no room for any freedom of opinion. Governmental theory was vaguely derived from the old functionalist doctrines. The state was thought of as a single organism with a single head, a single brain, and a single purpose. Anything not compulsory was forbidden. "Honest so help me," claimed Magee, "you can't go to bed in that place without finding one of their damned secret police between the sheets."

"But at that," he continued, "it's an easier place to live than with the Angels."

"The Angels?"

"Sure. We still got 'em. Must have been two or three thousand die-hards that chose to go to Coventry after the Revolution—you know that. There's still a colony up in the hills to the north, complete with Prophet Incarnate and the works. They aren't bad hombres, but they'll pray you into heaven even if it kills you."

All three states had one curious characteristic in common—each one claimed to be the only legal government of the entire United Stares, and each looked forward to some future day when they would reclaim the "unredeemed" portion; i.e., outside Coventry. To the Angels, this was an event which would occur when the First Prophet returned to earth to lead them again. In New America it was hardly more than a convenient campaign plank, to be forgotten after each election. But in the Free State it was a fixed policy.

Pursuant to this purpose there had been a whole series of wars between the Free State and New America. The Liberator held, quite logically, that New America was an unredeemed section, and that it was necessary to bring it under the rule of the Free State before the advantages of their culture could be extended to the outside.

Magee's words demolished MacKinnon's dream of finding an anarchistic utopia within the barrier, but he could not let his fond illusion die without a protest. "But see here, Fader," he persisted, "isn't there some place where a man can live quietly by himself without all this insufferable interference?"

"No—" considered Fader, "no . . . not unless you took to the hills and hid. Then you 'ud be all right, as long as you steered clear of the Angels. But it would be pretty slim pickin's, living off the country. Ever tried it?"

"No . . . not exactly—but I've read all the classics: Zane Grey, and Emerson Hough, and so forth."

"Well . . . maybe you could do it. But if you really want to go off and be a hermit, you 'ud do better to try it on the Outside, where there aren't so many objections to it."

"No"—MacKinnon's backbone stiffened at once—"no, I'll never do that. I'll never submit to psychological reorientation just to have a chance to be let alone. If I could go back to where I was before a couple of months ago, before I was arrested, it might be all right to go off to the Rockies, or look up an abandoned farm somewhere . . . But with that diagnosis staring me in the face . . . after being told I wasn't fit for human society until I had had my emotions re-tailored to fit a cautious little pattern, I couldn't face it. Not if it meant going to a sanatarium—"

"I see," agreed Fader, nodding, "you want to go to Coventry, but you don't want the Barrier to shut you off from the rest of the world."

"No, that's not quite fair . . . Well, maybe, in a way. Say, you don't think I'm not fit to associate with, do you?"

"You look all right to me," Magee reassured him, with a grin, "but I'm in Coventry too, remember. Maybe I'm no judge."

"You don't talk as if you liked it much. Why are you here?"

Magee held up a gently admonishing finger. "Tut! Tut! That is the one question you must never ask a man here. You must assume that he came here because he knew how swell everything is here."

"Still . . . you don't seem to like it."

"I didn't say I didn't like it. I do like it; it has flavor. Its little incongruities are a source of innocent merriment. And anytime they turn on the heat I can always go back through the Gate and rest up for a while in a nice quiet hospital, until things quiet down."

MacKinnon was puzzled again. "Turn on the heat? Do they supply too hot weather here?"

"Huh? Oh, I didn't mean weather control—there isn't any of that here, except what leaks over from outside. I was just using an old figure of speech."

"What does it mean?"

Magee smiled to himself. "You'll find out."

After supper—bread, stew in a metal dish, a small apple—Magee introduced MacKinnon to the mysteries of cribbage. Fortunately, MacKinnon had no cash to lose. Presently Magee put the cards down without shuffling them. "Dave," he said, "are you enjoying the hospitality offered by this institution?"

"Hardly— Why?"

"I suggest that we check out."

"A good idea, but how?"

"That's what I've been thinking about. Do you suppose you could take another poke on that battered phiz of yours, in a good cause?"

MacKinnon cautiously fingered his face. "I suppose so—if necessary. It can't do me much more harm, anyhow."

"That's mother's little man! Now listen—this guard, Lefty, in addition to being kind o' unbright, is sensitive about his appearance. When they turn out the lights, you—"

"Let me out of here! Let me out of here!" MacKinnon beat on the bars and screamed. No answer came. He renewed the racket, his voice an hysterical falsetto. Lefty arrived to investigate, grumbling.

"What the hell's eating on you?" he demanded, peering through the bars.

MacKinnon changed to tearful petition. "Oh, Lefty, please let me out of here. Please! I can't stand the dark.

It's dark in here—please don't leave me alone." He flung himself, sobbing, on the bars.

The guard cursed to himself. "Another slugnutty. Listen, you—shut up, and go to sleep, or I'll come in there, and give you something to yelp for!" He started to leave.

MacKinnon changed instantly to the vindictive, unpredictable anger of the irresponsible. "You big ugly baboon! You rat-faced idiot! Where'd you get that nose?"

Lefty turned back, fury in his face. He started to speak. MacKinnon cut him short. "Yah! Yah! Yah!" he gloated, like a nasty little boy. "Lefty's mother was scared by a warthog—"

The guard swung at the spot where MacKinnon's face was pressed between the bars of the door. MacKinnon ducked and grabbed simultaneously. Off balance at meeting no resistance, the guard rocked forward, thrusting his forearm between the bars. MacKinnon's fingers slid along his arm, and got a firm purchase on Lefty's wrist.

He threw himself backwards, dragging the guard with him, until Lefty was jammed up against the outside of the barred door, with one arm inside, to the wrist of which MacKinnon clung as if welded.

The yell which formed in Lefty's throat miscarried; Magee had already acted. Out of the darkness, silent as death, his slim hands had snaked between the bars and imbedded themselves in the guard's fleshy neck. Lefty heaved, and almost broke free, but MacKinnon threw his weight to the right and twisted the arm he gripped in an agonizing, bone-breaking leverage.

It seemed to MacKinnon that they remained thus, like some grotesque game of statues, for an endless period. His pulse pounded in his ears until he feared that it must be heard by others, and bring rescue to Lefty. Magee spoke at last:

"That's enough," he whispered. "Go through his pockets."

He made an awkward job of it, for his hands were numb and trembling from the strain, and it was anything but convenient to work between the bars. But the keys were there, in the last pocket he tried. He passed them to Magee, who let the guard slip to the floor, and accepted them.

Magee made a quick job of it. The door swung open with a distressing creak. Dave stepped over Lefty's body, but Magee kneeled down, unhooked a truncheon from the guard's belt, and cracked him behind the ear with it. MacKinnon paused.

"Did you kill him?" he asked.

"Cripes, no," Magee answered softly, "Lefty is a friend of mine. Let's go."

They hurried down the dimly lighted passageway between cells toward the door leading to the administrative offices—their only outlet. Lefty had carelessly left it ajar, and light shone through the crack, but as they silently approached it, they heard ponderous footsteps from the far side. Dave looked hurriedly for cover, but the best he could manage was to slink back into the corner formed by the cell block and the wall. He glanced around for Magee, but he had disappeared.

The door swung open; a man stepped through, paused, and looked around. MacKinnon saw that he was carrying a black-light, and wearing its complement—rectifying spectacles. He realized then that the darkness gave him no cover. The black-light swung his way; he tensed to spring—

He heard a dull *"clunk!"* The guard sighed, swayed gently, then collapsed into a loose pile. Magee stood over him, poised on the balls of his feet, and surveyed his work, while caressing the business end of the truncheon with the cupped fingers of his left hand.

"That will do," he decided. "Shall we go, Dave?"

He eased through the door without waiting for an answer; MacKinnon was close behind him. The lighted corridor led away to the right and ended in a large double door to the street. On the left wall, near the street door, a smaller office door stood open.

Magee drew MacKinnon to him. "It's a cinch," he whispered. "There'll be nobody in there now but the desk sergeant. We get past him, then out that door, and into the ozone—" He motioned Dave to keep behind him, and crept silently up to the office door. After drawing a small mirror from a pocket in his belt, he lay down on the floor, placed his head near the door frame, and cautiously extended the tiny mirror an inch or two past the edge.

Apparently he was satisfied with the reconnaissance the improvised periscope afforded, for he drew himself back onto his knees and turned his head so that MacKinnon could see the words shaped by his silent lips. "It's all right," he breathed, "there is only—"

Two hundred pounds of uniformed nemesis landed on his shoulders. A clanging alarm sounded through the corridor. Magee went down fighting, but he was out-classed and caught off guard. He jerked his head free and shouted, "Run for it, kid!"

MacKinnon could hear running feet somewhere, but could see nothing but the struggling figures before him. He shook his head and shoulders like a dazed animal, then kicked the larger of the two contestants in the face. The man screamed and let go his hold. MacKinnon grasped his small companion by the scruff of the neck and hauled him roughly to his feet.

Magee's eyes were still merry. "Well played, my lad," he commended in clipped syllables, as they burst out the street door, "—if hardly cricket! Where did you learn *La Savate*?"

MacKinnon had not time to answer, being fully occupied in keeping up with Magee's weaving, deceptively rapid progress. They ducked across the street, down an alley, and between two buildings.

The succeeding minutes, or hours, were confusion to MacKinnon. He remembered afterwards crawling along a roof top and letting himself down to crouch in the blackness of an interior court, but he could not remember how they had gotten on the roof. He also recalled spending an interminable period alone, compressed inside a most unsavory refuse bin, and his terror when footsteps approached the bin and a light flashed through a crack.

A crash and the sound of footsteps in flight immediately thereafter led him to guess that Fader had drawn the pursuit away from him. But when Fader did return, and open the top of the bin, MacKinnon almost throttled him before identification was established.

When the active pursuit had been shaken off, Magee guided him across town, showing a sophisticated knowledge of back ways and shortcuts, and a genius for taking full advantage of cover. They reached the outskirts of the town in a dilapidated quarter, far from the civic center. Magee stopped. "I guess this is the end of the line, kid," he told Dave. "If you follow this street, you'll come to open country shortly. That's what you wanted, wasn't it?"

"I suppose so," MacKinnon replied uneasily, and peered down the street. Then he turned back to speak again to Magee.

But Magee was gone. He had faded away into the shadows. There was neither sight nor sound of him.

MacKinnon started in the suggested direction with a heavy heart. There was no possible reason to expect Magee to stay with him; the service Dave had done him with a lucky kick had been repaid with interest—yet he had lost the only friendly companionship he had found in a strange place. He felt lonely and depressed.

He continued along, keeping to the shadows, and watching carefully for shapes that might be patrolmen. He had gone a few hundred yards, and was beginning to worry about how far it might be to open countryside, when he was startled into gooseflesh by a hiss from a dark doorway.

He did his best to repress the panic that beset him, and was telling himself that policemen never hiss, when a shadow detached itself from the blackness and touched him on the arm.

"Dave," it said softly.

MacKinnon felt a childlike sense of relief and well-being. "Fader!"

"I changed my mind, Dave. The gendarmes would have you in tow before morning. You don't know the ropes. . . . so I came back."

Dave was both pleased and crestfallen. "Hells bells, Fader," he protested, "you shouldn't worry about me. I'll get along."

Magee shook him roughly by the arm. "Don't be a chump. Green as you are, you'd start to holler about your civil rights, or something, and get clipped in the mouth again.

"Now see here," he went on, "I'm going to take you to some friends of mine who will hide you until you're smartened up to the tricks around here. But they're on the wrong side of the law, see? You'll have to be all three of the three sacred monkeys—see no evil, hear no evil, tell no evil. Think you can do it?"

"Yes, but—"

"No 'buts' about it. Come along!"

The entrance was in the rear of an old warehouse. Steps led down into a little sunken pit. From this open areaway—foul with accumulated refuse—a door let into the back wall of the building. Magee tapped lightly but systematically, waited and listened. Presently he whispered, "Pssst! It's the Fader."

The door opened quickly, and Magee was encircled by two great, fat arms. He was lifted off his feet, while the owner of those arms planted a resounding buss on his cheek. "Fader!" she exclaimed, "are you all right, lad? We've missed you."

"Now that's a proper welcome, Mother," he answered, when he was back on his own feet, "but I want you to meet a friend of mine. Mother Johnston, this is David MacKinnon."

"May I do you a service?" David acknowledged, with automatic formality, but Mother Johnston's eyes tightened with instant suspicion.

"Is he stooled?" she snapped.

"No, Mother, he's a new immigrant—but I vouch for him. He's on the dodge, and I've brought him here to cool."

She softened a little under his sweetly persuasive tones. "Well—"

Magee pinched her cheek. "That's a good girl! When are you going to marry me?"

She slapped his hand away. "Even if I were forty years younger, I'd not marry such a scamp as you! Come along then," she continued to MacKinnon, "as long as you're a friend of the Fader—though it's no credit to you!" She waddled quickly ahead of them, down a flight of stairs, while calling out for someone to open the door at its foot.

The room was poorly lighted and was furnished principally with a long table and some chairs, at which an odd dozen people were seated, drinking and talking. It reminded MacKinnon of prints he had seen of old English pubs in the days before the Collapse.

Magee was greeted with a babble of boisterous welcome. "Fader!"—"It's the kid himself!"—"How d'ja do it this time, Fader? Crawl down the drains?"—"Set 'em up, Mother—the Fader's back!"

He accepted the ovation with a wave of his hand and a shout of inclusive greeting, then turned to MacKinnon. "Folks," he said, his voice cutting through the confusion, "I want you to know Dave—the best pal that ever kicked a jailer at the right moment. If it hadn't been for Dave, I wouldn't be here."

Dave found himself seated between two others at the table and a stein of beer thrust into his hand by a not uncomely young woman. He started to thank her, but she had hurried off to help Mother Johnston take care of the sudden influx of orders. Seated opposite him was a rather surly young man who had taken little part in the greeting to Magee. He looked MacKinnon over with a face expressionless except for a recurrent tic which caused his right eye to wink spasmodically every few seconds.

"What's your line?" he demanded.

"Leave him alone, Alec," Magee cut in swiftly, but in a friendly tone. "He's just arrived inside; I told you that. But he's all right," he continued, raising his voice to include the others present, "he's been here less than twenty-four hours, but he's broken jail, beat up two customs busies, and sassed old Judge Fleishacker right to his face. How's that for a busy day?"

Dave was the center of approving interest, but the party with the tic persisted. "That's all very well, but I asked him a fair question: What's his line? If it's the same as mine, I won't stand for it—it's too crowded now."

"That cheap racket you're in is always crowded, but he's not in it. Forget about his line."

"Why don't he answer for himself," Alec countered suspiciously. He half stood up. "I don't believe he's stooled—"

It appeared that Magee was cleaning his nails with the point of a slender knife. "Put your nose back in your glass, Alec," he remarked in a conversational tone, without looking up, "—or must I cut it off and put it there?"

The other fingered something nervously in his hand. Magee seemed not to notice it, but nevertheless told him, "If you think you can use a vibrator on me faster than I use steel, go ahead—it will be an interesting experiment."

The man facing him stood uncertainly for a moment longer, his tic working incessantly. Mother Johnston came up behind him and pushed him down by the shoulders, saying, "Boys! Boys! Is that any way to behave?—and in front of a guest, too! Fader, put that toadsticker away—I'm ashamed of you."

The knife was gone from his hands. "You're right as always, Mother," he grinned. "Ask Molly to fill up my glass again."

An old chap sitting on MacKinnon's right had followed these events with alcoholic uncertainty, but he seemed to have gathered something of the gist of it, for now he fixed Dave with serum-filled eye, and enquired, "Boy, are you stooled to the rogue?" His sweetly sour breath reached MacKinnon as the old man leaned toward him and emphasized his question with a trembling, joint-swollen finger.

Dave looked to Magee for advice and enlightenment. Magee answered for him. "No, he's not—Mother Johnston knew that when she let him in. He's here for sanctuary—as our customs provide!"

An uneasy stir ran around the room. Molly paused in her serving and listened openly. But the old man seemed satisfied. "True . . . true enough," he agreed, and took another pull at his drink, "sanctuary may be given when needed, if—" His words were lost in a mumble.

The nervous tension slackened. Most of those present were subconsciously glad to follow the lead of the old man, and excuse the intrusion on the score of necessity. Magee turned back to Dave. "I thought that what you didn't know couldn't hurt you—or us—but the matter has been opened."

"But what did he mean?"

"Gramps asked you if you had been stooled to the rogue—whether or not you were a member of the ancient and honorable fraternity of thieves, cutthroats, and pickpockets!"

Magee stared into Dave's face with a look of sardonic amusement. Dave looked uncertainly from Magee to the others, saw them exchange glances, and wondered what answer was expected of him. Alec broke the pause. "Well," he sneered, "what are you waiting for? Go ahead and put the question to him—or are the great Fader's friends free to use this club without so much as a by-your-leave?"

"I thought I told you to quiet down, Alec," the Fader replied evenly. "Besides—you're skipping a requirement. All the comrades present must first decide whether or not to put the question at all."

A quiet little man with a chronic worried look in his eyes answered him. "I don't think that quite applies, Fader. If he had come himself, or fallen into our hands—in that case, yes. But you brought him here. I think I speak for all when I say he should answer the question. Unless someone objects, I will ask him myself." He allowed an interval to pass. No one spoke up. "Very well then . . . Dave, you have seen too much and heard too much. Will you leave us now—or will you stay and take the oath of our guild? I must warn you that once stooled you are stooled for life—and there is but one punishment for betraying the rogue."

He drew his thumb across his throat in an age-old deadly gesture. Gramps made an appropriate sound effect by sucking air wetly through his teeth, and chuckled.

Dave looked around. Magee's face gave him no help. "What is it that I have to swear to?" he temporized.

The parley was brought to an abrupt ending by the sound of pounding outside. There was a shout, muffled by two closed doors and a stairway, of "Open up down there!" Magee got lightly to his feet and beckoned to Dave.

"That's for us, kid," he said. "Come along."

He stepped over to a ponderous, old-fashioned radio-phonograph which stood against the wall, reached under it, fiddled for a moment, then swung out one side panel of it. Dave saw that the mechanism had been cunningly rearranged in such a fashion that a man could squeeze inside it. Magee urged him into it, slammed the panel closed, and left him.

His face was pressed up close to the slotted grill which was intended to cover the sound box. Molly had cleared off the two extra glasses from the table, and was dumping one drink so that it spread along the table top and erased the rings their glasses had made.

MacKinnon saw the Fader slide under the table, and reach up. Then he was gone. Apparently he had, in some fashion, attached himself to the underside of the table.

Mother Johnston made a great-to-do of opening up. The lower door she opened at once, with much noise. Then she clumped slowly up the steps, pausing, wheezing, and complaining aloud. He heard her unlock the outer door.

"A fine time to be waking honest people up!" she protested. "It's hard enough to get the work done and make both ends meet, without dropping what I'm doing every five minutes, and—"

"Enough of that, old girl," a man's voice answered, "just get along downstairs. We have business with you."

"What sort of business?" she demanded.

"It might be selling liquor without a license, but it's not—this time."

"I don't—this is a private club. The members own the liquor; I simply serve it to them."

"That's as may be. It's those members I want to talk to. Get out of the way now, and be spry about it."

They came pushing into the room with Mother Johnston, still voluble, carried along in by the van. The speaker was a sergeant of police; he was accompanied by a patrolman. Following them were two other uniformed men, but they were soldiers. MacKinnon judged by the markings on their kilts that they were corporal and private—provided the insignia in New America were similar to those used by the United States Army.

The sergeant paid no attention to Mother Johnston. "All right, you men," he called out, "line up!"

They did so, ungraciously but promptly. Molly and Mother Johnston watched them, and moved closer to each other. The police sergeant called out, "All right, corporal—take charge!"

The boy who washed up in the kitchen had been staring round-eyed. He dropped a glass. It bounced around on the hard floor, giving out bell-like sounds in the silence.

The man who had questioned Dave spoke up. "What's all this?"

The sergeant answered with a pleased grin. "Conscription—that's what it is. You are all enlisted in the army for the duration."

"Press gang!" It was an involuntary gasp that came from no particular source.

The corporal stepped briskly forward. "Form a column of twos," he directed. But the little man with the worried eyes was not done.

"I don't understand this," he objected. "We signed an armistice with the Free State three weeks ago."

"That's not your worry," countered the sergeant, "nor mine. We are picking up every able-bodied man not in essential industry. Come along."

"Then you can't take me."

"Why not?"

He held up the stump of a missing hand. The sergeant glanced from it to the corporal, who nodded grudgingly, and said, "Okay—but report to the office in the morning, and register."

He started to march them out when Alec broke ranks and backed up to the wall, screaming, "You can't do this to me! I won't go!" His deadly little vibrator was exposed in his hand, and the right side of his face was drawn up in a spastic wink that left his teeth bare.

"Get him, Steeves," ordered the corporal. The private stepped forward, but stopped when Alec brandished the vibrator at him. He had no desire to have a vibroblade between his ribs, and there was no doubt as to the uncontrolled dangerousness of his hysterical opponent.

The corporal, looking phlegmatic, almost bored, levelled a small tube at a spot on the wall over Alec's head. Dave heard a soft *pop!*, and a thin tinkle. Alec stood motionless for a few seconds, his face even more strained, as if he were exerting the limit of his will against some unseen force, then slid quietly to the floor. The chronic spasm in his face relaxed, and his features smoothed into those of a tired and petulant, and very bewildered, little boy.

"Two of you birds carry him," directed the corporal. "Let's get going."

The sergeant was the last to leave. He turned at the door and spoke to Mother Johnston. "Have you seen the Fader lately?"

"The Fader?" She seemed puzzled. "Why, he's in jail."

"Ah, yes . . . so he is." He went out.

Magee refused the drink that Mother Johnston offered him.

Dave was surprised to see that he appeared worried for the first time. "I don't understand it," Magee muttered, half to himself, then addressed the one-handed man. "Ed—bring me up to date."

"Not much news since they tagged you, Fader. The armistice was before that. I thought from the papers that things were going to be straightened out for once."

"So did I. But the government must expect war if they are going in for general conscription." He stood up. "I've got to have more data. Al!" The kitchen boy stuck his head into the room.

"What 'cha want, Fader?"

"Go out and make palaver with five or six of the beggars. Look up their 'king.' You know where he makes his pitch?"

"Sure—over by the auditorium."

"Find out what's stirring, but don't let them know I sent you."

"Right, Fader. It's in the bag." The boy swaggered out.

"Molly."

"Yes, Fader?"

"Will you go out, and do the same thing with some of the business girls? I want to know what they hear from their customers." She nodded agreement. He went on, "Better look up that little redhead that has her beat up on Union Square. She can get secrets out of a dead man. Here—" He pulled a wad of bills out of his pocket and handed her several. "You better take this grease . . . You might have to pay off a cop to get back out of the district."

Magee was not disposed to talk, and insisted that Dave get some sleep. He was easily persuaded, not having slept since he entered Coventry. That seemed like a lifetime past; he was exhausted. Mother Johnston fixed him a shakedown in a dark, stuffy room on the same underground level. It had none of the hygienic comforts to which he was accustomed—air-conditioning, restful music, hydraulic mattress, nor soundproofing—and he missed his usual relaxing soak and auto-massage, but he was too tired to care. He slept in clothing and under covers for the first time in his life.

He woke up with a headache, a taste in his mouth like tired sin, and a sense of impending disaster. At first he could not remember where he was—he thought he was still in detention Outside. His surroundings were inexplicably sordid; he was about to ring for the attendant and complain, when his memory pieced in the events of the day before. Then he got up and discovered that his bones and muscles were painfully sore, and—which was worse—that he was, by his standards, filthy dirty. He itched.

He entered the common room, and found Magee sitting at the table. He greeted Dave. "Hi, kid. I was about to wake you. You've slept almost all day. We've got a lot to talk about."

"Okay—shortly. Where's the 'fresher?"

"Over there."

It was not Dave's idea of a refreshing chamber, but he managed to take a sketchy shower in spite of the slimy floor. Then he discovered that there was no air blast installed, and he was forced to dry himself unsatisfactorily with his handkerchief. He had no choice in clothes. He must put back on the ones he had taken off, or go naked. He recalled that he had seen no nudity anywhere in Coventry, even at sports—a difference in customs, no doubt.

He put his clothes back on, though his skin crawled at the touch of the once-used linen.

But Mother Johnston had thrown together an appetizing breakfast for him. He let coffee restore his courage as Magee talked. It was, according to Fader, a serious situation. New America and the Free State had compromised their differences and had formed an alliance. They quite seriously proposed to break out of Coventry and attack the United States.

MacKinnon looked up at this. "That's ridiculous, isn't it? They would be outnumbered enormously. Besides, how about the Barrier?"

"I don't know—yet. But they have some reason to think that they can break through the Barrier . . . and there are rumors that whatever it is can be used as a weapon, too, so that a small army might be able to whip the whole United States."

MacKinnon looked puzzled. "Well," he observed, "I haven't any opinion of a weapon I know nothing about, but as to the Barrier. . . . I'm not a mathematical physicist, but I was always told that it was theoretically impossible to break the Barrier—that it was just a nothingness that there was no way to touch. Of course, you can fly over it, but even that is supposed to be deadly to life."

"Suppose they had found some way to shield from the effects of the Barrier's field?" suggested Magee. "Anyhow, that's not the point, for us. The point is: they've made this combine; the Free State supplies the techniques and most of the officers; and New America, with its bigger population, supplies most of the men. And that means to us that we don't dare show our faces any place, or we are in the army before you can blink.

"Which brings me to what I was going to suggest. I'm going to duck out of here as soon as it gets dark, and light out for the Gateway, before they send somebody after me who is bright enough to look under a table. I thought maybe you might want to come along."

"Back to the psychologists?" MacKinnon was honestly aghast.

"Sure—why not? What have you got to lose? This whole damn place is going to be just like the Free State in a couple of days—and a Joe of your temperament would be in hot water all the time. What's so bad about a nice, quiet hospital room as a place to hide out until things quiet down? You don't have to pay any attention to the psych boys—just make animal noises at 'em every time one sticks his nose into your room, until they get discouraged."

Dave shook his head. "No," he said slowly, "I can't do that."

"Then what will you do?"

"I don't know yet. Take to the hills I guess. Go live with the Angels if it comes to a showdown. I wouldn't mind them praying for my soul as long as they left my mind alone."

They were each silent for a while. Magee was mildly annoyed at MacKinnon's bullheaded stubbornness in the face of what seemed to him a reasonable offer. Dave continued busily to stow away grilled ham, while considering his position. He cut off another bite. "My, but this is good," he remarked, to break the awkward silence, "I don't know when I've had anything taste so good—Say!"

"What?" inquired Magee, looking up, and seeing the concern written on MacKinnon's face.

"This ham—is it synthetic, or is it *real meat*?"

"Why, it's real. What about it?"

Dave did not answer. He managed to reach the refreshing room before that which he had eaten departed from him.

Before he left, Magee gave Dave some money with which he could have purchased for him things that he would need in order to take to the hills. MacKinnon protested, but the Fader cut him short. "Quit being a damn fool, Dave. I can't use New American money on the Outside, and you can't stay alive in the hills without proper equipment. You lie doggo here for a few days while Al, or Molly, picks up what you need, and you'll stand a chance—unless you'll change your mind and come with me?"

Dave shook his head at this, and accepted the money.

It was lonely after Magee left. Mother Johnston and Dave were alone in the club, and the empty chairs reminded him depressingly of the men who had been impressed. He wished that Gramps or the one-handed man would show up. Even Alec, with his nasty temper, would have been company—he wondered if Alec had been punished for resisting the draft.

Mother Johnston inveigled him into playing checkers in an attempt to relieve his evident low spirits. He felt obligated to agree to her gentle conspiracy, but his mind wandered. It was all very well for the Senior Judge to tell him to seek adventure in interplanetary exploration, but only engineers and technicians were eligible for such billets. Perhaps he should have gone in for science, or engineering, instead of literature; then he might now be on Venus, contending against the forces of nature in high adventure, instead of hiding from uniformed bullies. It wasn't fair. No—he must not kid himself; there was no room for an expert in literary history in the raw frontier of the planets; that was not human injustice, that was a hard fact of nature, and he might as well face it.

He thought bitterly of the man whose nose he had broken, and thereby landed himself in Coventry. Maybe he was an "upholstered parasite" after all—but the recollection of the phrase brought back the same unreasoning anger that had gotten him into trouble. He was *glad* that he had socked that so-and-so! What right had he to go around sneering and calling people things like that?

He found himself thinking in the same vindictive spirit of his father, although he would have been at loss to explain the connection. The connection was not superficially evident, for his father would never have stooped to name-calling. Instead, he would have offered the sweetest of smiles, and quoted something nauseating in the way of sweetness-and-light. Dave's father was one of the nastiest little tyrants that ever dominated a household under the guise of loving-kindness. He was of the more-in-sorrow-than-in-anger, this-hurts-me-more-than-it-does-you school, and all his life had invariably been able to find an altruistic rationalization for always having his own way. Convinced of his own infallible righteousness, he had never valued his son's point of view on anything, but had dominated him in everything—always from the highest moralistic motives.

He had had two main bad effects on his son: the boy's natural independence, crushed at home, rebelled blindly at every sort of discipline, authority, or criticism which he encountered elsewhere and subconsciously identified with the not-to-be-criticized paternal authority. Secondly, through years of association Dave imitated his father's most dangerous social vice—that of passing unself-critical moral judgments on the actions of others.

When Dave was arrested for breaking a basic custom, to wit: atavistic violence, his father washed his hands of him with the statement that he had tried his best to "make a man of him," and could not be blamed for his son's failure to profit by his instruction.

A faint knock caused them to put away the checker board in a hurry. Mother Johnston paused before answering. "That's not our knock," she considered, "but it's not loud enough to be the nosies. Be ready to hide.'"

MacKinnon waited by the fox hole where he had hidden the night before, while Mother Johnston went to investigate. He heard her unbar and unlock the upper door, then she called out to him in a low but urgent voice, "Dave! Come here, Dave—hurry!"

It was Fader, unconscious, with his own bloody trail behind him.

Mother Johnston was attempting to pick up the limp form. MacKinnon crowded in, and between the two of them they managed to get him downstairs and to lay him on the long table. He came to for a moment as they straightened his limbs. "Hi, Dave," he whispered, managing to achieve the ghost of his debonair grin. "Somebody trumped my ace."

"You keep quiet!" Mother Johnston snapped at him, then in a lower voice to Dave, "Oh, the poor darling—Dave, we must get him to the Doctor."

"Can't . . . do . . . that," muttered the Fader. "Got . . . to get to the . . . Gate—" His voice trailed off. Mother Johnston's fingers had been busy all the while, as if activated by some separate intelligence. A small pair of scissors, drawn from some hiding place about her large person, clipped away at his clothing, exposing the superficial extent of the damage. She examined the trauma critically.

"This is no job for me," she decided, "and he must sleep while we move him. Dave, get that hypodermic kit out of the medicine chest in the 'fresher."

"No, Mother!" It was Magee, his voice strong and vibrant.

"Get me a pepper pill," he went on. "There's—"

"But Fader—"

He cut her short. "I've got to get to the Doctor all right, but how the devil will I get there if I don't walk?"

"We would carry you."

"Thanks, Mother," he told her, his voice softened, "I know you would—but the police would be curious. Get me that pill."

Dave followed her into the 'fresher, and questioned her while she rummaged through the medicine chest. "Why don't we just send for a doctor?"

"There is only one doctor we can trust, and that's *the* Doctor. Besides, none of the others are worth the powder to blast them."

Magee was out again when they came back into the room. Mother Johnston slapped his face until he came around, blinking and cursing. Then she fed him the pill.

The powerful stimulant, improbable offspring of common coal tar, took hold almost at once. To all surface appearance Magee was a well man. He sat up and tried his own pulse, searching it out in his left wrist with steady, sensitive fingers. "Regular as a metronome," he announced. "The old ticker can stand that dosage all right."

He waited while Mother Johnston applied sterile packs to his wounds, then said goodbye. MacKinnon looked at Mother Johnston. She nodded.

"I'm going with you," he told the Fader.

"What for? It will just double the risk."

"You're in no fit shape to travel alone—stimulant, or no stimulant."

"Nuts. *I'd* have to look after *you.*"

"I'm going with you."

Magee shrugged his shoulders and capitulated.

Mother Johnston wiped her perspiring face, kissed both of them.

Until they were well out of town their progress reminded MacKinnon of their nightmare flight of the previous evening. Thereafter they continued to the north-northwest by a highway which ran toward the foothills, and they left the highway only when necessary to avoid the sparse traffic. Once they were almost surprised by a police patrol car, equipped with black-light and almost invisible, but the Fader sensed it in time and they crouched behind a low wall which separated the adjacent field from the road.

Dave inquired bow he had known the patrol was near. Magee chuckled. "Damned if I know," he said, "but I believe I could smell a cop staked out in a herd of goats."

The Fader talked less and less as the night progressed. His usually untroubled countenance became lined and old as the effect of the drug wore off. It seemed to Dave as if this unaccustomed expression gave him a clearer insight into the man's character—that the mask of pain was his true face rather than the unworried features Magee habitually showed the world. He wondered for the ninth time what the Fader had done to cause a court to adjudge him socially insane.

This question was uppermost in his mind with respect to every person he met in Coventry. The answer was obvious in most cases; their types of instability were gross and showed up at once. Mother Johnston had been an enigma until she had explained it herself. She had followed her husband into Coventry. Now that she was a widow, she preferred to remain with the friends she knew and the customs and conditions she was adjusted to, rather than change for another and possibly less pleasing environment.

Magee sat down beside the road. "It's no use, kid," he admitted. "I can't make it."

"The hell we can't. I'll carry you."

Magee grinned faintly. "No, I mean it." Dave persisted. "How much farther is it?"

"Matter of two or three miles, maybe."

"Climb aboard." He took Magee pickaback and started on. The first few hundred yards were not too difficult; Magee was forty pounds lighter than Dave. After that the strain of the additional load began to tell. His arms cramped from supporting Magee's knees; his arches complained at the weight and the unnatural load distribution; and his breathing was made difficult by the clasp of Magee's arms around his neck.

Two miles to go—maybe more. Let your weight fall forward, and your foot must follow it, else you fall to the ground. It's automatic—as automatic as pulling teeth. How long is a mile? Nothing in a rocket ship, thirty seconds in a pleasure car, a ten minute crawl in a steel snail, fifteen minutes to trained troops in good condition. How far is it with a man on your back, on a rough road, when you are tired to start with?

Five thousand, two hundred, and eighty feet—a meaningless figure. But every step takes twenty-four inches off the total. The remainder is still incomprehensible—an infinity. Count them. Count them till you go crazy—till the figures speak themselves outside your head, and the jar! . . . jar! . . . jar! . . . of your enormous, benumbed feet beats in your brain. Count them backwards, subtracting two each time—no, that's worse; each remainder is still an unattainable, inconceivable figure.

His world closed in, lost its history and held no future. There was nothing, nothing at all, but the torturing necessity of picking up his foot again and placing it forward. No feeling but the heartbreaking expenditure of will necessary to achieve that meaningless act.

He was brought suddenly to awareness when Magee's arms relaxed from around his neck. He leaned forward, and dropped to one knee to keep from spilling his burden, then eased it slowly to the ground. He thought for a moment that the Fader was dead—he could not locate his pulse, and the slack face and limp body were sufficiently corpse-like, but he pressed an ear to Magee's chest, and heard with relief the steady *flub-dub* of his heart.

He tied Magee's wrists together with his handkerchief, and forced his own head through the encircled arms. But he was unable, in his exhausted condition, to wrestle the slack weight into position on his back. Fader regained consciousness while MacKinnon was struggling. His first words were, "Take it easy Dave. What's the trouble?"

Dave explained. "Better untie my wrists," advised the Fader, "I think I can walk for a while."

And walk he did, for nearly three hundred yards, before he was forced to give up again. "Look, Dave," he said, after he had partially recovered, "did you bring along any more of those pepper pills?"

"Yes—but you can't take any more dosage. It would kill you."

"Yeah, I know—so they say. But that isn't the idea— yet. I was going to suggest that you might take one."

"Why, of course! Good grief, Fader, but I'm dumb."

Magee seemed no heavier than a light coat, the morning star shone brighter, and his strength seemed inexhaustible. Even when they left the highway and started up the cart trail that led to the Doctor's home in the foothills, the going was tolerable and the burden not too great. MacKinnon knew that the drugs burned the working tissue of his body long after his proper reserves were gone, and that it would take him days to recover from the reckless expenditure, but he did not mind. No price was too high to pay for the moment when he at last arrived at the gate of the Doctor's home—on his own two feet, his charge alive and conscious.

MacKinnon was not allowed to see Magee for four days. In the meantime, he was encouraged to keep the routine of a semi-invalid himself in order to recover the twenty-five pounds he had lost in two days and two nights, and to make up for the heavy strain on his heart during the last night. A high-caloric diet, sun baths, rest, and peaceful surroundings plus his natural good health caused him to regain weight and strength rapidly, but he "enjoyed ill health" exceedingly because of the companionship of the Doctor himself—and Persephone.

Persephone's calendar age was fifteen. Dave never knew whether to think of her as much older, or much younger. She had been born in Coventry, and had lived her short life in the house of the Doctor, her mother having died in childbirth in that same house. She was completely childlike in many respects, being without experience in the civilized world Outside, and having had very little contact with the inhabitants of Coventry, except when she saw them as patients of the Doctor. But she had been allowed to read unchecked from the library of a sophisticated and protean-minded man of science. MacKinnon was continually being surprised at the extent of her academic and scientific knowledge—much greater than his own. She made him feel as if he were conversing with some aged and omniscient matriarch, then she would come out with some naive concept of the outer world, and he would be brought up sharply with the realization that she was, in fact, an inexperienced child.

He was mildly romantic about her. Not seriously, of course, in view of her barely nubile age, but she was pleasant to see, and he was hungry for feminine companionship. He was quite young enough himself to feel continual interest in the delightful differences, mental and physical, between male and female.

Consequently, it was a blow to his pride as sharp as had been the sentence to Coventry to discover that she classed him with the other inhabitants of Coventry as a poor unfortunate who needed help and sympathy because he was not quite right in his head.

He was furious and for one whole day he sulked

alone, but the human necessity for self-justification and approval forced him to seek her out and attempt to reason with her. He explained carefully and with emotional candor the circumstances leading up to his trial and conviction, and embellished the account with his own philosophy and evaluations, then confidently awaited her approval.

It was not forthcoming. "I don't understand your viewpoint," she said. "You broke his nose, yet he had done you no harm of any sort. You expect me to approve that?"

"But Persephone," he protested, "you ignore the fact that he called me a most insulting name."

"I don't see the connection," she said. "He made a noise with his mouth—a verbal label. If the label does not fit you, the noise is meaningless. If the label is true in your case—if you *are* the thing that the noise refers to, you are neither more, nor less, that thing by reason of some one uttering the verbal label. In short, he did not damage you.

"But what you did to him was another matter entirely. You broke his nose. That is damage. In self-protection the rest of society must seek you out, and determine whether or not you are so unstable as to be likely to damage some one else in the future. If you are, you must be quarantined for treatment, or leave society—whichever you prefer."

"You think I'm crazy, don't you?" he accused.

"Crazy? Not the way you mean it. You haven't paresis, or a brain tumor, or any other lesion that the Doctor could find. But from the viewpoint of your semantic reactions you are as socially *unsane* as any fanatic witchburner."

"Come now—that's not just!"

"What is justice?" She picked up the kitten she had been playing with. "I'm going in—it's getting chilly." Off she went into the house, her bare feet noiseless in the grass.

❖   ❖   ❖

Had the science of semantics developed as rapidly as psycho-dynamics and its implementing arts of propaganda and mob psychology, the United States might never have fallen into dictatorship, then been forced to undergo the Second Revolution. All of the scientific principles embodied in the Covenant which marked the end of the revolution were formulated as far back as the first quarter of the twentieth century.

But the work of the pioneer semanticists, C. K. Ogden, Alfred Korzybski, and others, were known to but a handful of students, whereas psychodynamics, under the impetus of repeated wars and the frenzy of high-pressure merchandising, progressed by leaps and bounds.

Semantics, "the meaning of meaning," gave a method for the first time of applying the scientific method to every act of everyday life. Because semantics dealt with spoken and written words as a determining aspect of human behavior it was at first mistakenly thought by many to be concerned *only* with words and of interest only to professional word manipulators, such as advertising copy writers and professors of etymology. A handful of unorthodox psychiatrists attempted to apply it to personal human problems, but their work was swept away by the epidemic mass psychoses that destroyed Europe and returned the United States to the Dark Ages.

The Covenant was the first scientific social document ever drawn up by man, and due credit must be given to its principal author, Dr. Micah Novak, the same Novak who served as staff psychologist in the revolution. The revolutionists wished to establish maximum personal liberty. How could they accomplish that to a degree of high mathematical probability?

First they junked the concept of "justice." Examined semantically "justice" has no referent—there is no observable phenomenon in the space-time-matter continuum to which one can point, and say, "This is justice."

Science can deal only with that which can be observed and measured. Justice is not such a matter; therefore it can never have the same meaning to one as to another; any "noises" said about it will only add to confusion.

But damage, physical or economic, can be pointed to and measured. Citizens were forbidden by the Covenant to damage another. Any act not leading to damage, physical or economic, to some particular person, they declared to be lawful.

Since they had abandoned the concept of "justice," there could be no rational standards of punishment. Penology took its place with lycanthropy and other forgotten witchcrafts. Yet, since it was not practical to permit a source of danger to remain in the community, social offenders were examined and potential repeaters were given their choice of psychological readjustment, or of having society withdraw itself from them—Coventry.

Early drafts of the Covenant contained the assumption that the socially unsane would naturally be hospitalized and readjusted, particularly since current psychiatry was quite competent to cure all non-lesional psychoses and cure or alleviate lesional psychoses, but Novak set his face against this.

"No!" he protested. "The government must never again be permitted to tamper with the mind of any citizen without his consent, or else we set up a greater tyranny than we had before. Every man must be free to accept, or reject, the Covenant, even though we think him insane!"

The next time David MacKinnon looked up Persephone he found her in a state of extreme agitation. His own wounded pride was forgotten at once. "Why, my dear," he said, "whatever in the world is the matter?"

Gradually he gathered that she had been present at

a conversation between Magee and the Doctor, and had heard, for the first time, of the impending military operation against the United States. He patted her hand. "So that's all it is," he observed in a relieved voice. "I thought something was wrong with you yourself."

"'That's all—' David MacKinnon, do you mean to stand there and tell me that you knew about this, and don't consider it worth worrying about?"

"Me? Why should I? And for that matter, what could I do?"

"What could you do? You could go outside and warn them—that's what you could do . . . As to why you should—Dave, you're impossible!" She burst into tears and ran from the room.

He stared after her, mouth open, then borrowed from his remotest ancestor by observing to himself that women are hard to figure out.

Persephone did not appear at lunch. MacKinnon asked the Doctor where she was.

"Had her lunch," the Doctor told him, between mouthfuls. "Started for the Gateway."

"What! Why did you let her do that?"

"Free agent. Wouldn't have obeyed me anyway. She'll be all right."

Dave did not hear that last, being already out of the room and running out of the house. He found her just backing her little monocycle runabout out of its shed. "Persephone!"

"What do you want?" she asked with frozen dignity beyond her years.

"You mustn't do this! That's where the Fader got hurt!"

"I am going. Please stand aside."

"Then I'm going with you."

"Why should you?"

"To take care of you."

She sniffed. "As if anyone would dare to touch me." There was a measure of truth in what she said. The

Doctor, and every member of his household, enjoyed a personal immunity unlike that of anyone else in Coventry. As a natural consequence of the set-up, Coventry had almost no competent medical men. The number of physicians who committed social damage was small. The proportion of such who declined psychiatric treatment was negligible, and this negligible remainder were almost sure to be unreliable bunglers in their profession. The Doctor was a natural healer, in voluntary exile in order that he might enjoy the opportunity to practice his art in the richest available field. He cared nothing for dry research; what he wanted was patients, the sicker the better, that he might make them well again.

He was above custom and above law. In the Free State the Liberator depended on him for insulin to hold his own death from diabetes at arm's length. In New America his beneficiaries were equally powerful. Even among the Angels of the Lord the Prophet himself accepted the dicta of the Doctor without question.

But MacKinnon was not satisfied. Some ignorant fool, he was afraid, might do the child some harm without realizing her protected status. He got no further chance to protest; she started the little runabout suddenly, and forced him to jump out of its path. When he had recovered his balance, she was far down the lane. He could not catch her.

She was back in less than four hours. He had expected that; if a person as elusive as Fader had not been able to reach the Gate at night, it was not likely that a young girl could do so in daylight.

His first feeling was one of simple relief, then he eagerly awaited an opportunity to speak to her. During her absence he had been turning over the situation in his mind. It was a foregone conclusion that she would fail; he wished to rehabilitate himself in her eyes; therefore, he would help her in the project nearest her heart—he himself would carry the warning to the Outside!

Perhaps she would ask for such help. In fact, it

seemed likely. By the time she returned he had convinced himself that she was certain to ask his help. He would agree—with simple dignity—and off he would go, perhaps to be wounded, or killed, but an heroic figure, even if he failed.

He pictured himself subconsciously as a blend of Sidney Carton, the White Knight, the man who carried the message to Garcia—and just a dash of d'Artagnan.

But she did not ask him—she would not even give him a chance to talk with her.

She did not appear at dinner. After dinner she was closeted with the Doctor in his study. When she reappeared she went directly to her room. He finally concluded that he might as well go to bed himself.

To bed, and then to sleep, and take it up again in the morning— But it's not as simple as that. The unfriendly walls stared back at him, and the other, critical half of his mind decided to make a night of it. Fool! She doesn't want your help. Why should she? What have you got that Fader hasn't got?—and better. To her, you are just one of the screwloose multitude you've seen all around you in this place.

But *I'm* not crazy!—just because I choose not to submit to the dictation of others doesn't make me *crazy*. Doesn't it, though? All the rest of them in here are lamebrains, what's so fancy about you? Not all of them—how about the Doctor, and— Don't kid yourself, chump, the Doctor and Mother Johnston are here for their own reasons; they weren't sentenced. And Persephone was born here.

How about Magee?—He was certainly rational—or seemed so. He found himself resenting, with illogical bitterness, Magee's apparent stability. Why should he be any different from the rest of us?

The rest of us? He had classed himself with the other inhabitants of Coventry. All right, all right, admit it, you fool—you're just like the rest of them; turned out because the decent people won't have you—and too damned stubborn to admit that you need treatment.

But the thought of treatment turned him cold, and made him think of his father again. Why should that be? He recalled something the Doctor had said to him a couple of days before: "What you need, son, is to stand up to your father and tell him off. Pity more children don't tell their parents to go to hell!"

He turned on the light and tried to read. But it was no use. Why should Persephone care what happened to the people Outside?—She didn't know them; she had no friends there. If *he* had no obligations to them, how could *she* possibly care? No obligations? You had a soft, easy life for many years—all they asked was that you behave yourself. For that matter, where would you be now, if the Doctor had stopped to ask whether or not he owed you anything?

He was still wearily chewing the bitter cud of self-examination when the first cold and colorless light of morning filtered in. He got up, threw a robe around him, and tiptoed down the hall to Magee's room. The door was ajar. He stuck his head in, and whispered, "Fader— Are you awake?"

"Come in, kid," Magee answered quietly. "What's the trouble? No can sleep?"

"No—"

"Neither can I. Sit down, and we'll carry the banner together."

"Fader, I'm going to make a break for it. I'm going Outside."

"Huh? When?"

"Right away."

"Risky business, kid. Wait a few days, and I'll try it with you."

"No, I can't wait for you to get well. I'm going out to warn the United States!"

Magee's eyes widened a little, but his voice was unchanged. "You haven't let that spindly kid sell you a bill of goods, Dave?"

"No. Not exactly. I'm doing this for myself—it's something I need to do. See here, Fader, what about this weapon? Have they really got something that could threaten the United States?"

"I'm afraid so," Magee admitted. "I don't know much about it, but it makes blasters look sick. More range—I don't know what they expect to do about the Barrier, but I saw 'em stringing heavy power lines before I got winged. Say, if you do get outside, here's a chap you might look up; in fact, be sure to. He's got influence." Magee scrawled something on a scrap of paper, folded the scrap, and handed it to MacKinnon, who pocketed it absent-mindedly and went on:

"How closely is the Gate guarded, Fader?"

"You can't get out the Gate; that's out of the question. Here's what you will have to do—" He tore off another piece of paper and commenced sketching and explaining.

Dave shook hands with Magee before he left. "You'll say goodbye for me, won't you? And thank the Doctor? I'd rather just slide out before anyone is up."

"Of course, kid," the Fader assured him.

MacKinnon crouched behind bushes and peered cautiously at the little band of Angels filing into the bleak, ugly church. He shivered, both from fear and from the icy morning air. But his need was greater than his fear. Those zealots had food—and he must have it.

The first two days after he left the house of the Doctor had been easy enough. True, he had caught cold from sleeping on the ground; it had settled in his lungs and slowed him down. But he did not mind that now if only he could refrain from sneezing or coughing until the little band of faithful were safe inside the temple. He watched them pass—dour-looking men, women in skirts that dragged the ground and whose work-lined faces were framed in shawls—sallow drudges with too many children. The light had gone out of their faces. Even the children were sober.

The last of them filed inside, leaving only the sexton in the churchyard, busy with some obscure duty. After an interminable time, during which MacKinnon pressed a finger against his upper lip in a frantic attempt to forestall a sneeze, the sexton entered the grim building and closed the doors.

MacKinnon crept out of his hiding place and hurried to the house he had previously selected, on the edge of the clearing, farthest from the church.

The dog was suspicious, but he quieted him. The house was locked, but the rear door could be forced. He was a little giddy at the sight of food when he found it—hard bread, and strong, unsalted butter made from goats' milk. A misstep two days before had landed him in a mountain stream. The mishap had not seemed important until he discovered that his food tablets were a pulpy mess. He had eaten them the rest of the day, then mold had taken them, and he had thrown the remainder away.

The bread lasted him through three more sleeps, but the butter melted and he was unable to carry it. He soaked as much of it as he could into the bread, then licked up the rest, after which he was very thirsty. Some hours after the last of the bread was gone, he reached his first objective—the main river to which all other streams in Coventry were tributary. Some place, down stream, it dived under the black curtain of the Barrier, and continued seaward. With the gateway closed and guarded, its outlet constituted the only possible egress to a man unassisted.

In the meantime it was water, and thirst was upon him again, and his cold was worse. But he would have to wait until dark to drink; there were figures down there by the bank—some in uniform, he thought. One of them made fast a little skiff to a landing. He marked it for his own and watched it with jealous eyes. It was still there when the sun went down.

The early morning sun struck his nose and he

sneezed. He came wide awake, raised his head, and looked around. The little skiff he had appropriated floated in midstream. There were no oars. He could not remember whether or not there had been any oars. The current was fairly strong; it seemed as if he should have drifted clear to the Barrier in the night. Perhaps he had passed under it—no, that was ridiculous.

Then he saw it, less than a mile away, black and ominous—but the most welcome sight he had seen in days. He was too weak and feverish to enjoy it, but it renewed the determination that kept him going.

The little boat scraped against bottom. He saw that the current at a bend had brought him to the bank. He hopped awkwardly out, his congealed joints complaining, and drew the bow of the skiff up onto the sand. Then he thought better of it, pushed it out once more, shoved as hard as he was able and watched it disappear around the meander. No need to advertise where he had landed.

He slept most of that day, rousing himself once to move out of the sun when it grew too hot. But the sun had cooked much of the cold out of his bones, and he felt much better by nightfall.

Although the Barrier was only a mile or so away, it took most of the night to reach it by following the river bank. He knew when he had reached it by the clouds of steam that rose from the water. When the sun came up, he considered the situation. The Barrier stretched across the water, but the juncture between it and the surface of the stream was hidden by billowing clouds. Someplace, down under the surface of the water—how far down he did not know—somewhere down there, the Barrier ceased, and its raw edge turned the water it touched to steam.

Slowly, reluctantly and most unheroically, he commenced to strip off his clothes. The time had come and he did not relish it. He came across the scrap of paper that Magee had handed him, and attempted to examine it. But it had been pulped by his involuntary dip in the mountain stream and was quite illegible. He chucked it away. It did not seem to matter.

He shivered as he stood hesitating on the bank, although the sun was warm. Then his mind was made up for him; he spied a patrol on the far bank.

Perhaps they had seen him, perhaps not. He dived.

Down, down, as far as his strength would take him. Down and try to touch bottom, to be sure of avoiding that searing, deadly base. He felt mud with his hands. Now to swim under it. Perhaps it was death to pass under it, as well as over it; he would soon know. But which way was it? There was no direction down here.

He stayed down until his congested lungs refused. Then he rose part way, and felt scalding water on his face. For a timeless interval of unutterable sorrow and loneliness he realized that he was trapped between heat and water—trapped under the Barrier.

Two private soldiers gossiped idly on a small dock which lay under the face of the Barrier. The river which poured out from beneath it held no interest for them, they had watched it for many dull tours of guard duty. An alarm clanged behind them and brought them to alertness. "What sector, Jack?"

"This bank. There he is now—see!"

They fished him out and had him spread out on the dock by the time the sergeant of the guard arrived. "Alive, or dead?" he enquired.

"Dead, I think," answered the one who was not busy giving artificial resuscitation.

The sergeant clucked in a manner incongruous to his battered face, and said, "Too bad. I've ordered the ambulance; send him up to the infirmary anyhow."

The nurse tried to keep him quiet, but MacKinnon made such an uproar that she was forced to get the ward surgeon. "Here! Here! What's all this nonsense?" the medico rebuked him, while reaching for his pulse. Dave managed to convince him that he would not quiet down, not accept a soporific until he had told his story. They struck a working agreement that MacKinnon was to be allowed to talk—"But keep it short, mind you!"—and the doctor would pass the word along to his next superior, and in return Dave would submit to a hypodermic.

The next morning two other men, unidentified, were brought to MacKinnon by the surgeon. They listened to his full story and questioned him in detail. He was transferred to corps area headquarters that afternoon by ambulance. There he was questioned again. He was regaining his strength rapidly, but he was growing quite tired of the whole rigamarole, and wanted assurance that his warning was being taken seriously. The latest of his interrogators reassured him. "Compose yourself," he told Dave, "you are to see the commanding officer this afternoon."

The corps area commander, a nice little chap with a quick, birdlike manner and a most unmilitary appearance, listened gravely while MacKinnon recited his story for what seemed to him the fiftieth time. He nodded agreement when David finished. "Rest assured, David MacKinnon, that all necessary steps are being taken."

"But how about their weapon?"

"That is taken care of—and as for the Barrier, it may not be as easy to break as our neighbors think. But your efforts are appreciated. May I do you some service?"

"Well, no—not for myself, but there are two of my friends in there—" He asked that something be done to rescue Magee, and that Persephone be enabled to come out, if she wished.

"I know of that girl," the general remarked. "We will get in touch with her. If at any time she wishes to become a citizen, it can be arranged. As for Magee, that is another matter—" He touched the stud of his desk visiphone. "Send Captain Randall in."

A neat, trim figure in the uniform of a captain of the

United States Army entered with a light step. MacKinnon glanced at him with casual, polite interest, then his expression went to pieces. "Fader!" he yelled.

Their mutual greeting was hardly sufficiently decorous for the private office of a commanding general, but the general did not seem to mind. When they had calmed down, MacKinnon had to ask the question uppermost in his mind "But see here, Fader, all this doesn't make sense—" He paused, staring, then pointed a finger accusingly, "I know! You're in the secret service!"

The Fader grinned cheerfully. "Did you think," he observed, "that the United States Army would leave a plague spot like that unwatched?"

The general cleared his throat. "What do you plan to do now, David MacKinnon?"

"Eh? Me? Why, I don't have any plans—" He thought for a moment, then turned to his friend. "Do you know, Fader, I believe I'll turn in for psychological treatment after all. You're on the Outside—"

"I don't believe that will be necessary," interrupted the general gently.

"No? Why not, sir?"

"You have cured yourself You may not be aware of it, but four psycho-technicians have interviewed you. Their reports agree. I am authorized to tell you that your status as a free citizen has been restored, if you wish it."

The general and Captain "the Fader" Randall managed tactfully between them to terminate the interview. Randall walked back to the infirmary with his friend. Dave wanted a thousand questions answered at once. "But Fader," he demanded, "you must have gotten out before I did."

"A day or two."

"Then my job was unnecessary!"

"I wouldn't say that," Randall contradicted. "I might not have gotten through. As a matter of fact, they had all the details even before I reported. There are others—

Anyhow," he continued, to change the subject, "now that you are here, what will you do?"

"Me? It's too soon to say . . . It won't be classical literature, that's a cinch. If I wasn't such a dumbie in math, I might still try for interplanetary."

"Well, we can talk about it tonight," suggested Fader, glancing at his chrono. "I've got to run along, but I'll stop by later, and we'll go over to the mess for dinner."

He was out the door with speed reminiscent of the thieves' kitchen. Dave watched him, then said suddenly, "Hey! Fader! Why couldn't I get into the secret ser—"

But the Fader was gone—he must ask himself.

Misfit

> "... for the purpose of conserving and improving our interplanetary resources, and providing useful, healthful occupations for the youth of this planet."
>
> Excerpt from the enabling act, H.R. 7118, setting up the Cosmic Construction Corps.

"Attention to muster!" The parade ground voice of a First Sergeant of Space Marines cut through the fog and drizzle of a nasty New Jersey morning. "As your names are called, answer 'Here', step forward with your baggage, and embark. Atkins!"

"Here!"

"Austin!"

"Hyar!"

"Ayres!"

"Here!"

One by one they fell out of ranks, shouldered the hundred and thirty pounds of personal possessions allowed them, and trudged up the gangway. They were

235

young—none more than twenty-two—in some cases luggage outweighed the owner.

"Kaplan!"

"Here!"

"Keith!"

"Heah!"

"Libby!"

"Here!" A thin gangling blonde had detached himself from the line, hastily wiped his nose, and grabbed his belongings. He slung a fat canvas bag over his shoulder, steadied it, and lifted a suitcase with his free hand. He started for the companionway in an unsteady dog trot. As he stepped on the gangway his suitcase swung against his knees. He staggered against a short wiry form dressed in the powder-blue of the Space Navy. Strong fingers grasped his arm and checked his fall.

"Steady, son. Easy does it." Another hand readjusted the canvas bag.

"Oh, excuse me, uh"—the embarrassed youngster automatically counted the four bands of silver braid below the shooting star—"Captain. I didn't—"

"Bear a hand and get aboard, son."

"Yes, sir."

The passage into the bowels of the transport was gloomy. When the lad's eyes adjusted he saw a gunner's mate wearing the brassard of a Master-at-Arms, who hooked a thumb towards an open airtight door.

"In there. Find your locker and wait by it." Libby hurried to obey. Inside he found a jumble of baggage and men in a wide low-ceilinged compartment. A line of glow-tubes ran around the junction of bulkhead and ceiling and trisected the overhead; the soft roar of blowers made a background to the voices of his shipmates. He picked his way through heaped luggage and located his locker, seven-ten, on the far wall outboard. He broke the seal on the combination lock, glanced at the combination, and opened it. The locker was very small, the middle of a tier of three. He considered what he should keep in it. A loudspeaker drowned out the surrounding voices and demanded his attention:

"Attention! Man all space details; first section. Raise ship in twelve minutes. Close air-tight doors. Stop blowers at minus two minutes. Special orders for passengers; place all gear on deck, and lie down on red signal light. Remain down until release is sounded. Masters-at-Arms check compliance."

The gunner's mate popped in, glanced around and immediately commenced supervising rearrangement of the baggage. Heavy items were lashed down. Locker doors were closed. By the time each boy had found a place on the deck and the Master-at-Arms had okayed the pad under his head, the glow-tubes turned red and the loudspeaker brayed out.

"All hands—Up Ship! Stand by for acceleration." The Master-at-Arms hastily reclined against two cruise bags, and watched the room. The blowers sighed to a stop. There followed two minutes of dead silence. Libby felt his heart commence to pound. The two minutes stretched interminably. Then the deck quivered and a roar like escaping high-pressure steam beat at his ear drums. He was suddenly very heavy and a weight lay across his chest and heart. An indefinite time later the glowtubes flashed white, and the announcer bellowed:

"Secure all getting underway details; regular watch, first section." The blowers droned into life. The Master-at-Arms stood up, rubbed his buttocks and pounded his arms, then said:

"Okay, boys." He stepped over and undogged the airtight door to the passageway. Libby got up and blundered into a bulkhead, nearly falling. His legs and arms had gone to sleep, besides which he felt alarmingly light, as if he had sloughed off at least half of his inconsiderable mass.

For the next two hours he was too busy to think, or to be homesick. Suitcases, boxes, and bags had to be passed down into the lower hold and lashed against angular acceleration. He located and learned how to use a waterless water closet. He found his assigned bunk and learned that it was his only eight hours in twenty-four; two other boys had the use of it too. The three sections ate in three shifts, nine shifts in all—twenty-four youths and a master-at-arms at one long table which jam-filled a narrow compartment off the galley.

After lunch Libby restowed his locker. He was standing before it, gazing at a photograph which he intended to mount on the inside of the locker door, when a command filled the compartment:

"Attention!"

Standing inside the door was the Captain flanked by the Master-at-Arms. The Captain commenced to speak. "At rest, men. Sit down. McCoy, tell control to shift this compartment to smoke filter." The gunner's mate hurried to the communicator on the bulkhead and spoke into it in a low tone. Almost at once the hum of the blowers climbed a half-octave and stayed there. "Now light up if you like. I'm going to talk to you.

"You boys are headed out on the biggest thing so far in your lives. From now on you're men, with one of the hardest jobs ahead of you that men have ever tackled. What we have to do is part of a bigger scheme. You, and hundreds of thousands of others like you, are going out as pioneers to fix up the solar system so that human beings can make better use of it.

"Equally important, you are being given a chance to build yourselves into useful and happy citizens of the Federation. For one reason or another you weren't happily adjusted back on Earth. Some of you saw the jobs you were trained for abolished by new inventions. Some of you got into trouble from not knowing what to do with the modern leisure. In any case you were misfits. Maybe you were called bad boys and had a lot of black marks chalked up against you.

"But everyone of you starts even today. The only record you have in this ship is your name at the top of a blank sheet of paper. It's up to you what goes on that page.

"Now about our job—We didn't get one of the easy repair-and-recondition jobs on the Moon, with weekends at Luna City, and all the comforts of home. Nor did we draw a high-gravity planet where a man can eat a full meal and expect to keep it down. Instead we've got to go out to Asteroid HS-5388 and turn it into Space Station E-M3. She has no atmosphere at all, and only about two percent Earth-surface gravity. We've got to play human fly on her for at least six months, no girls to date, no television, no recreation that you don't devise yourselves, and hard work every day. You'll get spacesick, and so homesick you can taste it, and agoraphobia. If you aren't careful you'll get ray-burnt. Your stomach will act up, and you'll wish to God you'd never enrolled.

"But if you behave yourself, and listen to the advice of the old spacemen, you'll come out of it strong and healthy, with a little credit stored up in the bank, and a lot of knowledge and experience that you wouldn't get in forty years on Earth. You'll be men, and you'll know it.

"One last word. It will be pretty uncomfortable to those that aren't used to it. Just give the other fellow a little consideration, and you'll get along all right. If you have any complaint and can't get satisfaction any other way, come see me. Otherwise, that's all. Any questions?"

One of the boys put up his hand. "Captain?" he enquired timidly.

"Speak up, lad, and give your name."

"Rogers, sir. Will we be able to get letters from home?"

"Yes, but not very often. Maybe every month or so. The chaplain will carry mail, and any inspection and supply ships."

The ship's loudspeaker blatted out, "All hands! Free

flight in ten minutes. Stand by to lose weight." The Master-at-Arms supervised the rigging of grab-lines. All loose gear was made fast, and little cellulose bags were issued to each man. Hardly was this done when Libby felt himself get light on his feet—a sensation exactly like that experienced when an express elevator makes a quick stop on an upward trip, except that the sensation continued and became more intense. At first it was a pleasant novelty, then it rapidly became distressing. The blood pounded in his ears, and his feet were clammy and cold. His saliva secreted at an abnormal rate. He tried to swallow, choked, and coughed. Then his stomach shuddered and contracted with a violent, painful, convulsive reflex and he was suddenly, disastrously nauseated. After the first excruciating spasm, he heard McCoy's voice shouting.

"Hey! Use your sick-kits like I told you. Don't let that stuff get in the blowers." Dimly Libby realized that the admonishment included him. He fumbled for his cellulose bag just as a second temblor shook him, but he managed to fit the bag over his mouth before the eruption occurred. When it subsided, he became aware that he was floating near the overhead and facing the door. The chief Master-at-Arms slithered in the door and spoke to McCoy.

"How are you making out?"

"Well enough. Some of the boys missed their kits."

"Okay. Mop it up. You can use the starboard lock." He swam out.

McCoy touched Libby's arm. "Here, Pinkie, start catching them butterflies." He handed him a handful of cotton waste, then took another handful himself and neatly dabbed up a globule of the slimy filth that floated about the compartment. "Be sure your sick-kit is on tight. When you get sick, just stop and wait until it's over." Libby imitated him as best as he could. In a few minutes the room was free of the worst of the sickening debris. McCoy looked it over, and spoke:

"Now peel off them dirty duds, and change your kits. Three or four of you bring everything along to the starboard lock."

At the starboard spacelock, the kits were put in first, the inner door closed, and the outer opened. When the inner door was opened again the kits were gone—blown out into space by the escaping air. Pinkie addressed McCoy.

"Do we have to throw away our dirty clothes too?"

"Huh uh, we'll just give them a dose of vacuum. Take 'em into the lock and stop 'em to those hooks on the bulkheads. Tie 'em tight."

This time the lock was left closed for about five minutes. When the lock was opened the garments were bone dry—all the moisture boiled out by the vacuum of space. All that remained of the unpleasant rejecta was a sterile powdery residue. McCoy viewed them with approval. "They'll do. Take them back to the compartment. Then brush them—hard—in front of the exhaust blowers."

The next few days were an eternity of misery. Homesickness was forgotten in the all-engrossing wretchedness of spacesickness. The Captain granted fifteen minutes of mild acceleration for each of the nine meal periods, but the respite accentuated the agony. Libby would go to a meal, weak and ravenously hungry. The meal would stay down until free flight resumed, then the sickness would hit him all over again.

On the fourth day he was seated against a bulkhead, enjoying the luxury of a few remaining minutes of weight while the last shift ate, when McCoy walked in and sat down beside him. The gunner's mate fitted a smoke filter over his face and lit a cigarette. He inhaled deeply and started to chat.

"How's it going, bud?"

"All right, I guess. This spacesickness— Say, McCoy, how do you ever get used to it?"

"You get over it in time. Your body acquires new reflexes, so they tell me. Once you learn to swallow without choking, you'll be all right. You even get so you like it. It's restful and relaxing. Four hours sleep is as good as ten."

Libby shook his head dolefully. "I don't think I'll ever get used to it."

"Yes, you will. You'd better anyway. This here asteroid won't have any surface gravity to speak of; the Chief Quartermaster says it won't run over two percent Earth normal. That ain't enough to cure spacesickness. And there won't be any way to accelerate for meals either."

Libby shivered and held his head between his hands.

Locating one asteroid among a couple of thousand is not as easy as finding Trafalgar Square in London—especially against the star-crowded backdrop of the galaxy. You take off from Terra with its orbital speed of about nineteen miles per second. You attempt to settle into a composite conoid curve that will not only intersect the orbit of the tiny fast-moving body, but also accomplish an exact rendezvous. Asteroid HS-5388, "Eighty-eight," lay about two and two-tenths astronomical units out from the sun, a little more than two hundred million miles; when the transport took off it lay beyond the sun better than three hundred million miles. Captain Doyle instructed the navigator to plot the basic ellipsoid to tack in free flight around the sun through an elapsed distance of some three hundred and forty million miles. The principle involved is the same as used by a hunter to wing a duck in flight by "leading" the bird in flight. But suppose that you face directly into the sun as you shoot; suppose the bird can not be seen from where you stand, and you have nothing to aim by but some old reports as to how it was flying when last seen?

On the ninth day of the passage Captain Doyle betook himself to the chart room and commenced punching keys on the ponderous integral calculator. Then he sent his orderly to present his compliments to the navigator and to ask him to come to the chartroom.

A few minutes later a tall heavyset form swam through the door, steadied himself with a grabline and greeted the captain.

"Good morning, Skipper."

"Hello, Blackie." The Old Man looked up from where he was strapped into the integrator's saddle. "I've been checking your corrections for the meal time accelerations."

"It's a nuisance to have a bunch of ground-lubbers on board, sir."

"Yes, it is, but we have to give those boys a chance to eat, or they couldn't work when we got there. Now I want to decelerate starting about ten o'clock, ship's time. What's our eight o'clock speed and co-ordinates?"

The Navigator slipped a notebook out of his tunic. "Three hundred fifty-eight miles per second; course is right ascension fifteen hours, eight minutes, twenty-seven seconds, declination minus seven degrees, three minutes; solar distance one hundred and ninety-two million four hundred eighty thousand miles. Our radial position is twelve degrees above course, and almost dead on course in R.A. Do you want Sol's co-ordinates?"

"No, not now." The captain bent over the calculator, frowned and chewed the tip of his tongue as he worked the controls. "I want you to kill the acceleration about one million miles inside Eighty-eight's orbit. I hate to waste the fuel, but the belt is full of junk and this damned rock is so small that we will probably have to run a search curve. Use twenty hours on deceleration and commence changing course to port after eight hours. Use normal asymptotic approach. You should have her in a circular trajectory abreast of Eighty-eight, and paralleling her orbit by six o'clock tomorrow morning. I shall want to be called at three."

"Aye aye, sir."

"Let me see your figures when you get em. I'll send up the order book later."

The transport decelerated on schedule. Shortly after three the Captain entered the control room and blinked his eyes at the darkness. The sun was still concealed by the hull of the transport and the midnight blackness was broken only by the dim blue glow of the instrument dials, and the crack of light from under the chart hood. The Navigator turned at the familiar tread.

"Good morning, Captain."

"Morning, Blackie. In sight yet?"

"Not yet. We've picked out half a dozen rocks, but none of them checked."

"Any of them close?"

"Not uncomfortably. We've overtaken a little sand from time to time."

"That can't hurt us—not on a stern chase like this. If pilots would only realize that the asteroids flow in fixed directions at computable speeds nobody would come to grief out here." He stopped to light a cigarette. "People talk about space being dangerous. Sure, it used to be; but I don't know of a case in the past twenty years that couldn't be charged up to some fool's recklessness."

"You're right, Skipper. By the way, there's coffee under the chart hood."

"Thanks; I had a cup down below." He walked over by the lookouts at stereoscopes and radar tanks and peered up at the star-flecked blackness. Three cigarettes later the lookout nearest him called out.

"Light ho!"

"Where away?"

His mate read the exterior dials of the stereoscope. "Plus point two, abaft one point three, slight drift astern." He shifted to radar and added, "Range seven nine oh four three."

"Does that check?"

"Could be, Captain. What is her disk?" came the Navigator's muffled voice from under the hood. The first lookout hurriedly twisted the knobs of his instrument, but the Captain nudged him aside.

"I'll do this, son." He fitted his face to the double eye guards and surveyed a little silvery sphere, a tiny moon. Carefully he brought two illuminated cross-hairs up until they were exactly tangent to the upper and lower limbs of the disc. "Mark!"

The reading was noted and passed to the Navigator, who shortly ducked out from under the hood.

"That's our baby, Captain."

"Good."

"Shall I make a visual triangulation?"

"Let the watch officer do that. You go down and get some sleep. I'll ease her over until we get close enough to use the optical range finder."

"Thanks, I will."

Within a few minutes the word had spread around the ship that Eighty-eight had been sighted. Libby crowded into the starboard troop deck with a throng of excited mess mates and attempted to make out their future home from the view port. McCoy poured cold water on their excitement.

"By the time that rock shows up big enough to tell anything about it with your naked eye we'll all be at our grounding stations. She's only about a hundred miles thick, yuh know."

And so it was. Many hours later the ship's announcer shouted:

"All hands! Man your grounding stations. Close all air-tight doors. Stand by to cut blowers on signal."

McCoy forced them to lie down throughout the ensuing two hours. Short shocks of rocket blasts alternated with nauseating weightlessness. Then the blowers stopped and check valves clicked into their seats. The ship dropped free for a few moments—a final quick blast—five seconds of falling, and a short, light, grinding bump. A single bugle note came over the announcer, and the blowers took up their hum.

McCoy floated lightly to his feet and poised, swaying, on his toes. "All out, troops—this is the end of the line."

A short chunky lad, a little younger than most of them, awkwardly emulated him, and bounded toward the door, shouting as he went, "Come on, fellows! Let's go outside and explore!"

The Master-at-Arms squelched him. "Not so fast, kid. Aside from the fact that there is no air out there, go right ahead. You'll freeze to death, burn to death, and explode like a ripe tomato. Squad leader, detail six men to break out spacesuits. The rest of you stay here and stand by."

The working party returned shortly loaded down with a couple of dozen bulky packages. Libby let go the four he carried and watched them float gently to the deck. McCoy unzipped the envelope from one suit, and lectured them about it.

"This is a standard service type, general issue, Mark IV, Modification 2." He grasped the suit by the shoulders and shook it out so that it hung like a suit of long winter underwear with the helmet lolling helplessly between the shoulders of the garment. "It's self-sustaining for eight hours, having an oxygen supply for that period. It also has a nitrogen trim tank and a carbon-dioxide-water-vapor cartridge filter."

He droned on, repeating practically verbatim the description and instructions given in training regulations. McCoy knew these suits like his tongue knew the roof of his mouth; the knowledge had meant his life on more than one occasion.

"The suit is woven from glass fibre laminated with nonvolatile asbestocellutite. The resulting fabric is flexible, very durable; and will turn all rays normal to solar space outside the orbit of Mercury. It is worn over your regular clothing, but notice the wire-braced accordion pleats at the major joints. They are so designed as to keep the internal volume of the suit nearly constant when the arms or legs are bent. Otherwise the gas pressure inside would tend to keep the suit blown up in an erect position, and movement while wearing the suit would be very fatiguing.

"The helmet is moulded from a transparent silicone, leaded and polarized against too great ray penetration. It may be equipped with external visors of any needed type. Orders are to wear not less than a number-two amber on this body. In addition, a lead plate covers the cranium and extends on down the back of the suit, completely covering the spinal column.

"The suit is equipped with two-way telephony. If your radio quits, as these have a habit of doing, you can talk by putting your helmets in contact. Any questions?"

"How do you eat and drink during the eight hours?"

"You don't stay in 'em any eight hours. You can carry sugar balls in a gadget in the helmet, but you boys will always eat at the base. As for water, there's a nipple in the helmet near your mouth which you can reach by turning your head to the left. It's hooked to a built-in canteen. But don't drink any more water when you're wearing a suit than you have to. These suits ain't got any plumbing."

Suits were passed out to each lad, and McCoy illustrated how to don one. A suit was spread supine on the deck, the front zipper that stretched from neck to crotch was spread wide and one sat down inside this opening, whereupon the lower part was drawn on like long stockings. Then a wiggle into each sleeve and the heavy flexible gauntlets were smoothed and patted into place. Finally an awkward backward stretch of the neck with shoulders hunched enabled the helmet to be placed over the head.

Libby followed the motions of McCoy and stood up in his suit. He examined the zipper which controlled the suit's only opening. It was backed by two soft gaskets which would be pressed together by the zipper and sealed by internal air pressure. Inside the helmet a composition mouthpiece for exhalation led to the filter.

McCoy bustled around, inspecting them, tightening a belt here and there, instructing them in the use of the external controls. Satisfied, he reported to the conning room that his section had received basic instruction and was ready to disembark. Permission was received to take them out for thirty minutes acclimatization.

Six at a time, he escorted them through the air lock, and out on the surface of the planetoid. Libby blinked his eyes at the unaccustomed luster of sunshine on rock. Although the sun lay more than two hundred million miles away and bathed the little planet with radiation only one fifth as strong as that lavished on mother Earth, nevertheless the lack of atmosphere resulted in a glare that made him squint. He was glad to have the protection of his amber visor. Overhead the sun, shrunk to penny size, shone down from a dead black sky in which unwinking stars crowded each other and the very sun itself.

The voice of a mess mate sounded in Libby's earphones, "Jeepers! That horizon looks close. I'll bet it ain't more'n a mile away.

Libby looked out over the flat bare plain and subconsciously considered the matter. "It's less," he commented, "than a third of a mile away."

"What the hell do you know about it, Pinkie? And who asked you, anyhow?"

Libby answered defensively, "As a matter of fact, it's one thousand six hundred and seventy feet, figuring that my eyes are five feet three inches above ground level."

"Nuts. Pinkie, you are always trying to show off how much you think you know."

"Why, I am not," Libby protested. "If this body is a hundred miles thick and as round as it looks: why, naturally the horizon *has* to be just that far away."

"Says *who?*"

McCoy interrupted.

"Pipe down! Libby is a lot nearer right than you were."

"He is exactly right," put in a strange voice. "I had to look it up for the navigator before I left control."

"Is that so?"—McCoy's voice again—"If the Chief Quartermaster says you're right, Libby, you're right. How did you know?"

Libby flushed miserably. "I—I don't know. That's the only way it could be."

The gunner's mate and the quartermaster stared at him but dropped the subject.

By the end of the "day" (ship's time, for Eighty-eight had a period of eight hours and thirteen minutes), work was well under way. The transport had grounded close by a low range of hills. The Captain selected a little bowl-shaped depression in the hills, some thousand feet long and half as broad, in which to establish a permanent camp. This was to be roofed over, sealed, and an atmosphere provided.

In the hill between the ship and the valley, quarters were to be excavated; dormitories, mess hall, officers' quarters, sick bay, recreation room, offices, store rooms, and so forth. A tunnel must be bored through the hill, connecting the sites of these rooms, and connecting with a ten foot airtight metal tube sealed to the ship's portside air-lock. Both the tube and tunnel were to be equipped with a continuous conveyor belt for passengers and freight.

Libby found himself assigned to the roofing detail. He helped a metalsmith struggle over the hill with a portable atomic heater, difficult to handle because of a mass of eight hundred pounds, but weighing here only sixteen pounds. The rest of the roofing detail were breaking out and preparing to move by hand the enormous translucent tent which was to be the "sky" of the little valley.

The metalsmith located a landmark on the inner slope of the valley, set up his heater, and commenced

cutting a deep horizontal groove or step in the rock.
He kept it always at the same level by following a chalk
mark drawn along the rock wall. Libby enquired how
the job had been surveyed so quickly.

"Easy," he was answered, "two of the quarter-masters
went ahead with a transit, leveled it just fifty feet above
the valley floor, and clamped a searchlight to it. Then
one of 'em ran like hell around the rim, making chalk
marks at the height at which the beam struck."

"Is this roof going to be just fifty feet high?"

"No, it will average maybe a hundred. It bellies up
in the middle from the air pressure."

"Earth normal?"

"Half Earth normal."

Libby concentrated for an instant, then looked
puzzled. "But look— This valley is a thousand feet long
and better than five hundred wide. At half of fifteen
pounds per square inch, and allowing for the arch of
the roof, that's a load of one and an eighth billion
pounds. What fabric can take that kind of a load?"

"Cobwebs."

"Cobwebs?"

"Yeah, cobwebs. Strongest stuff in the world, stronger than the best steel. Synthetic spider silk. This gauge
we're using for the roof has a tensile strength of four
thousand pounds a running inch."

Libby hesitated a second, then replied, "I see. With
a rim about eighteen hundred thousand inches around,
the maximum pull at the point of anchoring would be
about six hundred and twenty-five pounds per inch.
Plenty safe margin."

The metalsmith leaned on his tool and nodded.
"Something like that. You're pretty quick at arithmetic,
aren't you, bud?"

Libby looked startled. "I just like to get things
straight."

They worked rapidly around the slope, cutting a clean
smooth groove to which the "cobweb" could be

anchored and sealed. The white-hot lava spewed out of the discharge vent and ran slowly down the hillside. A brown vapor boiled off the surface of the molten rock, arose a few feet and sublimed almost at once in the vacuum to white powder which settled to the ground. The metalsmith pointed to the powder.

"That stuff 'ud cause silicosis if we let it stay there, and breathed it later."

"What do you do about it?"

"Just clean it out with the blowers of the air conditioning plant."

Libby took this opening to ask another question. "Mister——?"

"Johnson's my name. No mister necessary."

"Well, Johnson, where do we get the air for this whole valley, not to mention the tunnels? I figure we must need twenty-five million cubic feet or more. Do we manufacture it?"

"Naw, that's too much trouble. We brought it with us."

"On the transport?"

"Uh huh, at fifty atmospheres."

Libby considered this. "I see—that way it would go into a space eighty feet on a side."

"Matter of fact it's in three specially constructed holds—giant air bottles. This transport carried air to Ganymede. I was in her then—a recruit, but in the air gang even then."

In three weeks the permanent camp was ready for occupancy and the transport cleared of its cargo. The storerooms bulged with tools and supplies. Captain Doyle had moved his administrative offices underground, signed over his command to his first officer, and given him permission to proceed on "duty assigned"—in this case; return to Terra with a skeleton crew.

Libby watched them take off from a vantage point on the hillside. An overpowering homesickness took possession of him. Would he ever go home? He honestly believed at the time that he would swap the rest of his life for thirty minutes each with his mother and with Betty.

He started down the hill toward the tunnel lock. At least the transport carried letters to them, and with any luck the chaplain would be by soon with letters from Earth. But tomorrow and the days after that would be no fun. He had enjoyed being in the air gang, but tomorrow he went back to his squad. He did not relish that—the boys in his squad were all right, he guessed, but he just could not seem to fit in.

This company of the C.C.C. started on its bigger job; to pock-mark Eighty-eight with rocket tubes so that Captain Doyle could push this hundred-mile marble out of her orbit and herd her in to a new orbit between Earth and Mars, to be used as a space station—a refuge for ships in distress, a haven for life boats, a fueling stop, a naval outpost.

Libby was assigned to a heater in pit H-16. It was his business to carve out carefully calculated emplacements in which the blasting crew then set off the minute charges which accomplished the major part of the excavating. Two squads were assigned to H-16, under the general supervision of an elderly marine gunner. The gunner sat on the edge of the pit, handling the plans, and occasionally making calculations on a circular slide rule which hung from a lanyard around his neck.

Libby had just completed a tricky piece of cutting for a three-stage blast, and was waiting for the blasters, when his phones picked up the gunner's instructions concerning the size of the charge. He pressed his transmitter button.

"Mr. Larsen! You've made a mistake!"

"Who said that?"

"This is Libby. You've made a mistake in the charge. If you set off that charge, you'll blow this pit right out of the ground, and us with it."

Marine Gunner Larsen spun the dials on his slide rule before replying, "You're all het up over nothing, son. That charge is correct."

"No, I'm not, sir," Libby persisted, "you've multiplied where you should have divided."

"Have you had any experience at this sort of work?"

"No, sir."

Larsen addressed his next remark to the blasters. "Set the charge."

They started to comply. Libby gulped, and wiped his lips with his tongue. He knew what he had to do, but he was afraid. Two clumsy stiff-legged jumps placed him beside the blasters. He pushed between them and tore the electrodes from the detonator. A shadow passed over him as he worked, and Larsen floated down beside him. A hand grasped his arm.

"You shouldn't have done that, son. That's direct disobedience of orders. I'll have to report you." He commenced reconnecting the firing circuit.

Libby's ears burned with embarrassment, but he answered back with the courage of timidity at bay. "I had to do it, sir. You're still wrong."

Larsen paused and ran his eyes over the dogged face. "Well—it's a waste of time, but I don't like to make you stand by a charge you're afraid of. Let's go over the calculation together."

Captain Doyle sat at his ease in his quarters, his feet on his desk. He stared at a nearly empty glass tumbler.

"That's good beer, Blackie. Do you suppose we could brew some more when it's gone?"

"I don't know, Cap'n. Did we bring any yeast?"

"Find out, will you?" He turned to a massive man who occupied the third chair. "Well, Larsen, I'm glad it wasn't any worse than it was."

"What beats me, Captain, is how I could have made such a mistake. I worked it through twice. If it had been a nitro explosive, I'd have known off hand that I was wrong. If this kid hadn't had a hunch, I'd have set it off."

Captain Doyle clapped the old warrant officer on the shoulder. "Forget it, Larsen. You wouldn't have hurt anybody; that's why I require the pits to be evacuated even for small charges. These isotope explosives are tricky at best. Look what happened in pit A-9. Ten days' work shot with one charge, and the gunnery officer himself approved that one. But I want to see this boy. What did you say his name was?"

"Libby, A. J."

Doyle touched a button on his desk. A knock sounded at the door. A bellowed "Come in!" produced a stripling wearing the brassard of Corpsman Mate-of-the-Deck.

"Have Corpsman Libby report to me."

"Aye aye, sir."

Some few minutes later Libby was ushered into the Captain's cabin. He looked nervously around, and noted Larsen's presence, a fact that did not contribute to his peace of mind. He reported in a barely audible voice, "Corpsman Libby, sir."

The Captain looked him over. "Well, Libby, I hear that you and Mr. Larsen had a difference of opinion this morning. Tell me about it."

"I—I didn't mean any harm, sir."

"Of course not. You're not in any trouble; you did us all a good turn this morning. Tell me, how did you know that the calculation was wrong? Had any mining experience?"

"No, sir. I just saw that he had worked it out wrong."

"But how?"

Libby shuffled uneasily. "Well, sir, it just seemed wrong—It didn't fit."

"Just a second, Captain. May I ask this young man a couple of questions?" It was Commander "Blackie" Rhodes who spoke.

"Certainly. Go ahead."

"Are you the lad they call 'Pinkie'?"

Libby blushed. "Yes, sir."

"I've heard some rumors about this boy." Rhodes pushed his big frame out of his chair, went over to a bookshelf, and removed a thick volume. He thumbed through it, then with open book before him, started to question Libby.

"What's the square root of ninety-five?"

"Nine and seven hundred forty-seven thousandths."

"What's the cube root?"

"Four and five hundred sixty-three thousandths."

"What's its logarithm?"

"Its what, sir?"

"Good Lord, can a boy get through school today without knowing?"

The boy's discomfort became more intense. "I didn't get much schooling, sir. My folks didn't accept the Covenant until Pappy died, and we had to."

"I see. A logarithm is a name for a power to which you raise a given number, called the base, to get the number whose logarithm it is. Is that clear?"

Libby thought hard. "I don't quite get it, sir."

"I'll try again. If you raise ten to the second power—square it—it gives one hundred. Therefore the logarithm of a hundred to the base ten is two. In the same fashion the logarithm of a thousand to the base ten is three. Now what is the logarithm of ninety-five?"

Libby puzzled for a moment. "I can't make it come out even. It's a fraction."

"That's okay."

"Then it's one and nine hundred seventy-eight thousandths—just about."

Rhodes turned to the Captain. "I guess that about proves it, sir."

Doyle nodded thoughtfully. "Yes, the lad seems to have intuitive knowledge of arithmetical relationships. But let's see what else he has."

"I am afraid we'll have to send him back to Earth to find out properly."

Libby caught the gist of this last remark. "Please, sir, you aren't going to send me home? Maw 'ud be awful vexed with me."

"No, no, nothing of the sort. When your time is up, I want you to be checked over in the psychometrical laboratories. In the meantime I wouldn't part with you for a quarter's pay. I'd give up smoking first. But let's see what else you can do."

In the ensuing hour the Captain and the Navigator heard Libby: one, deduce the Pythagorean proposition; two, derive Newton's laws of motion and Kepler's laws of ballistics from a statement of the conditions in which they obtained; three, judge length, area, and volume by eye with no measurable error. He had jumped into the idea of relativity and non-rectilinear space-time continua, and was beginning to pour forth ideas faster than he could talk, when Doyle held up a hand.

"That's enough, son. You'll be getting a fever. You run along to bed now, and come see me in the morning. I'm taking you off field work."

"Yes, sir."

"By the way, what is your full name?"

"Andrew Jackson Libby, sir."

"No, your folks wouldn't have signed the Covenant. Good night."

"Good night, sir."

After he had gone, the two older men discussed their discovery.

"How do you size it up, Captain?"

"Well, he's a genius, of course—one of those wild talents that will show up once in a blue moon. I'll turn him loose among my books and see how he shapes up. Shouldn't wonder if he were a page-at-a-glance reader, too."

"It beats me what we turn up among these boys— and not a one of 'em any account back on Earth."

Doyle nodded. "That was the trouble with these kids. They didn't feel needed."

❖   ❖   ❖

Eighty-eight swung some millions of miles further around the sun. The pock-marks on her face grew deeper, and were lined with durite, that strange close-packed laboratory product which (usually) would confine even atomic disintegration. Then Eighty-eight received a series of gentle pats, always on the side headed along her course. In a few weeks' time the rocket blasts had their effect and Eighty-eight was plunging in an orbit toward the sun.

When she reached her station one and three-tenths the distance from the sun of Earth's orbit, she would have to be coaxed by another series of pats into a circular orbit. Thereafter she was to be known as E-M3, Earth-Mars Space Station Spot Three.

Hundreds of millions of miles away two other C.C.C. companies were inducing two other planetoids to quit their age-old grooves and slide between Earth and Mars to land in the same orbit as Eighty-eight. One was due to ride this orbit one hundred and twenty degrees ahead of Eighty-eight, the other one hundred and twenty degrees behind. When E-M1, E-M2, and E-M3 were all on station no hard-pushed traveler of the spaceways on the Earth-Mars passage would ever again find himself far from land—or rescue.

During the months that Eighty-eight fell free toward the sun, Captain Doyle reduced the working hours of his crew and turned them to the comparatively light labor of building a hotel and converting the little roofed-in valley into a garden spot. The rock was broken down into soil, fertilizers applied, and cultures of anaerobic bacteria planted. Then plants, conditioned by thirty-odd generations of low gravity at Luna City, were set out and tenderly cared for. Except for the low gravity, Eighty-eight began to feel like home.

But when Eighty-eight approached a tangent to the hypothetical future orbit of E-M3, the company went back to maneuvering routine, watch on and watch off, with the Captain living on black coffee and catching catnaps in the plotting room.

Libby was assigned to the ballistic calculator, three tons of thinking metal that dominated the plotting room. He loved the big machine. The Chief Fire Controlman let him help adjust it and care for it. Libby subconsciously thought of it as a person—his own kind of person.

On the last day of the approach, the shocks were more frequent. Libby sat in the right-hand saddle of the calculator and droned out the predictions for the next salvo, while gloating over the accuracy with which the machine tracked. Captain Doyle fussed around nervously, occasionally stopping to peer over the Navigator's shoulder. Of course the figures were right, but what if it didn't work? No one had ever moved so large a mass before. Suppose it plunged on and on—and on. Nonsense! It couldn't. Still he would be glad when they were past the critical speed.

A marine orderly touched his elbow. "Helio from the Flagship, sir."

"Read it."

"Flag to Eighty-eight; private message, Captain Doyle; am lying off to watch you bring her in.—Kearney."

Doyle smiled. Nice of the old geezer. Once they were on station, he would invite the Admiral to ground for dinner and show him the park.

Another salvo cut loose, heavier than any before. The room trembled violently. In a moment the reports of the surface observers commenced to trickle in. "Tube nine, clear! Tube ten, clear!"

But Libby's drone ceased.

Captain Doyle turned on him. "What's the matter, Libby? Asleep? Call the polar stations. I have to have a parallax."

"Captain—" The boy's voice was low and shaking. "Speak up, man!"

"Captain—the machine isn't tracking."

"Spiers!" The grizzled head of the Chief Fire Controlman appeared from behind the calculator.

"I'm already on it, sir. Let you know in a moment."

He ducked back again. After a couple of long minutes he reappeared. "Gyros tumbled. It's a twelve hour calibration job, at least."

The Captain said nothing, but turned away, and walked to the far end of the room. The Navigator followed him with his eyes. He returned, glanced at the chronometer, and spoke to the Navigator.

"Well, Blackie, if I don't have that firing data in seven minutes, we're sunk. Any suggestions?"

Rhodes shook his head without speaking.

Libby timidly raised his voice. "Captain—"

Doyle jerked around. "Yes?"

"The firing data is tube thirteen, seven point six three; tube twelve, six point nine oh; tube fourteen, six point eight nine."

Doyle studied his face. "You sure about that, son?"

"It *has* to be that, Captain."

Doyle stood perfectly still. This time he did not look at Rhodes but stared straight ahead. Then he took a long pull on his cigarette, glanced at the ash, and said in a steady voice,

"Apply the data. Fire on the bell."

Four hours later, Libby was still droning out firing data, his face grey, his eyes closed. Once he had fainted but when they revived him he was still muttering figures. From time to time the Captain and the Navigator relieved each other, but there was no relief for him.

The salvos grew closer together, but the shocks were lighter.

Following one faint salvo, Libby looked up, stared at the ceiling, and spoke.

"That's all, Captain."

"Call polar stations!"

The reports came back promptly, "Parallax constant, sidereal-solar rate constant."

The Captain relaxed into a chair. "Well, Blackie, we did it—thanks to Libby!" Then he noticed a worried, thoughtful look spread over Libby's face. "What's the matter, man? Have we slipped up?"

"Captain, you know you said the other day that you wished you had Earth-normal gravity in the park?"

"Yes. What of it?"

"If that book on gravitation you lent me is straight dope, I think I know a way to accomplish it."

The Captain inspected him as if seeing him for the first time. "Libby, you have ceased to amaze me. Could you stop doing that sort of thing long enough to dine with the Admiral?"

"Gee, Captain, that would be swell!"

The audio circuit from Communications cut in.

"Helio from Flagship: 'Well, done, Eighty-eight.'"

Doyle smiled around at them all. "That's pleasant confirmation."

The audio brayed again.

"Helio from Flagship: 'Cancel last signal, stand by for correction.'"

A look of surprise and worry sprang into Doyle's face—then the audio continued:

"Helio from Flagship: 'Well done, E-M3.'"

Concerning Stories Never Written: Postscript

This aside is addressed primarily to you who have read the first two volumes of this series rather grandly titled "Future History." Volume One, *The Man Who Sold the Moon,* is laid from right now until the closing years of this century and ends with mankind's first faltering steps toward space. Some of the stories are so close to the present time as already to be outdated by events—an occupational hazard I share with weather forecasters and fortune tellers. Volume Two, *The Green Hills of Earth,* is concerned with the great days of exploration of the Solar System. All of the stories take place somewhere close around the year 2000 A.D. If you refer to the chart in the flyleaf of this volume, you will see that this second group of stories appears to cover about twenty-five years, but this appearance is a deceptive shortcoming of typography—printing the titles on the chart requires a certain minimum of space. Nor does the order matter materially—some of the stories overlap in time but concern different characters in differing scenes.

This present Volume Three starts about seventy-five

years later than the end of the last story in Volume Two—and a great amount of "Future History" has taken place between the two volumes. *Green Hills* ended with the United States a leading power in a systemwide imperialism embracing all the habitable planets. But the very first page of the first story in this book finds the United States plunged in a new Dark Ages, no longer space minded, isolationist even with respect to this planet, and under a theocracy as absolute as that of Communism.

The effect on the reader could be a little like that which sometimes results from unskillful editing of magazine serials—the sort of thing in which one installment ends with the hero hanging by his heels over the snake pit while the sinister villain leers at him from above, only to have the next installment start with our hero walking up Fifth Avenue, debonair and undamaged.

I could plead the excuse that these stories were never meant to be a definitive history of the future (concerning which I know no more than you do), nor are they installments of a long serial (since each is intended to be entirely independent of all the others). They are just stories, meant to amuse and written to buy groceries.

Nevertheless, I think that you who are kind enough to buy this volume are entitled to more explanation as to the great hiatus between the second and the third volume. On the chart you will see three titles in parentheses between the last story in *Green Hills* and the first story in this book; these three stories, had they ever been written, would have covered the intervening three quarters of a century and might well have been an additional volume in this series.

The first of these unwritten stories, *The Sound of His Wings* starts shortly before *Logic of Empire* and continues for several years beyond the ending of *Logic;* it would have recounted the early life, rise as a television evangelist, and subsequent political career of the Reverend Nehemiah Scudder, the "First Prophet," President of the United States and destroyer of its Constitution, founder of the Theocracy.

The second story, *Eclipse*, parallels somewhat both the American Revolution and the break-up of colonialism taking place on this planet today, for it is concerned with the colonies on Mars and on Venus becoming self-sufficient and politically mature and breaking away from Mother Earth, followed by almost complete cessation of interplanetary travel. *Logic of Empire* suggests some of the forces that led to the breakdown. Interplanetary travel will be tremendously expensive at first; if the home planet is no longer in a position to exploit the colonies, trade and communication might dwindle almost to zero for a long period—indeed the infant nations might pass "Non-Intercourse Acts."

The Stone Pillow was intended to fill the gap between the establishment of the Theocracy and its overthrow in the Second American Revolution. It was to have been concerned with the slow build-up of a counter-revolutionary underground. It gets its name from the martyrs of the underground, those who rested their heads on pillows of stone—in or out of prison. These revolutionaries would be in much the same nearly hopeless position that anti-Communists have found themselves in these thirty years past in the U.S.S.R., but the story would have concerned itself with the superiority of the knife to the atom bomb under some circumstances and with the inadvisability of swatting mosquitoes with an axe.

These three stories will probably never be written. In the case of *Eclipse* I have dealt with the themes involved at greater length in two novels which were not bound by the Procrustean Bed of a fictional chart; it would be tedious for both you and me to deal with the same themes again. As for the other two stories, they both have the disadvantage of being "down beat" stories, their outcomes are necessarily not pleasant. I am not opposed to tragedy and have written quite a bit of it, but today we can find more than enough of it in the headlines. I don't want to write tragedy just now and I doubt if you want to read it. Perhaps in another and sunnier year we will both feel differently.

In any case, I feel that even Caruso, Cleopatra, or Santa Claus could overstay their welcomes; it may be that this pseudohistory has already taken more curtain calls than the applause justifies.

I am aware that the themes of the unwritten stories linking the second and this the third volume thus briefly stated above have not been elaborated sufficiently to lend conviction, particularly with reference to two notions; the idea that space travel, once apparently firmly established, could fall into disuse, and secondly the idea that the United States could lapse into a dictatorship of superstition. As for the first, consider the explorations of the Vikings a thousand years ago and the colonies they established in North America. Their labors were fruitless; Columbus and his successors had to do it all over again. Space travel in the near future is likely to be a marginal proposition at best, subsidized for military reasons. It could die out—then undergo a renascence through new techniques and through new economic and political pressures. I am not saying these things will happen, I do say they could happen.

As for the second notion, the idea that we could lose our freedom by succumbing to a wave of religious hysteria, I am sorry to say that I consider it possible. I hope that it is not probable. But there is a latent deep strain of religious fanaticism in this, our culture; it is rooted in our history and it has broken out many times in the past. It is with us now; there has been a sharp rise in strongly evangelical sects in this country in recent years, some of which hold beliefs theocratic in the extreme, anti-intellectual, anti-scientific, and anti-libertarian.

It is a truism that almost any sect, cult, or religion will legislate its creed into law if it acquires the political power to do so, and will follow it by suppressing opposition, subverting all education to seize early the minds of the young, and by killing, locking up, or driving underground all heretics. This is equally true whether the faith is Communism or Holy-Rollerism; indeed it is the bounden duty of the faithful to do so. The custodians of the True Faith cannot logically admit tolerance of heresy to be a virtue.

Nevertheless this business of legislating religious beliefs into law has never been more than sporadically successful in this country—Sunday closing laws here and there, birth control legislation in spots, the Prohibition experiment, temporary enclaves of theocracy such as Voliva's Zion, Smith's Nauvoo, a few others. The country is split up into such a variety of faiths and sects that a degree of uneasy tolerance now exists from expedient compromise; the minorities constitute a majority of opposition against each other.

Could it be otherwise here? Could any one sect obtain a working majority at the polls and take over the country? Perhaps not—but a combination of a dynamic evangelist, television, enough money, and modern techniques of advertising and propaganda might make Billy Sunday's efforts look like a corner store compared to Sears Roebuck. Throw in a depression for good measure, promise a material heaven here on earth, add a dash of anti-Semitism, anti-Catholicism, anti-Negroism, and a good large dose of anti-"furriners" in general and anti-intellectuals here at home and the result might be something quite frightening—particularly when one recalls that our voting system is such that a minority distributed as pluralities in enough states can constitute a working majority in Washington.

I imagined Nehemiah Scudder as a backwoods evangelist who combined some of the features of John Calvin, Savonarola, Judge Rutherford and Huey Long. His influence was not national until after the death of Mrs. Rachel Biggs, an early convert who had the single virtue of being the widow of an extremely wealthy man who shared none of her religious myopia—she left Brother Scudder several millions of dollars with which to establish a television station. Shortly thereafter he teamed up with an ex-Senator from his home state; they placed their affairs in the hands of a major advertising agency and were on their way to fame and fortune. Presently they needed stormtroopers; they revived the Ku Klux Klan in everything but the name—sheets, passwords, grips and all. It was a "good gimmick" once and it still served. Blood at the polls and blood in the streets, but Scudder won the election. The next election was never held.

Impossible? Remember the Klan in the 'Twenties—and how far it got without even a dynamic leader. Remember Karl Marx and note how close that unscientific piece of nonsense called *Das Kapital* has come to smothering out all freedom of thought on half a planet, without—mind you—the emotional advantage of calling it a religion. The capacity of the human mind for swallowing nonsense and spewing it forth in violent and repressive action has never yet been plumbed.

No. I probably never will write the story of Nehemiah Scudder; I dislike him too thoroughly. But I hope that you will go along with me in the idea that he *could* happen, for the sake of the stories which follow. Whether you believe in the possibility of the postulates of these stories or not, I hope that you will enjoy them—at my age it would be very inconvenient to have to go back to working for a living.

ROBERT A. HEINLEIN
Colorado Springs, Colorado
October 1952

To Edward E. Smith, PhD.

Methuselah's Children

To Edward E. Smith, Ph.D.

PART ONE

1

"Mary Sperling, you're a fool not to marry him!"

Mary Sperling added up her losses and wrote a check before answering, "There's too much difference in age." She passed over her credit voucher. "I shouldn't gamble with you—sometimes I think you're a sensitive."

"Nonsense! You're just trying to change the subject. You must be nearly thirty . . . and you won't be pretty forever."

Mary smiled wryly. "Don't I know it!"

"Bork Vanning can't be much over forty and he's a plus citizen. You should jump at the chance."

"You jump at it. I must run now. Service, Ven."

"Service," Ven answered, then frowned at the door as it contracted after Mary Sperling. She itched to know why Mary would not marry a prime catch like the Honorable Bork Vanning and was almost as curious as to why and where Mary was going, but the custom of privacy stopped her.

Mary had no intention of letting anyone know where she was going. Outside her friend's apartment she dropped down a bounce tube to the basement, claimed her car from the robopark, guided it up the ramp and set the controls for North Shore. The car waited for a break in the traffic, then dived into the high-speed stream and hurried north. Mary settled back for a nap.

When its setting was about to run out, the car beeped for instructions; Mary woke up and glanced out. Lake Michigan was a darker band of darkness on her right. She signaled traffic control to let her enter the local traffic lane; it sorted out her car and placed her there, then let her resume manual control. She fumbled in the glove compartment.

The license number which traffic control automatically photographed as she left the controlways was not the number the car had been wearing.

She followed a side road uncontrolled for several miles, turned into a narrow dirt road which led down to the shore, and stopped. There she waited, lights out, and listened. South of her the lights of Chicago glowed; a few hundred yards inland the controlways whined, but here there was nothing but the little timid noises of night creatures. She reached into the glove compartment, snapped a switch; the instrument panel glowed, uncovering other dials behind it. She studied these while making adjustments. Satisfied that no radar watched her and that nothing was moving near her, she snapped off the instruments, sealed the window by her and started up again.

What appeared to be a standard Camden speedster rose quietly up, moved out over the lake, skimming it— dropped into the water and sank. Mary waited until she was a quarter mile off shore in fifty feet of water, then called a station. "Answer," said a voice.

"'Life is short—'"

"'—but the years are long.'"

"'Not,'" Mary responded, "'while the evil days come not.'"

"I sometimes wonder," the voice answered conversationally. "Okay, Mary. I've checked you."

"Tommy?"

"No—Cecil Hedrick. Are your controls cast loose?"

"Yes. Take over."

Seventeen minutes later the car surfaced in a pool which occupied much of an artificial cave. When the car was beached, Mary got out, said hello to the guards and went on through a tunnel into a large underground room where fifty or sixty men and women were seated. She chatted until a clock announced midnight, then she mounted a rostrum and faced them.

"I am," she stated, "one hundred and eighty-three years old. Is there anyone here who is older?"

No one spoke. After a decent wait she went on, "Then in accordance with our customs I declare this meeting opened. Will you choose a moderator?"

Someone said, "Go ahead, Mary." When no one else spoke up, she said, "Very well." She seemed indifferent to the honor and the group seemed to share her casual attitude—an air of never any hurry, of freedom from the tension of modern life.

"We are met as usual," she announced, "to discuss our welfare and that of our sisters and brothers. Does any Family representative have a message from his family? Or does anyone care to speak for himself?"

A man caught her eye and spoke up, "Ira Weatheral, speaking for the Johnson Family. We've met nearly two months early. The trustees must have a reason. Let's hear it."

She nodded and turned to a prim little man in the first row. "Justin . . . if you will, please."

The prim little man stood up and bowed stiffly. Skinny legs stuck out below his badly-cut kilt. He looked and acted like an elderly, dusty civil servant, but his black hair and the firm, healthy tone of his skin said that he was a man in his prime. "Justin Foote," he said precisely, "reporting for the trustees. It has been eleven years since the Families decided on the experiment of letting the public know that there were, living among them, persons who possessed a probable life expectancy far in excess of that anticipated by the average man, as well as other persons who had proved the scientific truth of such expectation by having lived more than twice the normal life span of human beings."

Although he spoke without notes he sounded as if he were reading aloud a prepared report. What he was saying they all knew but no one hurried him; his audience had none of the febrile impatience so common elsewhere. "In deciding," he droned on, "to reverse the previous long-standing policy of silence and concealment as to the peculiar aspect in which we differ from the balance of the human race, the Families were moved by several considerations. The reason for the original adoption of the policy of concealment should be noted:

"The first offspring resulting from unions assisted by the Howard Foundation were born in 1875. They aroused no comment, for they were in no way remarkable. The Foundation was an openly-chartered non-profit corporation—"

On March 17, 1874, Ira Johnson, medical student, sat in the law offices of Deems, Wingate, Alden, & Deems and listened to an unusual proposition. At last he interrupted the senior partner. "Just a moment! Do I understand that you are trying to *hire* me to marry one of these women?"

The lawyer looked shocked. "Please, Mr. Johnson. Not at all."

"Well, it certainly sounded like it."

"No, no, such a contract would be void, against public policy. We are simply informing you, as administrators of a trust, that should it come about that you *do* marry one of the young ladies on this list it would then be our pleasant duty to endow each child of such a union according to the scale here set forth. But there would be no contract with us involved, nor is there any 'proposition' being made to you—and we certainly do not urge any course of action on you. We are simply informing you of certain facts."

Ira Johnson scowled and shuffled his feet. "What's it all about? Why?"

"That is the business of the Foundation. One might put it that we approve of your grandparents."

"Have you discussed me with them?" Johnson said sharply. He felt no affection for his grandparents. A tight-fisted foursome—if any one of them had had the grace to die at a reasonable age he would not now be worried about money enough to finish medical school.

"We have talked with them, yes. But not about you."

The lawyer shut off further discussion and young Johnson accepted gracelessly a list of young women, all strangers, with the intention of tearing it up the moment he was outside the office. Instead, that night he wrote seven drafts before he found the right words in which to start cooling off the relation between himself and his girl back home. He was glad that he had never actually popped the question to her—it would have been deucedly awkward.

When he did marry (from the list) it seemed a curious but not too remarkable coincidence that his wife as well as himself had four living, healthy active grandparents.

"—an openly chartered non-profit corporation," Foote continued, "and its avowed purpose of encouraging births among persons of sound American stock was consonant with the customs of that century. By the simple expedient of being closemouthed about the true purpose of the Foundation no unusual methods of concealment were necessary until late in the period during the World Wars sometimes loosely termed 'The Crazy Years—'"

Selected headlines April to June 1969:

BABY BILL BREAKS BANK
2-year toddler youngest winner $1,000,000 TV
jackpot White House phones congrats

COURT ORDERS STATEHOUSE SOLD
Colorado Supreme Bench Rules State Old Age
Pension Has First Lien All State Property

N.Y. YOUTH MEET DEMANDS UPPER LIMIT
ON FRANCHISE

"U.S. BIRTH RATE 'TOP SECRET'"
—DEFENSE SEC

CAROLINA CONGRESSMAN
COPS BEAUTY CROWN
"Available for draft for President"
she announces while starting tour
to show her qualifications

IOWA RAISES VOTING AGE TO FORTY-ONE
Rioting on Des Moines Campus

EARTH-EATING FAD MOVES WEST: CHI-
CAGO PARSON EATS CLAY SANDWICH IN
PULPIT
"Back to simple things," he advises flock.

LOS ANGELES HI-SCHOOL MOB
DEFIES SCHOOL BOARD
"Higher pay, Shorter Hours, no Homework—
We Demand Our Right to Elect
Teachers, Coaches."

SUICIDE RATE UP NINTH SUCCESSIVE
YEAR
AEC Denies Fall-Out to Blame

"'—The Crazy Years.' The trustees of that date decided—correctly, we now believe—that any minority during that period of semantic disorientation and mass hysteria was a probable target for persecution, discriminatory legislation, and even of mob violence. Furthermore the disturbed financial condition of the country and in particular the forced exchange of trust securities for government warrants threatened the solvency of the trust.

"Two courses of action were adopted: the assets of the Foundation were converted into real wealth and distributed widely among members of the Families to be held by them as owners-of-record; and the so-called 'Masquerade' was adopted as a permanent policy. Means were found to simulate the death of any member of the Families who lived to a socially embarrassing age and to provide him with a new identity in another part of the country.

"The wisdom of this later policy, though irksome to some, became evident at once during the Interregnum of the Prophets. The Families at the beginning of the reign of the First Prophet had ninety-seven per cent of their members with publicly avowed ages of less than fifty years. The close public registration enforced by the secret police of the Prophets made changes of public identity difficult, although a few were accomplished with the aid of the revolutionary Cabal.

"Thus, a combination of luck and foresight saved our secret from public disclosure. This was well—we may be sure that things would have gone harshly at that time for any group possessing a prize beyond the power of the Prophet to confiscate.

"The Families took no part as such in the events leading up to the Second American Revolution, but many members participated and served with credit in the Cabal and in the fighting which preceded the fall of New Jerusalem. We took advantage of the period of disorganization which followed to readjust the ages of our kin who had grown conspicuously old. In this we were aided by certain members of the Families who, as members of the Cabal, held key posts in the Reconstruction.

"It was argued by many at the Families' meeting of 2075, the year of the Covenant, that we should reveal ourselves, since civil liberty was firmly re-established. The majority did not agree at that time . . . perhaps through long habits of secrecy and caution. But the renascence of culture in the ensuing fifty years, the steady growth of tolerance and good manners, the semantically sound orientation of education, the increased respect for the custom of privacy and for the dignity of the individual— all of these things led us to believe that the time had at last come when it was becoming safe to reveal ourselves and to take our rightful place as an odd but nonetheless respected minority in society.

"There were compelling reasons to do so. Increasing numbers of us were finding the 'Masquerade' socially intolerable in a new and better society. Not only was it upsetting to pull up roots and seek a new background every few years but also it grated to have to live a lie in a society where frank honesty and fair dealing were habitual with most people. Besides that, the Families as a group had learned many things through our researches in the bio-sciences, things which could be of great benefit to our poor short-lived brethren. We needed freedom to help them.

"These and similar reasons were subject to argument. But the resumption of the custom of positive physical identification made the 'Masquerade' almost untenable. Under the new orientation a sane and peaceful citizen welcomes positive identification under appropriate circumstances even though jealous of his right of privacy at all other times—so we dared not object; it would have aroused curiosity, marked us as an eccentric group, set apart, and thereby have defeated the whole purpose of the 'Masquerade.'

"We necessarily submitted to personal identification. By the time of the meeting of 2125, eleven years ago, it had become extremely difficult to counterfeit new identities for the ever-increasing number of us holding public ages incompatible with personal appearance; we decided on the experiment of letting volunteers from this group up to ten per cent of the total membership of the Families reveal themselves for what they were and observe the consequences, while maintaining all other secrets of the Families' organization.

"The results were regrettably different from our expectations."

Justin Foote stopped talking. The silence had gone on for several moments when a solidly built man of medium height spoke up. His hair was slightly grizzled—unusual in that group—and his face looked space tanned. Mary Sperling had noticed him and had wondered who he was—his live face and gusty laugh had interested her. But any member was free to attend the conclaves of the Families' council; she had thought no more of it.

He said, "Speak up, Bud. What's your report?"

Foote made his answer to the chair. "Our senior psychometrician should give the balance of the report. My remarks were prefatory."

"For the love o'—" the grizzled stranger exclaimed. "Bud, do you mean to stand there and admit that all you had to say were things we already knew?"

"My remarks were a foundation . . . and my name is Justin Foote, not 'Bud.'"

Mary Sperling broke in firmly. "Brother," she said to the stranger, "since you are addressing the Families, will you please name yourself? I am sorry to say that I do not recognize you."

"Sorry, Sister. Lazarus Long, speaking for myself."

Mary shook her head. "I still don't place you."

"Sorry again—that's a 'Masquerade' name I took at the time of the First Prophet . . . it tickled me. My Family name is Smith . . . Woodrow Wilson Smith."

"'Woodrow Wilson Sm—' *How old are you?*"

"Eh? Why, I haven't figured it lately. One hun . . . no, two hundred and—thirteen years. Yeah, that's right, two hundred and thirteen."

There was a sudden, complete silence. Then Mary said quietly, "Did you hear me inquire for anyone older than myself?"

"Yes. But shucks, Sister, you were doing all right. I ain't attended a meeting of the Families in over a century. Been some changes."

"I'll ask you to carry on from here." She started to leave the platform.

"Oh no!" he protested. But she paid no attention and found a seat. He looked around, shrugged and gave in. Sprawling one hip over a corner of the speaker's table he announced, "All right, let's get on with it. Who's next?"

Ralph Schultz of the Schultz Family looked more like a banker than a psychometrician. He was neither shy nor absent-minded and he had a flat, underemphasized way of talking that carried authority. "I was part of the group that proposed ending the 'Masquerade.' I was wrong. I believed that the great majority of our fellow citizens, reared under modern educational methods, could evaluate any data without excessive emotional disturbance. I anticipated that a few abnormal people would dislike us, even hate us; I even predicted that most people would envy us—everybody who enjoys life would like to live a long time. But I did not anticipate any serious trouble. Modern attitudes have done away with inter-racial friction; any who still harbor race prejudice are ashamed to voice it. I believed that our society was so tolerant that we could live peacefully and openly with the short-lived.

"I was wrong.

"The Negro hated and envied the white man as long as the white man enjoyed privileges forbidden the Negro by reason of color. This was a sane, normal reaction.

When discrimination was removed, the problem solved itself and cultural assimilation took place. There is a similar tendency on the part of the short-lived to envy the long-lived. We assumed that this expected reaction would be of no social importance in most people once it was made clear that we owe our peculiarity to our genes—no fault nor virtue of our own, just good luck in our ancestry.

"This was mere wishful thinking. By hindsight it is easy to see that correct application of mathematical analysis to the data would have given a different answer, would have spotlighted the false analogy. I do not defend the misjudgment, no defense is possible. We were led astray by our hopes.

"What actually happened was this: we showed our short-lived cousins the greatest boon it is possible for a man to imagine . . . then we told them it could never be theirs. This faced them with an unsolvable dilemma. They have rejected the unbearable facts, they refuse to believe us. Their envy now turns to hate, with an emotional conviction that we are depriving them of their rights . . . deliberately, maliciously.

"That rising hate has now swelled into a flood which threatens the welfare and even the lives of all our revealed brethren . . . and which is potentially as dangerous to the rest of us. The danger is very great and very pressing." He sat down abruptly.

They took it calmly, with the unhurried habit of years. Presently a female delegate stood up. "Eve Barstow, for the Cooper Family. Ralph Schultz, I am a hundred and nineteen years old, older, I believe, than you are. I do not have your talent for mathematics and human behavior but I have known a lot of people. Human beings are inherently good and gentle and kind. Oh, they have their weaknesses but most of them are decent enough if you give them half a chance. I cannot believe that they would hate me and destroy me simply because I have lived a long time. What have you to go on? You admit one mistake—why not two?"

Schultz looked at her soberly and smoothed his kilt. "You're right, Eve. I could easily be wrong again. That's the trouble with psychology: it is a subject so terribly complex, so many unknowns, such involved relationships, that our best efforts sometimes look silly in the bleak light of later facts." He stood up again, faced the others, and again spoke with flat authority. "But I am not making a long-range prediction this time; I am talking about facts, not guesses, not wishful thinking—and with those facts a prediction so short-range that it is like predicting that an egg will break when you see it already on its way to the floor. But Eve is right . . . as far as she went. Individuals are kind and decent . . . as individuals and to other individuals. Eve is in no danger from her neighbors and friends, and I am in no danger from mine. But she is in danger from *my* neighbors and friends—and I from hers. Mass psychology is not simply a summation of individual psychologies; that is a prime theorem of social psychodynamics—not just my opinion; no exception has ever been found to this theorem. It is the social mass-action rule, the mob-hysteria law, known and used by military, political, and religious leaders, by advertising men and prophets and propagandists, by rabble rousers and actors and gang leaders, for generations before it was formulated in mathematical symbols. It works. It is working now.

"My colleagues and I began to suspect that a mob-hysteria trend was building up against us several years ago. We did not bring our suspicions to the council for action because we could not prove anything. What we observed then could have been simply the mutterings of the crackpot minority present in even the healthiest society. The trend was at first so minor that we could not be sure it existed, for all social trends are intermixed with other social trends, snarled together like a plate of spaghetti—worse than that, for it takes an abstract topological space of many dimensions (ten or twelve are not uncommon and hardly adequate) to describe mathematically the interplay of social forces. I cannot overemphasize the complexity of the problem.

"So we waited and worried and tried statistical sampling, setting up our statistical universes with great care.

"By the time we were sure, it was almost too late. Sociopsychological trends grow or die by a 'yeast growth' law, a complex power law. We continued to hope that other favorable factors would reverse the trend—Nelson's work in symbiotics, our own contributions to geriatrics, the great public interest in the opening of the Jovian satellites to immigration. Any major break-through offering longer life and greater hope to the short-lived could end the smouldering resentment against us.

"Instead the smouldering has burst into flame, into an uncontrolled forest fire. As nearly as we can measure it, the rate has doubled in the past thirty-seven days and the rate itself is accelerated. I can't guess how far or how fast it will go—and that's why we asked for the emergency session. Because we can expect trouble at any moment." He sat down hard, looking tired.

Eve did not argue with him again and no one else argued with him at all; not only was Ralph Schultz considered expert in his own field but also every one of them each from his own viewpoint, had seen the grosser aspects of the trend building up against their revealed kin. But, while the acceptance of the problem was unanimous, there were as many opinions about what to do about it as there were people present. Lazarus let the discussion muddle along for two hours before he held up a hand. "We aren't getting anywhere," he stated, "and it looks like we won't get anywhere tonight. Let's take an over-all look at it, hitting just the high spots:

"We can—" He started ticking plans off on his fingers—"do nothing, sit tight, and see what happens.

"We can junk the 'Masquerade' entirely, reveal our full numbers, and demand our rights politically.

"We can sit tight on the surface and use our organization and money to protect our revealed brethren, maybe haul 'em back into the 'Masquerade.'

"We can reveal ourselves and ask for a place to colonize where we can live by ourselves.

"Or we can do something else. I suggest that you sort yourselves out according to those four major points of view—say in the corners of the room, starting clockwise in that far right hand corner—each group hammer out a plan and get it ready to submit to the Families. And those of you who don't favor any of those four things gather in the middle of the room and start scrappin' over just what it is you do think. Now, if I hear no objection, I am going to declare this lodge recessed until midnight tomorrow night. How about it?"

No one spoke up. Lazarus Long's streamlined version of parliamentary procedure had them somewhat startled; they were used to long, leisurely discussions until it became evident that one point of view had become unanimous. Doing things in a hurry was slightly shocking.

But the man's personality was powerful, his years gave him prestige, and his slightly archaic way of speaking added to his patriarchal authority; nobody argued.

"Okay," Lazarus announced, clapping his hands once. "Church is out until tomorrow night." He stepped down from the platform.

Mary Sperling came up to him. "I would like to know you better," she said, looking him in the eyes.

"Sure, Sis. Why not?"

"Are you staying for discussion?"

"No."

"Could you come home with me?"

"Like to. I've no pressing business elsewhere."

"Come then." She led him through the tunnel to the underground pool connecting with Lake Michigan. He widened his eyes at the pseudo-Camden but said nothing until they were submerged.

"Nice little car you've got."

"Yes."

"Has some unusual features."

She smiled. "Yes. Among other things, it blows up—quite thoroughly—if anyone tries to investigate it."

"Good." He added, "You a designing engineer, Mary?"

"Me? Heavens, no! Not this past century, at least, and I no longer try to keep up with such things. But you can order a car modified the way this one is through the Families, if you want one. Talk to—"

"Never mind, I've no need for one. I just like gadgets that do what they were designed to do and do it quietly and efficiently. Some good skull sweat in this one."

"Yes." She was busy then, surfacing, making a radar check, and getting them back ashore without attracting notice.

When they reached her apartment she put tobacco and drink close to him, then went to her retiring room, threw off her street clothes and put on a soft loose robe that made her look even smaller and younger than she had looked before. When she rejoined Lazarus, he stood up, struck a cigarette for her, then paused as he handed it to her and gave a gallant and indelicate whistle.

She smiled briefly, took the cigarette, and sat down in a large chair, pulling her feet under her. "Lazarus, you reassure me."

"Don't you own a mirror, girl?"

"Not that," she said impatiently. "You yourself. You know that I have passed the reasonable life expectancy of our people—I've been expecting to die, been resigned to it, for the past ten years. Yet there you sit . . . years and *years* older than I am. You give me hope."

He sat up straight. "*You* expecting to die? Good grief, girl—you look good for another century."

She made a tired gesture. "Don't try to jolly me. You know that appearance has nothing to do with it. Lazarus, I don't *want* to die!"

Lazarus answered soberly, "I wasn't trying to kid you, Sis. You simply don't look like a candidate for corpse."

She shrugged gracefully. "A matter of biotechniques. I'm holding appearance at the early thirties."

"Or less, I'd say. I guess I'm not up on the latest dodges, Mary. You heard me say that I had not attended a get-together for more than a century. As a matter of fact I've been completely out of touch with the Families the whole time."

"Really? May I ask why?"

"A long story and a dull one. What it amounts to is that I got bored with them. I used to be a delegate to the annual meetings. But they got stuffy and set in their ways—or so it seemed to me. So I wandered off. I spent the Interregnum on Venus, mostly. I came back for a while after the Covenant was signed but I don't suppose I've spent two years on Earth since then. I like to move around."

Her eyes lit up. "Oh, tell me about it! I've never been out in deep space. Just Luna City, once."

"Sure," he agreed. "Sometime. But I want to hear more about this matter of your appearance. Girl, you sure don't look your age."

"I suppose not. Or, rather, of course I don't. As to how it's done, I can't tell you much. Hormones and symbiotics and gland therapy and some psychotherapy—things like that. What it adds up to is that, for members of the Families, senility is postponed and that senescence can be arrested at least cosmetically." She brooded for a moment. "Once they thought they were on the track of the secret of immortality, the true fountain of youth. But it was a mistake. Senility is simply postponed . . . and shortened. About ninety days from the first clear warning—then death from old age." She shivered. "Of course, most of our cousins don't wait—a couple of weeks to make certain of the diagnosis, then euthanasia."

"The hell you say! Well, *I* won't go that way. When the Old Boy comes to get *me*, he'll have to drag me—

and I'll be kicking and gouging eyes every step of the way!"

She smiled lopsidedly. "It does me good to hear you talk that way. Lazarus, I wouldn't let my guard down this way with anyone younger than myself. But your example gives me courage."

"We'll outlast the lot of 'em, Mary, never you fear. But about the meeting tonight: I haven't paid any attention to the news and I've only recently come earthside—does the chap Ralph Schultz know what he is talking about?"

"I think he must. His grandfather was a brilliant man and so is his father."

"I take it you know Ralph."

"Slightly. He is one of my grandchildren."

"That's amusing. He looks older than you do."

"Ralph found it suited him to arrest his appearance at about forty, that's all. His father was my twenty-seventh child. Ralph must be—let me see—oh, eighty or ninety years younger than I am, at least. At that, he is older than some of my children."

"You've done well by the Families, Mary."

"I suppose so. But they've done well by me, too. I've enjoyed having children and the trust benefits for my thirty-odd come to quite a lot. I have every luxury one could want." She shivered again. "I suppose that's why I'm in such a funk—I enjoy life."

"Stop it! I thought my sterling example and boyish grin had cured you of that nonsense."

"Well . . . you've helped."

"Mmm . . . look, Mary, why don't you marry again and have some more squally brats? Keep you too busy to fret."

"What? At my age? Now, really, Lazarus!"

"Nothing wrong with your age. You're younger than I am."

She studied him for a moment. "Lazarus, are you proposing a contract? If so, I wish you would speak more plainly."

His mouth opened and he gulped. "Hey, wait a minute! Take it easy! I was speaking in general terms . . . I'm not the domestic type. Why, every time I've married my wife has grown sick of the sight of me inside of a few years. Not but what I—well, I mean you're a very pretty girl and a man ought to—"

She shut him off by leaning forward and putting a hand over his mouth, while grinning impishly. "I didn't mean to panic you, cousin. Or perhaps I did—men are so funny when they think they are about to be trapped."

"Well—" he said glumly.

"Forget it, dear. Tell me, what plan do you think they will settle on?"

"That bunch tonight?"

"Yes."

"None, of course. They won't get anywhere. Mary, a committee is the only known form of life with a hundred bellies and no brain. But presently somebody with a mind of his own will bulldoze them into accepting his plan. I don't know what it will be."

"Well . . . what course of action do *you* favor?"

"Me? Why, none. Mary, if there is any one thing I have learned in the past couple of centuries, it's this: These things *pass*. Wars and depressions and Prophets and Covenants—they pass. The trick is to stay alive through them."

She nodded thoughtfully: "I think you are right."

"Sure I'm right. It takes a hundred years or so to realize just how good life is." He stood up and stretched. "But right now this growing boy could use some sleep."

"Me, too."

Mary's flat was on the top floor, with a sky view. When she had come back to the lounge she had cut the inside lighting and let the ceiling shutters fold back; they had been sitting, save for an invisible sheet of plastic, under the stars. As Lazarus raised his head in stretching, his eye had rested on his favorite constellation. "Odd," he commented. "Orion seems to have added a fourth star to his belt."

She looked up. "That must be the big ship for the Second Centauri Expedition. See if you can see it move."

"Couldn't tell without instruments."

"I suppose not," she agreed. "Clever of them to build it out in space, isn't it?"

"No other way to do it. It's too big to assemble on Earth. I can doss down right here, Mary. Or do you have a spare room?"

"Your room is the second door on the right. Shout if you can't find everything you need." She put her face up and kissed him goodnight, a quick peck. "'Night."

Lazarus followed her and went into his own room.

Mary Sperling woke at her usual hour the next day. She got up quietly to keep from waking Lazarus, ducked into her 'fresher, showered and massaged, swallowed a grain of sleep surrogate to make up for the short night, followed it almost as quickly with all the breakfast she permitted her waistline, then punched for the calls she had not bothered to take the night before. The phone played back several calls which she promptly forgot, then she recognized the voice of Bork Vanning. "'Hello,'" the instrument said. "'Mary, this is Bork, calling at twenty-one o'clock. I'll be by at ten o'clock tomorrow morning, for a dip in the lake and lunch somewhere. Unless I hear from you it's a date. 'Bye, my dear. Service.'"

"Service," she repeated automatically. Drat the man! Couldn't he take no for an answer? Mary Sperling, you're slipping!—a quarter your age and yet you can't seem to handle him.

Call him and leave word that—no, too late; he'd be here any minute. Bother!

❖   ❖   ❖

2

When Lazarus went to bed he stepped out of his kilt and chucked it toward a wardrobe . . . which snagged it, shook it out, and hung it up neatly. "Nice catch," he commented, then glanced down at his hairy thighs and smiled wryly, the kilt had concealed a blaster strapped to one thigh, a knife to the other. He was aware of the present gentle custom against personal weapons, but he felt naked without them. Such customs were nonsense anyhow, foolishness from old women—there was no such thing as a "dangerous weapon," there were only dangerous men.

When he came out of the 'fresher, he put his weapons where he could reach them before sprawling in sleep.

He came instantly wide awake with a weapon in each hand . . . then remembered where he was, relaxed, and looked around to see what had wakened him.

It was a murmur of voices through the air duct. Poor soundproofing, he decided, and Mary must be entertaining callers—in which case he should not be slug-a-bed. He got up, refreshed himself, strapped his best friends back on his thighs, and went looking for his hostess.

As the door to the lounge dilated noiselessly in front of him the sound of voices became loud and very interesting. The lounge was el-shaped and he was out of sight; he hung back and listened shamelessly. Eavesdropping had saved his skin on several occasions; it worried him not at all—he enjoyed it.

A man was saying, "Mary you're completely unreasonable! You know you're fond of me, you admit that marriage to me would be to your advantage. So why *won't* you?"

"I told you, Bork. Age difference."

"That's foolish. What do you expect? Adolescent romance? Oh, I admit that I'm not as young as you are . . . but a woman needs an older man to look up to and keep her steady. I'm not too old for you; I'm just at my prime."

Lazarus decided that he already knew this chap well enough to dislike him. Sulky voice—

Mary did not answer. The man went on: "Anyhow, I have a surprise for you on that point. I wish I could tell you now, but . . . well, it's a state secret."

"Then don't tell me. It can't change my mind in any case, Bork."

"Oh, but it would! Mmm . . . I *will* tell you—I know *you* can be trusted."

"Now, Bork, you shouldn't assume that—"

"It doesn't matter; it will be public knowledge in a few days anyhow. Mary . . . *I'll never grow old on you!*"

"What do you mean?" Lazarus decided that her tone was suddenly suspicious.

"Just what I said. Mary, they've found the secret of eternal youth!"

"*What?* Who? How? When?"

"Oh, so now you're interested, eh? Well, I won't keep you waiting. You know these old Johnnies that call themselves the Howard Families?"

"Yes . . . I've heard of them, of course," she admitted slowly. "But what of it? They're fakes."

"Not at all. I *know*. The Administration has been quietly investigating their claims. Some of them are unquestionably more than a hundred years old—and *still young!*"

"That's very hard to believe."

"Nevertheless it's true."

"Well . . . how do they do it?"

"Ah! That's the point. They claim that it is a simple matter of heredity, that they live a long time because they come from long lived stock. But that's preposterous, scientifically incompatible with the established facts. The Administration checked most carefully and the answer is certain: they have the secret of staying young."

"You can't be sure of that."

"Oh, come, Mary! You're a dear girl but you're questioning the expert opinion of the best scientific brains in the world. Never mind. Here's the part that is confidential. We don't have their secret yet—but we will have it shortly. Without any excitement or public notice, they are to be picked up and questioned. We'll get the secret—and you and I will never grow old! What do you think of *that?* Eh?"

Mary answered very slowly, almost inaudibly, "It would be nice if everyone could live a long time."

"Huh? Yes, I suppose it would. But in any case you and I will receive the treatment, whatever it is. Think about *us,* dear. Year after year after year of happy, youthful marriage. Not less than a century. Maybe even—"

"Wait a moment, Bork. This 'secret.' It wouldn't be for everybody?"

"Well now . . . that's a matter of high policy. Population pressure is a pretty unwieldy problem even now. In practice it might be necessary to restrict it to essential personnel—and their wives. But don't fret your lovely head about it; you and I will have it."

"You mean I'll have it *if* I marry you."

"Mmm . . . that's a nasty way to put it, Mary. I'd do anything in the world for you that I could—because I *love* you. But it would be utterly simple if you were married to me. So say you will."

"Let's let that be for the moment. How do you propose to get this 'secret' out of them?"

Lazarus could almost hear his wise nod. "Oh, they'll talk!"

"Do you mean to say you'd send them to Coventry if they didn't?"

"Coventry? Hm! You don't understand the situation at all, Mary; this isn't any minor social offense. This is *treason*—treason against the whole human race. We'll use means! Ways that the Prophets used . . . if they don't cooperate willingly."

"Do you mean that? Why, that's against the Covenant!"

"Covenant be damned! This is a matter of life and death—do you think we'd let a scrap of paper stand in our way? You can't bother with petty legalities in the fundamental things men live by—not something they will fight to the death for. And that is precisely what this is. These . . . these dog-in-the-manger scoundrels are trying to keep life itself from us. Do you think we'll bow to 'custom' in an emergency like this?"

Mary answered in a hushed and horrified voice: "Do you really think the Council will violate the Covenant?"

"*Think* so? The Action-in-Council was recorded last night. We authorized the Administrator to use 'full expediency.'"

Lazarus strained his ears through a long silence. At last Mary spoke. "Bork—"

"Yes, my dear?"

"You've got to do something about this. You must stop it."

"Stop it? You don't know what you're saying. I couldn't . . . and I would not if I could."

"But you *must*. You must convince the Council. They're making a mistake, a tragic mistake. There is nothing to be gained by trying to coerce those poor people. *There is no secret!*"

"What? You're getting excited, my dear. You're setting your judgment up against some of the best and wisest men on the planet. Believe me, we know what we are doing. We don't relish using harsh methods any more than you do, but it's for the general welfare. Look, I'm sorry I ever brought it up. Naturally you are soft and gentle and warmhearted and I love you for it. Why not marry me and not bother your head about matters of public policy?"

"Marry *you?* Never!"

"Aw, Mary—you're upset. Give me just one good reason why not?"

"I'll tell you why! Because I am one of those people you want to persecute!"

There was another pause. "Mary . . . you're not well."

"Not well, am I? I am as well as a person can be at my age. Listen to me, you fool! I have grandsons twice your age. I was here when the First Prophet took over the country. I was here when Harriman launched the first Moon rocket. You weren't even a squalling brat—your *grandparents* hadn't even met, when I was a woman grown and married. And you stand there and glibly propose to push around, even to torture, me and my kind. Marry *you?* I'd rather marry one of my own grandchildren!"

Lazarus shifted his weight and slid his right hand inside the flap of his kilt; he expected trouble at once. You can depend on a woman, he reflected, to blow her top at the wrong moment.

He waited. Bork's answer was cool; the tones of the experienced man of authority replaced those of thwarted passion. "Take it easy, Mary. Sit down, I'll look after you. First I want you to take a sedative. Then I'll get the best psychotherapist in the city—in the whole country. You'll be all right."

"Take your hands off me!"

"Now, Mary . . ."

Lazarus stepped out into the room and pointed at Vanning with his blaster. "This monkey giving you trouble, Sis?"

Vanning jerked his head around. "Who are you?" he demanded indignantly. "What are you doing here?"

Lazarus still addressed Mary. "Say the word, Sis, and I'll cut him into pieces small enough to hide."

"No, Lazarus," she answered with her voice now under control. "Thanks just the same. Please put your gun away. I wouldn't want anything like that to happen."

"Okay." Lazarus holstered the gun but let his hand rest on the grip.

"Who are you?" repeated Vanning. "What's the meaning of this intrusion?"

"I was just about to ask you that, Bud," Lazarus said mildly, "but we'll let it ride. I'm another one of those old Johnnies you're looking for . . . like Mary here."

Vanning looked at him keenly. "I wonder—" he said. He looked back at Mary. "It can't be, it's preposterous. Still . . . it won't hurt to investigate your story. I've plenty to detain you on, in any event, I've never seen a clearer case of anti-social atavism." He moved toward the videophone.

"Better get away from that phone, Bud," Lazarus said quickly, then added to Mary, "I won't touch my gun, Sis. I'll use my knife."

Vanning stopped. "Very well," he said in annoyed tones, "put away that vibroblade. I won't call from here."

"Look again, it ain't a vibroblade. It's steel. Messy."

Vanning turned to Mary Sperling. "I'm leaving. If you are wise, you'll come with me." She shook her head. He looked annoyed, shrugged, and faced Lazarus Long. "As for you, sir, your primitive manners have led you into serious trouble. You will be arrested shortly."

Lazarus glanced up at the ceiling shutters. "Reminds me of a patron in Venusburg who wanted to have me arrested."

"Well?"

"I've outlived him quite a piece."

Vanning opened his mouth to answer—then turned suddenly and left so quickly that the outer door barely had time to clear the end of his nose. As the door snapped closed Lazarus said musingly, "Hardest man to reason with I've met in years. I'll bet he never used an unsterilized spoon in his life."

Mary looked startled, then giggled. He turned toward her. "Glad to see you sounding perky, Mary. Kinda thought you were upset."

"I was. I hadn't known you were listening. I was forced to improvise as I went along."

"Did I queer it?"

"No. I'm glad you came in—thanks. But we'll have to hurry now."

"I suppose so. I think he meant it—there'll be a proctor looking for me soon. You, too, maybe."

"That's what I meant. So let's get out of here."

Mary was ready to leave in scant minutes but when they stepped out into the public hall they met a man whose brassard and hypo kit marked him as a proctor. "Service," he said. "I'm looking for a citizen in company with Citizen Mary Sperling. Could you direct me?"

"Sure," agreed Lazarus. "She lives right down there." He pointed at the far end of the corridor. As the peace officer looked in that direction, Lazarus tapped him carefully on the back of the head, a little to the left, with the butt of his blaster, and caught him as he slumped.

Mary helped Lazarus wrestle the awkward mass into her apartment. He knelt over the cop, pawed through his hypo kit, took a loaded injector and gave him a shot. "There," he said, "that'll keep him sleepy for a few hours." Then he blinked thoughtfully at the hypo kit, detached it from the proctor's belt. "This might come in handy again. Anyhow, it won't hurt to take it." As an afterthought he removed the proctor's peace brassard and placed it, too, in his pouch.

They left the apartment again and dropped to the parking level. Lazarus noticed as they rolled up the ramp that Mary had set the North Shore combination. "Where are we going?" he asked.

"The Families' Seat. No place else to go where we won't be checked on. But we'll have to hide somewhere in the country until dark."

Once the car was on beamed control headed north Mary asked to be excused and caught a few minutes sleep. Lazarus watched a few miles of scenery, then nodded himself.

They were awakened by the jangle of the emergency alarm and by the speedster slowing to a stop. Mary reached up and shut off the alarm. "All cars resume local control," intoned a voice. "Proceed at speed twenty to the nearest traffic control tower for inspection. All cars resume local control. Proceed at—"

She switched that off, too. "Well, that's us," Lazarus said cheerfully. "Got any ideas?"

Mary did not answer. She peered out and studied their surroundings. The steel fence separating the high-speed control way they were on from the uncontrolled local-traffic strip lay about fifty yards to their right but no changeover ramp broke the fence for at least a mile ahead—where it did, there would be, of course, the control tower where they were ordered to undergo inspection. She started the car again, operating it manually, and wove through stopped or slowly moving traffic while speeding up. As they got close to the barrier Lazarus felt himself shoved into the cushions; the car surged and lifted, clearing the barrier by inches. She set it down rolling on the far side.

A car was approaching from the north and they were slashing across his lane. The other car was moving no more than ninety but its driver was taken by surprise—he had no reason to expect another car to appear out of nowhere against him on a clear road. Mary was forced to duck left, then right, and left again; the car slewed and reared up on its hind wheel, writhing against the steel grip of its gyros. Mary fought it back into control to the accompaniment of a teeth-shivering grind of Herculean against glass as the rear wheel fought for traction.

Lazarus let his jaw muscles relax and breathed out gustily. "*Whew!*" he sighed. "I hope we won't have to do *that* again."

Mary glanced at him, grinning. "Women drivers make you nervous?"

"Oh, no, no, not at all! I just wish you would warn me when something like that is about to happen."

"I didn't know myself," she admitted, then went on worriedly, "I don't know quite what to do now. I thought we could lie quiet out of town until dark . . . but I had to show my hand a little when I took that fence. By now somebody will be reporting to the tower. Mmm. . . ."

"Why wait until dark?" he asked. "Why not just bounce over to the lake in this Dick Dare contraption of yours and let it swim us home?"

"I don't like to," she fretted. "I've attracted too much attention already. A trimobile faked up to look like a goundster is handy, but . . . well, if anyone sees us taking it under water and the proctors hear of it, somebody is going to guess the answer. Then they'll start fishing—everything from seismo to sonar and Heaven knows what else."

"But isn't the Seat shielded?"

"Of course. But anything that big they can find—if they know what they're looking for and keep looking."

"You're right, of course," Lazarus admitted slowly. "Well, we certainly don't want to lead any nosy proctors to the Families' Seat. Mary, I think we had better ditch your car and get lost." He frowned. "Anywhere but the Seat."

"No, it has to be the Seat," she answered sharply.

"Why? If you chase a fox, he—"

"Quiet a moment! I want to try something." Lazarus shut up; Mary drove with one hand while she fumbled in the glove compartment.

"Answer," a voice said.

"Life is short—" Mary replied.

They completed the formula. "Listen," Mary went on hurriedly, "I'm in trouble—get a fix on me."

"Okay."

"Is there a sub in the pool?"

"Yes."

"Good! Lock on me and home them in." She explained hurriedly the details of what she wanted, stopping once to ask Lazarus if he could swim. "That's all," she said at last, "but move! We're short on minutes."

"Hold it, Mary!" the voice protested. "You know I can't send a sub out in the daytime, certainly not on a calm day. It's too easy to—"

"Will you, or won't you!"

A third voice cut in. "I was listening, Mary—Ira Barstow. We'll pick you up."

"But—" objected the first voice.

"Stow it, Tommy. Just mind your burners and home me in. See you, Mary."

"Right, Ira!"

While she had been talking to the Seat, Mary had turned off from the local-traffic strip into the unpaved road she had followed the night before, without slowing and apparently without looking. Lazarus gritted his teeth and hung on. They passed a weathered sign reading CONTAMINATED AREA—PROCEED AT YOUR OWN RISK and graced with the conventional purple trefoil. Lazarus blinked at it and shrugged—he could not see how, at the moment, his hazard could be increased by a neutron or so.

Mary slammed the car to a stop in a clump of stunted trees near the abandoned road. The lake lay at their feet, just beyond a low bluff. She unfastened her safety belt, struck a cigarette, and relaxed. "Now we wait. It'll take at least half an hour for them to reach us no matter how hard Ira herds it. Lazarus, do you think we were seen turning off into here?"

"To tell the truth, Mary, I was too busy to look."

"Well . . . nobody ever comes here, except a few reckless boys."

("—and girls," Lazarus added to himself.) Then he went on aloud, "I noted a 'hot' sign back there. How high is the count?"

"That? Oh, pooh. Nothing to worry about unless you decided to build a house here. We're the ones who are hot. If we didn't have to stay close to the communicator, we—"

The communicator spoke. "Okay, Mary. Right in front of you."

She looked startled. "Ira?"

"This is Ira speaking but I'm still at the Seat. Pete Hardy was available in the Evanston pen, so we homed him in on you. Quicker."

"Okay—thanks!" She was turning to speak to Lazarus when he touched her arm.

"Look behind us."

A helicopter was touching down less than a hundred yards from them. Three men burst out of it. They were dressed as proctors.

Mary jerked open the door of the car and threw off her gown in one unbroken motion. She turned and called, "Come on!" as she thrust a hand back inside and tore a stud loose from the instrument panel. She ran.

Lazarus unzipped the belt of his kilt and ran out of it as he followed her to the bluff. She went dancing down it; he came after with slightly more caution, swearing at sharp stones. The blast shook them as the car exploded, but the bluff saved them.

They hit the water together.

The lock in the little submarine was barely big enough for one at a time; Lazarus shoved Mary into it first and tried to slap her when she resisted, and discovered that slapping will not work under water. Then he spent an endless time, or so it seemed, wondering whether or not he could breathe water. "What's a fish got that I ain't got?" he was telling himself, when the outer latch moved under his hand and he was able to wiggle in.

Eleven dragging seconds to blow the lock clear of water and he had a chance to see what damage, if any, the water had done to his blaster.

Mary was speaking urgently to the skipper. "Listen, Pete—there are three proctors back up there with a whirly. My car blew up in their faces just as we hit the water. But if they aren't all dead or injured, there will be a smart boy who will figure out that there was only one place for us to go—under water. We've got to be away from here before they take to the air to look for us."

"It's a losing race," Pete Hardy complained slapping his controls as he spoke. "Even if it's only a visual search, I'll have to get outside and stay outside the circle of total reflection faster than he can gain altitude—and I can't." But the little sub lunged forward reassuringly.

Mary worried about whether or not to call the Seat from the sub. She decided not to; it would just increase the hazard both to the sub and to the Seat itself. So she calmed herself and waited, huddled small in a passenger seat too cramped for two. Peter Hardy swung wide into deep water, hugging the bottom, picking up the Muskegon-Gary bottom beacons and conned himself in blind.

By the time they surfaced in the pool inside the Seat she had decided against any physical means of communication, even the carefully shielded equipment at the Seat. Instead she hoped to find a telepathic sensitive ready and available among the Families' dependents cared for there. Sensitives were as scarce among healthy members of the Howard Families as they were in the rest of the population, but the very inbreeding which had conserved and reinforced the abnormal longevity had also conserved and reinforced bad genes as well as good; they had an unusually high percentage of physical and mental defectives. Their board of genetic control plugged away at the problem of getting rid of bad strains while conserving the longevity strain, but for many generations they would continue to pay for their long lives with an excess of defectives.

But almost five percent of these defectives were telepathically sensitive.

Mary went straight to the sanctuary in the Seat where some of these dependents were cared for, with Lazarus

Long at her heels. She braced the matron. "Where's Little Stephen? I need him."

"Keep your voice down," the matron scolded. "Rest hour—you can't."

"Janice, I've got to see him," Mary insisted. "This won't wait. I've got to get a message out to all the Families—at once."

The matron planted her hands on her hips. "Take it to the communication office. You can't come here disturbing my children at all hours. I won't have it."

"Janice, please! I don't dare use anything but telepathy. You know I wouldn't do this unnecessarily. Now take me to Stephen."

"It wouldn't do you any good if I did. Little Stephen has had one of his bad spells today."

"Then take me to the strongest sensitive who can possibly work. Quickly, Janice! The safety of every member may depend on it."

"Did the trustees send you?"

"No, no! There wasn't time!"

The matron still looked doubtful. While Lazarus was trying to recall how long it had been since he had socked a lady, she gave in. "All right—you can see Billy, though I shouldn't let you. Mind you, don't tire him out." Still bristling, she led them along a corridor past a series of cheerful rooms and into one of them. Lazarus looked at the thing on the bed and looked away.

The matron went to a cupboard and returned with a hypodermic injector. "Does he work under a hypnotic?" Lazarus asked.

"No," the matron answered coldly, "he has to have a stimulant to be aware of us at all." She swabbed skin on the arm of the gross figure and made the injection. "Go ahead," she said to Mary and lapsed into grim-mouthed silence.

The figure on the bed stirred, its eyes rolled loosely, then seemed to track. It grinned. "Aunt Mary!" it said. "Oooh! Did you bring Billy Boy something?"

"No," she said gently. "Not this time, hon. Aunt Mary was in too much of a hurry. Next time? A surprise? Will that do?"

"All right," it said docilely.

"That's a good boy." She reached out and tousled its hair; Lazarus looked away again. "Now will Billy Boy do something for Aunt Mary? A big, *big* favor?"

"Sure."

"Can you hear your friends?"

"Oh, sure."

"All of them?"

"Uh huh. Mostly they don't say anything," it added.

"Call to them."

There was a very short silence. "They heard me."

"Fine! Now listen carefully, Billy Boy: All the Families—urgent warning! Elder Mary Sperling speaking. Under an Action-in-Council the Administrator is about to arrest every revealed member. The Council directed him to use 'full expedience'—and it is my sober judgment that they are determined to use any means at all, regardless of the Covenant, to try to squeeze out of us the so-called secret of our long lives. They even intend to use the tortures developed by the inquisitors of the Prophets!" Her voice broke. She stopped and pulled herself together. "Now get busy! Find them, warn them, hide them! You may have only minutes left to save them!"

Lazarus touched her arm and whispered; she nodded and went on:

"If any cousin is arrested, rescue him *by any means at all!* Don't try to appeal to the Covenant, don't waste time arguing about justice . . . rescue him! Now *move!*"

She stopped and then spoke in a tired, gentle voice, "Did they hear us, Billy Boy?"

"Sure."

"Are they telling their folks?"

"Uh huh. All but Jimmie-the-Horse. He's mad at me," it added confidentially.

" 'Jimmie-the-Horse'? Where is he?"

"Oh, where he lives."

"In Montreal," put in the matron. "There are two other sensitives there, your message got through. Are you finished?"

"Yes . . ." Mary said doubtfully. "But perhaps we had better have some other Seat relay it back."

"No!"

"But, Janice—"

"I won't permit it. I suppose you had to send it but I want to give Billy the antidote now. So get out."

Lazarus took her arm. "Come on, kid. It either got through or it didn't; you've done your best. A good job, girl."

Mary went on to make a full report to the Resident Secretary; Lazarus left her on business of his own. He retraced his steps, looking for a man who was not too busy to help him; the guards at the pool entrance were the first he found. "Service—" he began.

"Service to you," one of them answered. "Looking for someone?" He glanced curiously at Long's almost complete nakedness, glanced away again—how anybody dressed or did not dress, was a private matter.

"Sort of," admitted Lazarus. "Say, Bud, do you know of anyone around here who would lend me a kilt?"

"You're looking at one," the guard answered pleasantly. "Take over, Dick—back in a minute." He led Lazarus to bachelors' quarters, outfitted him, helped him to dry his pouch and contents, and made no comment about the arsenal strapped to his hairy thighs. How elders behaved was no business of his and many of them were even touchier about their privacy than most people. He had seen Aunt Mary Sperling arrive stripped for swimming but had not been surprised as he had heard Ira Barstow briefing Pete for the underwater pickup; that the elder with her chose to take a dip in the lake weighed down by hardware did surprise him but not enough to make him forget his manners.

"Anything else you need?" he asked. "Do those shoes fit?"

"Well enough. Thanks a lot, Bud." Lazarus smoothed the borrowed kilt. It was a little too long for him but it comforted him. A loin strap was okay, he supposed—if you were on Venus. But he had never cared much for Venus customs. Damn it, a man liked to be *dressed*. "I feel better," he admitted. "Thanks again. By the way, what's your name?"

"Edmund Hardy, of the Foote Family."

"That so? What's your line?"

"Charles Hardy and Evelyn Foote. Edward Hardy-Alice Johnson and Terence Briggs-Eleanor Weatheral. Oliver—"

"That's enough. I sorta thought so. You're one of my great-great-grandsons.

"Why, that's interesting," commented Hardy agreeably. "Gives us a sixteenth of kinship, doesn't it—not counting convergence. May I ask your name?"

"Lazarus Long."

Hardy shook his head. "Some mistake. Not in my line."

"Try Woodrow Wilson Smith instead. It was the one I started with."

"Oh, that one! Yes, surely. But I thought you were . . . uh—"

"Dead? Well, I ain't."

"Oh, I didn't mean that at all," Hardy protested, blushing at the blunt Anglo-Saxon monosyllable. He hastily added, "I'm glad to have run across you, Gran'ther. I've always wanted to hear the straight of the story about the Families' Meeting in 2012."

"That was before you were born, Ed," Lazarus said gruffly, "and don't call me 'Gran'ther.'"

"Sorry, sir—I mean 'Sorry, Lazarus.' Is there any other service I can do for you?"

"I shouldn't have gotten shirty. No—yes, there is, too. Where can I swipe a bite of breakfast? I was sort of rushed this morning."

"Certainly." Hardy took him to the bachelors' pantry, operated the autochef for him, drew coffee for his watch mate and himself, and left. Lazarus consumed his "bite of breakfast"—about three thousand calories of sizzling sausages, eggs, jam, hot breads, coffee with cream, and ancillary items, for he worked on the assumption of always topping off his reserve tanks because you never knew how far you might have to lift before you had another chance to refuel. In due time he sat back, belched, gathered up his dishes and shoved them into the incinerator, then went looking for a newsbox.

He found one in the bachelors' library, off their lounge. The room was empty save for one man who seemed to be about the same age as that suggested by Lazarus' appearance. There the resemblance stopped; the stranger was slender, mild in feature, and was topped off by finespun carroty hair quite unlike the grizzled wiry bush topping Lazarus. The stranger was bending over the news receiver with his eyes pressed to the microviewer.

Lazarus cleared his throat loudly and said, "Howdy."

The man jerked his head up and exclaimed, "Oh! Sorry—I was startled. Do y' a service?"

"I was looking for the news box. Mind if we throw it on the screen?"

"Not at all." The smaller man stood up, pressed the rewind button, and set the controls for projection. "Any particular subject?"

"I wanted to see," said Lazarus, "if there was any news about us—the Families."

"I've been watching for that myself. Perhaps we had better use the sound track and let it hunt."

"Okay," agreed Lazarus, stepping up and changing the setting to audio. "What's the code word?"

"'Methuselah.'"

Lazarus punched in the setting; the machine chattered and whined as it scanned and rejected the track speeding through it, then it slowed with a triumphant click. "The DAILY DATA," it announced. "The only midwest news service subscribing to every major grid. Leased videochannel to Luna City. Tri-S correspondents throughout the System. First, Fast, and Most! Lincoln, Nebraska—Savant Denounces Oldsters! Dr. Witwell Oscarsen, President Emeritus of Bryan Lyceum, calls for official reconsideration of the status of the kin group styling themselves the 'Howard Families.' 'It is proved,' he says, 'that these people have solved the age-old problem of extending, perhaps indefinitely, the span of human life. For that they are to be commended; it is a worthy and potentially fruitful research. But their claim that their solution is no more than hereditary predisposition defies both science and common sense. Our modern knowledge of the established laws of genetics enables us to deduce with certainty that they are withholding from the public some secret technique or techniques whereby they accomplish their results.

"'It is contrary to our customs to permit scientific knowledge to be held as a monopoly for the few. When concealing such knowledge strikes at life itself the action becomes treason to the race. As a citizen, I call on the Administration to act forcefully in this matter and I remind them that the situation is not one which could possibly have been foreseen by the wise men who drew up the Covenant and codified our basic customs. Any custom is man-made and is therefore a finite attempt to describe any infinity of relationships. It follows as the night from day that any custom necessarily has its exceptions. To be bound by them in the face of new—'"

Lazarus pressed the HOLD button. "Had enough of that guy?"

"Yes, I had already heard it." The stranger sighed. "I have rarely heard such complete lack of semantic rigor. It surprises me—Dr. Oscarsen has done sound work in the past."

"Reached his dotage," Lazarus stated, as he told the machine to try again. "Wants what he wants when he wants it—and thinks that constitutes a natural law."

The machine hummed and clicked and again spoke up. "The DAILY DATA, the only midwest news—"

"Can't we scramble that commercial?" suggested Lazarus.

His companion peered at the control panel. "Doesn't seem to be equipped for it."

"Ensenada, Baja California. Jeffers and Lucy Weatheral today asked for special proctor protection, alleging that a group of citizens had broken into their home, submitted them to personal indignity and committed other asocial acts. The Weatherals are, by their own admission, members of the notorious Howard Families and claim that the alleged incident could be traced to that supposed fact. The district provost points out that they have offered no proof and has taken the matter under advisement. A town mass meeting has been announced for tonight which will air—"

The other man turned toward Lazarus. "Cousin, did we hear what I thought we heard? That is the first case of asocial group violence in more than twenty years . . . yet they reported it like a breakdown in a weather integrator."

"Not quite," Lazarus answered grimly. "The connotations of the words used in describing us were loaded."

"Yes, true, but loaded cleverly. I doubt if there was a word in that dispatch with an emotional index, taken alone, higher than one point five. The newscasters are allowed two zero, you know."

"You a psychometrician?"

"Uh, no. I should have introduced myself. I'm Andrew Jackson Libby."

"Lazarus Long."

"I know. I was at the meeting last night."

"'Libby . . . Libby,'" Lazarus mused. "Don't seem to place it in the Families. Seems familiar, though."

"My case is a little like yours—"

"Changed it during the Interregnum, eh?"

"Yes and no. I was born after the Second Revolution. But my people had been converted to the New Crusade and had broken with the Families and changed their name. I was a grown man before I knew I was a Member."

"The deuce you say! That's interesting—how did you come to be located . . . if you don't mind my asking?"

"Well, you see I was in the Navy and one of my superior officers—"

"Got it! Got it! I *thought* you were a spaceman. You're Slipstick Libby, the Calculator."

Libby grinned sheepishly. "I have been called that."

"Sure, sure. The last can I piloted was equipped with your paragravitic rectifier. And the control bank used your fractional differential on the steering jets. But I installed that myself—kinda borrowed your patent."

Libby seemed undisturbed by the theft. His face lit up. "You are interested in symbolic logic?"

"Only pragmatically. But look, I put a modification on your gadget that derives from the rejected alternatives in your thirteenth equation. It helps like this: suppose you are cruising in a field of density 'x' with an n-order gradient normal to your course and you want to set your optimum course for a projected point of rendezvous capital 'A' at matching-in vector 'rho' using automatic selection the entire jump, then if—"

They drifted entirely away from Basic English as used by earthbound laymen. The newsbox beside them continued to hunt; three times it spoke up, each time Libby touched the rejection button without consciously hearing it.

"I see your point," he said at last. "I had considered a somewhat similar modification but concluded that it was not commercially feasible, too expensive for anyone but enthusiasts such as yourself. But your solution is cheaper than mine."

"How do you figure that?"

"Why, it's obvious from the data. Your device contains sixty-two moving parts, which should require, if we assume standardized fabrication processes, a probable—" Libby hesitated momentarily as if he were programming the problem. "—a probable optimax of five thousand two hundred and eleven operations in manufacture assuming null-therblig automation, whereas mine—"

Lazarus butted in. "Andy," he inquired solicitously, "does your head ever ache?"

Libby looked sheepish again. "There's nothing abnormal about my talent," he protested. "It is theoretically possible to develop it in any normal person."

"Sure," agreed Lazarus, "and you can teach a snake to tap dance once you get shoes on him. Never mind, I'm glad to have fallen in with you. I heard stories about you way back when you were a kid. You were in the Cosmic Construction Corps, weren't you?"

Libby nodded. "Earth-Mars Spot Three."

"Yeah, that was it—chap on Mars gimme the yarn. Trader at Drywater. I knew your maternal grandfather, too. Stiffnecked old coot."

"I suppose he was."

"He was, all right. I had quite a set-to with him at the Meeting in 2012. He had a powerful vocabulary." Lazarus frowned slightly. "Funny thing, Andy . . . I recall that vividly, I've always had a good memory—yet it seems to be getting harder for me to keep things straight. Especially this last century."

"Inescapable mathematical necessity," said Libby.

"Huh? Why?"

"Life experience is linearly additive, but the correlation of memory impressions is an unlimited expansion. If mankind lived as long as a thousand years, it would be necessary to invent some totally different method of memory association in order to be effectively time-binding. A man would otherwise flounder helplessly in the wealth of his own knowledge, unable to evaluate. Insanity, or feeblemindedness."

"That so?" Lazarus suddenly looked worried. "Then we'd better get busy on it."

"Oh, it's quite possible of solution."

"Let's work on it. Let's not get caught short."

The newsbox again demanded attention, this time with the buzzer and flashing light of a spot bulletin: "Hearken to the DATA. Flash! High Council Suspends Covenant! Under the Emergency Situation clause of the Covenant an unprecedented Action-in-Council was announced today directing the Administrator to detain and question all members of the so-called Howard Families—*by any means expedient!* The Administrator authorized that the following statement be released by all licensed news outlets: (I quote) 'The suspension of the Covenant's civil guarantees applies only to the group known as the Howard Families except that government agents are empowered to act as circumstances require to apprehend speedily the persons affected by the Action-in-Council. Citizens are urged to tolerate cheerfully any minor inconvenience this may cause them; your right of privacy will be respected in every way possible; your right of free movement may be interrupted temporarily, but full economic restitution will be made."

"Now, Friends and Citizens, what does this mean?— to you and you and also you! The DAILY DATA brings you now your popular commentator, Albert Reifsnider:

"Reifsnider reporting: Service, Citizens! There is no cause for alarm. To the average free citizen this emergency will be somewhat less troublesome than a low-pressure minimum too big for the weather machines. Take it easy! Relax! Help the proctors when requested and tend to your private affairs. If inconvenienced, don't stand on custom—coöperate with Service!

"That's what it means today. What does it mean tomorrow and the day after that? Next year? It means that your public servants have taken a forthright step

to obtain for you the boon of a longer and happier life!
Don't get your hopes too high . . . but it looks like the
dawn of a new day. Ah, indeed it does! The jealously
guarded secret of a selfish few will soon—"

Long raised an eyebrow at Libby, then switched it
off.

"I suppose that," Libby said bitterly, "is an example
of 'factual detachment in news reporting.'"

Lazarus opened his pouch and struck a cigarette
before replying. "Take it easy, Andy. There are bad times
and good times. We're overdue for bad times. The
people are on the march again . . . this time at us."

3

The burrow known as the Families' Seat became
jammed as the day wore on. Members kept trickling
in, arriving by tunnels from downstate and from Indi-
ana. As soon as it was dark a traffic jam developed
at the underground pool entrance—sporting subs, fake
ground cars such as Mary's, ostensible surface cruisers modified to dive, each craft loaded with refugees
some half suffocated from lying in hiding on deep
bottom most of the day while waiting for a chance to
sneak in.

The usual meeting room was much too small to
handle the crowd; the resident staff cleared the largest room, the refectory, and removed partitions separating if from the main lounge. There at midnight
Lazarus climbed onto a temporary rostrum. "Okay," he
announced, "let's pipe down. You down in front sit on
the floor so the rest can see. I was born in 1912.
Anybody older?"

He paused, then added, "Nominations for
chairman . . . speak up."

Three were proposed; before a fourth could be offered the last man nominated got to his feet. "Axel Johnson, of the Johnson Family, I want my name withdrawn and I suggest that the others do likewise. Lazarus cut through the fog last night; let him handle it. This is no time for Family politics."

The other names were withdrawn; no more were offered. Lazarus said, "Okay if that's the way you want it. Before we get down to arguing, I want a report from the Chief Trustee. How about it, Zack? Any of our kinfolk get nabbed?"

Zaccur Barstow did not need to identify himself; he simply said, "Speaking for the Trustees: our report is not complete, but we do not as yet know that any Member has been arrested. Of the nine thousand two hundred and eighty-five revealed Members, nine thousand one hundred and six had been reported, when I left the communication office ten minutes ago, as having reached hiding, in other Family strongholds, or in the homes of unrevealed Members, or elsewhere. Mary Sperling's warning was amazingly successfully in view of how short the time was from the alarm to the public execution of the Action-in-Council—but we still have one hundred and seventy-nine revealed cousins unreported. Probably most of these will trickle in during the next few days. Others are probably safe but unable to get in touch with us."

"Get to the point, Zack," Lazarus insisted. "Any reasonable chance that all of them will make it home safe?"

"Absolutely none."

"Why?"

"Because three of them are known to be in public conveyances between here and the Moon, traveling under their revealed identities. Others we don't know about are almost certainly caught in similar predicaments."

"Question!" A cocky little man near the front stood up and pointed his finger at the Chief Trustee. "Were

all those Members now in jeopardy protected by
hypnotic injunction?"

"No. There was no—"

"I demand to know why not!"

"Shut up!" bellowed Lazarus. "You're out of order.
Nobody's on trial here and we've got no time to waste
on spilled milk. Go ahead, Zack."

"Very well. But I will answer the question to this
extent: everyone knows that a proposal to protect our
secrets by hypnotic means was voted down at the Meeting
which relaxed the 'Masquerade.' I seem to recall that the
cousin now objecting helped then to vote it down."

"That is not true! And I insist that—"

"PIPE DOWN!" Lazarus glared at the heckler, than
looked him over carefully. "Bud, you strike me as a clear
proof that the Foundation should 'a' bred for brains
instead of age." Lazarus looked around at the crowd.
"Everybody will get his say, but in order as recognized
by the chair. If he butts in again, I'm going to gag him
with his own teeth—is my ruling sustained?"

There was a murmur of mixed shock and approval;
no one objected. Zaccur Barstow went on, "On the
advice of Ralph Schultz the trustees have been proceeding quietly for the past three months to persuade
revealed Members to undergo hypnotic instruction. We
were largely successful." He paused.

"Make it march, Zack," Lazarus. "Are we covered?
Or not?"

"We are *not*. At least two of our cousins certain to
be arrested are not so protected."

Lazarus shrugged. "That tears it. Kinfolk, the game's
over. One shot in the arm of babble juice and the 'Masquerade' is over. It's a new situation—or will be in a
few hours. What do you propose to do about it?"

In the control room of the Antipodes Rocket *Wallaby*,
South Flight, the telecom hummed, went *spung!* and
stuck out a tab like an impudent tongue. The copilot

rocked forward in his gymbals, pulled out the message and tore it off.

He read it, then reread it. "Skipper, brace yourself."

"Trouble?"

"Read it."

The captain did so, and whistled. "Bloody! I've never arrested anybody. I don't believe I've even *seen* anybody arrested. How do we start?"

"I bow to your superior authority."

"That so?" the captain said in nettled tones. "Now that you're through bowing you can tool aft and make the arrest."

"Uh? That's not what I meant. You're the bloke with the authority. I'll relieve you at the conn."

"You didn't read me. I'm delegating the authority. Carry out your orders."

"Just a moment, Al, I didn't sign up for—"

"Carry out your orders!"

"Aye Aye, sir!"

The copilot went aft. The ship had completed its reëntry, was in its long, flat, screaming approach-glide; he was able to walk—he wondered what an arrest in free-fall would be like. Snag him with a butterfly net? He located the passenger by seat check, touched his arm. "Service, sir. There's been a clerical error. May I see your ticket?"

"Why, certainly."

"Would you mind stepping back to the reserve stateroom? It's quieter there and we can both sit down."

"Not at all."

Once they were in the private compartment the chief officer asked the passenger to sit down, then looked annoyed. "Stupid of me!—I've left my lists in the control room." He turned and left. As the door slid to behind him, the passenger heard an unexpected click. Suddenly suspicious, he tried the door. It was locked.

Two proctors came for him at Melbourne. As they escorted him through the skyport he could hear remarks from a curious and surprisingly unfriendly crowd: "There's one of the laddies now!" "Him? My word, he doesn't look *old*." "What price ape glands?" "Don't stare, Herbert." "Why not? Not half bad enough for him."

They took him to the office of the Chief Provost, who invited him to sit down with formal civility. "Now then, sir," the Provost said with a slight local twang, "if you will help us by letting the orderly make a slight injection in your arm—"

"For what purpose?"

"You want to be socially cooperative, I'm sure. It won't hurt you."

"That's beside the point. I insist on an explanation. I am a citizen of the United States."

"So you are, but the Federation has concurrent jurisdiction in any member state—and I am acting under its authority. Now bare your arm, please."

"I refuse. I stand on my civil rights."

"Grab him, lads."

It took four men to do it. Even before the injector touched his skin, his jaw set and a look of sudden agony came into his face. He then sat quietly, listlessly, while the peace officers waited for the drug to take effect. Presently the Provost gently rolled back one of the prisoner's eyelids and said, "I think he's ready. He doesn't weigh over ten stone: it has hit him rather fast. Where's that list of questions?"

A deputy handed it to him; he began, "Horace Foote, do you hear me?"

The man's lips twitched, he seemed about to speak. His mouth opened and blood gushed down his chest.

The Provost bellowed and grabbed the prisoner's head, made quick examination. "*Surgeon!* He's bitten his tongue half out of his head!"

The captain of the Luna City Shuttle *Moonbeam* scowled at the message in his hand. "What child's play is this?" He glared at his third officer. "Tell me that, Mister."

The third officer studied the overhead. Fuming, the captain held the message at arm's length, peered at it and read aloud: "—imperative that subject persons be prevented from doing themselves injury. You are directed to render them unconscious without warning them." He shoved the flimsy away from him. "What do they think I'm running? Coventry? Who do they think they are?—telling *me* in *my* ship what I must do with *my* passengers! I won't—so help me, I won't! There's no rule requiring me to . . . is there, Mister?"

The third officer went on silently studying the ship's structure.

The captain stopped pacing. "Purser! *Purser!* Why is that man never around when I want him?"

"I'm here, Captain."

"About time!"

"I've been here all along, sir."

"Don't argue with me. Here—attend to this." He handed the despatch to the purser and left.

A shipfitter, supervised by the purser, the hull officer, and the medical officer, made a slight change in the air-conditioning ducts to one cabin; two worried passengers sloughed off their cares under the influence of a non-lethal dose of sleeping gas.

"Another report, sir."

"Leave it," the Administrator said in a tired voice.

"And Councilor Bork Vanning presents his compliments and requests an interview."

"Tell him that I regret that I am too busy."

"He insists on seeing you, sir."

Administrator Ford answered snappishly, "Then you may tell the Honorable Mr. Vanning that he does not give orders in this office!" The aide said nothing; Administrator Ford pressed his fingertips wearily against his forehead and went on slowly, "No, Gerry, don't tell him that. Be diplomatic . . . but don't let him in.

"Yes, sir."

When he was alone, the Administrator picked up the report. His eye skipped over official heading, date line, and file number: "Synopsis of Interview with Conditionally Proscribed Citizen Arthur Sperling, full transcript attached. Conditions of Interview: Subject received normal dosage of neosco., having previously received unmeasured dosage of gaseous hypnotal. Antidote—" How the devil could you cure subordinates of wordiness? Was there something in the soul of a career civil servant that cherished red tape? His eye skipped on down:

"—stated that his name was Arthur Sperling of the Foote Family and gave his age as one hundred thirty-seven years. (Subject's apparent age is forty-five plus-or-minus four: see bio report attached.) Subject admitted that he was a member of the Howard Families. He stated that the Families numbered slightly more than one hundred thousand members. He was asked to correct this and it was suggested to him that the correct number was nearer ten thousand. He persisted in his original statement."

The Administrator stopped and reread this part.

He skipped on down, looking for the key part: "—insisted that his long life was the result of his ancestry and had no other cause. Admitted that artificial means had been used to preserve his youthful appearance but maintained firmly that his life expectancy was inherent, not acquired. It was suggested to him that his elder relatives had subjected him without his knowledge to treatment in his early youth to increase his life span. Subject admitted possibility. On being pressed for names of persons who might have performed, or might be performing, such treatments he returned to his original statement that no such treatments exist.

"He gave the names (surprise association procedure) and in some cases the addresses of nearly two hundred members of his kin group not previously identified as such in our records. (List attached) His strength ebbed under this arduous technique and he sank into full apathy from which he could not be roused by any stimuli within the limits of his estimated tolerance (see Bio Report).

"Conclusions under Expedited Analysis, Kelly-Holmes Approximation Method: Subject does not possess and does not believe in the Search Object. Does not remember experiencing Search Object but is mistaken. Knowledge of Search Object is limited to a small group, of the order of twenty. A member of this star group will be located through not more than triple-concatenation elimination search. (Probability of unity, subject to assumptions: first, that topologic social space is continuous and is included in the physical space of the Western Federation and, second, that at least one concatenative path exists between apprehended subjects and star group. Neither assumption can be verified as of this writing, but the first assumption is strongly supported by statistical analysis of the list of names supplied by Subject of previously unsuspected members of Howard kin group, which analysis also supports Subject's estimate of total size of group, and second assumption when taken negatively postulates that star group holding Search Object has been able to apply it with no social-space of contact, an absurdity.)

"Estimated Time for Search: 71 hrs, plus-or-minus 20 hrs. Prediction but not time estimate vouched for by cognizant bureau. Time estimate will be re—"

Ford slapped the report on a stack cluttering his old-fashioned control desk. The dumb fools! Not to recognize a negative report when they saw one—yet they called themselves *psychographers!*

He buried his face in his hands in utter weariness and frustration.

❖   ❖   ❖

Lazarus rapped on the table beside him, using the butt of his blaster as a gavel. "Don't interrupt the speaker," he boomed, then added, "Go ahead but cut it short."

Bertram Hardy nodded curtly. "I say again, these mayflies we see around us have no rights that we of the Families are bound to respect. We should deal with them with stealth, with cunning, with guile, and when we eventually consolidate our position . . . with *force!* We are no more obligated to respect their welfare than a hunter is obliged to shout a warning at his quarry. The—"

There was a catcall from the rear of the room. Lazarus again banged for order and tried to spot the source. Hardy ploughed steadily on. "The so-called human race has split in two; it is time we admitted it. On one side, *Homo vivens*, ourselves . . . on the other— *Homo moriturus!* With the great lizards, with the sabertooth tiger and the bison, their day is done. We would no more mix our living blood with theirs than we would attempt to breed with apes. I say temporize with them, tell them any tale, assure them that we will bathe them in the fountain of youth—gain time, so that when these two naturally antagonistic races join battle, *as they inevitably must*, the victory will be ours!"

There was no applause but Lazarus could see wavering uncertainty in many faces. Bertram Hardy's ideas ran counter to thought patterns of many years of gentle living yet his words seemed to ring with destiny. Lazarus did not believe in destiny: he believed in . . . well, never mind—but he wondered how Brother Bertram would look with both arms broken.

Eve Barstow got up. "If that is what Bertram means by the survival of the fittest," she said bitterly, "I'll go live with the asocials in Coventry. However, he has offered a plan; I'll have to offer another plan if I won't take his. I won't accept any plan which would have us live at the expense of our poor transient neighbors.

Furthermore it is clear to me now that our mere presence, the simple fact of our rich heritage of life, is damaging to the spirit of our poor neighbor. Our longer years and richer opportunities make his best efforts seem futile to him—any effort save a hopeless struggle against an appointed death. Our mere presence saps his strength, ruins his judgment, fills him with panic fear of death.

"So I propose a plan. Let's disclose ourselves, tell *all* the truth, and ask for our share of the Earth, some little corner where we may live apart. If our poor friends wish to surround it with a great barrier like that around Coventry, so be it—it is better that we never meet face to face."

Some expressions of doubt changed to approval. Ralph Schultz stood up. "Without prejudice to Eve's basic plan, I must advise you that it is my professional opinion that the psychological insulation she proposes cannot be accomplished that easily. As long as we're on this planet they won't be able to put us out of their minds. Modern communications—"

"Then we must move to another planet!" she retorted.

"Where?" demanded Bertram Hardy. "Venus? I'd rather live in a steam bath. Mars? Worn-out and worthless."

"We will rebuild it," she insisted.

"Not in your lifetime nor mine. No, my dear Eve, your tenderheartedness sounds well but it doesn't make sense. There is only one planet in the System fit to live on—we're standing on it."

Something in Bertram Hardy's words set off a response in Lazarus Long's brain, then the thought escaped him. Something . . . something that he had heard or said just a day or two ago . . . or was it longer than? Somehow it seemed to be associated with his first trip out into space, too, well over a century ago. Thunderation! It was maddening to have his memory play tricks on him like that—

Then he had it—the starship! The interstellar ship they were putting the finishing touches on out there between Earth and Luna. "Folks," he drawled, "before we table this idea of moving to another planet, let's consider all the possibilities." He waited until he had their full attention. "Did you ever stop to think that not all the planets swing around this one Sun?"

Zaccur Barstow broke the silence. "Lazarus . . . are you making a serious suggestion?"

"Dead serious."

"It does not sound so. Perhaps you had better explain."

"I will." Lazarus faced the crowd "There's a spaceship hanging out there in the sky, a roomy thing, built to make the long jumps between stars. Why don't we take it and go looking for our own piece of real estate?"

Bertram Hardy was first to recover. "I don't know whether our chairman is lightening the gloom with another of his wisecracks or not, but, assuming that he is serious, I'll answer. My objection to Mars applies to this wild scheme ten times over. I understand that the reckless fools who are actually intending to man that ship expect to make the jump in about a century—then maybe their grandchildren will find something, or maybe they won't. Either way, I'm not interested. I don't care to spend a century locked up in a steel tank, nor do I expect to live that long. I won't buy it."

"Hold it," Lazarus told him. "Where's Andy Libby?"

"Here," Libby answered, standing up.

"Come on down front. Slipstick, did you have anything to do with designing the new Centaurus ship?"

"No. Neither this one nor the first one."

Lazarus spoke to the crowd. "That settles it. If that ship didn't have Slipstick's finger in the drive design, then she's not as fast as she could be, not by a good big coefficient. Slipstick, better get busy on the problem, son. We're likely to need a solution."

"But Lazarus, you mustn't assume that—"

"Aren't there theoretical possibilities?"

"Well, you know there are, but—"

"Then get that carrot top of yours working on it."

"Well . . . all right." Libby blushed as pink as his hair.

"Just a moment, Lazarus." It was Zaccur Barstow. "I like this proposal and I think we should discuss it at length . . . not let ourselves be frightened off by Brother Bertram's distaste for it. Even if Brother Libby fails to find a better means of propulsion—and frankly, I don't think he will; I know a little something of field mechanics—even so, I shan't let a century frighten me. By using cold-rest and manning the ship in shifts, most of us should be able to complete one hop. There is—"

"What makes you think," demanded Bertram Hardy, "that they'll let *us* man the ship anyhow?"

"Bert," Lazarus said coldly, "address the chair when you want to sound off. You're not even a Family delegate. Last warning."

"As I was saying," Barstow continued, "there is an appropriateness in the long-lived exploring the stars. A mystic might call it our true vocation." He pondered. "As for the ship Lazarus suggested, perhaps they will not let us have that . . . but the Families are rich. If we need a starship—or ships—we can build them, we can pay for them. I think we had better hope that they will let us do this . . . for it may be that there is no way, not another way of any sort, out of our dilemma which does not include our own extermination."

Barstow spoke these last words softly and slowly, with great sadness. They bit into the company like damp chill. To most of them the problem was so new as not yet to be real; no one had voiced the possible consequence of failing to find a solution satisfactory to the short-lived majority. For their senior trustee to speak soberly of his fear that the Families might be exterminated—hunted down and killed—stirred up in each one the ghost they never mentioned.

"Well," Lazarus said briskly when the silence had

grown painful, "before we work this idea over, let's hear what other plan anyone has to offer. Speak up."

A messenger hurried in and spoke to Zaccur Barstow. He looked startled and seemed to ask to have the message repeated. He then hurried across the rostrum to Lazarus, whispered to him. Lazarus looked startled. Barstow hurried out.

Lazarus looked back at the crowd. "We'll take a recess," he announced. "Give you time to think about other plans . . . and time for a stretch and a smoke." He reached for his pouch.

"What's up?" someone called out.

Lazarus struck a cigarette, took a long drag, let it drift out. "We'll have to wait and see," he said. "I don't know. But at least half a dozen of the plans put forward tonight we won't have to bother to vote on. The situation has changed again—how much, I couldn't say."

"What do you mean?"

"Well," Lazarus drawled, "it seems the Federation Administrator wanted to talk to Zack Barstow right away. He asked for him by name . . . *and he called over our secret Families' circuit.*"

"Huh? That's impossible!"

"Yep. So is a baby, son."

<h1 style="text-align:center">4</h1>

Zaccur Barstow tried to quiet himself down as he hurried into the phone booth.

At the other end of the same videophone circuit the Honorable Slayton Ford was doing the same thing—trying to calm his nerves. He did not underrate himself. A long and brilliant public career crowned by years as Administrator for the Council and under the Covenant of the Western Administration had made Ford aware of his own superior ability and unmatched experience; no ordinary man could possibly make him feel at a disadvantage in negotiation.

But this was different.

What would a man be like who had lived more than two ordinary lifetimes? Worse than that—a man who had had four or five times the adult experience that Ford himself had had? Slayton Ford knew that his own opinions had changed and changed again since his own boyhood; he knew that the boy he had been, or even the able young man he had been, would be no match for the mature man he had become. So what would this Barstow be like? Presumably he was the most able, the most astute, of a group all of whom had had much more experience than Ford could possibly have—how could he guess such a man's evaluations, intentions, ways of thinking, his possible resources?

Ford was certain of only one thing: he did not intend to trade Manhattan Island for twenty-four dollars and a case of whisky, nor sell humanity's birthright for a mess of pottage.

He studied Barstow's face as the image appeared in his phone. A good face and strong . . . it would be useless to try to bully this man. And the man looked young—why, he looked younger than Ford himself! The subconscious image of the Administrator's own stern and implacable grandfather faded out of his mind and his tension eased off. He said quietly, "You are Citizen Zaccur Barstow?"

"Yes, Mister Administrator."

"You are chief executive of the Howard Families?"

"I am the current speaker trustee of our Families' Foundation, but I am responsible to my cousins rather than in authority over them."

Ford brushed it aside. "I assume that your position carries with it leadership. I can't negotiate with a hundred thousand people."

Barstow did not blink. He saw the power play in the

sudden admission that the administration knew the true numbers of the Families and discounted it. He had already adjusted himself to the shock of learning that the Families' secret headquarters was no longer secret and the still more upsetting fact that the Administrator knew how to tap into their private communication system; it simply proved that one or more Members had been caught and forced to talk.

So it was now almost certain that the authorities already knew every important fact about the Families.

Therefore it was useless to try to bluff—just the same, don't volunteer any information; they might not have all the facts this soon.

Barstow answered without noticeable pause. "What is it you wish to discuss with me, sir?"

"The policy of the Administration toward your kin group. The welfare of yourself and your relatives."

Barstow shrugged. "What can we discuss? The Convenant has been tossed aside and you have been given power to do as you like with us—to squeeze a secret out of us that we don't have. What can we do but pray for mercy?"

"Please!" The Administrator gestured his annoyance. "Why fence with me? We have a problem, you and I. Let's discuss it openly and try to reach a solution. Yes?"

Barstow answered slowly, "I would like to . . . and I believe that you would like to, also. But the problem is based on a false assumption, that we, the Howard Families, know how to lengthen human life. We don't."

"Suppose I tell you that I know there is no such secret?"

"Mmm . . . I would like to believe you. But how can you reconcile that with the persecution of my people? You've been harrying us like rats."

Ford made a wry face. "There is an old, old story about a theologian who was asked to reconcile the doctrine of Divine mercy with the doctrine of infant damnation. 'The Almighty,' he explained, 'finds it necessary to do things in His official and public capacity which in His private and personal capacity He deplores.' "

Barstow smiled in spite of himself "I see the analogy. Is it actually pertinent?"

"I think it is."

"So. You didn't call me simply to make a headsman's apology?"

"No. I hope not. You keep in touch with politics? I'm sure you must; your position would require it." Barstow nodded; Ford explained at length:

Ford's administration had been the longest since the signing of the Covenant; he had lasted through four Councils. Nevertheless his control was now so shaky that he could not risk forcing a vote of confidence—certainly not over the Howard Families. On that issue his nominal majority was already a minority. If he refused the present decision of the Council, forced it to a vote of confidence, Ford would be out of office and the present minority leader would take over as administrator. "You follow me? I can either stay in office and try to cope with this problem while restricted by a Council directive with which I do not agree . . . or I can drop out and let my successor handle it."

"Surely you're not asking my advice?"

"No, no! Not on that. I've made my decision. The Action-in-Council would have been carried out in any case, either by me or by Mr. Vanning—so I decided to do it. The question is: will I have your help, or will I not?"

Barstow hesitated, while rapidly reviewing Ford's political career in his mind. The earlier part of Ford's long administration had been almost a golden age of statesmanship. A wise and practical man, Ford had shaped into workable rules the principles of human freedom set forth by Novak in the language of the Covenant. It had been a period of good will, of prosperous expansion, of civilizing processes which seemed to be permanent, irreversible.

Nevertheless a setback had come and Barstow understood the reasons at least as well as Ford did. Whenever the citizens fix their attention on one issue to the exclusion of others, the situation is ripe for scalawags, demagogues, ambitious men on horseback. The Howard Families, in all innocence, had created the crisis in public morals from which they now suffered, through their own action, taken years earlier, in letting the short-lived learn of their existence. It mattered not at all that the "secret" did not exist; the corrupting effect did exist.

Ford at least understood the true situation—

"We'll help," Barstow answered suddenly.

"Good. What do you suggest?"

Barstow chewed his lip. "Isn't there some way you can stall off this drastic action, this violation of the Covenant itself?"

Ford shook his head. "It's too late."

"Even if you went before the public and told the citizens, face to face that you knew that—"

Ford cut him short. "I wouldn't last in office long enough to make the speech. Nor would I be believed. Besides that—understand me clearly, Zaccur Barstow—no matter what sympathy I may have personally for you and your people, I would not do so if I could. This whole matter is a cancer eating into vitals of our society; it must be settled. I have had my hand forced, true . . . but there is no turning back. It must be pressed on to a solution."

In at least one respect Barstow was a wise man; he knew that another man could oppose him and not be a villain. Nevertheless he protested, "My people are being persecuted."

"Your people," Ford said forcefully, "are a fraction of a tenth of one per cent of all the people . . . and I must find a solution for all! I've called on you to find out if you have any suggestions toward a solution for everyone. Do you?"

"I'm not sure," Barstow answered slowly. "Suppose I concede that you must go ahead with this ugly business of arresting my people, of questioning them by unlawful means—I suppose I have no choice about that—"

"You have no choice. Neither have I." Ford frowned. "It will be carried out as humanely as I can manage it—I am not a free agent."

"Thank you. But, even though you tell me it would be useless for you yourself to go to the people, nevertheless you have enormous propaganda means at your disposal. Would it be possible, while we stall along, to build up a campaign to convince the people of the true facts? Prove to them that there *is* no secret?"

Ford answered, "Ask yourself: will it work?"

Barstow sighed. "Probably not."

"Nor would I consider it a solution even if it would! The people—even my trusted assistants—are clinging to their belief in a fountain of youth because the only alternative is too bitter to think about. Do you know what it would mean to them? For them to believe the bald truth?"

"Go on."

"Death has been tolerable to me only because Death has been the Great Democrat, treating all alike. But now Death plays favorites. Zaccur Barstow, can you understand the bitter, bitter jealousy of the ordinary man of—oh, say 'fifty'—who looks on one of your sort? Fifty years . . . twenty of them he is a child, he is well past thirty before he is skilled in his profession. He is forty before he is established and respected. For not more than the last ten years of his fifty he has really amounted to something."

Ford leaned forward in the screen and spoke with sober emphasis: "And now, when he has reached his goal, what is his prize? His eyes are failing him, his bright young strength is gone, his heart and wind are 'not what they used to be.' He is not senile yet . . . but he feels the chill of the first frost. He knows what is in store for him. He knows—he knows!"

"But it was inevitable and each man learned to be resigned to it."

"Now *you* come along," Ford went on bitterly. "You shame him in his weakness, you humble him before his children. He dares not plan for the future; you blithely undertake plans that will not mature for fifty years—for a hundred. No matter what success he has achieved, what excellence he has attained, you will catch up with him, pass him—outlive him. In his weakness you are *kind* to him.

"Is it any wonder that he hates you?"

Barstow raised his head wearily. "Do *you* hate me, Slayton Ford?"

"No. No, I cannot afford to hate anyone. But I can tell you this," Ford added suddenly, "had there been a secret, I would have it out of you if I had to tear you to pieces!"

"Yes. I understand that." Barstow paused to think. "There is little that we of the Howard Families can do. We did not plan it this way; it was planned for us. But there is one thing we can offer."

"Yes?"

Barstow explained.

Ford shook his head. "Medically what you suggest is feasible and I have no doubt that a half interest in your heritage would lengthen the span of human life. But even if women were willing to accept the germ plasm of your men—I do not say that they would—it would be psychic death for all other men. There would be an outbreak of frustration and hatred that would split the human race to ruin. No, no matter what we wish, our customs are what they are. We can't breed men like animals; they won't stand for it."

"I know it," agreed Barstow, "but it is all we have to offer . . . a share in our fortune through artificial impregnation."

"Yes. I suppose I should thank you but I feel no thanks and I shan't. Now let's be practical. Individually you old ones are doubtless honorable, lovable men. But as a group you are as dangerous as carriers of plague. So you must be quarantined."

Barstow nodded. "My cousins and I had already reached that conclusion."

Ford looked relieved. "I'm glad you're being sensible about it."

"We can't help ourselves. Well? A segregated colony? Some remote place that would be a Coventry of our own? Madagascar, perhaps? Or we might take the British Isles, build them up again and spread from there into Europe as the radioactivity died down."

Ford shook his head. "Impossible. That would simply leave the problem for my grandchildren to solve. By that time you and yours would have grown in strength; you might defeat us. No, Zaccur Barstow, you and your kin must leave this planet entirely!"

Barstow looked bleak. "I knew it would come to that. Well, where shall we go?"

"Take your choice of the Solar System. Anywhere you like."

"But *where?* Venus is no prize, but even if we chose it, would they accept us? The Venerians won't take orders from Earth; that was settled in 2020. Yes, they now accept screened immigrants under the Four Planets Convention . . . but would they accept a hundred thousand whom Earth found too dangerous to keep? I doubt it."

"So do I. Better pick another planet."

"What planet? In the whole system there is not another body that will support human life as it is. It would take almost superhuman effort, even with unlimited money and the best of modern engineering, to make the most promising of them fit for habitation."

"Make the effort. We will be generous with help."

"I am sure you would. But is that any better solution in the long run than giving us a reservation on Earth? Are you going to put a stop to space travel?"

Ford sat up suddenly. "Oh! I see your thought. I had not followed it through, but let's face it. Why not? Would it not be better to give up space travel than to let this situation degenerate into open war? It was given up once before."

"Yes, when the Venerians threw off their absentee landlords. But it started up again and Luna City is rebuilt and ten times more tonnage moves through the sky than ever did before. Can you stop it? If you can, will it stay stopped?"

Ford turned it over and over in his mind. He could not stop space travel, no administration could. But could an interdict be placed on whatever planet these oldsters were shipped to? And would it help? One generation, two, three . . . what difference would it make? Ancient Japan had tried some solution like that; the foreign devils had come sailing in anyhow. Cultures could not be kept apart forever, and when they did come in contact, the hardier displaced the weaker; that was a natural law.

A permanent and effective quarantine was impossible. That left only one answer—an ugly one. But Ford was tough-minded; he could accept what was necessary. He started making plans, Barstow's presence in the screen forgotten. Once he gave the Chief Provost the location of the Howard Families headquarters it should be reduced in an hour, two at the most . . . unless they had extraordinary defenses—but anywise it was just a matter of time. From those who would be arrested at their headquarters it should be possible to locate and arrest every other member of their group. With luck he would have them all in twenty-four to forty-eight hours.

The only point left undecided in his mind was whether to liquidate them all, or simply to sterilize them. Either would be a final solution and there was no third solution. But which was the more humane?

Ford knew that this would end his career. He would leave office in disgrace, perhaps be sent to Coventry, but he gave it no thought; he was so constituted as to be unable to weigh his own welfare against his concept of his public duty.

Barstow could not read Ford's mind but he did sense that Ford had reached a decision and he surmised correctly how bad that decision must be for himself and his kin. Now was the time, he decided, to risk his one lone trump.

"Mister Administrator—"

"Eh? Oh, sorry! I was preoccupied." That was a vast understatement; he was shockingly embarrassed to find himself still facing a man he had just condemned to death. He gathered formality about him like a robe. "Thank you, Zaccur Barstow, for talking with me. I am sorry that—"

"Mister Administrator!"

"Yes?"

"I propose that you move us entirely out of the Solar System."

"*What?*" Ford blinked. "Are you speaking seriously?"

Barstow spoke rapidly, persuasively, explaining Lazarus Long's half-conceived scheme, improvising details as he went along, skipping over obstacles and emphasizing advantages.

"It might work." Ford at last said slowly. "There are difficulties you have not mentioned, political difficulties and a terrible hazard of time. Still, it might." He stood up. "Go back to your people. Don't spring this on them yet. I'll talk with you later."

Barstow walked back slowly while wondering what he could tell the Members. They would demand a full report; technically he had no right to refuse. But he was strongly inclined to coöperate with the Administrator as long as there was any chance of a favorable outcome. Suddenly making up his mind, he turned, went to his office, and sent for Lazarus.

"Howdy, Zack," Long said as he came in. "How'd the palaver go?"

"Good and bad," Barstow replied. "Listen—" He gave him a brief, accurate résumé. "Can you go back in there and tell them something that will hold them?"

"Mmm . . . reckon so."

"Then do it and hurry back here."

They did not like the stall Lazarus gave them. They did not want to keep quiet and they did not want to adjourn the meeting. "Where is Zaccur?"—"We demand a report!"—"Why all the mystification?"

Lazarus shut them up with a roar. "Listen to me, you damned idiots! Zack'll talk when he's ready—don't joggle his elbow. He knows what he's doing."

A man near the back stood up. "I'm going home!"

"Do that," Lazarus urged sweetly. "Give my love to the proctors."

The man looked startled and sat down.

"Anybody else want to go home?" demanded Lazarus. "Don't let me stop you. But it's time you bird-brained dopes realized that you have been outlawed. The only thing that stands between you and the proctors is Zack Barstow's ability to talk sweet to the Administrator. So do as you like . . . the meeting's adjourned."

"Look, Zack," said Lazarus a few minutes later, "let's get this straight. Ford is going to use his extraordinary powers to help us glom onto the big ship and make a getaway. Is that right?"

"He's practically committed to it."

"Hmmm—He'll have to do this while pretending to the Council that everything he does is just a necessary step in squeezing the 'secret' out of us—he's going to double-cross 'em. That right?"

"I hadn't thought that far ahead. I—"

"But that's true, isn't it?"

"Well . . . yes, it must be true."

"Okay. Now, is our boy Ford bright enough to realize what he is letting himself in for and tough enough to go through with it?"

Barstow reviewed what he knew of Ford and added his impressions from the interview. "Yes," he decided, "he knows and he's strong enough to face it."

"All right. Now how about you, pal? Are *you* up to it, too?" Lazarus' voice was accusing.

"Me? What do you mean?"

"You're planning on double-crossing *your* crowd, too, aren't you? Have you got the guts to go through with it when the going gets tough?"

"I don't understand you, Lazarus," Barstow answered worriedly. "I'm not planning to deceive anyone—at least, no member of the Families."

"Better look at your cards again," Lazarus went on remorselessly. "Your part of the deal is to see to it that every man, woman and child takes part in this exodus. Do you expect to sell the idea to each one of them separately and get a hundred thousand people to agree? *Unanimously?* Shucks, you couldn't get that many to whistle 'Yankee Doodle' unanimously."

"But they will *have* to agree," protested Barstow. "They have no choice. We either emigrate, or they hunt us down and kill us. I'm certain that is what Ford intends to do. And he will."

"Then why didn't you walk into the meeting and tell 'em that? Why did you send me in to give 'em a stall?"

Barstow rubbed a hand across his eyes. "I don't know."

"I'll tell you why," continued Lazarus. "You think better with your hunches than most men do with the tops of their minds. You sent me in there to tell 'em a tale because you knew damn well the truth wouldn't serve. If you told 'em it was get out or get killed, some would get panicky and some would get stubborn. And some old-woman-in-kilts would decide to go home and stand on his Covenant rights. Then he'd spill the scheme before it ever dawned on him that the government was playing for keeps. That's right, isn't it?"

Barstow shrugged and laughed unhappily. "You're

right. I didn't have it figured out but you're absolutely right."

"But you did have it figured out," Lazarus assured him. "You had the right answers. Zack, I like your hunches; that's why I'm stringing along. All right, you and Ford are planning to pull a whizzer on every man jack on this globe—I'm asking you again: *have you got the guts to see it through?*"

5

The Members stood around in groups, fretfully. "I can't understand it," the Resident Archivist was saying to a worried circle around her. "The Senior Trustee never interfered in my work before. But he came bursting into my office with that Lazarus Long behind him and ordered me out."

"What did he say?" asked one of her listeners.

"Well, *I* said, 'May I do you a service, Zaccur Barstow?' and he said, 'Yes, you may. Get out and take your girls with you.' Not a word of ordinary courtesy!"

"A lot you've got to complain about," another voice added gloomily. It was Cecil Hedrick, of the Johnson Family, chief communications engineer. "Lazarus Long paid a call on me, and he was a damned sight less polite."

"What did he do?"

"He walks into the communication cell and tells me he is going to take over my board—Zaccur's orders. I told him that nobody could touch my burners but me and my operators, and anyhow, where was his authority? You know what he did? You won't believe it but he pulled a blaster on me."

"You don't mean it!"

"I certainly do. I tell you, that man is dangerous. He

ought to go for psycho adjustment. He's an atavism if I ever saw one."

Lazarus Long's face stared out of the screen into that of the Administrator. "Got it all canned?" he demanded.

Ford cut the switch on the facsimulator on his desk. "Got it all," he confirmed.

"Okay," the image of Lazarus replied. "I'm clearing." As the screen went blank Ford spoke into his interoffice circuit.

"Have the High Chief Provost report to me at once—in corpus."

The public safety boss showed up as ordered with an expression on his lined face in which annoyance struggled with discipline. He was having the busiest night of his career, yet the Old Man had sent orders to report in the flesh. What the devil were viewphones for, anyway, he thought angrily—and asked himself why he had ever taken up police work. He rebuked his boss by being coldly formal and saluting unnecessarily. "You sent for me, sir."

Ford ignored it. "Yes, thank you. Here." He pressed a stud; a film spool popped out of the facsimulator. "This is a complete list of the Howard Families. Arrest them."

"Yes, sir." The Federation police chief stared at the spool and debated whether or not to ask how it had been obtained—it certainly hadn't come through *his* office . . . did the Old Man have an intelligence service he didn't even know about?

"It's alphabetical, but keyed geographically," the Administrator was saying. "After you put it through sorters, send the—no, *bring* the original back to me. You can stop the psycho interviews, too," he added. "Just bring them in and hold them. I'll give you more instructions later."

The High Chief Provost decided that this was not a good time to show curiosity. "Yes, sir." He saluted stiffly and left.

Ford turned back to his desk controls and sent word that he wanted to see the chiefs of the bureaus of land resources and of transportation control. On afterthought he added the chief of the bureau of consumption logistics.

Back in the Families' Seat a rump session of the trustees was meeting; Barstow was absent. "I don't like it," Andrew Weatheral was saying. "I could understand Zaccur deciding to delay reporting to the Members but I had supposed that he simply wanted to talk to us first. I certainly did expect him to consult us. What do you make of it, Philip?"

Philip Hardy chewed his lip. "I don't know. Zaccur's got a head on his shoulders . . . but it certainly seems to me that he should have called us together and advised with us. Has he spoken with you, Justin?"

"No, he has not," Justin Foote answered frigidly.

"Well, what should we do? We can't very well call him in and demand an accounting unless we are prepared to oust him from office and if he refuses, I, for one, am reluctant to do that."

They were still discussing it when the proctors arrived.

Lazarus heard the commotion and correctly interpreted it—no feat, since he had information that his brethren lacked. He was aware that he should submit peacefully and conspicuously to arrest—set a good example. But old habits die hard; he postponed the inevitable by ducking into the nearest men's 'fresher.

It was a dead end. He glanced at the air duct—no, too small. While thinking he fumbled in his pouch for a cigarette; his hand found a strange object, he pulled it out. It was the brassard he had "borrowed" from the proctor in Chicago.

When the proctor working point of the mop-squad covering that wing of the Seat stuck his head into that 'fresher, he found another "proctor" already there. "Nobody in here," announced Lazarus. "I've checked it."

"How the devil did you get ahead of me?"

"Around your flank. Stoney Island Tunnel and through their air vents." Lazarus trusted that the real cop would be unaware that there was no Stoney Island Tunnel. "Got a cigarette on you?"

"Huh? This is no time to catch a smoke."

"Shucks," said Lazarus, "my legate is a good mile away."

"Maybe so," the proctor replied, "but mine is right behind us."

"So? Well, skip it—I've got something to tell him anyhow." Lazarus started to move past but the proctor did not get out of his way. He was glancing curiously at Lazarus' kilt. Lazarus had turned it inside out and its blue lining made a fair imitation of a proctor's service uniform if not inspected closely.

"What station did you say you were from?" inquired the proctor.

"This one," answered Lazarus and planted a short jab under the man's breastbone. Lazarus' coach in rough-and-tumble had explained to him that a solar plexus blow was harder to dodge than one to the jaw; the coach had been dead since the roads strike of 1966, his skill lived on.

Lazarus felt more like a cop with a proper uniform kilt and a bandolier of paralysis bombs slung under his left arm. Besides, the proctor's kilt was a better fit. To the right the passage outside led to the Sanctuary and a dead end; he went to the left by Hobson's choice although he knew he would run into his unconscious benefactor's legate. The passage gave into a hall which was crowded with Members herded into a group of proctors. Lazarus ignored his kin and sought out the harassed officer in charge. "Sir," he reported, saluting smartly, "There's sort of a hospital back there. You'll need fifty or sixty stretchers."

"Don't bother me, tell your legate. We've got our hands full."

Lazarus almost did not answer; he had caught Mary Sperling's eye in the crowd—she stared at him and looked away. He caught himself and answered, "Can't tell him, sir. Not available."

"Well go on outside and tell the first-aid squad."

"Yes, sir." He moved away, swaggering a little, his thumbs hooked in the band of his kilt. He was far down the passage leading to the transbelt tunnel serving the Waukegan outlet when he heard shouts behind him. Two proctors were running to overtake him.

Lazarus stopped in the archway giving into the transbelt tunnel and waited for them. "What's the trouble?" he asked easily as they came up.

"The legate—" began one. He got no further; a paralysis bomb tinkled and popped at his feet. He looked surprised as the radiations wiped all expression from his face; his mate fell across him.

Lazarus waited behind a shoulder of the arch, counted seconds up to fifteen: "Number one jet fire! Number two jet fire! Number three jet fire!"—added a couple to be sure the paralyzing effect had died away. He had cut it finer than he liked. He had not ducked quite fast enough and his left foot tingled from exposure.

He then checked. The two were unconscious, no one else was in sight. He mounted the transbelt. Perhaps they had not been looking for him in his proper person, perhaps no one had given him away. But he did not hang around to find out. One thing he was damn well certain of, he told himself, if anybody had squealed on him, it wasn't Mary Sperling.

It took two more parabombs and a couple of hundred words of pure fiction to get him out into the open air. Once he was there and out of immediate observation the brassard and the remaining bombs went into his pouch and the bandolier ended up behind some bushes; he then looked up a clothing store in Waukegan.

He sat down in a sales booth and dialed the code for kilts. He let cloth designs flicker past in the screen while he ignored the persuasive voice of the catalogue until a pattern showed up which was distinctly unmilitary and not blue, whereupon he stopped the display and punched an order for his size. He noted the price, tore an open-credit voucher from his wallet, stuck it into the machine and pushed the switch. Then he enjoyed a smoke while the tailoring was done.

Ten minutes later he stuffed the proctor's kilt into the refuse hopper of the sales booth and left, nattily and loudly attired. He had not been in Waukegan the past century but he found a middle-priced autel without drawing attention by asking questions, dialed its registration board for a standard suite and settled down for seven hours of sound sleep.

He breakfasted in his suite, listening with half an ear to the news box; he was interested, in a mild way, in hearing what might be reported concerning the raid on the Families. But it was a detached interest; he had already detached himself from it in his own mind. It had been a mistake, he now realized, to get back in touch with the Families—a darn good thing he was clear of it all with his present public identity totally free of any connection with the whing-ding.

A phrase caught his attention: "—including Zaccur Barstow, alleged to be their tribal chief.

"The prisoners are being shipped to a reservation in Oklahoma, near the ruins of the Okla-Orleans road city about twenty-five miles east of Harriman Memorial Park. The Chief Provost describes it as a 'Little Coventry,' and has ordered all aircraft to avoid it by ten miles laterally. The Administrator could not be reached for a statement but a usually reliable source inside the administration informs us that the mass arrest was accomplished in order to speed up the investigations whereby the administration expects to obtain the 'Secret of the Howard Families'—their techniques for indefinitely prolonging life. This forthright action in arresting and transporting every member of the outlaw group is expected to have a salutary effect in breaking down the resistance of their leaders to the legitimate demands of society. It will bring home forcibly to them that the civil rights enjoyed by decent citizens must not be used as a cloak behind which to damage society as a whole.

"The chattels and holdings of the members of this criminal conspiracy have been declared subject to the Conservator General and will be administered by his agents during the imprisonment of—"

Lazarus switched it off. "Damnation!" he thought. "Don't fret about things you can't help." Of course, he had expected to be arrested himself . . . but he had escaped. That was that. It wouldn't do the Families any good for him to turn himself in—and besides, he owed the Families nothing, not a tarnation thing.

Anyhow, they were better off all arrested at once and quickly placed under guard. If they had been smelled out one at a time, anything could have happened—lynchings, even pogroms. Lazarus knew from hard experience how close under the skin lay lynch law and mob violence in the most sweetly civilized; that was why he had advised Zack to rig it—that and the fact that Zack and the Administrator had to have the Families in one compact group to stand a chance of carrying out their scheme. They were well off . . . and no skin off his nose.

But he wondered how Zack was getting along, and what he would think of Lazarus' disappearance. And what Mary Sperling thought—it must have been a shock to her when he turned up making a noise like a proctor. He wished he could straighten that out with her.

Not that it mattered what any of them thought. They would all either be light-years away very soon . . . or dead. A closed book.

He turned to the phone and called the post office. "Captain Aaron Sheffield," he announced, and gave his postal number. "Last registered with Goddard Field post office. Will you please have my mail sent to—" He leaned closer and read the code number from the suite's mail receptacle.

"Service," assented the voice of the clerk. "Right away, Captain."

"Thank you."

It would take a couple of hours, he reflected, for his mail to catch up with him—a half hour in trajectory, three times that in fiddle-faddle. Might as well wait here . . . no doubt the search for him had lost itself in the distance but there was nothing in Waukegan he wanted. Once the mail showed up he would hire a U-push-it and scoot down to—

To where? What was he going to do now?

He turned several possibilities over in his mind and came at last to the blank realization that there was nothing, from one end of the Solar System to the other, that he really wanted to do.

It scared him a little. He had once heard, and was inclined to credit, that a loss of interest in living marked the true turning point in the battle between anabolism and catabolism—old age. He suddenly envied normal short-lived people—at least they could go make nuisances of themselves to their children. Filial affection was not customary among Members of the Families; it was not a feasible relationship to maintain for a century or more. And friendship, except between Members, was bound to be regarded as a passing and shallow matter. There was no one whom Lazarus wanted to see.

Wait a minute . . . who was that planter on Venus? The one who knew so many folk songs and who was so funny when he was drunk? He'd go look him up. It would make a nice hop and it would be fun, much as he disliked Venus.

Then he recalled with cold shock that he had not seen the man for—how long? In any case, he was certainly dead by now.

Libby had been right, he mused glumly, when he
spoke of the necessity for a new type of memory association for the long-lived. He hoped the lad would push
ahead with the necessary research and come up with
an answer before Lazarus was reduced to counting on
his fingers. He dwelt on the notion for a minute or two
before recalling that he was most unlikely ever to see
Libby again.

The mail arrived and contained nothing of importance. He was not surprised; he expected no personal
letters. The spools of advertising went into the refuse
chute; he read only one item, a letter from Pan-Terra
Docking Corp. telling him that his convertible cruiser
I Spy had finished her overhaul and had been moved
to a parking dock, rental to start forthwith. As instructed, they had not touched the ship's astrogational
controls—was that still the Captain's pleasure?

He decided to pick her up later in the day and head
out into space. Anything was better than sitting Earthbound and admitting that he was bored.

Paying his score and finding a jet for hire occupied
less than twenty minutes. He took off and headed for
Goddard Field, using the low local-traffic level to avoid
entering the control pattern with a flight plan. He was
not consciously avoiding the police because he had no
reason to think that they could be looking for "Captain
Sheffield"; it was simply habit, and it would get him
to Goddard Field soon enough.

But long before he reached there, while over east-
ern Kansas, he decided to land and did so.

He picked the field of a town so small as to be
unlikely to rate a full-time proctor and there he sought
out a phone booth away from the field. Inside it, he
hesitated. How did you go about calling up the head
man of the entire Federation—and get him? If he simply called Novak Tower and asked for Administrator
Ford, he not only would not be put through to him
but his call would be switched to the Department of

Public Safety for some unwelcome inquiries, sure as taxes.

Well, there was only one way to beat that and that was to call the Department of Safety himself and, somehow, get the Chief Provost on the screen—after that he would play by ear.

"Department of Civil Safety," a voice answered. "What service, citizen?"

"Service to you," he began in his best control-bridge voice. "I am Captain Sheffield. Give me the Chief." He was not overbearing; his manner simply assumed obedience.

Short silence—"What is it about, please?"

"I said I was *Captain Sheffield.*" This time Lazarus' voice showed restrained annoyance.

Another short pause—"I'll connect you with the Chief Deputy's office," the voice said doubtfully.

This time the screen came to life. "Yes?" asked the Chief Deputy, looking him over.

"Get me the Chief—hurry."

"What's it about?"

"Good Lord, man—get me the Chief! I'm *Captain Sheffield!*"

The Chief Deputy must be excused for connecting him; he had had no sleep and more confusing things had happened in the last twenty-four hours than he had been able to assimilate. When the High Chief Provost appeared in the screen, Lazarus spoke first. "Oh, there you are! I've had the damnedest time cutting through your red tape. Get me the Old Man and *move!* Use your closed circuit."

"What the devil do you mean? Who are you?"

"Listen, brother," said Lazarus in tones of slow exasperation, "I would not have routed through your damned hide-bound department if I hadn't been in a jam. Cut me in to the Old Man. *This is about the Howard Families.*"

The police chief was instantly alert. "Make your report."

"Look," said Lazarus in tired tones, "I know you would like to look over the Old Man's shoulder, but this isn't a good time to try. If you obstruct me and force me to waste two hours by reporting in corpus, I will. But the Old Man will want to know why and you can bet your pretty parade kit I'll tell him."

The Chief Provost decided to take a chance—cut this character in on a three-way; then, if the Old Man didn't burn this joker off the screen in about three seconds, he'd know he had played safe and guessed lucky. If he did—well, you could always blame it on a cross-up in communications. He set the combo.

Administrator Ford looked flabbergasted when he recognized Lazarus in the screen. "You?" he exclaimed. "How on Earth—Did Zaccur Barstow—"

"Seal your circuit!" Lazarus cut in.

The Chief Provost blinked as his screen went dead and silent. So the Old Man *did* have secret agents outside the department . . . interesting—and not to be forgotten.

Lazarus gave Ford a quick and fairly honest account of how he happened to be at large, then added, "So you see, I could have gone to cover and escaped entirely. In fact I still can. But I want to know this: is the deal with Zaccur Barstow to let us emigrate still on?"

"Yes, it is."

"Have you figured out how you are going to get a hundred thousand people inboard the *New Frontiers* without tipping your hand? You can't trust your own people, you know that."

"I know. The present situation is a temporary expedient while we work it out."

"And I'm the man for the job. I've got to be, I'm the only agent on the loose that either one of you can afford to trust. Now listen—"

Eight minutes later Ford was nodding his head slowly and saying, "It might work. It might. Anyway, you start your preparations. I'll have a letter of credit waiting for you at Goddard."

"Can you cover your tracks on that? I can't flash a letter of credit from the Administrator; people would wonder."

"Credit me with some intelligence. By the time it reaches you it will appear to be a routine banking transaction."

"Sorry. Now how can I get through to you when I need to?"

"Oh, yes—note this code combination." Ford recited it slowly. "That puts you through to my desk without relay. No, don't write it down; memorize it."

"And how can I talk to Zack Barstow?"

"Call me and I'll hook you in. You can't call him directly unless you can arrange a sensitive circuit."

"Even if I could, I can't cart a sensitive around with me. Well, cheerio—I'm clearing."

"Good luck!"

Lazarus left the phone booth with restrained haste and hurried back to reclaim his hired ship. He did not know enough about current police practice to guess whether or not the High Chief Provost had traced the call to the Administrator; he simply took it for granted because he himself would have done so in the Provost's shoes. Therefore the nearest available proctor was probably stepping on his heels—time to move, time to mess up the trail a little.

He took off again and headed west, staying in the local, uncontrolled low level until he reached a cloud bank that walled the western horizon. He then swung back and cut air for Kansas City, staying carefully under the speed limit and flying as low as local traffic regulations permitted. At Kansas City he turned his ship in to the local U-push-it agency and flagged a ground taxi, which carried him down the controlway to Joplin. There he boarded a local jet bus from St. Louis without buying a ticket first, thereby insuring that his flight would not be recorded until the bus's trip records were turned in on the west coast.

Instead of worrying he spent the time making plans.

One hundred thousand people with an average mass of a hundred and fifty—no, make it a hundred and sixty pounds, Lazarus reconsidered—a hundred and sixty each made a load of sixteen million pounds, eight thousand tons. The *I Spy* could boost such a load against one gravity but she would be as logy as baked beans. It was out of the question anyhow; people did not stow like cargo; the *I Spy* could lift that dead weight—but "dead" was the word, for that was what they would be.

He needed a transport.

Buying a passenger ship big enough to ferry the Families from Earth up to where the *New Frontiers* hung in her construction orbit was not difficult; Four Planets Passenger Service would gladly unload such a ship at a fair price. Passenger trade competition being what it was, they were anxious to cut their losses on older ships no longer popular with tourists. But a passenger ship would not do; not only would there be unhealthy curiosity in what he intended to do with such a ship, but—and this settled it—he could not pilot it single-handed. Under the Revised Space Precautionary Act, passenger ships were required to be built for human control throughout on the theory that no automatic safety device could replace human judgment in an emergency.

It would have to be a freighter.

Lazarus knew the best place to find one. Despite efforts to make the Moon colony ecologically self-sufficient, Luna City still imported vastly more tonnage than she exported. On Earth this would have resulted in "empties coming back"; in space transport it was sometimes cheaper to let empties accumulate, especially on Luna where an empty freighter was worth more as metal than it had cost originally as a ship back Earthside.

He left the bus when it landed at Goddard City, went to the space field, paid his bills, and took possession of the *I Spy*, filed a request for earliest available departure for Luna. The slot he was assigned was two days from then, but Lazarus did not let it worry him; he simply went back to the docking company and indicated that he was willing to pay liberally for a swap in departure time. In twenty minutes he had oral assurance that he could boost for Luna that evening.

He spent the remaining several hours in the maddening red tape of interplanetary clearance. He first picked up the letter of credit Ford had promised him and converted it into cash. Lazarus would have been quite willing to use a chunk of the cash to speed up his processing just as he had paid (quite legally) for a swap in slot with another ship. But he found himself unable to do so. Two centuries of survival had taught him that a bribe must be offered as gently and as indirectly as a gallant suggestion is made to a proud lady; in a very few minutes he came to the glum conclusion that civic virtue and public honesty could be run into the ground—the functionaries at Goddard Field seemed utterly innocent of the very notion of cumshaw, squeeze, or the lubricating effect of money in routine transactions. He admired their incorruptibility; he did not have to like it—most especially when filling out useless forms cost him the time he had intended to devote to a gourmet's feast in the Skygate Room.

He even let himself be vaccinated again rather than go back to the *I Spy* and dig out the piece of paper that showed he had been vaccinated on arrival Earthside a few weeks earlier.

Nevertheless, twenty minutes before his revised slot time, he lay at the controls of the *I Spy*, his pouch bulging with stamped papers and his stomach not bulging with the sandwich he had managed to grab. He had worked out the "Hohmann's-S" trajectory he would use;

the results had been fed into the autopilot. All the lights on his board were green save the one which would blink green when field control started his count down. He waited in the warm happiness that always filled him when about to boost.

A thought hit him and he raised up against his straps. Then he loosened the chest strap and sat up, reached for his copy of the current *Terra Pilot and Traffic Hazards supplement*. Mmm . . .

New Frontiers hung in a circular orbit of exactly twenty-four hours, keeping always over meridian 106° west at declination zero at a distance from Earth center of approximately twenty-six thousand miles.

Why not pay her a call, scout out the lay of the land?

The *I Spy*, with tanks topped off and cargo spaces empty, had many mile-seconds of reserve boost. To be sure, the field had cleared him for Luna City, not for the interstellar ship . . . but, with the Moon in its present phase, the deviation from his approved flight pattern would hardly show on a screen, probably would not be noticed until the film record was analyzed at some later time—at which time Lazarus would receive a traffic citation, perhaps even have his license suspended. But traffic tickets had never worried him . . . and it was certainly worthwhile to reconnoiter.

He was already setting up the problem in his ballistic calculator. Aside from checking the orbit elements of the *New Frontiers* in the *Terra Pilot* Lazarus could have done it in his sleep; satellite-matching maneuvers were old hat for any pilot and a doubly-tangent trajectory for a twenty-four hour orbit was one any student pilot knew by heart.

He fed the answers into his autopilot during the count down, finished with three minutes to spare, strapped himself down again and relaxed as the acceleration hit him. When the ship went into free fall, he checked his position and vector via the field's transponder. Satisfied, he locked his board, set the alarm for rendezvous, and went to sleep.

6

About four hours later the alarm woke him. He switched it off; it continued to ring—a glance at his screen showed him why. The Gargantuan cylindrical body of the *New Frontiers* lay close aboard. He switched off the radar alarm circuit as well and completed matching with her by the seat of his pants, not bothering with the ballistic calculator. Before he had completed the maneuver the communications alarm started beeping. He slapped a switch; the rig hunted frequencies and the vision screen came to life. A man looked at him. "*New Frontiers* calling: what ship are you?"

"Private vessel *I Spy*, Captain Sheffield. My compliments to your commanding officer. May I come inboard to pay a call?"

They were pleased to have visitors. The ship was completed save for inspection, trials, and acceptance; the enormous gang which had constructed her had gone to Earth and there was no one aboard but the representatives of the Jordan Foundation and a half dozen engineers employed by the corporation which had been formed to build the ship for the foundation. These few were bored with inactivity, bored with each other, anxious to quit marking time and get back to the pleasures of Earth; a visitor was a welcome diversion.

When the *I Spy*'s airlock had been sealed to that of the big ship, Lazarus was met by the engineer in charge—technically "captain" since the *New Frontiers* was a ship under way even though not under power. He introduced himself and took Lazarus on a tour of the ship. They floated through miles of corridors, visited laboratories, storerooms, libraries containing hundreds of thousands of spools, acres of hydroponic tanks for growing food and replenishing oxygen, and comfortable, spacious, even luxurious quarters for a crew colony of ten thousand people. "We believe that the *Vanguard* expedition was somewhat undermanned," the skipper-engineer explained. "The socio-dynamicists calculate that this colony will be able to maintain the basics of our present level of culture."

"Doesn't sound like enough," Lazarus commented. "Aren't there more than ten thousand types of specialization?"

"Oh, certainly! But the idea is to provide experts in all basic arts and indispensable branches of knowledge. Then, as the colony expands, additional specializations can be added through the aid of the reference libraries—anything from tapdancing to tapestry weaving. That's the general idea though it's out of my line. Interesting subject, no doubt, for those who like it."

"Are you anxious to get started?" asked Lazarus.

The man looked almost shocked. "Me? D'you mean to suggest that *I* would go in this thing? My dear sir, I'm an engineer, not a damn fool."

"Sorry."

"Oh, I don't mind a reasonable amount of spacing when there's a reason for it—I've been to Luna City more times than I can count and I've even been to Venus. But you don't think the man who built the *Mayflower* sailed her, do you? For my money the only thing that will keep these people who signed up for it from going crazy before they get there is that it's a dead cinch they're all crazy before they start."

Lazarus changed the subject. They did not dally in the main drive space, nor in the armored cell housing the giant atomic converter, once Lazarus learned that they were unmanned, fully-automatic types. The total absence of moving parts in each of these divisions, made possible by recent developments in parastatics, made their inner workings of intellectual interest only, which could wait. What Lazarus did want to see was the control room, and there he lingered, asking endless questions until his host was plainly bored and remaining only out of politeness.

Lazarus finally shut up, not because he minded imposing on this host but because he was confident that he had learned enough about the controls to be willing to chance conning the ship.

He picked up two other important data before he left the ship: in nine Earth days the skeleton crew was planning a weekend on Earth, following which the acceptance trials would be held. But for three days the big ship would be empty, save possibly for a communications operator—Lazarus was too wary to be inquisitive on this point. But there would be no guard left in her because no need for a guard could be imagined. One might as well guard the Mississippi River.

The other thing he learned was how to enter the ship from the outside without help from the inside; he picked that datum up through watching the mail rocket arrive just as he was about to leave the ship.

At Luna City, Joseph McFee, factor for Diana Terminal Corp., subsidiary of Diana Freight Lines, welcomed Lazarus warmly. "Well! Come in, Cap'n, and pull up a chair. What'll you drink?" He was already pouring as he talked—tax-free paint-remover from his own amateur vacuum still. "Haven't seen you in . . . well, too long. Where d'you raise from last and what's the gossip there? Heard any new ones?"

"From Goddard," Lazarus answered and told him what the skipper had said to the V.I.P. McFee answered with the one about the old maid in free fall, which Lazarus pretended not to have heard. Stories led to politics, and McFee expounded his notion of the "only possible solution" to the European question, a solution predicated on a complicated theory of McFee's as to why the Covenant could not be extended to any culture below a certain level of industrialization. Lazarus did not give a hoot either way but he knew better than to hurry McFee; he nodded at the right places, accepted more of the condemned rocket juice when offered, and waited for the right moment to come to the point.

"Any company ships for sale now, Joe?"

"Are there? I should hope to shout. I've got more steel sitting out on that plain and cluttering my inventory than I've had in ten years. Looking for some? I can make you a sweet price."

"Maybe. Maybe not. Depends on whether you've got what I want."

"You name it, I've got it. Never saw such a dull market. Some days you can't turn an honest credit." McFee frowned. "You know what the trouble is? Well, I'll tell you—it's this Howard Families commotion. Nobody wants to risk any money until he knows where he stands. How can a man make plans when he doesn't know whether to plan for ten years or a hundred? You mark my words: if the administration manages to sweat the secret loose from those babies, you'll see the biggest boom in long-term investments ever. But if not . . . well, long-term holdings won't be worth a peso a dozen and there will be an eat-drink-and-be-merry craze that will make the Reconstruction look like a tea party."

He frowned again. "What kind of metal you looking for?"

"I don't want metal, I want a ship."

McFee's frown disappeared, his eyebrows shot up. "So? What sort?"

"Can't say exactly. Got time to look 'em over with me?"

They suited up and left the dome by North Tunnel, then strolled around grounded ships in the long, easy strides of low gravity. Lazarus soon saw that just two ships had both the lift and the air space needed. One was a tanker and the better buy, but a mental calculation showed him that it lacked deck space, even including the floor plates of the tanks, to accommodate eight thousand tons of passengers. The other was an older ship with cranky piston-type injection meters, but she was fitted for general merchandise and had enough deck space. Her pay load was higher than necessary for the job, since passengers weigh little for the cubage they clutter—but that would make her lively, which might be critically important.

As for the injectors, he could baby them—he had herded worse junk than this.

Lazarus haggled with McFee over terms, not because he wanted to save money but because failure to do so would have been out of character. They finally reached a complicated three-cornered deal in which McFee bought the *I Spy* for himself, Lazarus delivered clear title to it unmortgaged and accepted McFee's unsecured note in payment, then purchased the freighter by endorsing McFee's note back to him and adding cash. McFee in turn would be able to mortgage the *I Spy* at the Commerce Clearance Bank in Luna City, use the proceeds plus cash or credit of his own to redeem his own paper—presumably before his accounts were audited, though Lazarus did not mention that.

It was not quite a bribe. Lazarus merely made use of the fact that McFee had long wanted a ship of his own and regarded the *I Spy* as the ideal bachelor's go-buggy for business or pleasure; Lazarus simply held the price down to where McFee could swing the deal. But the arrangements made certain that McFee would not gossip about the deal, at least until he had time to redeem his note. Lazarus further confused the issue by asking McFee to keep his eyes open for a good buy in trade tobacco . . . which made McFee sure that Captain Sheffield's mysterious new venture involved Venus, that being the only major market for such goods.

Lazarus got the freighter ready for space in only four days through lavish bonuses and overtime payments. At last he dropped Luna City behind him, owner and master of the *City of Chillicothe*. He shortened the

name in his mind to *Chili* in honor of a favorite dish
he had not tasted in a long time—fat red beans, plenty
of chili powder, chunks of meat . . . real meat, not the
synthetic pap these youngsters call "meat." He thought
about it and his mouth watered.

He had not a care in the world.

As he approached Earth, he called traffic control and
asked for a parking orbit, as he did not wish to put the
Chili down; it would waste fuel and attract attention.
He had no scruples about orbiting without permission
but there was a chance that the *Chili* might be spotted, charted, and investigated as a derelict during his
absence; it was safer to be legal.

They gave him an orbit; he matched in and steadied down, then set the *Chili*'s identification beacon to
his own combination, made sure that the radar of the
ship's gig could trip it, and took the gig down to the
auxiliary small-craft field at Goddard. He was careful
to have all necessary papers with him this time; by letting the gig be sealed in bond he avoided customs and
was cleared through the space port quickly. He had no
destination in mind other than to find a public phone
and check in with Zack and Ford—then, if there was
time, try to find some real chili. He had not called the
Administrator from space because ship-to-ground
required relay, and the custom of privacy certainly would
not protect them if the mixer who handled the call
overheard a mention of the Howard Families.

The Administrator answered his call at once, although
it was late at night in the longitude of Novak Tower.
From the puffy circles under Ford's eyes Lazarus judged
that he had been living at his desk. "Hi," said Lazarus,
"better get Zack Barstow on a three-way. I've got things
to report."

"So it's you," Ford said grimly. "I thought you had
run out on us. Where have you been?"

"Buying a ship," Lazarus answered. "As you knew.
Let's get Barstow."

Ford frowned, but turned to his desk. By split screen, Barstow joined them. He seemed surprised to see Lazarus and not altogether relieved. Lazarus spoke quickly:

"What's the matter, pal? Didn't Ford tell you what I was up to?"

"Yes, he did," admitted Barstow, "but we didn't know where you were or what you were doing. Time dragged on and you didn't check in . . . so we decided we had seen the last of you."

"Shucks," complained Lazarus, "you know I wouldn't ever do anything like *that*. Anyhow, here I am and here's what I've done so far—" He told them of the *Chili* and of his reconnaissance of the *New Frontiers*. "Now here's how I see it: sometime this weekend, while the *New Frontiers* is sitting out there with nobody inboard her, I set the *Chili* down in the prison reservation, we load up in a hurry, rush out to the *New Frontiers*, grab her, and scoot. Mr. Administrator, that calls for a lot of help from you. Your proctors will have to look the other way while I land and load. Then we need to sort of slide past the traffic patrol. After that it would be a whole lot better if no naval craft was in a position to do anything drastic about the *New Frontiers*—if there is a communication watch left in her, they may be able to holler for help before we can silence them."

"Give me credit for some foresight," Ford answered sourly. "I know you will have to have a diversion to stand any chance of getting away with it. The scheme is fantastic at the best."

"Not too fantastic," Lazarus disagreed, "if you are willing to use your emergency powers to the limit at the last minute."

"Possibly. But we can't wait four days."

"Why not?"

"The situation won't hold together that long."

"Neither will mine," put in Barstow.

Lazarus looked from one to the other. "Huh? What's the trouble? What's up?"

They explained:

Ford and Barstow were engaged in a preposterously improbable task, that of putting over a complex and subtle fraud, a triple fraud with a different face for the Families, for the public, and for the Federation Council. Each aspect presented unique and apparently insurmountable difficulties.

Ford had no one whom he dared take into his confidence, for even his most trusted personal staff member might be infected with the mania of the delusional Fountain of Youth . . . or might not be, but there was no way to know without compromising the conspiracy. Despite this, he had to convince the Council that the measures he was taking were the best for achieving the Council's purpose.

Besides that, he had to hand out daily news releases to convince the citizens that their government was just about to gain for them the "secret" of living forever. Each day the statements had to be more detailed, the lies more tricky. The people were getting restless at the delay; they were sloughing off the coat of civilization, becoming a mob.

The Council was feeling the pressure of the people. Twice Ford had been forced to a vote of confidence; the second he had won by only two votes. "I won't win another one—we've got to *move.*"

Barstow's troubles were different but just as sticky. He had to have confederates, because his job was to prepare all the hundred thousand members for the exodus. They had to know, before the time came to embark, if they were to leave quietly and quickly. Nevertheless he did not dare tell them the truth too soon because among so many people there were bound to be some who were stupid and stubborn . . . and it required just one fool to wreck the scheme by spilling it to the proctors guarding them.

Instead he was forced to try to find leaders whom he could trust, convince them, and depend on them to convince others. He needed almost a thousand dependable "herdsmen" to be sure of getting his people to follow him when the time came. Yet the very number of confederates he needed was so great as to make certain that somebody would prove weak.

Worse than that, he needed other confederates for a still touchier purpose. Ford and he had agreed on a scheme, weak at best, for gaining time. They were doling out the techniques used by the Families in delaying the symptoms of senility under the pretense that the sum total of these techniques was the "secret." To put over this fraud Barstow had to have the help of the biochemists, gland therapists, specialists in symbiotics and in metabolism, and other experts among the Families, and these in turn had to be prepared for police interrogation by the Families' most skilled psychotechnicians . . . because they had to be able to put over the fraud even under the influence of babble drugs. The hypnotic false indoctrination required for this was enormously more complex than that necessary for a simple block against talking. Thus far the swindle had worked . . . fairly well. But the discrepancies became more hard to explain each day.

Barstow could not keep these matters juggled much longer. The great mass of the Families, necessarily kept in ignorance, were getting out of hand even faster than the public outside. They were rightfully angry at what had been done to them; they expected anyone in authority to do something about it—and do it now!

Barstow's influence over his kin was melting away as fast as that of Ford over the Council.

"It can't be four days," repeated Ford. "More like twelve hours . . . twenty-four at the outside. The Council meets again tomorrow afternoon."

Barstow looked worried. "I'm not sure I can prepare them in so short a time. I may have trouble getting them aboard."

"Don't worry about it," Ford snapped.

"Why not?"

"Because," Ford said bluntly, "any who stay behind will be dead—if they're lucky."

Barstow said nothing and looked away. It was the first time that either one of them had admitted explicitly that this was no relatively harmless piece of political chicanery but a desperate and nearly hopeless attempt to avoid a massacre . . . and that Ford himself was on both sides of the fence.

Well," Lazarus broke in briskly, "now that you boys have settled that, let's get on with it. I can ground the *Chili* in—" He stopped and estimated quickly where she would be in orbit, how long it would take him to rendezvous. "—well, by twenty-two Greenwich. Add an hour to play safe. How about seventeen o'clock Oklahoma time tomorrow afternoon? That's today, actually."

The other two seemed relieved. "Good enough," agreed Barstow. "I'll have them in the best shape I can manage."

"All right," agreed Ford, "if that's the fastest it can be done." He thought for a moment. "Barstow, I'll withdraw at once all proctors and government personnel now inside the reservation barrier and shut you off. Once the gate contracts, you can tell them all."

"Right. I'll do my best."

"Anything else before we clear?" asked Lazarus. "Oh, yes—Zack, we'd better pick a place for me to land, or I may shorten a lot of lives with my blast."

"Uh, yes. Make your approach from the west. I'll rig a standard berth marker. Okay?"

"Okay."

"Not okay," denied Ford. "We'll have to give him a pilot beam to come in on."

"Nonsense," objected Lazarus. "I could set her down on top of the Washington Monument."

"Not this time, you couldn't. Don't be surprised at the weather."

✧   ✧   ✧

As Lazarus approached his rendezvous with the *Chili* he signaled from the gig; the *Chili's* transponder echoed, to his relief—he had little faith in gear he had not personally overhauled and a long search for the *Chili* at this point would have been disastrous.

He figured the relative vector, gunned the gig, flipped, and gunned to brake—homed-in three minutes off estimate, feeling smug. He cradled the gig, hurried inside, and took her down.

Entering the stratosphere and circling two-thirds of the globe took no longer than he had estimated. He used part of the hour's leeway he had allowed himself by being very stingy in his maneuvers in order to spare the worn, obsolescent injection meters. Then he was down in the troposphere and making his approach, with skin temperatures high but not dangerously so. Presently he realized what Ford had meant about the weather. Oklahoma and half of Texas were covered with deep, thick clouds. Lazarus was amazed and somehow pleased; it reminded him of other days, when weather was something experienced rather than controlled. Life had lost some flavor, in his opinion, when the weather engineers had learned how to harness the elements. He hoped that their planet—if they found one!—would have some nice, lively weather.

Then he was down in it and too busy to meditate. In spite of her size the freighter bucked and complained. Whew! Ford must have ordered this little charivari the minute the time was set—and, at that, the integrators must have had a big low-pressure area close at hand to build on.

Somewhere a pattern controlman was shouting at him; he switched it off and gave all his attention to his approach radar and the ghostly images in the infra-red rectifier while comparing what they told him with his inertial tracker. The ship passed over a miles-wide scar on the landscape—the ruins of the Okla-Orleans Road

City. When Lazarus had last seen it, it had been noisy with life. Of all the mechanical monstrosities the human race had saddled themselves with, he mused, those dinosaurs easily took first prize.

Then the thought was cut short by a squeal from his board; the ship had picked up the pilot beam.

He wheeled her in, cut his last jet as she scraped and slapped a series of switches; the great cargo ports rumbled open and rain beat in.

Eleanor Johnson huddled into herself, half crouching against the storm, and tried to draw her cloak more tightly about the baby in the crook of her left arm. When the storm had first hit, the child had cried endlessly, stretching her nerves taut. Now it was quiet, but that seemed only new cause for alarm.

She herself had wept, although she had tried not to show it. In all her twenty-seven years she had never been exposed to weather like this; it seemed symbolic of the storm that had overturned her life, swept her away from her cherished first home of her own with its homey old-fashioned fireplace, its shiny service cell, its thermostat which she could set to the temperature she liked without consulting others—a tempest which had swept her away between two grim proctors, arrested like some poor psychotic, and landed her after terrifying indignities here in the cold sticky red clay of this Oklahoma field.

Was it true? Could it possibly be true? Or had she not yet borne her baby at all and this was another of the strange dreams she had while carrying it?

But the rain was too wetly cold, the thunder too loud; she could never have slept through such a dream. Then what the Senior Trustee had told them must be true, to—it had to be true; she had seen the ship ground with her own eyes, its blast bright against the black of the storm. She could no longer see it but the crowd around her moved slowly forward; it must be in front of her.

She was close to the outskirts of the crowd; she would be one of the last to get aboard.

It was very necessary to board the ship—Elder Zaccur Barstow had told them with deep solemnness what lay in store for them if they failed to board. She had believed his earnestness; nevertheless she wondered how it could possibly be true—could anyone be so wicked, so deeply and terribly wicked as to want to kill anyone as harmless and helpless as herself and her baby?

She was struck by panic terror—suppose there was no room left by the time she got up to the ship? She clutched her baby more tightly; the child cried again at the pressure.

A woman in the crowd moved closer and spoke to her. "You must be tired. May I carry the baby for a while?"

"No. No, thank you. I'm all right." A flash of lightning showed the woman's face; Eleanor Johnson recognized her—Elder Mary Sperling.

But the kindness of the offer steadied her. She knew now what she must do. If they were filled up and could take not more, she must pass her baby forward, hand to hand over the heads of the crowd. They could not refuse space to anything as little as her baby.

Something brushed her in the dark. The crowd was moving forward again.

When Barstow could see that loading would be finished in a few more minutes he left his post at one of the cargo doors and ran as fast as he could through the splashing sticky mud to the communications shack. Ford had warned him to give notice just before they raised ship; it was necessary to Ford's plan for diversion. Barstow fumbled with an awkward unpowered door, swung it open and rushed in. He set the private combination which should connect him directly to Ford's control desk and pushed the key.

He was answered at once but it was not Ford's face on the screen. Barstow burst out with, "Where is the

Administrator? I want to talk with him," before he recognized the face in front of him.

It was a face well known to all the public—Bork Vanning, Leader of the Minority in the Council. "You're talking to the Administrator," Vanning said and grinned coldly. "The new Administrator. Now who the devil are you and why are you calling?"

Barstow thanked all gods, past and present, that recognition was one-sided. He cut the connection with one unaimed blow and plunged out of the building.

Two cargo ports were already closed; stragglers were moving through the other two. Barstow hurried the last of them inside with curses and followed them, slammed pell-mell to the control room. "Raise ship!" he shouted to Lazarus. "Fast!"

"What's all the shootin' fer?" asked Lazarus, but he was already closing and sealing the ports. He tripped the acceleration screamer, waited a scant ten seconds . . . and gave her power.

"Well," he said conversationally six minutes later, "I hope everybody was lying down. If not, we've got some broken bones on our hands. What's that you were saying?"

Barstow told him about his attempt to report to Ford.

Lazarus blinked and whistled a few bars of *Turkey in the Straw*. "It looks like we've run out of minutes. It does look like it." He shut up and gave his attention to his instruments, one eye on his ballistic track, one on radar-aft.

7

Lazarus had his hands full to jockey the *Chili* into just the right position against the side of the *New Frontiers*; the overstrained meters made the smaller craft skittish as a young horse. But he did it. The magnetic anchors clanged home; the gas-tight seals slapped into place; and their ears popped as the pressure in the *Chili* adjusted to that in the giant ship. Lazarus dived for the drop hole in the deck of the control room, pulled himself rapidly hand over hand to the port of contact, and reached the passenger lock of the *New Frontiers* to find himself facing the skipper-engineer.

The man looked at him and snorted. "You again, eh? Why the deuce didn't you answer our challenge? You can't lock onto us without permission; this is private property. What do you mean by it?"

"It means," said Lazarus, "that you and your boys are going back to Earth a few days early—in this ship."

"Why, that's ridiculous!"

"Brother," Lazarus said gently, his blaster suddenly growing out of his left fist, "I'd sure hate to hurt you after you were so nice to me . . . but I sure will, unless you knuckle under awful quick."

The official simply stared unbelievingly. Several of his juniors had gathered behind him; one of them sunfished in the air, started to leave. Lazarus winged him in the leg, at low power; he jerked and clutched at nothing. "Now you'll have to take care of him," Lazarus observed.

That settled it. The skipper called together his men from the announcing system microphone at the passenger lock; Lazarus counted them as they arrived—twenty-nine, a figure he had been careful to learn on his first visit. He assigned two men to hold each of them. Then he took a look at the man he had shot.

"You aren't really hurt, bub," he decided shortly and turned to the skipper-engineer. "Soon as we transfer you, get some radiation salve on that burn. The Red Cross kit's on the after bulkhead of the control room."

"This is piracy! You can't get away with this."

"Probably not," Lazarus agreed thoughtfully. "But I

sort of hope we do." He turned his attention back to his job. "Shake it up there! Don't take all day."

The *Chili* was slowly being emptied. Only the one exit could be used but the pressure of the half hysterical mob behind them forced along those in the bottleneck of the trunk joining the two ships; they came boiling out like bees from a disturbed hive.

Most of them had never been in free fall before this trip; they burst out into the larger space of the giant ship and drifted helplessly, completely disoriented. Lazarus tried to bring order into it by grabbing anyone he could see who seemed to be able to handle himself in zero gravity, ordered him to speed things up by shoving along the helpless ones—shove them anywhere, on back into the big ship, get them out of the way, make room for the thousands more yet to come. When he had conscripted a dozen or so such herdsmen he spotted Barstow in the emerging throng, grabbed him and put him in charge. "Keep 'em moving, just anyhow. I've got to get for'ard to the control room. If you spot Andy Libby, send him after me."

A man broke loose from the stream and approached Barstow. "There's a ship trying to lock onto ours. I saw it through a port."

"Where?" demanded Lazarus.

The man was handicapped by slight knowledge of ships and shipboard terms, but he managed to make himself understood. "I'll be back," Lazarus told Barstow. "Keep 'em moving—and don't let any of those babies get away—our guests there." He holstered his blaster and fought his way back through the swirling mob in the bottleneck.

Number three port seemed to be the one the man had meant. Yes, there was something there. The port had an armor-glass bull's-eye in it, but instead of stars beyond Lazarus saw a lighted space. A ship of some sort had locked against it.

Its occupants either had not tried to open the *Chili's*

port or just possibly did not know how. The port was
not locked from the inside; there had been no reason
to bother. It should have opened easily from either side
once pressure was balanced . . . which the tell-tale,
shining green by the latch, showed to be the case.

Lazarus was mystified.

Whether it was a traffic control vessel, a Naval craft,
or something else, its presence was bad news. But why
didn't they simply open the door and walk in? He was
tempted to lock the port from the inside, hurry and lock
all the others, finish loading and try to run for it.

But his monkey ancestry got the better of him; he
could not leave alone something he did not understand.
So he compromised by kicking the blind latch into place
that would keep them from opening the port from outside, then slithered cautiously alongside the bull's-eye
and sneaked a peep with one eye.

He found himself staring at Slayton Ford.

He pulled himself to one side, kicked the blind latch
open, pressed the switch to open the port. He waited
there, a toe caught in a handhold, blaster in one hand,
knife in the other.

One figure emerged. Lazarus saw that it was Ford,
pressed the switch again to close the port, kicked the
blind latch into place, while never taking his blaster off
his visitor. "Now what the hell?" he demanded. "What
are you doing here? And who else is here? Patrol?"

"I'm alone."

"Huh?"

"I want to go with you . . . if you'll have me."

Lazarus looked at him and did not answer. Then he
went back to the bull's-eye and inspected all that he
could see. Ford appeared to be telling the truth, for
no one else was in sight. But that was not what held
Lazarus' eye.

Why, the ship wasn't a proper deep-space craft at all.
It did not have an airlock but merely a seal to let it
fasten to a larger ship; Lazarus was staring right into

the body of the craft. It looked like—yes, it was a "Joyboat Junior," a little private stratoyacht, suitable only for point-to-point trajectory, or at the most for rendezvous with a satellite provided the satellite could refuel it for the return leg.

There was no fuel for it here. A lightning pilot possibly could land that tin toy without power and still walk away from it . . . provided he had the skill to play Skip-to-M'Lou in and out of the atmosphere while nursing his skin temperatures—but Lazarus wouldn't want to try it. No, sir! He turned to Ford. "Suppose we turned you down. How did you figure on getting back?"

"I didn't figure on it," Ford answered simply.

"Mmm—Tell me about it, but make it march; we're minus on minutes."

Ford had burned all bridges. Turned out of office only hours earlier, he had known that, once all the facts came out, life-long imprisonment in Coventry was the best he could hope for—if he managed to avoid mob violence or mind-shattering interrogation.

Arranging the diversion was the thing that finally lost him his thin margin of control. His explanations for his actions were not convincing to the Council. He had excused the storm and the withdrawing of proctors from the reservation as a drastic attempt to break the morale of the Families—a possible excuse but not too plausible. His orders to Naval craft, intended to keep them away from the *New Frontiers*, had apparently not been associated in anyone's mind with the Howard Families affair; nevertheless the apparent lack of sound reason behind them had been seized on by the opposition as another weapon to bring him down. They were watching for anything to catch him out— one question asked in Council concerned certain monies from the Administrator's discretionary fund which had been paid indirectly to one Captain Aaron Sheffield; were these monies in fact expended in the public interest?

Lazarus' eyes widened. "You mean they were onto me?"

"Not quite. Or you wouldn't be here. But they were close behind you. I think they must have had help from a lot of my people at the last."

"Probably. But we made it, so let's not fret. Come on. The minute everybody is out of this ship and into the big girl, we've got to boost." Lazarus turned to leave.

"You're going to let me go along?"

Lazarus checked his progress, twisted to face Ford. "How else?" He had intended at first to send Ford down in the *Chili*. It was not gratitude that changed his mind, but respect. Once he had lost office Ford had gone straight to Huxley Field north of Novak Tower, cleared for the vacation satellite *Monte Carlo*, and had jumped for the *New Frontiers* instead. Lazarus liked that. "Go for broke" took courage and character that most people didn't have. Don't grab a toothbrush, don't wind the cat—just do it! "Of course you're coming along," he said easily. "You're my kind of boy, Slayton."

The *Chili* was more than half emptied now but the spaces near the interchange were still jammed with frantic mobs. Lazarus cuffed and shoved his way through, trying not to bruise women and children unnecessarily but not letting the possibility slow him up. He scrambled through the connecting trunk with Ford hanging onto his belt, pulled aside once they were through and paused in front of Barstow.

Barstow stared past him. "Yeah, it's him," Lazarus confirmed. "Don't stare—it's rude. He's going with us. Have you seen Libby?"

"Here I am, Lazarus." Libby separated himself from the throng and approached with the ease of a veteran long used to free fall. He had a small satchel strapped to one wrist.

"Good. Stick around. Zack, how long till you're all loaded?"

"God knows. I can't count them. An hour, maybe."

"Make it less. If you put some husky boys on each side of the hole, they can snatch them through faster than they are coming. We've got to shove out of here a little sooner than is humanly possible. I'm going to the control room. Phone me there the instant you have everybody in, our guests here out, and the *Chili* broken loose. Andy! Slayton! Let's go."

"Lazarus—"

"Later, Andy. We'll talk when we get there."

Lazarus took Slayton Ford with him because he did not know what else to do with him and felt it would be better to keep him out of sight until some plausible excuse could be dreamed up for having him along. So far no one seemed to have looked at him twice, but once they quieted down, Ford's well-known face would demand explanation.

The control room was about a half mile forward of where they had entered the ship. Lazarus knew that there was a passenger belt leading to it but he didn't have time to look for it; he simply took the first passageway leading forward. As soon as they got away from the crowd they made good time even though Ford was not as skilled in the fishlike maneuvers of free fall as were the other two.

Once there, Lazarus spent the enforced wait in explaining to Libby the extremely ingenious but unorthodox controls of the star ship. Libby was fascinated and soon was putting himself through dummy runs. Lazarus turned to Ford. "How about you, Slayton? Wouldn't hurt to have a second relief pilot."

Ford shook his head. "I've been listening but I could never learn it. I'm not a pilot."

"*Huh?* How did you get here?"

"Oh. I do have a license, but I haven't had time to keep in practice. My chauffeur always pilots me. I haven't figured a trajectory in many years."

Lazarus looked him over. "And yet you plotted an orbit rendezvous? With no reserve fuel?"

"Oh, that. I had to."

"I see. The way the cat learned to swim. Well, that's one way." He turned back to speak to Libby, was interrupted by Barstow's voice over the announcing system:

"Five minutes, Lazarus! Acknowledge."

Lazarus found the microphone, covered the light under it with his hand and answered, "Okay, Zack! Five minutes." Then he said, "Cripes, I haven't even picked a course. What do you think, Andy? Straight out from Earth to shake the busies off our tail? Then pick a destination? How about it, Slayton? Does that fit with what you ordered Navy craft to do?"

"No, Lazarus, no!" protested Libby.

"Huh? Why not?"

"You should head right straight down for the Sun."

"For the Sun? For Pete's sake, why?"

"I tried to tell you when I first saw you. It's because of the space drive you asked me to develop."

"But, Andy, we haven't got it."

"Yes, we have. Here." Libby shoved the satchel he had been carrying toward Lazarus.

Lazarus opened it.

Assembled odd bits of other equipment, looking more like the product of a boy's workshop than the output of a scientist's laboratory, the gadget which Libby referred to as a "space drive" underwent Lazarus' critical examination. Against the polished sophisticated perfection of the control room it looked uncouth, pathetic, ridiculously inadequate.

Lazarus poked at it tentatively. "What is it?" he asked. "Your model?"

"No, no. That's it. That's the space drive."

Lazarus looked at the younger man not unsympathetically. "Son," he asked slowly, "have you come unzipped?"

"No, no, no!" Libby sputtered. "I'm as sane as you are. This is a radically new notion. That's why I want you to take us down near the Sun. If it works at all, it will work best where light pressure is strongest."

"And if it doesn't work," inquired Lazarus, "what does that make us? Sunspots?"

"Not straight down into the Sun. But head for it now and as soon as I can work out the data, I'll give you corrections to warp you into your proper trajectory. I want to pass the Sun in a very flat hyperbola, well inside the orbit of Mercury, as close to the photosphere as this ship can stand. I don't know how close that is, so I couldn't work it out ahead of time. But the data will be here in the ship and there will be time to correlate them as we go."

Lazarus looked again at the giddy little cat's cradle of apparatus. "Andy . . . if you are sure that the gears in your head are still meshed, I'll take a chance. Strap down, both of you." He belted himself into the pilot's couch and called Barstow. "How about it, Zack?"

"Right now!"

"Hang on tight!" With one hand Lazarus covered a light in his leftside control panel; acceleration warning shrieked throughout the ship. With the other he covered another; the hemisphere in front of them was suddenly spangled with the starry firmament, and Ford gasped.

Lazarus studied it. A full twenty degrees of it was blanked out by the dark circle of the nightside of Earth. "Got to duck around a comer, Andy. We'll use a little Tennessee windage." He started easily with a quarter gravity, just enough to shake up his passengers and make them cautious, while he started a slow operation of precessing the enormous ship to the direction he needed to shove her in order to get out of Earth's shadow. He raised acceleration to a half gee, then to a gee.

Earth changed suddenly from a black silhouette to a slender crescent as the half-degree white disc of the Sun came out from behind her. "I want to clip her about a thousand miles out, Slipstick," Lazarus said tensely, "at two gees. Gimme a temporary vector."

Libby hesitated only momentarily and gave it to him. Lazarus again sounded acceleration warning and boosted to twice Earth-normal gravity. Lazarus was tempted to raise the boost to emergency-full but he dared not do so with a shipload of ground-lubbers; even two gees sustained for a long period might be too much of a strain for some of them. Any Naval pursuit craft ordered to intercept them could boost at much higher gee and their selected crews could stand it. But it was just a chance they would have to take . . . and anyhow, he reminded himself, a Navy ship could not maintain a high boost for long; her mile-seconds were strictly limited by her reaction-mass tanks.

The *New Frontiers* had no such old fashioned limits, no tanks; her converter accepted any mass at all, turned it into pure radiant energy. Anything would serve—meteors, cosmic dust, stray atoms gathered in by her sweep field, or anything from the ship herself, such as garbage, dead bodies, deck sweepings, anything at all. Mass was energy. In dying, each tortured gram gave up nine hundred million trillion ergs of thrust.

The crescent of Earth waxed and swelled and slid off toward the left edge of the hemispherical screen while the Sun remained dead ahead. A little more than twenty minutes later, when they were at closest approach and the crescent, now at half phase, was sliding out of the bowl screen, the ship-to-ship circuit came to life. *"New Frontiers!"* a forceful voice sounded. "Maneuver to orbit and lay to! This is an official traffic control order."

Lazarus shut it off. "Anyhow," he said cheerfully, "if they try to catch us, they won't like chasing us down into the Sun! Andy, it's a clear road now and time we corrected, maybe. You want to compute it? Or will you feed me the data?"

"I'll compute it," Libby answered. He had already

discovered that the ship's characteristics pertinent to astrogation, including her "black body" behavior, were available at both piloting stations. Armed with this and with the running data from instruments he set out to calculate the hyperboloid by which he intended to pass the Sun. He made a half-hearted attempt to use the ship's ballistic calculator but it baffled him; it was a design he was not used to, having no moving parts of any sort, even in the exterior controls. So he gave it up as a waste of time and fell back on the strange talent for figures lodged in his brain. His brain had no moving parts, either, but he was used to it.

Lazarus decided to check on their popularity rating. He switched on the ship-to-ship again, found that it was still angrily squawking, although a little more faintly. They knew his own name now—one of his names—which caused him to decide that the boys in the *Chili* must have called traffic control almost at once. He tut-tutted sadly when he learned that "Captain Sheffield's" license to pilot had been suspended. He shut it off and tried the Naval frequencies . . . then shut them off also when he was able to raise nothing but code and scramble, except that the words *"New Frontiers"* came through once in clear.

He said something about "Sticks and stones may break my bones—" and tried another line of investigation. Both by long-range radar and by paragravitic detector he could tell that there were ships in their neighborhood but this alone told him very little; there were bound to be ships this close to Earth and he had no easy way to distinguish, from these data alone, an unarmed liner or freighter about her lawful occasions from a Naval cruiser in angry pursuit.

But the *New Frontiers* had more resources for analyzing what was around her than had an ordinary ship; she had been specially equipped to cope unassisted with any imaginable strange conditions. The hemispherical control room in which they lay was an enormous multiscreened television receiver which could duplicate the starry heavens either in view-aft or view-forward at the selection of the pilot. But it also had other circuits, much more subtle; simultaneously or separately it could act as an enormous radar screen as well, displaying on it the blips of any body within radar range.

But that was just a starter. Its inhuman senses could apply differential analysis to doppler data and display the result in a visual analog. Lazarus studied his left hand control bank, tried to remember everything he had been told about it, made a change in the set up.

The simulated stars and even the Sun faded to dimness; about a dozen lights shined brightly.

He ordered the board to check them for angular rate; the bright lights turned cherry red, became little comets trailing off to pink tails—all but one, which remained white and grew no tail. He studied the others for a moment, decided that their vectors were such that they would remain forever strangers, and ordered the board to check the line-of-sight doppler on the one with a steady bearing.

It faded to violet, ran halfway through the spectrum and held steady at blue-green. Lazarus thought a moment, subtracted from the inquiry their own two gees of boost; it turned white again. Satisfied he tried the same tests with view-aft.

"Lazarus—"

"Yeah, Lib?"

"Will it interfere with what you are doing if I give you the corrections now?"

"Not at all. I was just taking a look-see. If this magic lantern knows what it's talking about, they didn't manage to get a pursuit job on our tail in time."

"Good. Well, here are the figures . . ."

"Feed 'em in yourself, will you? Take the conn for a while. I want to see about coffee and sandwiches. How about you? Feel like some breakfast?"

Libby nodded absent-mindedly, already starting to

revise the ship's trajectory. Ford spoke up eagerly, the
first word he had uttered in a long time. "Let me get
it. I'd be glad to." He seemed pathetically anxious to
be useful.

"Mmm . . . you might get into some kind of trouble,
Slayton. No matter what sort of a selling job Zack did,
your name is probably 'Mud' with most of the members. I'll phone aft and raise somebody."

"Probably nobody would recognize me under these
circumstances," Ford argued. "Anyway, it's a legitimate
errand—I can explain that."

Lazarus saw from his face that it was necessary to
the man's morale. "Okay . . . if you can handle yourself under two gees."

Ford struggled heavily up out of the acceleration
couch he was in. "I've got space legs. What kind of sandwiches?"

"I'd say corned beef, but it would probably be some
damned substitute. Make mine cheese, with rye if
they've got it and use plenty of mustard. And a gallon
of coffee. What are you having, Andy?"

"Me? Oh, anything that is convenient."

Ford started to leave, bracing himself heavily against
double weight, then he added, "Oh—it might save time
if you could tell me where to go."

"Brother," said Lazarus, "if this ship isn't pretty well
crammed with food, we've all made a terrible mistake.
Scout around. You'll find some."

Down, down, down toward the Sun, with speed
increasing by sixty-four feet per second for every second elapsed. Down and still down for fifteen endless
hours of double weight. During this time they traveled
seventeen million miles and reached the inconceivable
speed of six hundred and forty miles per second. The
figures mean little—think instead of New York to Chicago, a half hour's journey even by stratomail, done in
a single heartbeat.

Barstow had a rough time during heavy weight. For all of the others it was a time to lie down, try hopelessly to sleep, breathe painfully and seek new positions in which to try to rest from the burdens of their own bodies. But Zaccur Barstow was driven by his sense of responsibility; he kept going though the Old Man of the Sea sat on his neck and raised his weight to three hundred and fifty pounds.

Not that he could do anything for them, except crawl wearily from one compartment to another and ask about their welfare. Nothing could be done, no organization to relieve their misery was possible, while high boost continued. They lay where they could, men, women, and children crowded together like cattle being shipped, without even room to stretch out, in spaces never intended for such extreme overcrowding.

The only good thing about it, Barstow reflected wearily, was that they were all too miserable to worry about anything but the dragging minutes. They were too beaten down to make trouble. Later on there would be doubts raised, he was sure, about the wisdom of fleeing; there would be embarrassing questions asked about Ford's presence in the ship, about Lazarus' peculiar and sometimes shady actions, about his own contradictory role. But not yet.

He really must, he decided reluctantly, organize a propaganda campaign before trouble could grow. If it did—and it surely would if he didn't move to offset it, and . . . well, that would be the last straw. It would be.

He eyed a ladder in front of him, set his teeth, and struggled up to the next deck. Picking his way through the bodies there he almost stepped on a woman who was clutching a baby too tightly to her. Barstow noticed that the infant was wet and soiled and he thought of ordering its mother to take care of the matter, since she seemed to be awake. But he let it go—so far as he knew there was not a clean diaper in millions of miles. Or there might be ten thousand of them on the deck above . . . which seemed almost as far away.

He plodded on without speaking to her. Eleanor Johnson had not been aware of his concern. After the first great relief at realizing that she and her baby were safe inside the ship she had consigned all her worries to her elders and now felt nothing but the apathy of emotional reaction and of inescapable weight. Baby had cried when that awful weight had hit them, then had become quiet, too quiet. She had roused herself enough to listen for its heartbeat; then, sure that he was alive, she had sunk back into stupor.

Fifteen hours out, with the orbit of Venus only four hours away, Libby cut the boost. The ship plunged on, in free fall, her terrific speed still mounting under the steadily increasing pull of the Sun. Lazarus was awakened by no weight. He glanced at the copilot's couch and said, "On the curve?"

"As plotted."

Lazarus looked him over. "Okay, I've got it. Now get out of here and get some sleep. Boy, you look like a used towel."

"I'll just stay here and rest."

"You will like hell. You haven't slept even when I had the conn; if you stay here, you'll be watching instruments and figuring. So beat it! Slayton, chuck him out."

Libby smiled shyly and left. He found the spaces abaft the control room swarming with floating bodies but he managed to find an unused corner, passed his kilt belt through a handhold, and slept at once.

Free fall should have been as great a relief to everyone else; it was not, except to the fraction of one per cent who were salted spacemen. Free-fall nausea, like seasickness, is a joke only to those not affected; it would take a Dante to describe a hundred thousand cases of it. There were anti-nausea drugs aboard, but they were not found at once; there were medical men among the Families, but they were sick, too. The misery went on.

Barstow, himself long since used to free flight, floated forward to the control room to pray relief for the less fortunate. "They're in bad shape," he told Lazarus. "Can't you put spin on the ship and give them some let-up? It would help a lot."

"And it would make maneuvering difficult, too. Sorry. Look, Zack, a lively ship will be more important to them in a pinch than just keeping their suppers down. Nobody dies from seasickness anyhow . . . they just wish they could."

The ship plunged on down, still gaining speed as it fell toward the Sun. The few who felt able continued slowly to assist the enormous majority who were ill.

Libby continued to sleep, the luxurious return-to-the-womb sleep of those who have learned to enjoy free fall. He had had almost no sleep since the day the Families had been arrested; his overly active mind had spent all its time worrying the problem of a new space drive.

The big ship precessed around him; he stirred gently and did not awake. It steadied in a new altitude and the acceleration warning brought him instantly awake. He oriented himself, placed himself flat against the after bulkhead, and waited; weight hit him almost at once—three gees this time and he knew that something was badly wrong. He had gone almost a quarter mile aft before he found a hide-away; nevertheless he struggled to his feet and started the unlikely task of trying to climb that quarter mile—now straight up—at three times his proper weight, while blaming himself for having let Lazarus talk him into leaving the control room.

He managed only a portion of the trip . . . but an heroic portion, one about equal to climbing the stairs of a ten-story building while carrying a man on each shoulder . . . when resumption of free fall relieved him. He zipped the rest of the way like a salmon returning home and was in the control room quickly. "What happened?"

Lazarus said regretfully, "Had to vector, Andy."
Slayton Ford said nothing but looked worried.

"Yes, I know. But why?" Libby was already strapping
himself against the copilot's couch while studying the
astrogational situation.

"Red lights on the screen." Lazarus described the display, giving coördinates and relative vectors.

Libby nodded thoughtfully. "Naval craft. No commercial vessels would be in such trajectories. A
minelaying bracket."

"That's what I figured. I didn't have time to consult
you; I had to use enough mile-seconds to be sure they
wouldn't have boost enough to reposition on us."

"Yes, you had to." Libby looked worried. "I thought
we were free of any possible Naval interference."

"They're not ours," put in Slayton Ford. "They can't
be ours no matter what orders have been given since
I—uh, since I left. They must be Venerian craft."

"Yeah," agreed Lazarus, "they must be. Your pal, the
new Administrator, hollered to Venus for help and they
gave it to him—just a friendly gesture of interplanetary
good will."

Libby was hardly listening. He was examining data
and processing it through the calculator inside his skull.
"Lazarus . . . this new orbit isn't too good."

"I know," Lazarus agreed sadly. "I had to duck . . .
ducked the only direction they left open to me—closer
to the Sun."

"Too close, perhaps."

The Sun is not a large star, nor is it very hot. But
it is hot with reference to men, hot enough to strike
them down dead if they are careless about tropic noon-
day ninety-two million miles away from it, hot enough
that we who are reared under its rays nevertheless dare
not look directly at it.

At a distance of two and a half million miles the Sun
beats out with a glare fourteen hundred times as bright
as the worst ever endured in Death Valley, the Sahara,

or Aden. Such radiance would not be perceived as heat or light; it would be death more sudden than the full power of a blaster. The Sun is a hydrogen bomb, a naturally occurring one; the *New Frontiers* was skirting the limits of its circle of total destruction.

It was hot inside the ship. The Families were protected against instant radiant death by the armored walls but the air temperature continued to mount. They were relieved of the misery of free fall but they were doubly uncomfortable, both from heat and from the fact that the bulkheads slanted crazily; there was no level place to stand or lie. The ship was both spinning on its axis and accelerating now; it was never intended to do both at once and the addition of the two accelerations, angular and linear, make "down" the direction where outer and after bulkheads met. The ship was being spun through necessity to permit some of the impinging radiant energy to re-radiate on the "cold" side. The forward acceleration was equally from necessity, a forlorn-hope maneuver to pass the Sun as far out as possible and as fast as possible, in order to spend least time at perihelion, the point of closest approach.

It was hot in the control room. Even Lazarus had voluntarily shed his kilt and shucked down to Venus styles. Metal was hot to the touch. On the great stellarium screen an enormous circle of blackness marked where the Sun's disc should have been; the receptors had cut out automatically at such a ridiculous demand.

Lazarus repeated Libby's last words. "Thirty-seven minutes to perihelion.' We can't take it, Andy. The ship can't take it."

"I know. I never intended us to pass this close."

"Of course you didn't. Maybe I shouldn't have maneuvered. Maybe we would have missed the mines anyway. Oh, well——" Lazarus squared his shoulders and filed it with the might-have-beens. "It looks to me, son, about time to try out your gadget." He poked a thumb at Libby's uncouth-looking "space drive." "You say that all you have to do is to hook up that one connection?"

"That is what is intended. Attach that one lead to any portion of the mass to be affected. Of course I don't really know that it will work," Libby admitted. "There is no way to test it."

"Suppose it doesn't?"

"There are three possibilities," Libby answered methodically. "In the first place, nothing may happen."

"In which case we fry."

"In the second place, we and the ship may cease to exist as matter as we know it."

"Dead, you mean. But probably a pleasanter way."

"I suppose so. I don't know what death is. In the third place, if my hypotheses are correct, we will recede from the Sun at a speed just under that of light."

Lazarus eyed the gadget and wiped sweat from his shoulders. "It's getting hotter, Andy. Hook it up—and it had better be good!"

Andy hooked it up.

"Go ahead," urged Lazarus. "Push the button, throw the switch, cut the beam. Make it march."

"I have," Libby insisted. "Look at the Sun."

"Huh? *Oh!*"

The great circle of blackness which had marked the position of the Sun on the star-speckled stellarium was shrinking rapidly. In a dozen heartbeats it lost half its diameter; twenty seconds later it had dwindled to a quarter of its original width.

"It worked," Lazarus said softly. "Look at it, Slayton! Sign me up as a purple baboon—it *worked!*"

"I rather thought it would," Libby answered seriously. "It should, you know."

"Hmm— That may be evident to you, Andy. It's not to me. How fast are we going?"

"Relative to what?"

"Uh, relative to the Sun."

"I haven't had opportunity to measure it, but it

seems to be just under the speed of light. It can't be greater."

"Why not? Aside from theoretical considerations."

"We still see." Libby pointed at the stellarium bowl.

"Yeah, so we do," Lazarus mused. "Hey! We shouldn't be able to. It ought to doppler out."

Libby looked blank, then smiled. "But it dopplers right back in. Over on that side, toward the Sun, we're seeing by short radiations stretched to visibility. On the opposite side we're picking up something around radio wavelengths dopplered down to light."

"And in between?"

"Quit pulling my leg, Lazarus. I'm sure you can work out relativity vector additions quite as well as I can."

"*You* work it out," Lazarus said firmly. "I'm just going to sit here and admire it. Eh, Slayton?"

"Yes. Yes indeed."

Libby smiled politely. "We might as well quit wasting mass on the main drive." He sounded the warner, then cut the drive. "Now we can return to normal conditions." He started to disconnect his gadget.

Lazarus said hastily, "Hold it, Andy! We aren't even outside the orbit of Mercury yet. Why put on the brakes?"

"Why, this won't stop us. We have acquired velocity; we will keep it."

Lazarus pulled at his cheek and stared. "Ordinarily I would agree with you. First Law of Motion. But with this pseudo-speed I'm not so sure. We got it for nothing and we haven't paid for it—in energy, I mean. You seem to have declared a holiday with respect to inertia; when the holiday is over, won't all that free speed go back where it came from?"

"I don't think so," Libby answered. "Our velocity isn't 'pseudo' anything; it's as real as velocity can be. You are attempting to apply verbal anthropomorphic logic to a field in which it is not pertinent. You would not expect us to be transported instantaneously back

to the lower gravitational potential from which we
started, would you?"

"Back to where you hooked in your space drive? No,
we've moved."

"And we'll keep on moving. Our newly acquired
gravitational potential energy of greater height above the
Sun is no more real than our present kinetic energy of
velocity. They both exist."

Lazarus looked baffled. The expression did not suit
him. "I guess you've got me, Andy. No matter how I
slice it, we seemed to have picked up energy from somewhere. But *where?* When I went to school, they taught
me to honor the Flag, vote the straight party ticket, and
believe in the law of conservation of energy. Seems like
you're violated it. How about it?"

"Don't worry about it," suggested Libby. "The so-called
law of conservation of energy was merely a working hypothesis, unproved and unprovable, used to describe gross
phenomena. Its terms apply only to the older, dynamic
concept of the world. In a plenum conceived as a static
grid of relationships, a 'violation' of that 'law' is nothing
more startling than a discontinuous function, to be noted
and described. That's what I did. I saw a discontinuity
in the mathematical model of the aspect of mass-energy
called inertia. I applied it. The mathematical model
turned out to be similar to the real world. That was the
only hazard, really—one never knows that a mathematical
model is similar to the real world until you try it."

"Yeah, yeah, sure, you can't tell the taste till you bite
it—but, Andy, I still don't see what *caused* it!" He
turned toward Ford. "Do you, Slayton?"

Ford shook his head. "No. I would like to know but
I doubt if I could understand it."

"You and me both. Well, Andy?"

Now Libby looked baffled. "But, Lazarus, causality
has nothing to do with the real plenum. A fact simply
is. Causality is merely an old-fashioned postulate of a
pre-scientific philosophy."

"I guess," Lazarus said slowly, "I'm old fashioned."
Libby said nothing. He disconnected his apparatus.
The disc of black continued to shrink. When it had
shrunk to about one sixth its greatest diameter, it
changed suddenly from black to shining white, as the
ship's distance from the Sun again was great enough to
permit the receptors to manage the load.

Lazarus tried to work out in his head the kinetic
energy of the ship—one-half the square of the velocity of light (minus a pinch, he corrected) times the
mighty tonnage of the *New Frontiers*. The answer did
not comfort him, whether he called it ergs or apples.

8

"First things first," interrupted Barstow. "I'm as fascinated by the amazing scientific aspects of our present
situation as any of you, but we've got work to do. We've
got to plan a pattern for daily living at once. So let's
table mathematical physics and talk about organization."

He was not speaking to the trustees but to his own
personal lieutenants, the key people in helping him put
over the complex maneuvers which had made their
escape possible—Ralph Schultz, Eve Barstow, Mary
Sperling, Justin Foote, Clive Johnson, about a dozen
others.

Lazarus and Libby were there. Lazarus had left Slayton
Ford to guard the control room, with orders to turn away
all visitors and, above all, not to let anyone touch the
controls. It was a make-work job, it being Lazarus' notion
of temporary occupational therapy. He had sensed in Ford
a mental condition that he did not like. Ford seemed to
have withdrawn into himself. He answered when spoken
to, but that was all. It worried Lazarus.

"We need an executive," Barstow went on, "someone

who, for the time being, will have very broad powers to give orders and have them carried out. He'll have to make decisions, organize us, assign duties and responsibilities, get the internal economy of the ship working. It's a big job and I would like to have our brethren hold an election and do it democratically. That'll have to wait; somebody has to give orders now. We're wasting food and the ship is—well, I wish you could have seen the 'fresher I tried to use today."

"Zaccur . . ."

"Yes, Eve?"

"It seems to me that the thing to do is to put it up to the trustees. We haven't any authority; we were just an emergency group for something that is finished now."

"Ahrrumph—" It was Justin Foote, in tones as dry and formal as his face. "I differ somewhat from our sister. The trustees are not conversant with the full background; it would take time we can ill afford to put them into the picture, as it were, before they would be able to judge the matter. Furthermore, being one of the trustees myself, I am able to say without bias that the trustees, as an organized group, can have no jurisdiction because legally they no longer exist."

Lazarus looked interested. "How do you figure that, Justin?"

"Thusly: the board of trustees were the custodians of a foundation which existed as a part of and in relation to a society. The trustees were never a government; their sole duties had to do with relations between the Families and the rest of that society. With the ending of relationship between the Families and terrestrial society, the board of trustees, *ipso facto*, ceases to exist. It is one with history. Now we in this ship are not yet a society, we are an anarchistic group. This present assemblage has as much—or as little—authority to initiate a society as has any part group."

Lazarus cheered and clapped. "Justin," he applauded,

"that is the neatest piece of verbal juggling I've heard in a century. Let's get together sometime and have a go at solipsism."

Justin Foote looked pained. "Obviously—" he began.

"Nope! Not another word! You've convinced me, don't spoil it. If that's how it is, let's get busy and pick a bull moose. How about you, Zack? You look like the logical candidate."

Barstow shook his head. "I know my limitations. I'm an engineer, not a political executive; the Families were just a hobby with me. We need an expert in social administration."

When Barstow had convinced them that he meant it, other names were proposed and their qualifications debated at length. In a group as large as the Families there were many who had specialized in political science, many who had served in public office with credit.

Lazarus listened; he knew four of the candidates. At last he got Eve Barstow aside and whispered with her. She looked startled, then thoughtful, finally nodded.

She asked for the floor. "I have a candidate to propose," she began in her always gentle tones, "who might not ordinarily occur to you, but who is incomparably better fitted, by temperament, training, and experience, to do this job than is anyone as yet proposed. For civil administrator of the ship I nominate Slayton Ford."

They were flabbergasted into silence, then everybody tried to talk at once. "Has Eve lost her mind? Ford is back on Earth!"—"No, no, he's not. I've seen him—*here*—in the ship."—"But it's out of the question!"—"Him? The Families would never accept him!"—"Even so, he's not one of us."

Eve patiently kept the floor until they quieted. "I know my nomination sounds ridiculous and I admit the difficulties. But consider the advantages. We all know Slayton Ford by reputation and by performance. You know, every member of the Families knows, that Ford is a genius in his field. It is going to be hard enough to work out plans for living together in this badly over-crowded ship; the best talent we can draw on will be no more than enough."

Her words impressed them because Ford was that rare thing in history, a statesman whose worth was almost universally acknowledged in his own lifetime. Contemporary historians credited him with having saved the Western Federation in at least two of its major development crises; it was his misfortune rather than his personal failure that his career was wrecked on a crisis not solvable by ordinary means.

"Eve," said Zaccur Barstow, "I agree with your opinion of Ford and I myself would be glad to have him as our executive. But how about all of the others? To the Families—everyone except ourselves here present—Mr. Administrator Ford symbolizes the persecution they have suffered. I think that makes him an impossible candidate."

Eve was gently stubborn. "I don't think so. We've already agreed that we will have to work up a campaign to explain away a lot of embarrassing facts about the last few days. Why don't we do it thoroughly and convince them that Ford is a martyr who sacrificed himself to save them? He is, you know."

"Mmm . . . yes, he is. He didn't sacrifice himself primarily on our account, but there is no doubt in my mind that his personal sacrifice saved us. But whether or not we can convince the others, convince them strongly enough that they will accept him and take orders from him . . . when he is now a sort of personal devil to them—well, I just don't know. I think we need expert advice. How about it, Ralph? Could it be done?"

Ralph Schultz hesitated. "The truth of a proposition has little or nothing to do with its psychodynamics. The notion that 'truth will prevail' is merely a pious wish; history doesn't show it. The fact that Ford really is a martyr to whom we owe gratitude is irrelevant to the purely technical question you put to me." He stopped to think. "But the proposition *per se* has certain sentimentally dramatic aspects which lend it to propaganda manipulation, even in the face of the currently accepted strong counterproposition. Yes . . . yes, I think it could be sold."

"How long would it take you to put it over?"

"Mmm . . . the social space involved is both 'tight' and 'hot' in the jargon we use; I should be able to get a high positive 'k' factor on the chain reaction—if it works at all. But it's an unsurveyed field and I don't know what spontaneous rumors are running around the ship. If you decide to do this, I'll want to prepare some rumors before we adjourn, rumors to repair Ford's reputation—then about twelve hours from now I can release another one that Ford is actually aboard . . . because he intended from the first to throw his lot in with us."

"Uh, I hardly think he did, Ralph."

"Are you *sure*, Zaccur?"

"No, but— Well . . ."

"You see? The truth about his original intentions is a secret between him and his God. You don't know and neither do I. But the dynamics of the proposition are a separate matter. Zaccur, by the time my rumor gets back to you three or four times, even you will begin to wonder." The psychometrician paused to stare at nothing while he consulted an intuition refined by almost a century of mathematical study of human behavior. "Yes, it will work. If you all want to do it, you will be able to make a public announcement inside of twenty-four hours."

"I so move!" someone called out.

A few minutes later Barstow had Lazarus fetch Ford to the meeting place. Lazarus did not explain to him why his presence was required; Ford entered the compartment like a man come to judgment, one with a bitter certainty that the outcome will be against him. His manner showed fortitude but not hope. His eyes were unhappy.

Lazarus had studied those eyes during the long hours they had been shut up together in the control room. They bore an expression Lazarus had seen many times before in his long life. The condemned man who has lost his final appeal, the fully resolved suicide, little furry things exhausted and defeated by struggle with the unrelenting steel of traps—the eyes of each of these hold a single expression, born of hopeless conviction that his time has run out.

Ford's eyes had it.

Lazarus had seen it grow and had been puzzled by it. To be sure, they were all in a dangerous spot, but Ford no more than the rest. Besides, awareness of danger brings a *live* expression; why should Ford's eyes hold the signal of death?

Lazarus finally decided that it could only be because Ford had reached the dead-end state of mind where suicide is necessary. But why? Lazarus mulled it over during the long watches in the control room and reconstructed the logic of it to his own satisfaction. Back on Earth, Ford had been important among his own kind, the short-lived. His paramount position had rendered him then almost immune to the feeling of defeated inferiority which the long-lived stirred up in normal men. But now he was the *only* ephemeral in a race of Methuselahs.

Ford had neither the experience of the elders nor the expectations of the young; he felt inferior to them both, hopelessly outclassed. Correct or not, he felt himself to be a useless pensioner, an impotent object of charity.

To a person of Ford's busy useful background the situation was intolerable. His very pride and strength of character were driving him to suicide.

As he came into the conference room Ford's glance sought out Zaccur Barstow. "You sent for me, sir?"

"Yes, Mr. Administrator." Barstow explained briefly

the situation and the responsibility they wanted him to assume. "You are under no compulsion," he concluded, "but we need your services if you are willing to serve. Will you?"

Lazarus' heart felt light as he watched Ford's expression change to amazement. "Do you really mean that?" Ford answered slowly. "You're not joking with me?"

"Most certainly we mean it!"

Ford did not answer at once and when he did, his answer seemed irrelevant. "May I sit down?"

A place was found for him; he settled heavily into the chair and covered his face with his hands. No one spoke. Presently he raised his head and said in a steady voice, "If that is your will, I will do my best to carry out your wishes."

The ship required a captain as well as a civil administrator. Lazarus had been, up to that time, her captain in a very practical, piratical sense but he balked when Barstow proposed that it be made a formal title. "Huh *uh!* Not me. I may just spend this trip playing checkers. Libby's your man. Serious-minded, conscientious, former naval officer—just the type for the job."

Libby blushed as eyes turned toward him. "Now, really," he protested, "while it is true that I have had to command ships in the course of my duties, it has never suited me. I am a staff officer by temperament. I don't *feel* like a commanding officer."

"Don't see how you can duck out of it," Lazarus persisted. "You invented the go-fast gadget and you are the only one who understands how it works. You've got yourself a job, boy."

"But that does not follow at all," pleaded Libby. "I am perfectly willing to be astrogator, for that is consonant with my talents. But I very much prefer to serve under a commanding officer."

Lazarus was smugly pleased then to see how Slayton Ford immediately moved in and took charge; the sick man was gone, here again was the executive. "It isn't a matter of your personal preference, Commander Libby; we each must do what we can. I have agreed to direct social and civil organization; that is consonant with *my* training. But I can't command the ship as a ship; I'm not trained for it. You are. You must do it."

Libby blushed pinker and stammered. "I would if I were the only one. But there are hundreds of spacemen among the Families and dozens of them certainly have more experience and talent for command than I have. If you'll look for him, you'll find the right man."

Ford said, "What do you think, Lazarus?"

"Um. Andy's got something. A captain puts spine into his ship . . . or doesn't, as the case may be. If Libby doesn't hanker to command, maybe we'd better look around."

Justin Foote had a microed roster with him but there was no scanner at hand with which to sort it. Nevertheless the memories of the dozen and more present produced many candidates. They finally settled on Captain Rufus "Ruthless" King.

Libby was explaining the consequences of his light-pressure drive to his new commanding officer. "The loci of our attainable destinations are contained in a sheaf of paraboloids having their apices tangent to our present course. This assumes that acceleration by means of the ship's normal drive will always be applied so that the magnitude of our present vector, just under the speed of light, will be held constant. This will require that the ship be slowly precessed during the entire maneuvering acceleration. But it will not be too fussy because of the enormous difference in magnitude between our present vector and the maneuvering vectors being impressed on it. One may think of it roughly as accelerating at right angles to our course."

"Yes, yes, I see that," Captain King cut in, "but why

do you assume that the resultant vectors must always be equal to our present vector?"

"Why, it need not be if the Captain decides otherwise," Libby answered, looking puzzled, "but to apply a component that would reduce the resultant vector below our present speed would simply be to cause us to backtrack a little without increasing the scope of our present loci of possible destinations. The effect would only increase our flight time, to generations, even to centuries, if the resultant—"

"Certainly, certainly! I understand basic ballistics, Mister. But why do you reject the other alternative? Why not increase our speed? Why can't I accelerate directly along my present course if I choose?"

Libby looked worried. "The Captain may, if he so orders. But it would be an attempt to exceed the speed of light. That has been assumed to be impossible—"

"That's exactly what I was driving at. 'Assumed.' I've always wondered if that assumption was justified. Now seems like a good time to find out."

Libby hesitated, his sense of duty struggling against the ecstatic temptations of scientific curiosity. "If this were a research ship, Captain, I would be anxious to try it. I can't visualize what the conditions would be if we did pass the speed of light, but it seems to me that we would be cut off entirely from the electromagnetic spectrum insofar as other bodies are concerned. How could we see to astrogate?" Libby had more than theory to worry him; they were "seeing" now only by electronic vision. To the human eye itself the hemisphere behind them along their track was a vasty black; the shortest radiations had dopplered to wavelengths too long for the eye. In the forward direction stars could still be seen but their visible "light" was made up of longest Hertzian waves crowded in by the ship's incomprehensible speed. Dark "radio stars" shined at first magnitude; stars poor in radio wavelengths had faded to obscurity. The familiar constellations were changed beyond easy recognition. The fact that they were seeing by vision distorted by Doppler's effect was confirmed by spectrum analysis; Fraunhofer's lines had not merely shifted toward the violet end, they had passed beyond, out of sight, and previously unknown patterns replaced them.

"Hmm . . ." King replied. "I see what you mean. But I'd certainly like to try it, damme if I wouldn't! But I admit it's out of the question with passengers inboard. Very well, prepare for me roughed courses to type 'G' stars lying inside this trumpet-flower locus of yours and not too far away. Say ten light-years for your first search."

"Yes, sir. I have. I can't offer anything in that range in the 'G' types."

"So? Lonely out here, isn't it? Well?"

"We have Tau Ceti inside the locus at eleven light-years."

"A G5, eh? Not too good."

"No, sir. But we have a true Sol type, a G2—catalog ZD9817. But it's more than twice as far away."

Captain King chewed a knuckle. "I suppose I'll have to put it up to the elders. How much subjective time advantage are we enjoying?"

"I don't know, sir."

"Eh? Well, work it out! Or give me the data and I will. I don't claim to be the mathematician you are, but any cadet could solve that one. The equations are simple enough."

"So they are, sir. But I don't have the data to substitute in the time-contraction equation . . . because I have no way now to measure the ship's speed. The violet shift is useless to use; we don't know what the lines mean. I'm afraid we must wait until we have worked up a much longer baseline."

King sighed. "Mister, I sometimes wonder why I got into this business. Well, are you willing to venture a best guess? Long time? Short time?"

"Uh . . . a long time, sir. Years."

"So? Well, I've sweated it out in worse ships. Years, eh? Play any chess?"

"I have, sir." Libby did not mention that he had given up the game long ago for lack of adequate competition.

"Looks like we'd have plenty of time to play. King's pawn to king four."

"King's knight to bishop three."

"An unorthodox player, eh? Well, I'll answer you later. I suppose I had better try to sell them the G2 even though it takes longer . . . and I suppose I had better caution Ford to start some contests and things. Can't have 'em getting coffin fever."

"Yes, sir. Did I mention deceleration time? It works out to just under one Earth year, subjective, at a negative one gee, to slow us to stellar speeds."

"Eh? We'll decelerate the same way we accelerated—with your light-pressure drive."

Libby shook his head. "I'm sorry, sir. The drawback of the light-pressure drive is that it makes no difference what your previous course and speed may be; if you go inertialess in the near neighborhood of a star, its light pressure kicks you away from it like a cork hit by a stream of water. Your previous momentum is canceled out when you cancel your inertia."

"Well," King conceded, "let's assume that we will follow your schedule. I can't argue with you yet; there are still some things about that gadget of yours that I don't understand."

"There are lots of things about it," Libby answered seriously, "that I don't understand either."

The ship had flicked by Earth's orbit less than ten minutes after Libby cut in his space drive. Lazarus and he had discussed the esoteric physical aspects of it all the way to the orbit of Mars—less than a quarter hour. Jupiter's path was far distant when Barstow called the organization conference. But it killed an hour to find them all in the crowded ship; by the time he called them to order they were a billion miles out, beyond the orbit of Saturn—elapsed time from *"Go!"* less than an hour and a half.

But the blocks get longer after Saturn. Uranus found them still in discussion. Nevertheless Ford's name was agreed on and he had accepted before the ship was as far from the Sun as is Neptune. King had been named captain, had toured his new command with Lazarus as guide, and was already in conference with his astrogator when the ship passed the orbit of Pluto nearly four billion miles deep into space, but still less than six hours after the Sun's light had blasted them away.

Even then they were not outside the Solar System, but between them and the stars lay nothing but the winter homes of Sol's comets and hiding places of hypothetical trans-Plutonian planets—space in which the Sun holds options but can hardly be said to own in fee simple. But even the nearest stars were still light-years away. *New Frontiers* was headed for them at a pace which crowded the heels of light—weather cold, track fast.

Out, out, and still farther out . . . out to the lonely depths where world lines are almost straight, undistorted by gravitation. Each day, each month . . . each year . . . their headlong flight took them farther from all humanity.

PART TWO

1

The ship lunged on, alone in the desert of night, each light-year as empty as the last. The Families built up a way of life in her.

The *New Frontiers* was approximately cylindrical. When not under acceleration, she was spun on her axis to give pseudo-weight to passengers near the outer skin of the ship; the outer or "lower" compartments were living quarters while the innermost or "upper" compartments were storerooms and so forth. 'Tween compartments were shops, hydroponic farms and such. Along the axis, fore to aft, were the control room, the converter, and the main drive.

The design will be recognized as similar to that of the larger free-flight interplanetary ships in use today, but it is necessary to bear in mind her enormous size. She was a city, with ample room for a colony of twenty thousand, which would have allowed the planned complement of ten thousand to double their numbers during the long voyage to Proxima Centauri.

Thus, big as she was, the hundred thousand and more of the Families found themselves overcrowded fivefold.

They put up with it only long enough to rig for cold-sleep. By converting some recreation space on the lower levels to storage, room was squeezed out for the purpose. Somnolents require about one per cent the living room needed by active, functioning humans; in time the ship was roomy enough for those still awake. Volunteers for cold-sleep were not numerous at first— these people were more than commonly aware of death because of their unique heritage; cold-sleep seemed too much like the Last Sleep. But the great discomfort of extreme overcrowding combined with the equally extreme monotony of the endless voyage changed their minds rapidly enough to provide a steady supply for the little death as fast as they could be accommodated.

Those who remained awake were kept humping simply to get the work done—the ship's housekeeping, tending the hydroponic farms and the ship's auxiliary machinery and, most especially, caring for the somnolents themselves. Biomechanicians have worked out complex empirical formulas describing body deterioration and the measures which must be taken to offset it under various conditions of impressed acceleration, ambient temperature, the drugs used, and other factors such as metabolic age, body mass, sex, and so forth. By using the upper, low-weight compartments, deterioration caused by acceleration (that is to say, the simple weight of body tissues on themselves, the wear that leads to flat feet or bed sores) could be held to a minimum. But all the care of the somnolents had to be done by hand—turning them, massaging them, checking the blood sugar, testing the slow-motion heart actions, all the tests and services necessary to make sure that extremely reduced metabolism does not slide over into

death. Aside from a dozen stalls in the ship's infirmary
she had not been designed for cold-sleep passengers;
no automatic machinery had been provided. All this tedious care of tens of thousands of somnolents had to be
done by hand.

Eleanor Johnson ran across her friend, Nancy
Weatheral, in Refectory 9-D—called "The Club" by its
habitués, less flattering things by those who avoided it.
Most of its frequenters were young and noisy. Lazarus
was the only elder who ate there often. He did not mind
noise, he enjoyed it.

Eleanor swooped down on her friend and kissed the
back of her neck. "Nancy! So you are awake again! My,
I'm glad to see you!"

Nancy disentangled herself. "H'lo, babe. Don't spill
my coffee."

"Well! Aren't you glad to see *me*?"

"Of course I am. But you forget that while it's been
a year to you, it's only yesterday to me. And I'm still
sleepy."

"How long have you been awake, Nancy?"

"A couple of hours. How's that kid of yours?"

"Oh, he's fine!" Eleanor Johnson's face brightened.
"You wouldn't know him—he's shot up fast this past year.
Almost up to my shoulder and looking more like his
father every day."

Nancy changed the subject. Eleanor's friends made
a point of keeping Eleanor's deceased husband out of
the conversation. "What have you been doing while I
was snoozing? Still teaching primary?"

"Yes. Or rather 'No.' I stay with the age group my
Hubert is in. He's in junior secondary now."

"Why don't you catch a few months' sleep and skip
some of that drudgery, Eleanor? You'll make an old
woman out of yourself if you keep it up."

"No," Eleanor refused, "not until Hubert is old
enough not to need me."

"Don't be sentimental. Half the female volunteers are women with young children. I don't blame 'em a bit. Look at me—from my point of view the trip so far has lasted only seven months. I could do the rest of it standing on my head."

Eleanor looked stubborn. "No, thank you. That may be all right for you, but I am doing very nicely as I am."

Lazarus had been sitting at the same counter doing drastic damage to a sirloin steak surrogate. "She's afraid she'll miss something," he explained. "I don't blame her. So am I."

Nancy changed her tack. "Then have another child, Eleanor. That'll get you relieved from routine duties."

"It takes two to arrange that," Eleanor pointed out.

"That's no hazard. Here's Lazarus, for example. He'd make a plus father."

Eleanor dimpled. Lazarus blushed under his permanent tan. "As a matter of fact," Eleanor stated evenly, "I proposed to him and was turned down."

Nancy sputtered into her coffee and looked quickly from Lazarus to Eleanor. "Sorry. I didn't know."

"No harm," answered Eleanor. "It's simply because I am one of his granddaughters, four times removed."

"But . . ." Nancy fought a losing fight with the custom of privacy. "Well, goodness me, that's well within the limits of permissible consanguinity. What's the hitch? Or should I shut up?"

"You should," Eleanor agreed.

Lazarus shifted uncomfortably. "I know I'm old-fashioned," he admitted, "but I soaked up some of my ideas a long time ago. Genetics or no genetics, I just wouldn't feel *right* marrying one of my own grandchildren."

Nancy looked amazed. "I'll say you're old-fashioned!" She added, "Or maybe you're just shy. I'm tempted to propose to you myself and find out."

Lazarus glared at her. "Go ahead and see what a surprise you get!"

Nancy looked him over coolly. "Mmm . . ." she meditated.

Lazarus tried to outstare her, finally dropped his eyes. "I'll have to ask you ladies to excuse me," he said nervously. "Work to do."

Eleanor laid a gentle hand on his arm. "Don't go, Lazarus. Nancy is a cat and can't help it. Tell her about the plans for landing."

"What's that? Are we going to land? When? Where?"

Lazarus, willing to be mollified, told her. The type G2, or Sol-type star, toward which they had bent their course years earlier was now less than a light-year away—a little over seven light-months—and it was now possible to infer by parainterferometric methods that the star (ZD9817, or simply "our" star) had planets of some sort.

In another month, when the star would be a half light-year away, deceleration would commence. Spin would be taken off the ship and for one year she would boost backwards at one gravity, ending near the star at interplanetary rather than interstellar speed, and a search would be made for a planet fit to support human life. The search would be quick and easy as the only planets they were interested in would shine out brilliantly then, like Venus from Earth; they were not interested in elusive cold planets, like Neptune or Pluto, lurking in distant shadows, nor in scorched cinders like Mercury, hiding in the flaming skirts of the mother star.

If no Earthlike planet was to be had, then they must continue on down really close to the strange sun and again be kicked away by light pressure, to resume hunting for a home elsewhere—with the difference that this time, not harassed by police, they could select a new course with care.

Lazarus explained that the *New Frontiers* would not actually land in either case; she was too big to land, her weight would wreck her. Instead, if they found a planet, she would be thrown into a parking orbit around her and exploring parties would be sent down in ship's boats.

As soon as face permitted Lazarus left the two young women and went to the laboratory where the Families continued their researches in metabolism and gerontology. He expected to find Mary Sperling there; the brush with Nancy Weatheral had made him feel a need for her company. If he ever did marry again, he thought to himself, Mary was more his style. Not that he seriously considered it; he felt that a liaison between Mary and himself would have a ridiculous flavor of lavender and old lace.

Mary Sperling, finding herself cooped up in the ship and not wishing to accept the symbolic death of cold-sleep, had turned her fear of death into constructive channels by volunteering to be a laboratory assistant in the continuing research into longevity. She was not a trained biologist but she had deft fingers and an agile mind; the patient years of the trip had shaped her into a valuable assistant to Dr. Gordon Hardy, chief of the research.

Lazarus found her servicing the deathless tissue of chicken heart known to the laboratory crew as "Mrs. 'Awkins." Mrs. 'Awkins was older than any member of the Families save possibly Lazarus himself; she was a growing piece of the original tissue obtained by the Families from the Rockefeller Institute in the twentieth century, and the tissues had been alive since early in the twentieth century even then. Dr. Hardy and his predecessors had kept their bit of it alive for more than two centuries now, using the Carrel-Lindbergh-O'Shaug techniques—and still Mrs. 'Awkins flourished.

Gordon Hardy had insisted on taking the tissue and the apparatus which cherished it with him to the reservation when he was arrested; he had been equally stubborn about taking the living tissue along during the escape in the *Chili*. Now Mrs. 'Awkins still lived and grew in the *New Frontiers*, fifty or sixty pounds of her—blind, deaf, and brainless, but still alive.

Mary Sperling was reducing her size. "Hello, Lazarus," she greeted him. "Stand back. I've got the tank open."

He watched her slice off excess tissue. "Mary," he mused, "what keeps that silly thing alive?"

"You've got the question inverted," she answered, not looking up; "the proper form is: why should it die? Why shouldn't it go on forever?"

"I wish to the Devil it would die!" came the voice of Dr. Hardy from behind them. "Then we could observe and find out why."

"You'll never find out why from Mrs. 'Awkins, boss," Mary answered, hands and eyes still busy. "The key to the matter is in the gonads—she hasn't any."

"Hummph! What do you know about it?"

"A woman's intuition. What do *you* know about it?"

"Nothing, absolutely nothing!—which puts me ahead of you and your intuition."

"Maybe. At least," Mary added slyly, "I knew you before you were housebroken."

"A typical female argument. Mary, that lump of muscle cackled and laid eggs before either one of us was born, yet it doesn't know anything." He scowled at it. "Lazarus, I'd gladly trade it for one pair of carp, male and female."

"Why carp?" asked Lazarus.

"Because carp don't seem to die. They get killed, or eaten, or starve to death, or succumb to infection, but so far as we know they don't die."

"Why not?"

"That's what I was trying to find out when we were rushed off on this damned safari. They have unusual intestinal flora and it may have something to do with that. But I think it has to do with the fact that they never stop growing."

Mary said something inaudibly. Hardy said, "What are you muttering about? Another intuition?"

"I said, 'Amebas don't die.' You said yourself that every ameba now alive has been alive for, oh, fifty million years or so. Yet they don't grow indefinitely larger and they certainly can't have intestinal flora."

"No guts," said Lazarus and blinked.

"What a terrible pun, Lazarus. But what I said is true. They don't die. They just twin and keep on living."

"Guts or no guts;" Hardy said impatiently, "there may be a structural parallel. But I'm frustrated for lack of experimental subjects. Which reminds me: Lazarus, I'm glad you dropped in. I want you to do me a favor."

"Speak up. I might be feeling mellow."

"You're an interesting case yourself, you know. You didn't follow our genetic pattern; you anticipated it. I don't want your body to go into the converter; I want to examine it."

Lazarus snorted "S'all right with me, bud. But you'd better tell your successor what to look for—you may not live that long. And I'll bet you anything that you like that nobody'll find it by poking around in my cadaver!"

The planet they had hoped for was there when they looked for it, green, lush, and young, and looking as much like Earth as another planet could. Not only was it Earthlike but the rest of the system duplicated roughly the pattern of the Solar System—small terrestrial planets near the sun, large Jovian planets farther out. Cosmologists had never been able to account for the Solar System; they had alternated between theories of origin which had failed to stand up and "sound" mathematico-physical "proofs" that such a system could never have originated in the first place. Yet here was another enough like it to suggest that its paradoxes were not unique, might even be common.

But more startling and even more stimulating and certainly more disturbing was another fact brought out by telescopic observation as they got close to the planet. The planet held life . . . intelligent life . . . civilized life.

Their cities could be seen. Their engineering works, strange in form and purpose, were huge enough to be seen from space just as ours can be seen.

Nevertheless, though it might mean that they must again pursue their weary hegira, the dominant race did not appear to have crowded the available living space. There might be room for their little colony on those broad continents. If a colony was welcome—

"To tell the truth," Captain King fretted, "I hadn't expected anything like this. Primitive aborigines perhaps, and we certainly could expect dangerous animals, but I suppose I unconsciously assumed that man was the only really civilized race. We're going to have to be very cautious."

King made up a scouting party headed by Lazarus; he had come to have confidence in Lazarus' practical sense and will to survive. King wanted to head the party himself, but his concept of his duty as a ship's captain forced him to forego it. But Slayton Ford could go; Lazarus chose him and Ralph Schultz as his lieutenants. The rest of the party were specialists—biochemist, geologist, ecologist, stereographer, several sorts of psychologists and sociologists to study the natives including one authority in McKelvy's structural theory of communication whose task would be to find some way to talk with the natives.

No weapons—

King flatly refused to arm them. "Your scouting party is expendable," he told Lazarus bluntly; "for we cannot risk offending them by any sort of fighting for any reason, even in self-defense. You are ambassadors, not soldiers. Don't forget it."

Lazarus returned to his stateroom, came back and gravely delivered to King one blaster. He neglected to mention the one still strapped to his leg under his kilt.

As King was about to tell them to man the boat and carry out their orders they were interrupted by Janice

Schmidt, chief nurse to the Families' congenital defectives. She pushed her way past and demanded the Captain's attention.

Only a nurse could have obtained it at that moment; she had professional stubbornness to match his and half a century more practice at being balky. He glared at her. "What's the meaning of this interruption?"

"Captain, I must speak with you about one of my children."

"Nurse, you are decidedly out of order. Get out. See me in my office—after taking it up with the Chief Surgeon."

She put her hands on her hips. "You'll see me now. This is the landing party, isn't it? I've got something you have to hear before they leave."

King started to speak, changed his mind, merely said, "Make it brief."

She did so. Hans Weatheral, a youth of some ninety years and still adolescent in appearance through a hyperactive thymus gland, was one of her charges. He had inferior but not moronic mentality, a chronic apathy, and a neuro-muscular deficiency which made him too weak to feed himself—and an acute sensitivity to telepathy.

He had told Janice that he knew all about the planet around which they orbited. His friends on the planet had told him about it . . . and they were expecting him.

The departure of the landing boat was delayed while King and Lazarus investigated. Hans was matter of fact about his information and what little they could check of what he said was correct. But he was not too helpful about his "friends." "Oh, just people," he said, shrugging at their stupidity. "Much like back home. Nice people. Go to work, go to school, go to church. Have kids and enjoy themselves. You'll like them."

But he was quite clear about one point: his friends were expecting him; therefore he must go along.

Against his wishes and his better judgment Lazarus saw added to his party Hans Weatheral, Janice Schmidt, and a stretcher for Hans.

✧ ✧ ✧

When the party returned three days later Lazarus made a long private report to King while the specialist reports were being analyzed and combined. "It's amazingly like Earth, Skipper, enough to make you homesick. But it's also different enough to give you the willies—like looking at your own face in the mirror and having it turn out to have three eyes and no nose. Unsettling."

"But how about the natives?"

"Let me tell it. We made a quick swing of the day side, for a bare eyes look. Nothing you haven't seen through the 'scopes. Then I put her down where Hans told me to, in a clearing near the center of one of their cities. I wouldn't have picked the place myself; I would have preferred to land in the bush and reconnoitre. But you told me to play Hans' hunches."

"You were free to use your judgment," King reminded him.

"Yes, yes. Anyhow we did it. By the time the techs had sampled the air and checked for hazards there was quite a crowd around us. They—well, you've seen the stereographs."

"Yes. Incredibly android."

"Android, hell! They're *men*. Not humans, but men just the same." Lazarus looked puzzled. "I don't like it."

King did not argue. The pictures had shown bipeds seven to eight feet tall, bilaterally symmetric, possessed of internal skeletal framework, distinct heads, lens-and-camera eyes. Those eyes were their most human and appealing features; they were large, limpid, and tragic, like those of a Saint Bernard dog.

It was well to concentrate on the eyes; their other features were not as tolerable. King looked away from the loose, toothless mouths, the bifurcated upper lips. He decided that it might take a long, long time to learn to be fond of these creatures. "Go ahead," he told Lazarus.

"We opened up and I stepped out alone, with my hands empty and trying to look friendly and peaceable. Three of them stepped forward—eagerly, I would say. But they lost interest in me at once; they seemed to be waiting for somebody else to come out. So I gave orders to carry Hans out.

"Skipper, you wouldn't believe it. They fawned over Hans like a long lost brother. No, that doesn't describe it. More like a king returning home in triumph. They were polite enough with the rest of us, in an offhand way, but they fairly slobbered over Hans." Lazarus hesitated. "Skipper? Do you believe in reincarnation?"

"Not exactly. I'm open-minded about it. I've read the report of the Frawling Committee, of course."

"I've never had any use for the notion myself. But how else could you account for the reception they gave Hans?"

"I don't account for it. Get on with your report. Do you think it is going to be possible for us to colonize here?"

"Oh," said Lazarus, "they left no doubt on that point. You see, Hans really can talk to them, telepathically. Hans tells us that their gods have authorized us to live here and the natives have already made plans to receive us."

"Eh?"

"That's right. They want us."

"Well! That's a relief."

"Is it?"

King studied Lazarus' glum features. "You've made a report favorable on every point. Why the sour look?"

"I don't know. I'd just rather we found a planet of our own. Skipper, anything this easy has a hitch in it."

2

The Jockaira (or Zhacheira, as some prefer) turned an entire city over to the colonists.

Such astounding coöperation, plus the sudden discovery by almost every member of the Howard Families that he was sick for the feel of dirt under foot and free air in his lungs, greatly speeded the removal from ship to ground. It had been anticipated that at least an Earth year would be needed for such transition and that somnolents would be waked only as fast as they could be accommodated dirtside. But the limiting factor now was the scanty ability of the ship's boats to transfer a hundred thousand people as they were roused.

The Jockaira city was not designed to fit the needs of human beings. The Jockaira were not human beings, their physical requirements were somewhat different, and their cultural needs as expressed in engineering were vastly different. But a city, any city, is a machine to accomplish certain practical ends: shelter, food supply, sanitation, communication; the internal logic of these prime requirements, as applied by different creatures to different environments, will produce an unlimited number of answers. But, as applied by any race of warm-blooded, oxygen-breathing androidal creatures to a particular environment, the results, although strange, are necessarily such that Terran humans can use them. In some ways the Jockaira city looked as wild as a pararealist painting, but humans have lived in igloos, grass shacks, and even in the cybernautomated burrow under Antarctica; these humans could and did move into the Jockaira city—and of course at once set about reshaping it to suit them better.

It was not difficult even though there was much to be done. There were buildings already standing—shelters with roofs on them, the artificial cave basic to all human shelter requirements. It did not matter what the Jockaira had used such a structure for; humans could use it for almost anything: sleeping, recreation, eating, storage, production. There were actual "caves" as well, for the Jockaira dig in more than we do. But humans easily turn troglodyte on occasion, in New York as readily as in Antarctica.

There was fresh potable water piped in for drinking and for limited washing. A major lack lay in plumbing; the city had no over-all drainage system. The "Jocks" did not water-bathe and their personal sanitation requirements differed from ours and were taken care of differently. A major effort had to be made to jury-rig equivalents of shipboard refreshers and adapt them to hook in with Jockaira disposal arrangements. Minimum necessity ruled; baths would remain a rationed luxury until water supply and disposal could be increased at least tenfold. But baths are not a necessity.

But such efforts at modification were minor compared with the crash program to set up hydroponic farming, since most of the somnolents could not be waked until a food supply was assured. The do-it-now crowd wanted to tear out every bit of hydroponic equipment in the *New Frontiers* at once, ship it down dirtside, set it up and get going, while depending on stored supplies during the change-over; a more cautious minority wanted to move only a pilot plant while continuing to grow food in the ship; they pointed out that unsuspected fungus or virus on the strange planet could result in disaster . . . starvation.

The minority, strongly led by Ford and Barstow and supported by Captain King, prevailed; one of the ship's hydroponic farms was drained and put out of service. Its machinery was broken down into parts small enough to load into ship's boats.

But even this never reached dirtside. The planet's native farm products turned out to be suitable for human food and the Jockaira seemed almost pantingly anxious to give them away. Instead, efforts were turned to establishing Earth crops in native soil in order to supplement Jockaira foodstuffs with sorts the humans were used to. The Jockaira moved in and almost took over that effort; they were superb "natural" farmers (they had no need for synthetics on their undepleted planet) and seemed delighted to attempt to raise anything their guests wanted.

Ford transferred his civil headquarters to the city as soon as a food supply for more than a pioneer group was assured, while King remained in the ship. Sleepers were awakened and ferried to the ground as fast as facilities were made ready for them and their services could be used. Despite assured food, shelter, and drinking water, much needed to be done to provide minimum comfort and decency. The two cultures were basically different. The Jockaira seemed always anxious to be endlessly helpful but they were often obviously baffled at what the humans tried to do. The Jockaira culture did not seem to include the idea of privacy; the buildings of the city had no partitions in them which were not loadbearing—and few that were; they tended to use columns or posts. They could not understand why the humans would break up these lovely open spaces into cubicles and passageways; they simply could not comprehend why any individual would ever wish to be alone for any purpose whatsoever.

Apparently (this is not certain for abstract communication with them never reached a subtle level) they decided eventually that being alone held a religious significance for Earth people. In any case they were again helpful; they provided thin sheets of material which could be shaped into partitions—with their tools and only with their tools. The stuff frustrated human engineers almost to nervous collapse. No corrosive known to our technology affected it; even the reactions that would break down the rugged fluorine plastics used in handling uranium compounds had no effect on it. Diamond saws went to pieces on it, heat did not melt it, cold did not make it brittle. It stopped light, sound, and all radiation they were equipped to try on it. Its tensile strength could not be defined because they could not break it. Yet Jockaira tools, even when handled by humans, could cut it, shape it, reweld it.

The human engineers simply had to get used to such frustrations. From the criterion of control over environment through technology the Jockaira were as civilized as humans. But their developments had been along other lines.

The important differences between the two cultures went much deeper than engineering technology. Although ubiquitously friendly and helpful the Jockaira were *not* human. They thought differently, they evaluated differently; their social structure and language structure reflected their unhuman quality and both were incomprehensible to human beings.

Oliver Johnson, the semantician who had charge of developing a common language, found his immediate task made absurdly easy by the channel of communication through Hans Weatheral. "Of course," he explained to Slayton Ford and to Lazarus, "Hans isn't exactly a genius; he just misses being a moron. That limits the words I can translate through him to ideas he can understand. But it does give me a basic vocabulary to build on."

"Isn't that enough?" asked Ford. "It seems to me that I have heard that eight hundred words will do to convey any idea."

"There's some truth in that," admitted Johnson. "Less than a thousand words will cover all ordinary situations. I have selected not quite seven hundred of their terms, operationals and substantives, to give us a working *lingua franca*. But subtle distinctions and fine discriminations will have to wait until we know them better and understand them. A short vocabulary cannot handle high abstractions."

"Shucks," said Lazarus, "seven hundred words ought to be enough. Me, I don't intend to make love to 'em, or try to discuss poetry."

This opinion seemed to be justified; most of the members picked up basic Jockairan in two weeks to a month after being ferried down and chattered in it to their hosts as if they had talked it all their lives. All of the Earthmen had had the usual sound grounding in mnemonics and semantics; a short-vocabulary auxiliary language was quickly learned under the stimulus of need and the circumstance of plenty of chance to practice—except, of course, by the usual percentage of unshakable provincials who felt that it was up to "the natives" to learn English.

The Jockaira did not learn English. In the first place not one of them showed the slightest interest. Nor was it reasonable to expect their millions to learn the language of a few thousand. But in any case the split upper lip of a Jockaira could not cope with "m," "p," and "b," whereas the gutturals, sibilants, dentals, and clicks they did use could be approximated by the human throat.

Lazarus was forced to revise his early bad impression of the Jockaira. It was impossible not to like them once the strangeness of their appearance had worn off. They were so hospitable, so generous, so friendly, so anxious to please. He became particularly attached to Kreel Sarloo, who acted as a sort of liaison officer between the Families and the Jockaira. Sarloo held a position among his own people which could be translated roughly as "chief," "father," "priest," or "leader" of the Kreel family or tribe. He invited Lazarus to visit him in the Jockaira city nearest the colony. "My people will like to see you and smell your skin," he said. "It will be a happy-making thing. The gods will be pleased."

Sarloo seemed almost unable to form a sentence without making reference to his gods. Lazarus did not mind; to another's religion he was tolerantly indifferent. "I will come, Sarloo, old bean. It will be a happy-making thing for me, too."

Sarloo took him in the common vehicle of the Jockaira, a wheelless wain shaped much like a soup bowl, which moved quietly and rapidly over the ground, skimming the surface in apparent contact. Lazarus squatted on the floor of the vessel while Sarloo caused it to speed along at a rate that made Lazarus' eyes water.

"Sarloo," Lazarus asked, shouting to make himself heard against the wind, "how does this thing work? What moves it?"

"The gods breathe on the—" Sarloo used a word not in their common language, "—and cause it to need to change its place."

Lazarus started to ask for a fuller explanation, then shut up. There had been something familiar about that answer and he now placed it; he had once given a very similar answer to one of the water people of Venus when he was asked to explain the diesel engine used in an early type of swamp tractor. Lazarus had not meant to be mysterious; he had simply been tongue-tied by inadequate common language.

Well, there was a way to get around that—

"Sarloo, I want to see pictures of what happens inside," Lazarus persisted, pointing. "You have pictures?"

"Pictures are," Sarloo acknowledged, "in the temple. You must not enter the temple." His great eyes looked mournfully at Lazarus, giving him a strong feeling that the Jockaira chief grieved over his friend's lack of grace. Lazarus hastily dropped the subject.

But the thought of Venerians brought another puzzler to mind. The water people, cut off from the outside world by the eternal clouds of Venus, simply did not believe in astronomy. The arrival of Earthmen had caused them to readjust their concept of the cosmos a little, but there was reason to believe that their revised explanation was no closer to the truth. Lazarus wondered what the Jockaira thought about visitors from space. They had shown no surprise—or had they?

"Sarloo," he asked, "do you know where my brothers and I come from?"

"I know," Sarloo answered. "You come from a distant sun—so distant that many seasons would come and go while light traveled that long journey."

Lazarus felt mildly astonished. "Who told you that?"

"The gods tell us. Your brother Libby spoke on it."

Lazarus was willing to lay long odds that the gods had not got around to mentioning it until after Libby explained it to Kreel Sarloo. But he held his peace. He still wanted to ask Sarloo if he had been surprised to have visitors arrive from the skies but he could think of no Jockairan term for surprise or wonder. He was still trying to phrase the question when Sarloo spoke again:

"The fathers of my people flew through the skies as you did, but that was before the coming of the gods. The gods, in their wisdom, bade us stop."

And that, thought Lazarus, is one damn big lie, from pure swank. There was not the slightest indication that the Jockaira had ever been off the surface of their planet.

At Sarloo's home that evening Lazarus sat through a long session of what he assumed was entertainment for the guest of honor, himself. He squatted beside Sarloo on a raised portion of the floor of the vast common room of the clan Kreel and listened to two hours of howling that might have been intended as singing. Lazarus felt that better music would result from stepping on the tails of fifty assorted dogs but he tried to take it in the spirit in which it seemed to be offered.

Libby, Lazarus recalled, insisted that this mass howling which the Jockaira were wont to indulge in was, in fact, music, and that men could learn to enjoy it by studying its interval relationships.

Lazarus doubted it.

But he had to admit that Libby understood the Jockaira better than he did in some ways. Libby had been delighted to discover that the Jockaira were excellent and subtle mathematicians. In particular they had a grasp of numbers that paralleled his own wild talent. Their arithmetics were incredibly involved for normal humans. A number, any number large or small, was to them a unique entity, to be grasped in itself and not merely as a grouping of smaller numbers. In consequence they used any convenient positional or exponential notation with any base, rational, irrational, or variable—or none at all.

It was supreme luck, Lazarus mused, that Libby was available to act as mathematical interpreter between the Jockaira and the Families, else it would have been impossible to grasp a lot of the new technologies the Jockaira were showing them.

He wondered why the Jockaira showed no interest in learning human technologies they were offered in return.

The howling discords died away and Lazarus brought his thoughts back to the scene around him. Food was brought in; the Kreel family tackled it with the same jostling enthusiasm with which Jockaira did everything. Dignity, thought Lazarus, is an idea which never caught on here. A large bowl, fully two feet across and brimful of an amorphous mess, was placed in front of Kreel Sarloo. A dozen Kreels crowded around it and started grabbing, giving no precedence to their senior. But Sarloo casually slapped a few of them out of the way and plunged a hand into the dish, brought forth a gob of the ration and rapidly kneaded it into a ball in the palm of his double-thumbed hand. Done, he shoved it towards Lazarus' mouth.

Lazarus was not squeamish but he had to remind himself, first, that food for Jockaira was food for men, and second, that he could not catch anything from them anyhow, before he could bring himself to try the proffered morsel.

He took a large bite. Mmmm . . . not too bad—rather bland and sticky, no particular flavor. Not good, either, but it could be swallowed. Grimly determined to uphold the honor of his race, he ate on, while promising himself a proper meal in the near future. When he felt that to swallow another mouthful would be to invite physical and social disaster, he thought of a possible way out. Reaching into the common plate he scooped up a large handful of the stuff, molded it into a ball and offered it to Sarloo.

It was inspired diplomacy. For the rest of the meal Lazarus fed Sarloo, fed him until his arms were tired, until he marveled at his host's ability to tuck it away.

After eating they slept and Lazarus slept with the family, literally. They slept where they had eaten, without beds and disposed as casually as leaves on a path or puppies in a pen. To his surprise, Lazarus slept well and did not wake until false suns in the cavern roof glowed in mysterious sympathy to the new dawn. Sarloo was still asleep near him and giving out most human-like snores. Lazarus found that one infant Jockaira was cuddled spoon fashion against his own stomach.

He felt a movement behind his back, a rustle at his thigh. He turned cautiously and found that another Jockaira—a six-year-old in human equivalence—had extracted his blaster from its holster and now gazing curiously into its muzzle.

With hasty caution Lazarus removed the deadly toy from the child's unwilling fingers, noted with relief that the safety was still on, and reholstered it. Lazarus received a reproachful look; the kid seemed about to cry. "Hush," whispered Lazarus, "you'll wake your old man. Here—" He gathered the child into his left arm and cradled it against his side. The little Jockaira snuggled up to him, laid a soft moist mouth against his hide, and promptly went to sleep.

Lazarus looked down at him. "You're a cute little devil," he said softly. "I could grow right fond of you if I could ever get used to your smell."

Some of the incidents between the two races would have been funny had they not been charged with potential trouble: for example, the case of Eleanor Johnson's son Hubert. This gangling adolescent was a confirmed sidewalk superintendent. One day he was watching two technicians, one human and one Jockaira, adapt a Jockaira power source to the needs of Earth-type machinery. The Jockaira was apparently amused by the boy and, in an obviously friendly spirit, picked him up.

Hubert began to scream.

His mother, never far from him, joined battle. She lacked strength and skill to do the utter destruction she was bent on; the big nonhuman was unhurt, but it created a nasty situation.

Administrator Ford and Oliver Johnson tried very hard to explain the incident to the amazed Jockaira. Fortunately, they seemed grieved rather than vengeful.

Ford then called in Eleanor Johnson. "You have endangered the entire colony by your stupidity—"

"But I—"

"Keep *quiet!* If you hadn't spoiled the boy rotten, he would have behaved himself. If you weren't a maudlin fool, you would have kept your hands to yourself. The boy goes to the regular development classes henceforth and you are to let him alone. At the slightest sign of animosity on your part toward any of the natives, I'll have you subjected to a few years' cold-rest. Now get out!"

Ford was forced to use almost as strong measures on Janice Schmidt. The interest shown in Hans Weatheral by the Jockaira extended to all of the telepathic defectives. The natives seemed to be reduced to a state of quivering adoration by the mere fact that these could communicate with them directly. Kreel Sarloo informed Ford that he wanted the sensitives to be housed separately from the other defectives in the evacuated temple of the Earthmen's city and that the Jockaira wished to wait on them personally. It was more of an order than a request.

Janice Schmidt submitted ungracefully to Ford's insistence that the Jockaira be humored in the matter in return for all that they had done, and Jockaira nurses took over under her jealous eyes.

Every sensitive of intelligence higher than the semimoronic Hans Weatheral promptly developed spontaneous and extreme psychoses while being attended by Jockaira.

So Ford had another headache to straighten out. Janice Schmidt was more powerfully and more intelligently vindictive than was Eleanor Johnson. Ford was forced to bind Janice over to keep the peace under the threat of retiring her completely from the care of her beloved "children." Kreel Sarloo, distressed and apparently shaken to his core, accepted a compromise whereby Janice and her junior nurses resumed care of the poor psychotics while Jockaira continued to minister to sensitives of moron level and below.

But the greatest difficulty arose over . . . surnames.

Jockaira each had an individual name and a surname. Surnames were limited in number, much as they were in the Families. A native's surname referred equally to his tribe and to the temple in which he worshipped.

Kreel Sarloo took up the matter with Ford. "High Father of the Strange Brothers," he said, "the time has come for you and your children to choose your surnames." (The rendition of Sarloo's speech into English necessarily contains inherent errors.)

Ford was used to difficulties in understanding the Jockaira. "Sarloo, brother and friend," he answered. "I hear your words but I do not understand. Speak more fully."

Sarloo began over. "Strange brother, the seasons come and the seasons go and there is a time of ripening. The gods tell us that you, the Strange Brothers, have reached the time in your education (?) when you must select your tribe and your temple. I have come to arrange with you the preparations (ceremonies?) by which each will choose his surname. I speak for the gods in this. But let me say for myself that it would make me happy if you, my brother Ford, were to choose the temple Kreel."

Ford stalled while he tried to understand what was implied. "I am happy that you wish me to have your surname. But my people already have their own surnames."

Sarloo dismissed that with a flip of his lips. "Their present surnames are words and nothing more. Now they must choose their real surnames, each the name of his temple and of the god whom he will worship. Children grow up and are no longer children."

Ford decided that he needed advice. "Must this be done at once?"

"Not today, but in the near future. The gods are patient."

Ford called in Zaccur Barstow, Oliver Johnson, Lazarus Long, and Ralph Schultz, and described the interview. Johnson played back the recording of the conversation and strained to catch the sense of the words. He prepared several possible translations but failed to throw any new light on the matter.

"It looks," said Lazarus, "like a case of join the church or get out."

"Yes," agreed Zaccur Barstow, "that much seems to come through plainly. Well, I think we can afford to go through the motions. Very few of our people have religious prejudices strong enough to forbid their paying lip service to the native gods in the interests of the general welfare."

"I imagine you are correct," Ford said. "I, for one, have no objection to adding Kreel to my name and taking part in their genuflections if it will help us to live in peace." He frowned. "But I would not want to see our culture submerged in theirs."

"You can forget that," Ralph Schultz assured him. "No matter what we have to do to please them, there is absolutely no chance of any real cultural assimilation. Our brains are not like theirs—just how different I am only beginning to guess."

"Yeah," said Lazarus, "'just how different.'"

Ford turned to Lazarus. "What do you mean by that? What's troubling you?"

"Nothing. Only," he added, "I never did share the general enthusiasm for this place."

They agreed that one man should take the plunge first, then report back. Lazarus tried to grab the assignment on seniority, Schultz claimed it as a professional right; Ford overruled them and appointed himself, asserting that it was his duty as the responsible executive.

Lazarus went with him to the doors of the temple where the induction was to take place. Ford was as bare of clothing as the Jockaira, but Lazarus, since he was not to enter the temple, was able to wear his kilt. Many of the colonists, sunstarved after years in the ship, went bare when it suited them, just as the Jockaira did. But Lazarus never did. Not only did his habits run counter to it, but a blaster is an extremely conspicuous object on a bare thigh.

Kreel Sarloo greeted them and escorted Ford inside. Lazarus called out after them, "Keep your chin up, pal!"

He waited. He struck a cigarette and smoked it. He walked up and down. He had no way to judge how long it would be; it seemed, in consequence, much longer than it was.

At last the doors slid back and natives crowded out through them. They seemed curiously worked up about something and none of them came near Lazarus. The press that still existed in the great doorway separated, formed an aisle, and a figure came running headlong through it and out into the open.

Lazarus recognized Ford.

Ford did not stop where Lazarus waited but plunged blindly on past. He tripped and fell down. Lazarus hurried to him.

Ford made no effort to get up. He lay sprawled face down, his shoulders heaving violently, his frame shaking with sobs.

Lazarus knelt by him and shook him. "Slayton," he demanded, "what's happened? What's wrong with you?" Ford turned wet and horror-stricken eyes to him, checking his sobs momentarily. He did not speak but he seemed to recognize Lazarus. He flung himself on Lazarus, clung to him, wept more violently than before.

Lazarus wrenched himself free and slapped Ford hard. "Snap out of it!" he ordered. "Tell me what's the matter."

Ford jerked his head at the slap and stopped his outcries but he said nothing. His eyes looked dazed. A shadow fell across Lazarus' line of sight; he spun around, covering with his blaster. Kreel Sarloo stood a few feet away and did not come any closer—not because of the weapon; he had never seen one before.

"You!" said Lazarus. "For the—What did you do to him?"

He checked himself and switched to speech that Sarloo could understand. "What has happened to my brother Ford?"

"Take him away," said Sarloo, his lips twitching. "This is a bad thing. This is a very bad thing."

"You're telling me!" said Lazarus. He did not bother to translate.

3

The same conference as before, minus its chairman, met as quickly as possible. Lazarus told his story, Schultz reported on Ford's condition. "The medical staff can't find anything wrong with him. All I can say with certainty is that the Administrator is suffering from an undiagnosed extreme psychosis. We can't get into communication with him."

"Won't he talk at all?" asked Barstow.

"A word or two, on subjects as simple as food or water. Any attempt to reach the cause of his trouble drives him into incoherent hysteria."

"No diagnosis?"

"Well, if you want an unprofessional guess in loose language, I'd say he was scared out of his wits. But," Schultz added, "I've seen fear syndromes before. Never anything like this."

"I have," Lazarus said suddenly.

"You have? Where? What were the circumstances?"

"Once," said Lazarus, "when I was a kid, a couple of hundred years back, I caught a grown coyote and penned him up. I had a notion I could train him to be a hunting dog. It didn't work.

"Ford acts just the way the coyote did."

An unpleasant silence followed. Schultz broke it with, "I don't quite see what you mean. What is the parallel?"

"Well," Lazarus answered slowly, "this is just my guess. Slayton is the only one who knows the true answer and he can't talk. But here's my opinion: we've had these Jockaira doped out all wrong from scratch. We made the mistake of thinking that because they looked like us, in a general way, and were about as civilized as we are, that they were *people*. But they aren't people at all. They are . . . *domestic animals*.

"Wait a minute now!" he added. "Don't get in a rush. There are people on this planet, right enough. Real people. They lived in the temples and the Jockaira called them gods. They *are* gods!"

Lazarus pushed on before anyone could interrupt. "I know what you're thinking. Forget it. I'm not going metaphysical on you; I'm just putting it the best I can. I mean that there is something living in those temples and whatever it is, it is such heap big medicine that it can pinch-hit for gods, so you might as well call 'em that. Whatever they are, they are the true dominant race on this planet—its *people!* To them, the rest of us, Jocks or us, are just animals, wild or tame. We made the mistake of assuming that a local religion was merely superstition. It ain't."

Barstow said slowly, "And you think this accounts for what happened to Ford?"

"I do. He met one, the one called Kreel, and it drove him crazy."

"I take it," said Schultz, "that it is your theory that any man exposed to this . . . this *presence* . . . would become psychotic?"

"Not exactly," answered Lazarus. "What scares me a damn sight more is the fear that I might *not* go crazy!"

That same day the Jockaira withdrew all contact with the Earthmen. It was well that they did so, else there would have been violence. Fear hung over the city, fear of horror worse than death, fear of some terrible thing, the mere knowledge of which could turn a man into a broken mindless animal. The Jockaira no longer seemed harmless friends, rather clownish despite their scientific attainments, but puppets, decoys, bait for the unseen potent beings who lurked in the "temples."

There was no need to vote on it; with the single-mindedness of a crowd stampeding from a burning building the Earthmen wanted to leave this terrible place. Zaccur Barstow assumed command. "Get King on the screen. Tell him to send down every boat at once. We'll get out of here as fast as we can." He ran his fingers worriedly though his hair. "What's the most we can load on each trip, Lazarus? How long will the evacuation take?"

Lazarus muttered.

"What did you say?"

"I said, 'It ain't a case of how long; it's a case of will we be let.' Those things in the temples may want more domestic animals—us!"

Lazarus was needed as a boat pilot but he was needed more urgently for his ability to manage a crowd. Zaccur Barstow was telling him to conscript a group of emergency police when Lazarus looked past Zaccur's shoulder and exclaimed, "Oh oh! Hold it, Zack—school's out."

Zaccur turned his head quickly and saw, approaching with stately dignity across the council hall, Kreel Sarloo. No one got in his way.

They soon found out why. Zaccur moved forward to greet him, found himself stopped about ten feet from the Jockaira. No clue to the cause; just that—stopped.

"I greet you, unhappy brother," Sarloo began.

"I greet you, Kreel Sarloo."

"The gods have spoken. Your kind can never be civilized (?). You and your brothers are to leave this world."

Lazarus let out a deep sigh of relief.

"We are leaving, Kreel Sarloo," Zaccur answered soberly.

"The gods require that you leave. Send your brother Libby to me."

Zaccur sent for Libby, then turned back to Sarloo. But the Jockaira had nothing more to say to them; he seemed indifferent to their presence. They waited.

Libby arrived. Sarloo held him in a long conversation. Barstow and Lazarus were both in easy earshot and could see their lips move, but heard nothing. Lazarus found the circumstance very disquieting. Damn my eyes, he thought, I could figure several ways to pull that trick with the right equipment but I'll bet none of 'em is the right answer—and I don't see any equipment.

The silent discussion ended, Sarloo stalked off without farewell. Libby turned to the others and spoke; now his voice could be heard. "Sarloo tells me," he began, brow wrinkled in puzzlement, "that we are to go to a planet, uh, over thirty-two light-years from here. The gods have decided it." He stopped and bit his lip.

"Don't fret about it," advised Lazarus. "Just be glad they want us to leave. My guess is that they could have squashed us flat just as easily. Once we're out in space we'll pick our own destination."

"I suppose so. But the thing that puzzles me is that he mentioned a time about three hours away as being our departure from this system."

"Why that's utterly unreasonable," protested Barstow. "Impossible. We haven't the boats to do it."

Lazarus said nothing. He was ceasing to have opinions.

Zaccur changed his opinion quickly. Lazarus acquired one, born of experience. While urging his cousins toward the field where embarkation was proceeding, he found himself lifted up, free of the ground. He struggled, his arms and legs met no resistance but the ground dropped away. He closed his eyes, counted ten jets, opened them again. He was at least two miles in the air.

Below him, boiling up from the city like bats from a cave, were uncountable numbers of dots and shapes, dark against the sunlit ground. Some were close enough for him to see that they were men, Earthmen, the Families.

The horizon dipped down, the planet became a sphere, the sky turned black. Yet his breathing seemed normal, his blood vessels did not burst.

They were sucked into clusters around the open ports of the *New Frontiers* like bees swarming around a queen. Once inside the ship Lazarus gave himself over to a case of the shakes. *Whew!* he sighed to himself, watch that first step—it's a honey!

Libby sought out Captain King as soon as he was inboard and had recovered his nerve. He delivered Sarloo's message.

King seemed undecided. "I don't know," he said. "You know more about the natives than I do, inasmuch as I have hardly put foot to the ground. But between ourselves, Mister, the way they sent my passengers back has me talking to myself. That was the most remarkable evolution I have ever seen performed."

"I might add that it was remarkable to experience, sir," Libby answered unhumorously. "Personally I would prefer to take up ski jumping. I'm glad you had the ship's access ports open."

"I didn't," said King tersely. "They were opened for me."

They went to the control room with the intention of getting the ship under boost and placing a long distance between it and the planet from which they had been evicted; thereafter they would consider destination and course. "This planet that Sarloo described to you," said King, "does it belong to a G-type star?"

"Yes," Libby confirmed, "an Earth-type planet accompanying a Sol-type star. I have its coördinates and could identify from the catalogues. But we can forget it; it is too far away."

"So . . ." King activated the vision system for the stellarium. Then neither of them said anything for several moments. The images of the heavenly bodies told their own story.

With no orders from King, with no hands at the controls, the *New Frontiers* was on her long way again, headed out, as if she had a mind of her own.

"I can't tell you much," admitted Libby some hours later to a group consisting of King, Zaccur Barstow and Lazarus Long. "I was able to determine, before we passed the speed of light—or appeared to—that our course then was compatible with the idea that we have been headed toward the star named by Kreel Sarloo as the destination ordered for us by his gods. We continued to accelerate and the stars faded out. I no longer have any astrogational reference points and I am unable to say where we are or where we are going."

"Loosen up, Andy," suggested Lazarus. "Make a guess."

"Well . . . if our world line is a smooth function—
if it is, and I have no data—then we may arrive in the
neighborhood of star PK3722, where Kreel Sarloo said
we were going."

"Rummph!" Lazarus turned to King. "Have you tried
slowing down?"

"Yes," King said shortly. "The controls are dead."

"Mmm . . . Andy, when do we get there?"

Libby shrugged helplessly. "I have no frame of reference. What is time without a space reference?"

Time and space, inseparable and one—Libby thought
about it long after the others had left. To be sure, he
had the space framework of the ship itself and therefore there necessarily was ship's time. Clocks in the ship
ticked or hummed or simply marched; people grew
hungry, fed themselves, got tired, rested. Radioactives
deteriorated, physiochemical processes moved toward
states of greater entropy, his own consciousness perceived duration.

But the background of the stars, against which every
timed function in the history of man had been measured,
was gone. So far as his eyes or any instrument in the
ship could tell him, they had become unrelated to the
rest of the universe.

What universe?

There was no universe. It was gone.

Did they move? Can there be motion when there is
nothing to move past?

Yet the false weight achieved by the spin of the ship
persisted. Spin with reference to *what?* thought Libby.
Could it be that space held a true, absolute,
nonrelational texture of its own, like that postulated for
the long-discarded "ether" that the classic Michelson-
Morley experiments had failed to detect? No, more than
that—had denied the very possibility of its existence?

—had for that matter denied the possibility of speed
greater than light. Had the ship actually passed the
speed of light? Was it not more likely that this was a

coffin, with ghosts as passengers, going nowhere at no time?

But Libby itched between his shoulder blades and was forced to scratch; his left leg had gone to sleep; his stomach was beginning to speak insistently for food—if this was death, he decided, it did not seem materially different from life.

With renewed tranquility, he left the control room and headed for his favorite refectory, while starting to grapple with the problem of inventing a new mathematics which would include all the new phenomena. The mystery of how the hypothetical gods of the Jockaira had teleported the families from ground to ship he discarded. There had been no opportunity to obtain significant data, *measured* data; the best that any honest scientist could do, with epistemological rigor, was to include a note that recorded the fact and stated that it was unexplained. It *was* a fact; here he was who shortly before had been on the planet; even now Schultz's assistants were overworked trying to administer depressant drugs to the thousands who had gone to pieces emotionally under the outrageous experience.

But Libby could not explain it and, lacking data, felt no urge to try. What he did want to do was to deal with world lines in a plenum, the basic problem of field physics.

Aside from his penchant for mathematics Libby was a simple person. He preferred the noisy atmosphere of the "Club," refectory 9-D, for reasons different from those of Lazarus. The company of people younger than himself reassured him; Lazarus was the only elder he felt easy with.

Food, he learned, was not immediately available at the Club; the commissary was still adjusting to the sudden change. But Lazarus was there and others whom he knew; Nancy Weatheral scrunched over and made room for him. "You're just the man I want to see," she said. "Lazarus is being most helpful. Where are we going this time and when do we get there?"

Libby explained the dilemma as well as he could. Nancy wrinkled her nose. "That's a pretty prospect, I must say! Well, I guess that means back to the grind for little Nancy."

"What do you mean?"

"Have you ever taken care of a somnolent? No, of course you haven't. It gets tiresome. Turn them over, bend their arms, twiddle their tootsies, move their heads, close the tank and move on to the next one. I get so sick of human bodies that I'm tempted to take a vow of chastity."

"Don't commit yourself too far," advised Lazarus.

"Why would you care, you old false alarm?"

Eleanor Johnson spoke up. "I'm *glad* to be in the ship again. Those slimy Jockaira—ugh!"

Nancy shrugged. "You're prejudiced, Eleanor. The Jocks are okay, in their way. Sure, they aren't exactly like us, but neither are dogs. You don't dislike dogs, do you?"

"That's what they are," Lazarus said soberly. "Dogs."

"Huh?"

"I don't mean that they are anything like dogs in most ways—they aren't even vaguely canine and they certainly are our equals and possibly our superiors in some things . . . but they are dogs just the same. Those things they call their 'gods' are simply their masters, their owners. We couldn't be domesticated, so the owners chucked us out."

Libby was thinking of the inexplicable telekinesis the Jockaira—or their masters—had used. "I wonder what it would have been like," he said thoughtfully, "if they had been able to domesticate us. They could have taught us a lot of wonderful things."

"Forget it," Lazarus said sharply. "It's not a man's place to be property."

"What is a man's place?"

"It's a man's business to be what he is . . . and be it in style!" Lazarus got up. "Got to go."

Libby started to leave also, but Nancy stopped him. "Don't go. I want to ask you some questions. What year is it back on Earth?"

Libby started to answer, closed his mouth. He started to answer a second time, finally said, "I don't know how to answer that question. It's like saying, 'How high is up?'"

"I know I probably phrased it wrong," admitted Nancy. "I didn't do very well in basic physics, but I did gather the idea that time is relative and simultaneity is an idea which applies only to two points close together in the same framework. But just the same, I want to know something. We've traveled a lot faster and farther than anyone ever did before, haven't we? Don't our clocks slow down, or something?"

Libby got that completely baffled look which mathematical physicists wear whenever laymen try to talk about physics in nonmathematical language. "You're referring to the Lorentz-FitzGerald contraction. But, if you'll pardon me, anything one says about it in words is necessarily nonsense."

"Why?" she insisted.

"Because . . . well, because the language is inappropriate. The formulae used to describe the effect loosely called a contraction presuppose that the observer is part of the phenomenon. But verbal language contains the implicit assumption that we can stand outside the whole business and watch what goes on. The mathematical language denies the very possibility of any such outside viewpoint. Every observer has his own world line; he can't get outside it for a detached viewpoint."

"But suppose he did? Suppose we could see Earth right now?"

"There I go again," Libby said miserably. "I tried to talk about it in words and all I did was to add to the confusion. There is no way to measure time in any absolute sense when two events are separated in a continuum. All you can measure is interval."

"Well, what is interval? So much space and so much time?"

"No, no, no! It isn't that at all. Interval is . . . well, it's interval. I can write down formulae about it and show you how we use it, but it can't be defined in words. Look, Nancy, can you write the score for a full orchestration of a symphony in words?"

"No. Well, maybe you could but it would take thousands of times as long."

"And musicians still could not play it until you put it back into musical notation. That's what I meant," Libby went on, "when I said that the language was inappropriate. I got into a difficulty like this once before in trying to describe the light-pressure drive. I was asked why, since the drive depends on loss of inertia, we people inside the ship had felt no loss of inertia. There was no answer, in words. Inertia isn't a word; it is a mathematical concept used *mathematically* in certain aspects of a plenum. I was stuck."

Nancy looked baffled but persisted doggedly. "My question still means something, even if I didn't phrase it right. You can't just tell me to run along and play. Suppose we turned around and went back the way we came, all the way to Earth, exactly the same trip but in reverse—just double the ship's time it has been so far. All right, what year would it be on Earth when we got there?"

"It would be . . . let me see, now—" The almost automatic processes of Libby's brain started running off the unbelievably huge and complex problems in accelerations, intervals, nonuniform motion. He was approaching the answer in a warm glow of mathematical revery when the problem suddenly fell to pieces on him, became indeterminate. He abruptly realized that the problem had an unlimited number of equally valid answers.

But that was impossible. In the real world, not the fantasy world of mathematics, such a situation was absurd. Nancy's question had to have just one answer, unique and real.

Could the whole beautiful structure of relativity be an absurdity? Or did it mean that it was physically impossible ever to back-track an interstellar distance?

"I'll have to give some thought to that one," Libby said hastily and left before Nancy could object.

But solitude and contemplation gave him no clue to the problem. It was not a failure of his mathematical ability; he was capable, he knew of devising a mathematical description of any group of facts, whatever they might be. His difficulty lay in having too few facts. Until some observer traversed interstellar distances at speeds approximating the speed of light *and returned to the planet from which he had started* there could be no answer. Mathematics alone has no content, gives no answers.

Libby found himself wondering if the hills of his native Ozarks were still green, if the smell of wood smoke still clung to the trees in the autumn, then he recalled that the question lacked any meaning by any rules he knew of. He surrendered to an attack of homesickness such as he had not experienced since he was a youth in the Cosmic Construction Corps, making his first deep-space jump.

This feeling of doubt and uncertainty, the feeling of lostness and nostalgia, spread throughout the ship. On the first leg of their journey the Families had had the incentive that had kept the covered wagons crawling across the plains. But now they were going nowhere, one day led only to the next. Their long lives were become a meaningless burden.

Ira Howard, whose fortune established the Howard Foundation, was born in 1825 and died in 1873—of old age. He sold groceries to the Forty-niners in San Francisco, became a wholesale sutler in the American War of the Secession, multiplied his fortune during the tragic Reconstruction.

Howard was deathly afraid of dying. He hired the best doctors of his time to prolong his life. Nevertheless old age plucked him when most men are still young. But his will commanded that his money be used "to lengthen human life." The administrators of the trust found no way to carry out his wishes other than by seeking out persons whose family trees showed congenital predispositions toward long life and then inducing them to reproduce in kind. Their method anticipated the work of Burbank; they may or may not have known of the illuminating researches of the monk Gregor Mendel.

Mary Sperling put down the book she had been reading when Lazarus entered her stateroom. He picked it up. "What are you reading, Sis? 'Ecclesiastes.' Hmm . . . I didn't know you were religious." He read aloud:

"'Yea, though he live a thousand years twice told, yet hath he seen no good: do not all go to one place?'"

"Pretty grim stuff, Mary. Can't you find something more cheerful? Even in The Preacher?" His eyes skipped on down. "How about this one? 'For to him that is joined to all the living there is hope—' Or . . . mmmm, not too many cheerful spots. Try this: 'Therefore remove sorrow from thy heart, and put away evil from thy flesh: for childhood and youth are vanity.' That's more my style; I wouldn't be young again for overtime wages."

"I would."

"Mary, what's eating you? I find you sitting here, reading the most depressing book in the Bible, nothing but death and funerals. Why?"

She passed a hand wearily across her eyes. "Lazarus, I'm getting old. What else is there to think about?"

"You? Why, you're fresh as a daisy!"

She looked at him. She knew that he lied; her mirror showed her the greying hair, the relaxed skin; she felt it in her bones. Yet Lazarus was older than she . . . although she knew, from what she had learned of biology during the years she had assisted in the longevity research, that Lazarus should never have lived to be as old as he was now. When he was born the program had reached only the third generation, too few generations to eliminate the less durable strains—except through some wildly unlikely chance shuffling of genes.

But there he stood. "Lazarus," she asked, "how long do you expect to live?"

"Me? Now that's an odd question. I mind a time when I asked a chap that very same question—about me, I mean, not about him. Ever hear of Dr. Hugo Pinero?"

"'Pinero . . . Pinero . . .' Oh, yes, 'Pinero the Charlatan.'"

"Mary, he was no charlatan. He could do it, no foolin'. He could predict accurately when a man would die."

"But—Go ahead. What did he tell you?"

"Just a minute. I want you to realize that he was no fake. His predictions checked out right on the button—if he hadn't died, the life insurance companies would have been ruined. That was before you were born, but I was there and I know. Anyhow, Pinero took my reading and it seemed to bother him. So he took it again. Then he returned my money."

"What did he say?"

"Couldn't get a word out of him. He looked at me and he looked at his machine and he just frowned and clammed up. So I can't rightly answer your question."

"But what do *you* think about it, Lazarus? Surely you don't expect just to go on forever?"

"Mary," he said softly. "I'm not planning on dying. I'm not giving it any thought at all."

There was silence. At last she said, "Lazarus, I don't want to die. But what is the purpose of our long lives?

We don't seem to grow wiser as we grow older. Are we simply hanging on after our time has passed? Loitering in the kindergarten when we should be moving on? Must we die and be born again?"

"I don't know," said Lazarus, "and I don't have any way to find out . . . and I'm damned if I see any sense in my worrying about it. Or you either. I propose to hang onto this life as long as I can and learn as much as I can. Maybe wisdom and understanding are reserved for a later existence and maybe they aren't for us at all, ever. Either way, I'm satisfied to be living and enjoying it. Mary my sweet, carpe that old diem!—it's the only game in town."

The ship slipped back into the same monotonous routine that had obtained during the weary years of the first jump. Most of the Members went into cold-rest; the others tended them, tended the ship, tended the hydroponds. Among the somnolents was Slayton Ford; cold-rest was a common last-resort therapy for functional psychoses.

The flight to star PK3722 took seventeen months and three days, ship's time.

The ships officers had as little choice about the journey's end as about its beginning. A few hours before their arrival star images flashed back into being in the stellarium screens and the ship rapidly decelerated to interplanetary speeds. No feeling of slowing down was experienced; whatever mysterious forces were acting on them acted on all masses alike. The *New Frontiers* slipped into an orbit around a live green planet some hundred million miles from its sun; shortly Libby reported to Captain King that they were in a stable parking orbit.

Cautiously King tried the controls, dead since their departure. The ship surged; their ghostly pilot had left them.

Libby decided that the simile was incorrect; this trip had undoubtedly been planned for them but it was not necessary to assume that anyone or anything had shepherded them here. Libby suspected that the "gods" of the dog-people saw the plenum as static; their deportation was an accomplished fact to them before it began. Libby could visualize it as a mathematical concept—one regrettably studded with unknowns—but there were no appropriate words. Inadequately and incorrectly put into words, his concept was that of a "cosmic cam," a world line shaped for them which ran out of normal space and back into it; when the ship reached the end of its "cam" it returned to normal operation.

He tried to explain his concept to Lazarus and to the Captain, but he did not do well. He lacked data and also had not had time to refine his mathematical description into elegance; it satisfied neither him nor them.

Neither King nor Lazarus had time to give the matter much thought. Barstow's face appeared on an interstation viewscreen. "Captain!" he called out. "Can you come aft to lock seven? We have visitors!"

Barstow had exaggerated; there was only one. The creature reminded Lazarus of a child in fancy dress, masqueraded as a rabbit. The little thing was more android than were the Jockaira, though possibly not mammalian. It was unclothed but not naked, for its childlike body was beautifully clothed in short sleek golden fur. Its eyes were bright and seemed both merry and intelligent.

But King was too bemused to note such detail. A voice, a thought, was ringing in his head: ". . . so you are the group leader . . ." it said ". . . welcome to our world . . . we have been expecting you . . . the (blank) told us of your coming . . ."

Controlled telepathy—

A creature, a race, so gentle, so civilized, so free from enemies, from all danger and strife that they could afford to share their thoughts with others—to share more than their thoughts; these creatures were so gentle and so generous that they were offering the humans a homestead on their planet. This was why this messenger had come: to make the offer.

To King's mind this seemed remarkably like the prize package that had been offered by the Jockaira; he wondered what the boobytrap might be in this proposition.

The messenger seemed to read his thought. " . . . look into our hears . . . we hold no malice toward you . . . we share your love of life and we love the life in you . . ."

"We thank you," King answered formally and aloud. "We will have to confer." He turned to speak to Barstow, glanced back. The messenger was gone.

The Captain said to Lazarus, "Where did he go?"

"Huh? Don't ask me."

"But you were in front of the lock."

"I was checking the tell-tales. There's no boat sealed on outside this lock—so they show. I was wondering if they were working right. They are. How did he get into the ship? Where's his rig?"

"How did he *leave*?"

"Not past me!"

"Zaccur, he came in through this lock, didn't he?"

"I don't know."

"But he certainly went out through it."

"Nope," denied Lazarus. "This lock hasn't been opened. The deep-space seals are still in place. See for yourself."

King did. "You don't suppose," he said slowly "that he can pass through—"

"Don't look at me," said Lazarus. "I've got no more prejudices in the matter than the Red Queen. Where does a phone image go when you cut the circuit?" He left, whistling softly to himself. King did not recognize the tune. Its words, which Lazarus did not sing, started with:

> "Last night I saw upon the stair
> A little man who wasn't there—"

4

There was no catch to the offer. The people of the planet—they had no name since they had no spoken language and the Earthmen simply called them "The Little People"—the little creatures really did welcome them and help them. They convinced the Families of this without difficulty for there was no trouble in communication such as there had been with the Jockaira. The Little People could make even subtle thoughts known directly to the Earthmen and in turn could sense correctly any thought directed at them. They appeared either to ignore or not to be able to read any thought not directed at them; communication with them was as controlled as spoken speech. Nor did the Earthmen acquire any telepathic powers among themselves.

Their planet was even more like Earth than was the planet of the Jockaira. It was a little larger than the Earth but had a slightly lower surface gravitation, suggesting a lower average density—the Little People made slight use of metals in their culture, which may be indicative.

The planet rode upright in its orbit; it had not the rakish tilt of Earth's axis. Its orbit was nearly circular; aphelion differed from perihelion by less than one per cent. There were no seasons.

Nor was there a great heavy moon, such as Earth has, to wrestle its oceans about and to disturb the isostatic balance of its crust. Its hills were low, its winds were gentle, its seas were placid. To Lazarus' disappointment, their new home had no lively weather; it hardly had weather at all; it had climate, and that of the sort that California patriots would have the rest of the Earth believe exists in their part of the globe.

But on the planet of the Little People it really exists. They indicated to the Earth people where they were to land, a wide sandy stretch of beach running down to the sea. Back of the low break of the bank lay mile on mile of lush meadowland, broken by irregular clumps of bushes and trees. The landscape had a careless neatness, as if it were a planned park, although there was no evidence of cultivation.

It was here, a messenger told the first scouting party, that they were welcome to live.

There seemed always to be one of the Little People present when his help might be useful—not with the jostling inescapable overhelpfulness of the Jockaira, but with the unobtrusive readiness to hand of a phone or a pouch knife. The one who accompanied the first party of explorers confused Lazarus and Barstow by assuming casually that he had met them before, that he had visited them in the ship. Since his fur was rich mahogany rather than golden, Barstow attributed the error to misunderstanding, with a mental reservation that these people might be possibly be capable of chameleonlike changes in color. Lazarus reserved his judgment.

Barstow asked their guide whether or not his people had any preferences as to where and how the Earthmen were to erect buildings. The question had been bothering him because a preliminary survey from the ship had disclosed no cities. It seemed likely that the natives lived underground—in which case he wanted to avoid getting off on the wrong foot by starting something which the local government might regard as a slum.

He spoke aloud in words directed at their guide, they having learned already that such was the best way to insure that the natives would pick up the thought.

In the answer that the little being flashed back Barstow caught the emotion of surprise. " . . . must you sully the sweet countryside with interruptions? . . . to what purpose do you need to form buildings? . . ."

"We need buildings for many purposes," Barstow explained. "We need them as daily shelter, as places to sleep at night. We need them to grow our food and prepare it for eating." He considered trying to explain the processes of hydroponic farming, of food processing, and of cooking, then dropped it, trusting to the subtle sense of telepathy to let his "listener" understand. "We need buildings for many other uses, for workshops and laboratories, to house the machines whereby we communicate, for almost everything we do in our everyday life."

" . . . be patient with me . . ." the thought came, " . . . since I know so little of your ways . . . but tell me . . . do you prefer to sleep in such as *that?* . . ." He gestured toward the ship's boats they had come down in, where their bulges showed above the low bank. The thought he used for the boats was too strong to be bound by a word; to Lazarus' mind came a thought of a dead, constricted space—a jail that had once harbored him, a smelly public phone booth.

"It is our custom."

The creature leaned down and patted the turf. " . . . is this not a good place to sleep? . . ."

Lazarus admitted to himself that it was. The ground was covered with a soft spring turf, grass-like but finer than grass, softer, more even, and set more closely together. Lazarus took off his sandals and let his bare feet enjoy it, toes spread and working. It was, he decided, more like a heavy fur rug than a lawn.

" . . . as for food . . ." their guide went on, " . . . why struggle for that which the good soil gives freely? . . . come with me . . ."

He took them across a reach of meadow to where low bushy trees hung over a meandering brook. The "leaves" were growths the size of a man's hand, irregular in shape, and an inch or more in thickness. The little person broke off one and nibbled at it daintily.

Lazarus plucked one and examined it. It broke easily, like a well-baked cake. The inside was creamy yellow, spongy but crisp, and had a strong pleasant odor, reminiscent of mangoes.

"Lazarus, don't eat that!" warned Barstow. "It hasn't been analyzed."

". . . it is harmonious with your body . . ."

Lazarus sniffed it again. "I'm willing to be a test case, Zack."

"Oh, well—" Barstow shrugged. "I warned you. You will anyway."

Lazarus did. The stuff was oddly pleasing, firm enough to suit the teeth, piquant though elusive in flavor. It settled down happily in his stomach and made itself at home.

Barstow refused to let anyone else try the fruit until its effect on Lazarus was established. Lazarus took advantage of his exposed and privileged position to make a full meal— the best, he decided, that he had had in years.

" . . . will you tell me what you are in the habit of eating? . . ." inquired their little friend. Barstow started to reply but was checked by the creature's thought: " . . . all of you . . . think about it . . ." no further thought message came from him for a few moments, then he flashed, " . . . that is enough . . . my wives will take care of it . . ."

Lazarus was not sure the image meant "wives" but some similar close relationship was implied. It had not yet been established that the Little People were bisexual—or what.

Lazarus slept that night out under the stars and let their clean impersonal light rinse from him the claustrophobia of the ship. The constellations here were distorted out of easy recognition, although he could recognize, he decided, the cool blue of Vega and the orange glow of Antares. The one certainty was the Milky Way, spilling its cloudy arch across the sky just as at home. The Sun, he knew, could not be visible to the naked eye even if he knew where to look for it; its low absolute magnitude would not show up across the light-years. Have to get hold of Andy, he thought sleepily, work out its coördinates and pick it out with instruments. He fell asleep before it could occur to him to wonder why he should bother.

Since no shelter was needed at night they landed everyone as fast as boats could shuttle them down. The crowds were dumped on the friendly soil and allowed to rest, picnic fashion, until the colony could be organized. At first they ate supplies brought down from the ship, but Lazarus' continued good health caused the rule against taking chances with natural native foods to be relaxed shortly. After that they ate mostly of the boundless largesse of the plants and used ship's food only to vary their diets.

Several days after the last of them had been landed Lazarus was exploring alone some distance from the camp. He came across one of the little People; the native greeted him with the same assumption of earlier acquaintance which all of them seemed to show and led Lazarus to a grove of low trees still farther from the base. He indicated to Lazarus that he wanted him to eat.

Lazarus was not particularly hungry but he felt compelled to humor such friendliness, so he plucked and ate.

He almost choked in his astonishment. Mashed potatoes and brown gravy!

" . . . didn't we get it right? . . ." came an anxious thought.

"Bub," Lazarus said solemnly, "I don't know what you planned to do, but this is just fine!"

A warm burst of pleasure invaded his mind. " . . . try the next tree . . ."

Lazarus did so with cautious eagerness. Fresh brown bread and sweet butter seemed to be the combination, though a dash of ice cream seemed to have crept in from somewhere. He was hardly surprised when the third tree gave strong evidence of having both mushrooms and charcoal-broiled steak in its ancestry. " . . . we used your thought images almost entirely . . ." explained his companion. " . . . they were much stronger than those of any of your wives . . ."

Lazarus did not bother to explain that he was not married. The little person added, " . . . there has not yet been time to simulate the appearances and colors your thoughts showed . . . does it matter much to you? . . ."

Lazarus gravely assured him that it mattered very little.

When he returned to the base, he had considerable difficulty in convincing others of the seriousness of his report.

One who benefited greatly from the easy, lotus-land quality of their new home was Slayton Ford. He had awakened from cold rest apparently recovered from his breakdown except in one respect: he had no recollection of whatever it was he had experienced in the temple of Kreel. Ralph Schultz considered this a healthy adjustment to an intolerable experience and dismissed him as a patient.

Ford seemed younger and happier than he had appeared before his breakdown. He no longer held formal office among the Members—indeed there was little government of any sort; the Families lived in cheerful easy-going anarchy on this favored planet—but he was still addressed by his title and continued to be treated as an elder, one whose advice was sought, whose judgment was deferred to, along with Zaccur Barstow, Lazarus, Captain King, and others. The Families paid little heed to calendar ages; close friends might differ by a century. For years they had benefited from his skilled administration; now they continued to treat him as an elder statesman, even though two-thirds of them were older than was he.

The endless picnic stretched into weeks, into months. After being long shut up in the ship, sleeping or working, the temptation to take a long vacation was too strong to resist and there was nothing to forbid it. Food in abundance, ready to eat and easy to handle, grew almost everywhere; the water in the numerous streams was clean and potable. As for clothing, they had plenty if they wanted to dress but the need was esthetic rather than utilitarian; the Elysian climate made clothing for protection as silly as suits for swimming. Those who liked clothes wore them; bracelets and beads and flowers in the hair was quite enough for most of them and not nearly so much nuisance if one chose to take a dip in the sea.

Lazarus stuck to his kilt.

The culture and degree of enlightenment of the Little People was difficult to understand all at once, because their ways were subtle. Since they lacked outward signs, in Earth terms, of high scientific attainment—no great buildings, no complex mechanical transportation machines, no throbbing power plants—it was easy to mistake them for Mother Nature's children, living in a Garden of Eden.

Only one-eighth of an iceberg shows above water.

Their knowledge of physical science was not inferior to that of the colonists; it was incredibly superior. They toured the ship's boats with polite interest, but confounded their guides by inquiring why things were done *this* way rather than *that?*—and the way suggested invariably proved to be simpler and more efficient than Earth technique . . . when the astounded human technicians managed to understand what they were driving at.

The Little People understood machinery and all that machinery implied, but they simply had little use for it. They obviously did not need it for communication and had little need for it for transportation (although the full reason for that was not at once evident), and they had very little need for machinery in any of their activities. But when they had a specific need for a mechanical device they were quite capable of inventing, building it, using it once, and destroying it, performing the whole process with a smooth coöperation quite foreign to that of men.

But in biology their preëminence was the most startling. The Little People were masters in the manipulation of life forms. Developing plants in a matter of days which bore fruit duplicating not only in flavor but in nutrition values the foods humans were used to was not a miracle to them but a routine task any of their biotechnicians could handle. They did it more easily than an Earth horticulturist breeds for a certain strain of color or shape in a flower.

But their methods were different from those of any human plant breeder. Be it said for them that they did try to explain their methods, but the explanation simply did not come through. In our terms, they claimed to "think" a plant into the shape and character they desired. Whatever they meant by that, it is certainly true that they could take a dormant seedling plant and, without touching it or operating on it in any way perceptible to their human students, cause it to bloom and burgeon into maturity in the space of a few hours—with new characteristics not found in the parent line . . . and which bred true thereafter.

However the Little People differed from Earthmen only in degree with respect to scientific attainments. In an utterly basic sense they differed from humans in kind.

They were not individuals.

No single body of a native housed a discrete individual. Their individuals were multi-bodied; they had group "souls." The basic unit of their society was a telepathic rapport group of many parts. The number of bodies and brains housing one individual ran as high as ninety or more and was never less than thirty-odd.

The colonists began to understand much that had been utterly puzzling about the Little People only after they learned this fact. There is much reason to believe that the Little People found the Earthmen equally puzzling, that they, too, had assumed that their pattern of existence must be mirrored in others. The eventual discovery of the true facts on each side, brought about mutual misunderstandings over identity, seemed to arouse horror in the minds of the Little People. They withdrew themselves from the neighborhood of the Families' settlement and remained away for several days.

At length a messenger entered the camp site and sought out Barstow. " . . . we are sorry we shunned you . . . in our haste we mistook your fortune for your fault . . . we wish to help you . . . we offer to teach you that you may become like ourselves . . ."

Barstow pondered how to answer this generous overture. "We thank you for your wish to help us," he said at last, "but what you call our misfortune seems to be a necessary part of our makeup. Our ways are not your ways. I do not think we could understand your ways."

The thought that came back to him was very troubled. " . . . we have aided the beasts of the air and of the ground to cease their strife . . . but if you do not wish our help we will not thrust it on you . . ."

The messenger went away, leaving Zaccur Barstow troubled in his mind. Perhaps, he thought, he had been hasty in answering without taking time to consult the elders. Telepathy was certainly not a gift to be scorned; perhaps the Little People could train them in telepathy without any loss of human individualism. But what he knew of the sensitives among the Families did not encourage such hope; there was not a one of them who was emotionally healthy, many of them were mentally deficient as well—it did not seem like a safe path for humans.

It could be discussed later, he decided; no need to hurry.

"No need to hurry" was the spirit throughout the settlement. There was no need to strive, little that had to be done and rarely any rush about that little. The sun was warm and pleasant, each day was much like the next, and there was always the day after that. The Members, predisposed by their inheritance to take a long view of things began to take an eternal view. Time no longer mattered. Even the longevity research, which had continued throughout their memories, languished. Gordon Hardy tabled his current experimentation to pursue the vastly more fruitful occupation of learning what the Little People knew of the nature of life. He was forced to take it slowly, spending long hours in digesting new knowledge. As time trickled on, he was hardly aware that his hours of contemplation were becoming longer, his burst of active study less frequent.

One thing he did learn, and its implications opened up whole new fields of thought: the Little People had, in one sense, conquered death.

Since each of their egos was shared among many bodies, the death of one body involved no death for the ego. All memory experiences of that body remained intact, the personality associated with it was not lost, and the physical loss could be made up by letting a young native "marry" into the group. But a group ego, only of the personalities which spoke to the Earthmen, could not die, save possibly by the destruction of every body it lived in. They simply went on, apparently forever.

Their young, up to the time of "marriage" or group assimilation, seemed to have little personality and only rudimentary or possibly instinctive mental processes. Their elders expected no more of them in the way of intelligent behavior than a human expects of a child still in the womb. There were always many such uncompleted persons attached to any ego group; they were cared for like dearly beloved pets or helpless babies, although they were often as large and as apparently mature to Earth eyes as were their elders.

Lazarus grew bored with paradise more quickly than did the majority of his cousins. "It can't always," he complained to Libby, who was lying near him on the fine grass, "be time for tea."

"What's fretting you, Lazarus?"

"Nothing in particular." Lazarus set the point of his knife on his right elbow, flipped it with his other hand, watched it bury its point in the ground. "It's just that this place reminds me of a well-run zoo. It's got about as much future." He grunted scornfully. "It's 'Never-Never Land.'"

"But what in particular is worrying you?"

"Nothing. That's what worries me. Honest to goodness, Andy, don't you see anything wrong in being turned out to pasture like this?"

Libby grinned sheepishly. "I guess it's my hillbilly blood. 'When it don't rain, the roof don't leak; when it rains, I cain't fix it nohow,'" he quoted. "Seems to me we're doing tolerably well. What irks you?"

"Well—" Lazarus' pale-blue eyes stared far away; he paused in his idle play with his knife. "When I was a young man a long time ago, I was beached in the South Seas—"

"Hawaii?"

"No. Farther south. Damned if I know what they call it today. I got hard up, mighty hard up, and sold my sextant. Pretty soon—or maybe quite a while—I could have passed for a native. I lived like one. It didn't seem to matter. But one day I caught a look at myself in a mirror." Lazarus sighed gustily. "I beat my way out of that place shipmates to a cargo of green hides, which may give you some idea how scared and desperate I was!"

Libby did not comment. "What do *you* do with your time, Lib?" Lazarus persisted.

"Me? Same as always. Think about mathematics. Try to figure out a dodge for a space drive like the one that got us here."

"Any luck on that?" Lazarus was suddenly alert.

"Not yet. Gimme time. Or I just watch the clouds

integrate. There are amusing mathematical relationships
everywhere if you are on the lookout for them. In the
ripples on the water, or the shapes of breasts—elegant
fifth-order functions."

"Huh? You mean 'fourth order.'"

"Fifth order. You omitted the time variable. I like
fifth-order equations," Libby said dreamily. "You find
'em in fish, too."

"Hummph!" said Lazarus, and stood up suddenly.
"That may be all right for you, but it's not my pidgin."

"Going some place?"

"Goin' to take a walk."

Lazarus walked north. He walked the rest of that day,
slept on the ground as usual that night, and was up and
moving, still to the north, at dawn. The next day was
followed by another like it, and still another. The going
was easy, much like strolling in a park . . . too easy,
in Lazarus' opinion. For the sight of a volcano, or a really worthwhile waterfall, he felt willing to pay four bits
and throw in a jackknife.

The food plants were sometimes strange, but abun-
dant and satisfactory. He occasionally met one or more
of the Little People going about their mysterious affairs.
They never bothered him nor asked why he was simply traveling but simply greeted him with the usual
assumption of previous acquaintanceship. He began to
long for one who would turn out to be a stranger; he
felt watched.

Presently the nights grew colder, the days less balmy,
and the Little People less numerous. When at last he
had not seen one for an entire day, he camped for the
night, remained there the next day—took out his soul
and examined it.

He had to admit that he could find no reasonable
fault with the planet nor its inhabitants. But just as definitely it was not to his taste. No philosophy that he had
ever heard or read gave any reasonable purpose for
man's existence, nor any rational clue to his proper

conduct. Basking in the sunshine might be as good a thing to do with one's life as any other—but it was not for him and he knew it, even if he could not define how he knew it.

The hegira of the Families had been a mistake. It would have been a more human, a more mature and manly thing, to have stayed and fought for their rights, even if they had died insisting on them. Instead they had fled across half a universe (Lazarus was reckless about his magnitudes) looking for a place to light. They had found one, a good one—but already occupied by beings so superior as to make them intolerable for men . . . yet so supremely indifferent in their superiority to men that they had not even bothered to wipe them out, but had whisked them away to this—this overmanicured country club.

And that in itself was the unbearable humiliation. The *New Frontiers* was the culmination of five hundred years of human scientific research, the best that men could do—but it had been flicked across the deeps of space as casually as a man might restore a baby bird to its nest.

The Little People did not seem to want to kick them out but the Little People, in their own way, were as demoralizing to men as were the gods of the Jockaira. One at a time they might be morons but taken as groups each rapport group was a genius that threw the best minds that men could offer into the shade. Even Andy. Human beings could not hope to compete with that type of organization any more than a back-room shop could compete with an automated cybernated factory. Yet to form any such group identities, even if they could which he doubted, would be, Lazarus felt very sure, to give up whatever it was that made them *men*.

He admitted that he was prejudiced in favor of men. He *was* a man.

The uncounted days slid past while he argued with himself over the things that bothered him—problems that had made sad the soul of his breed since the first apeman had risen to self-awareness, questions never solved by full belly nor fine machinery. And the endless quiet days did no more to give him final answers than did all the soul searchings of his ancestors. Why? What shall it profit a man? No answer came back—save one: a firm unreasoned conviction that he was not intended for, or not ready for, this timeless snug harbor of ease.

His troubled reveries were interrupted by the appearance of one of the Little People. " . . . greetings, old friend . . . your wife King wishes you to return to your home . . . he has need of your advice . . ."

"What's the trouble?" Lazarus demanded.

But the little creature either could or would not tell him. Lazarus gave his belt a hitch and headed south. " . . . there is no need to go slowly . . ." a thought came after him.

Lazarus let himself be led to a clearing beyond a clump of trees. There he found an egg-shaped object about six feet long, featureless except for a door in the side. The native went in through the door, Lazarus squeezed his larger bulk in after him; the door closed.

It opened almost at once and Lazarus saw that they were on the beach just below the human settlement. He had to admit that it was a good trick.

Lazarus hurried to the ship's boat parked on the beach in which Captain King shared with Barstow a semblance of community headquarters. "You sent for me, Skipper. What's up?"

King's austere face was grave. "It's about Mary Sperling."

Lazarus felt a sudden cold tug at his heart. "Dead?"

"No. Not exactly. She's gone over to the Little People. 'Married' into one of their groups."

"*What?* But that's impossible!"

Lazarus was wrong. There was no faint possibility of interbreeding between Earthmen and natives but there was no barrier, if sympathy existed, to a human merging into one of their rapport groups, drowning his personality in the ego of the many.

Mary Sperling, moved by conviction of her own impending death, saw in the deathless group egos a way out. Faced with the eternal problem of life and death, she had escaped the problem by choosing neither . . . selflessness. She had found a group willing to receive her, she had crossed over.

"It raises a lot of new problems," concluded King. "Slayton and Zaccur and I all felt that you had better be here."

"Yes, yes, sure—but where is Mary?" Lazarus demanded and then ran out of the room without waiting for an answer. He charged through the settlement ignoring both greetings and attempts to stop him. A short distance outside the camp he ran across a native. He skidded to a stop. "Where is Mary Sperling?"

" . . . I am Mary Sperling . . ."

"For the love of—You *can't* be."

" . . . I am Mary Sperling and Mary Sperling is myself . . . do you not know me, Lazarus? . . . I know you . . ."

Lazarus waved his hands. "No! I want to see Mary Sperling who looks like an Earthman—like me!"

The native hesitated. " . . . follow me, then . . ."

Lazarus found her a long way from the camp; it was obvious that she had been avoiding the other colonists. "Mary!"

She answered him mind to mind: " . . . I am sorry to see you troubled . . . Mary Sperling is gone except in that she is part of us . . ."

"Oh, come off it, Mary! Don't give me that stuff! Don't you know me?"

" . . . of course I know you, Lazarus . . . it is you who do not know *me* . . . do not trouble your soul or grieve your heart with the sight of this body in front of you . . . I am not one of your kind . . . I am native to this planet . . ."

"Mary," he insisted, "you've got to undo this. You've got to come out of there!"

She shook her head, an oddly human gesture, for the face no longer held any trace of human expression; it was a mask of otherness. " . . . that is impossible . . . Mary Sperling is gone . . . the one who speaks with you is inextricably *myself* and not of your kind . . ." The creature who had been Mary Sperling turned and walked away.

"*Mary!*" he cried. His heart leapt across the span of centuries to the day his mother had died. He covered his face with his hands and wept the inconsolable grief of a child.

5

Lazarus found both King and Barstow waiting for him when he returned. King looked at his face. "I could have told you," he said soberly, "but you wouldn't wait."

"Forget it," Lazarus said harshly. "What now?"

"Lazarus, there is something else you have to see before we discuss anything," Zaccur Barstow answered.

"Okay. What?"

"Just come and see." They led him to a compartment in the ship's boat which was used as a headquarters. Contrary to Families' custom it was locked; King let them in. There was a woman inside, who, when she saw the three, quietly withdrew, locking the door again as she went out.

"Take a look at that," directed Barstow.

It was a living creature in an incubator—a child, but no such child as had ever been seen before. Lazarus stared at it, then said angrily, "What the devil is it?"

"See for yourself. Pick it up. You won't hurt it."

Lazarus did so, gingerly at first, then without shrinking from the contact as his curiosity increased. What it was, he could not say. It was not human; it was just as certainly not offspring of the Little People. Did this planet, like the last, contain some previously unsuspected race? It was manlike, yet certainly not a man child. It lacked even the button nose of a baby, nor were there evident external ears. There were organs in the usual locations of each but flush with the skull and protected with bony ridges. Its hands had too many fingers and there was an extra large one near each wrist which ended in a cluster of pink worms.

There was something odd about the torso of the infant which Lazarus could not define. But two other gross facts were evident: the legs ended not in human feet but in horny, toeless pediments—hoofs. And the creature was hermaphroditic—not in deformity but in healthy development, an androgyne.

"What is it?" he repeated, his mind filled with lively suspicion.

"That," said Zaccur, "is Marion Schmidt, born three weeks ago."

"Huh? What do you mean?"

"It means that the Little People are just as clever in manipulating us as they are in manipulating plants."

"What? But they agreed to leave us alone!"

"Don't blame them too quickly. We let ourselves in for it. The original idea was simply a few improvements."

"'Improvements!' That thing's an obscenity."

"Yes and no. My stomach turns whenever I have to look at it . . . but actually—well, it's sort of a superman. Its body architecture has been redesigned for greater efficiency, our useless simian hangovers have been left out, and its organs have been rearranged in a more sensible fashion. You can't say it's not human, for it *is* . . . an improved model. Take that extra appendage at the wrist. That's another hand, a miniature one . . . backed up by a microscopic eye. You can see how useful that would be, once you get used to the idea." Barstow stared at it. "But it looks horrid, to me."

"It'd look horrid to anybody," Lazarus stated. "It may be an improvement, but damn it, I say it ain't human."

"In any case it creates a problem."

"I'll say it does!" Lazarus looked at it again. "You say it has a second set of eyes in those tiny hands? That doesn't seem possible."

Barstow shrugged. "I'm no biologist. But every cell in the body contains a full bundle of chromosomes. I suppose that you could grow eyes, or bones, or anything you liked anywhere, if you knew how to manipulate the genes in the chromosomes. And they know."

"I don't want to be manipulated!"

"Neither do I."

Lazarus stood on the bank and stared out over the broad beach at a full meeting of the Families. "I am—" he started formally, then looked puzzled. "Come here a moment, Andy." He whispered to Libby; Libby looked pained and whispered back. Lazarus looked exasperated and whispered again. Finally he straightened up and started over.

"I am two hundred and forty-one years old—at least," he stated. "Is there anyone here who is older?" It was empty formality; he knew that he was the eldest; he felt twice that old. "The meeting is opened," he went on, his big voice rumbling on down the beach assisted by the speaker systems from the ship's boats. "Who is your chairman?"

"Get on with it," someone called from the crowd.

"Very well," said Lazarus. "Zaccur Barstow!"

Behind Lazarus a technician aimed a directional pickup at Barstow. "Zaccur Barstow," his voice boomed out, "speaking for myself. Some of us have come to believe that this planet, pleasant as it is, is not the place for us. You all know about Mary Sperling, you've seen stereos of Marion Schmidt; there have been other things and I won't elaborate. But emigrating again poses another question, the question of where? Lazarus Long proposes that we return to Earth. In such a—" His words were drowned by noise from the crowd.

Lazarus shouted them down. "Nobody is going to be forced to leave. But if enough of us want to leave to justify taking the ship, then we can. I say go back to Earth. Some say look for another planet. That'll have to be decided. But first—how many of you think as I do about leaving here?"

"I do!" The shout was echoed by many others. Lazarus peered toward the first man to answer, tried to spot him, glanced over his shoulder at the tech, then pointed. "Go ahead, bud," he ruled. "The rest of you pipe down."

"Name of Oliver Schmidt. I've been waiting for months for somebody to suggest this. I thought I was the only sorehead in the Families. I haven't any real reason for leaving—I'm not scared out by the Mary Sperling matter, nor Marion Schmidt. Anybody who likes such things is welcome to them—live and let live. But I've got a deep-down urge to see Cincinnati again. I'm fed up with this place. I'm tired of being a lotus eater. Damn it, I want to *work* for my living! According to the Families' geneticists I ought to be good for another century at least. I can't see spending that much time lying in the sun and daydreaming."

When he shut up, at last a thousand more tried to get the floor. "Easy! Easy!" bellowed Lazarus. "If everybody wants to talk, I'm going to have to channel it through your Family representatives. But let's get a sample here and there." He picked out another man, told him to sound off.

"I won't take long," the new speaker said, "as I agree with Oliver Schmidt. I just wanted to mention my own reason. Do any of you miss the Moon? Back home I used to sit out on my balcony on warm summer nights and smoke and look at the Moon. I didn't know it was important to me, but it is. I want a planet with a moon."

The next speaker said only, "This case of Mary Sperling has given me a case of nerves. I get nightmares that I've gone over myself."

The arguments went on and on. Somebody pointed out that they had been chased off Earth; what made anybody think that they would be allowed to return? Lazarus answered that himself. "We learned a lot from the Jockaira and now we've learned a lot more from the Little People—things that put us way out ahead of anything scientists back on Earth had even dreamed of. We can go back to Earth loaded for bear. We'll be in shape to demand our rights, strong enough to defend them."

"Lazarus Long—" came another voice.

"Yes," acknowledged Lazarus. "You over there, go ahead."

"I am too old to make any more jumps from star to star and much to old to fight at the end of such a jump. Whatever the ret of you do, I'm staying."

"In that case," said Lazarus, "there is no need to discuss it, is there?"

"I am entitled to speak."

"All right you've spoken. Now give someone else a chance."

The sun set and the stars came out and still the talk went on. Lazarus knew that it would never end unless he moved to end it. "All right," he shouted, ignoring the many who still wanted to speak. "Maybe we'll have to turn this back to the Family councils, but let's take a trial vote and see where we are. Everybody who wants to go back to Earth move way over to my right. Everybody who wants to stay here move down the beach to my left. Everybody who wants to go exploring for still another planet gather right here in front of me." He dropped back and said to the sound tech, "Give them some music to speed 'em up."

The tech nodded and the homesick strains of *Valse Triste* sighed over the beach. It was followed by *The*

Green Hills of Earth. Zaccur Barstow turned toward Lazarus. "You picked that music."

"Me?" Lazarus answered with bland innocence. "You know I ain't musical, Zack."

Even with music the separation took a long time. The last movement of the immortal Fifth had died away long before they at last had sorted themselves into three crowds.

On the left about a tenth of the total number were gathered, showing thereby their intention of staying. They were mostly the old and the tired, whose sands had run low. With them were a few youngsters who had never seen Earth, plus a bare sprinkling of other ages.

In the center was a very small group, not over three hundred, mostly men and a few younger women, who voted thereby for still newer frontiers.

But the great mass was on Lazarus' right. He looked at them and saw new animation in their faces; it lifted his heart, for he had been bitterly afraid that he was almost alone in his wish to leave.

He looked back at the small group nearest him. "It looks like you're outvoted," he said to them alone, his voice unamplified. "But never mind, there always comes another day." He waited.

Slowly the group in the middle began to break up. By ones and twos and threes they moved away. A very few drifted over to join those who were staying; most of them merged with the group on the right.

When this secondary division was complete Lazarus spoke to the smaller group on his left. "All right," he said very gently, "You . . . you old folks might as well go back up to the meadows and get your sleep. The rest of us have plans to make."

Lazarus then gave Libby the floor and let him explain to the majority crowd that the trip home would not be the weary journey the flight from Earth had been, nor even the tedious second jump. Libby placed all the credit

458 *Robert A. Heinlein*

where most of it belonged, with the Little People. They had straightened him out with his difficulties in dealing with the problem of speeds which appeared to exceed the speed of light. If the Little People knew what they were talking about—and Libby was sure that they did—there appeared to be no limits to what Libby chose to call "para-acceleration"—"para-" because, like Libby's own light-pressure drive, it acted on the whole mass uniformly and could no more be perceived by the senses than can gravitation, and "para-" also because, the ship would not go "through" but rather around or "beside" normal space. "It is not so much a matter of driving the ship as it is a selection of appropriate potential level in an n-dimensional hyperplenum of n-plus-one possible—"

Lazarus firmly cut him off. "That's your department, son, and everybody trusts you in it. We ain't qualified to discuss the fine points."

"I was only going to add—"

"I know. But you were already out of the world when I stopped you."

Someone from the crowd shouted one more question. "When do we get there?"

"I don't know," Libby admitted, thinking of the question the way Nancy Weatheral had put it to him long ago. "I can't say what year it will be . . . but it will seem like about three weeks from now."

The preparations consumed days simply because many round trips of the ship's boats were necessary to embark them. There was a marked lack of ceremonious farewell because those remaining behind tended to avoid those who were leaving. Coolness had sprung up between the two groups; the division on the beach had split friendships, had even broken up contemporary marriages, had caused many hurt feelings, unresolved bitterness. Perhaps the only desirable aspect of the division was that the parents of the mutant Marion Schmidt had elected to remain behind.

Lazarus was in charge of the last boat to leave. Shortly before he planned to boost he felt a touch at his elbow. "Excuse me," a young man said. "My name's Hubert Johnson. I want to go along but I've had to stay back with the other crowd to keep my mother from throwing fits. If I show up at the last minute, can I still go along?"

Lazarus looked him over. "You look old enough to decide without asking me."

"You don't understand. I'm an only child and my mother tags me around. I've got to sneak back before she misses me. How much longer—"

"I'm not holding this boat for anybody. And you'll never break away any younger. Get into the boat."

"But—"

"Git!" The young man did so, with one worried backward glance at the bank. There was a lot, thought Lazarus, to be said for ectogenesis.

Once inboard the *New Frontiers* Lazarus reported to Captain King in the control room. "All inboard?" asked King.

"Yeah. Some late deciders, pro and con, and one more passenger at the last possible split second—woman named Eleanor Johnson. Let's go!"

King turned to Libby. "Let's go, Mister."

The stars blinked out.

They flew blind, with only Libby's unique talent to guide them. If he had doubts as to his ability to lead them through the featureless blackness of other space he kept them to himself. On the twenty-third ship's day of the reach and the eleventh day of para-deceleration the stars reappeared, all in their old familiar ranges— the Big Dipper, giant Orion, lopsided Crux, the fairy Pleiades, and dead ahead of them, blazing against the frosty backdrop of the Milky Way, was a golden light that had to be the Sun.

Lazarus had tears in his eyes for the second time in a month.

They could not simply rendezvous with Earth, set a parking orbit, and disembark; they had to throw their hats in first. Besides that, they needed first to know what time it was.

Libby was able to establish quickly, through proper motions of nearest stars, that it was not later than about 3700 A.D.; without precise observatory instruments he refused to commit himself further. But once they were close enough to see the Solar planets he had another clock to read; the planets themselves make a clock with nine hands.

For any date there is a unique configuration of those "hands" since no planetary period is exactly commensurate with another. Pluto marks off an "hour" of a quarter of a millennium: Jupiter's clicks a cosmic minute of twelve years; Mercury whizzes a "second" of about ninety days. The other "hands" can refine these readings—Neptune's period is so cantankerously different from that of Pluto that the two fall into approximately repeated configuration only once in seven hundred and fifty-eight years. The great clock can be read with any desired degree of accuracy over any period—but it is not easy to read.

Libby started to read it as soon as any of the planets could be picked out. He muttered over the problem. "There's not a chance that we'll pick up Pluto," he complained to Lazarus, "and I doubt if we'll have Neptune. The inner planets give me in infinite series of approximations—you know as well as I do that "infinite" is a question-begging term. Annoying!"

"Aren't you looking at it the hard way, son? You can get a practical answer. Or move over and I'll get one."

"Of course I can get a practical answer," Libby said petulantly, "if you're satisfied with that. But—"

"But me no 'buts'—*what year is it, man!*"

"Eh? Let's put it this way. The time rate in the ship and duration on Earth have been unrelated three times. But now they are effectively synchronous again, such that slightly over seventy-four years have passed since we left.

Lazarus heaved a sigh. "Why didn't you say so?" He had been fretting that Earth might not be recognizable . . . they might have torn down New York or something like that. "Shucks, Andy, you shouldn't have scared me like that."

"Mmm . . ." said Libby. It was one of no further interest to him. There remained only the delicious problem of inventing a mathematics which would describe elegantly two apparently irreconcilable groups of facts: the Michelson-Morley experiments and the log of the *New Frontiers*. He set happily about it. Mmmm . . . what was the least number of para-dimensions indispensably necessary to contain the augmented plenum using a sheaf of postulates affirming—

It kept him contented for a considerable time—subjective time, of course.

The ship was placed in a temporary orbit half a billion miles from the Sun with a radius vector normal to the plane of the ecliptic. Parked thus at right angles to and far outside the flat pancake of the solar System they were safe from any long chance of being discovered. A ship's boat had been fitted with the neo-Libby drive during the jump and a negotiating party was sent down.

Lazarus wanted to go along; King refused to let him, which sent Lazarus into sulks. King had said curtly, "This isn't a raiding party, Lazarus; this is a diplomatic mission."

"Hell, man, I can be diplomatic when it pays!"

"No doubt. But we'll send a man who doesn't go armed to the 'fresher."

Ralph Schultz headed the party, since psychodynamic factors back on Earth were of first importance, but he was aided by legal, military, and technical specialists. If the Families were going to have to fight for living room it was necessary to know what sort

of technology, what sort of weapons, they would have
to meet—but it was even more necessary to find out
whether or not a peaceful landing could be arranged.
Schultz had been authorized by the elders to offer
a plan under which the Families would colonize the
thinly settled and retrograded European continent. But
it was possible, even likely, that this had already been
done in their absence, in view of the radioactive half-
lifes involved. Schultz would probably have to improvise some other compromise, depending on the
conditions he found.

Again there was nothing to do but wait.

Lazarus endured it in nail-chewing uncertainty. He
had claimed publicly that the Families had such great
scientific advantage that they could meet and defeat the
best the Earth could offer. Privately, he knew that this
was sophistry and so did any other Member competent
to judge the matter. Knowledge alone did not win wars.
The ignorant fanatics of Europe's Middle Ages had
defeated the incomparably higher Islamic culture;
Archimedes had been struck down by a common soldier; barbarians had sacked Rome. Libby, or some one,
might devise an unbeatable weapon from their mass of
new knowledge—or might not. And who knew what
strides military art had made on Earth in three quarters of a century?

King, trained in military art, was worried by the same
thing and still more worried by the personnel he would
have to work with. The Families were anything but
trained legions; the prospect of trying to whip those
cranky individualists into some semblance of a disci-
plined fighting machine ruined his sleep.

These doubts and fears King and Lazarus did not
mention even to each other; each was afraid that to
mention such things would be to spread a poison of fear
through the ship. But they were not alone in their
worries; half of the ship's company realized the weaknesses of their position and kept silent only because a

bitter resolve to go home, no matter what, made them willing to accept the dangers.

"Skipper," Lazarus said to King two weeks after Schultz's party had headed Earthside, "have you wondered how they're going to feel about the *New Frontiers* herself?"

"Eh? What do you mean?"

"Well, we hijacked her. Piracy."

King looked astounded. "Bless me, so we did! Do you know, it's been so long ago that it is hard for me to realize that she was ever anything but my ship . . . or to recall that I first came into her through an act of piracy." He looked thoughtful, then smiled grimly. "I wonder how conditions are in Coventry these days?"

"Pretty thin rations, I imagine," said Lazarus. "But we'll team up and make out. Never mind—they haven't caught us yet."

"Do you suppose that Slayton Ford will be connected with the matter? That would be hard lines after all he has gone through."

"There may not be any trouble about it at all," Lazarus answered soberly. "While the way we got this ship was kind of irregular, we *have* used it for the purpose for which it was built—to explore the stars. And we're returning it intact, long before they could have expected any results, and with a slick new space drive to boot. It's more for their money than they had any reason to expect—so they may just decide to forget it and trot out the fatted calf."

"I hope so," King answered doubtfully.

The scouting party was two days late. No signal was received from them until they emerged into normal spacetime, just before rendezvous, as no method had yet been devised for signalling from para-space to orthospace. While they were maneuvering to rendezvous, King received Ralph Schultz's face on the control-room screen. "Hello, Captain! We'll be boarding shortly to report."

"Give me a summary now!"

"I wouldn't know where to start. But it's all right—
we can go home!"

"Huh? How's that? Repeat!"

"Everything's all right. We are restored to the Covenant. You see, there isn't any difference any more.
Everybody is a member of the Families now."

"What do you mean?" King demanded.

"They've got it."

"Got what?"

"Got the secret of longevity."

"Huh? Talk sense. There isn't any secret. There never
was any secret."

"*We* didn't have any secret—but they thought we had.
So they found it."

"Explain yourself," insisted Captain King.

"Captain, can't this wait until we get back into the
ship?" Ralph Schultz protested. "I'm no biologist. We've
brought along a government representative—you can
quiz him, instead."

6

King received Terra's representative in his cabin. He
had notified Zaccur Barstow and Justin Foote to be
present for the Families and had invited Doctor Gordon Hardy because the nature of the startling news
was the biologist's business. Libby was there as the
ship's chief officer; Slayton Ford was invited because
of his unique status, although he had held no public
office in the Families since his breakdown in the
temple of Kreel.

Lazarus was there because Lazarus wanted to be
there, in own strictly private capacity. He had not been
invited, but even Captain King was somewhat diffident

about interfering with the assumed prerogatives of the eldest Member.

Ralph Schultz introduced Earth's ambassador to the assembled company. "This is Captain King, our commanding officer—and this is Miles Rodney, representing the Federation Council—minister plenipotentiary and ambassador extraordinary, I guess you would call him."

"Hardly that," said Rodney, "although I can agree to the 'extraordinary' part. This situation is quite without precedent. It is an honor to know you, Captain."

"Glad to have you inboard, sir."

"And this is Zaccur Barstow, representing the trustees of the Howard Families, and Justin Foote, secretary to the trustees—"

"Service."

"Service to you, gentlemen."

"—Andrew Jackson Libby, chief astrogational officer, Doctor Gordon Hardy, biologist in charge of our research into the causes of old age and death."

"Service to you, sir. So you are the chief biologist— there was a time when you could have done a service to the whole human race. Think of it, sir—think how different things could have been. But, happily, the human race was able to worry out the secret of extending life without the aid of the Howard Families."

Hardy looked vexed. "What do you mean, sir? Do you mean to say that you are still laboring under the delusion that we had some miraculous secret to impart, if we chose?"

Rodney shrugged and spread his hands. "Really, now, there is no need to keep up the pretense, is there? Your results have been duplicated, independently."

Captain King cut in. "Just a moment—Ralph Schultz, is the Federation still under the impression that there is some 'secret' to our long lives? Didn't you tell them?"

Schultz was looking bewildered. "Uh—this is ridiculous. The subject hardly came up. They themselves had achieved controlled longevity; they were no longer interested in us in that respect. It is true that there still existed a belief that our long lives derived from manipulation rather than from heredity, but I corrected that impression."

"Apparently not very thoroughly, from what Miles Rodney had just said."

"Apparently not. I did not spend much effort on it; it was beating a dead dog. The Howard Families and their long lives are no longer an issue on Earth. Interest, both public and official, is centered on the fact that we have accomplished a successful interstellar jump."

"I can confirm that," agreed Miles Rodney. "Every official, every news service, every citizen, every scientist in the system is waiting with utmost eagerness the arrival of the *New Frontiers*. It's the greatest, most sensational thing that has happened since the first trip to the Moon. You are famous, gentlemen—all of you."

Lazarus pulled Zaccur Barstow aside and whispered to him. Barstow looked perturbed, then nodded thoughtfully. "Captain—" Barstow said to King.

"Yes, Zack?"

"I suggest that we ask our guest to excuse us while we receive Ralph Schultz's report."

"Why?"

Barstow glanced at Rodney. "I think we will be better prepared to discuss matters if we are briefed by our own representative."

King turned to Rodney. "Will you excuse us, sir?"

Lazarus broke in. "Never mind, Skipper. Zack means well but he's too polite. Might as well let Comrade Rodney stick around and we'll lay it on the line. Tell me this, Miles; what proof have you got that you and your pals have figured out a way to live as long as we do?"

"Proof?" Rodney seemed dumbfounded. "Why do you ask—Whom am I addressing? Who are you sir?"

Ralph Schultz intervened. "Sorry—I didn't get a chance to finish the introductions. Miles Rodney, this is Lazarus Long, the Senior."

"Service. 'The Senior' what?"

"He just means 'the Senior,' period," answered Lazarus. "I'm the oldest Member. Otherwise I'm a private citizen."

"The oldest one of the Howard Families! Why—why, you must be the oldest man alive—think of that!"

"You think about it," retorted Lazarus. "I quit worrying about it a couple o' centuries ago. How about answering my question?"

"But I can't help being impressed. You make me feel like an infant—and I'm not a young man myself; I'll be a hundred and five this coming June."

"If you can prove that's your age, you can answer my question. I'd say you were about forty. How about it?"

"Well, dear me, I hardly expected to be interrogated on this point. Do you wish to see my identity card?"

"Are you kidding? I've had fifty-odd identity cards in my time, all with phony birth dates. What else can you offer?"

"Just a minute, Lazarus," put in Captain King. "What is the purpose of your question?"

Lazarus Long turned away from Rodney. "It's like this, Skipper—we hightailed it out of the Solar System to save our necks, because the rest of the yokels thought we had invented some way to live forever and proposed to squeeze it out of if they had to kill every one of us. Now everything is sweetness and light—so they say. But it seems mighty funny that the bird they send up to smoke the pipe of peace with us should still be convinced that we have that so-called secret.

"It got me to wondering.

"Suppose they hadn't figured out a way to keep from dying from old age but were still clinging to the idea that we had? What better way to keep us calmed down and unsuspicious than to tell us they had until they could get us where they wanted us in order to put the question to us again?"

Rodney snorted. "A preposterous idea! Captain, I don't think I'm called on to put up with this."

Lazarus stared coldly. "It was preposterous the first time, bub—but it happened. The burnt child is likely to be skittish."

"Just a moment, both of you," ordered King. "Ralph, how about it? Could you have been taken in by a put-up job?"

Schultz thought about it, painfully. "I don't think so." He paused. "It's rather difficult to say. I couldn't tell from appearance of course, any more than our own Members could be picked out from a crowd of normal persons."

"But you are a psychologist. Surely you could have detected indications of fraud, if there had been one."

"I may be a psychologist, but I'm not a miracle man and I'm not telepathic. I wasn't looking for fraud." He grinned sheepishly. "There was another factor. I was so excited over being home that I was not in the best emotional condition to note discrepancies, if there were any."

"Then you aren't sure?"

"No. I am emotionally convinced that Miles Rodney is telling the truth—"

"I am!"

"—and I believe that a few questions could clear the matter up. He claims to be one hundred and five years old. We can test that."

"I see," agreed King. "Hmm . . . you put the questions, Ralph?"

"Very well. You will permit, Miles Rodney?"

"Go ahead," Rodney answered stiffly.

"You must have been about thirty years old when we left Earth, since we have been gone nearly seventy-five years, Earth time. Do you remember the event?"

"Quite clearly. I was a clerk in Novak Tower at the time, in the offices of the Administrator."

Slayton Ford had remained in the background throughout the discussion, and had done nothing to call attention to himself. At Rodney's answer he sat up. "Just a moment, Captain—"

"Eh? Yes?"

"Perhaps I can cut this short. You'll pardon me, Ralph?" He turned to Terra's representative. "Who am I?"

Rodney looked at him in some puzzlement. His expression changed from one of simple surprise at the odd question to complete and unbelieving bewilderment. "Why, you . . . *you* are *Administrator Ford!*"

7

"One at a time! One at a time," Captain King was saying. "Don't everybody try to talk at once. Go on, Slayton; you have the floor. You know this man?"

Ford looked Rodney over. "No, I can't say that I do."

"Then it *is* a frame up." King turned to Rodney. "I suppose you recognized Ford from historical stereos— is that right?"

Rodney seemed about to burst. "No! I recognized him. He's changed but I knew him. Mr. Administrator—look at me, please! Don't you know me? I *worked* for you!"

"It seems fairly obvious that he doesn't," King said dryly.

Ford shook his head. "It doesn't prove anything, one way or the other, Captain. There were over two thousand civil service employees in my office. Rodney might have been one of them. His face looks vaguely familiar, but so do most faces."

"Captain—" Master Gordon Hardy was speaking. "If I can question Miles Rodney I might be able to give an opinion as to whether or not they actually have discovered anything new about the causes of old age and death."

Rodney shook his head. "I am not a biologist. You could trip me up in no time. Captain King, I ask you to arrange my return to Earth as quickly as possible. I'll not be subjected to any more of this. And let me add that I do not care a minim whether you and your—your pretty crew ever get back to civilization or not. I came here to help you, but I'm disgusted." He stood up.

Slayton Ford went toward him. "Easy, Miles Rodney, please! Be patient. Put yourself in their place. You would be just as cautious if you had been through what they have been through."

Rodney hesitated. "Mr. Administrator, what are *you* doing here?"

"It's a long and complicated story. I'll tell you later."

"You are a member of the Howard Families—you must be. That accounts for a lot of odd things."

Ford shook his head. "No, Miles Rodney, I am not. Later, please—I'll explain it. You worked for me once—when?"

"From 2109 until you, uh, disappeared."

"What was your job?"

"At the time of the crisis in 2113 I was an assistant correlation clerk in the division of Economic Statistics, Control Section."

"Who was your section chief?"

"Leslie Waldron."

"Old Waldron, eh? What was the color of his hair?"

"His hair? The Walrus was bald as an egg."

Lazarus whispered to Zaccur Barstow, "Looks like I was off base, Zack."

"Wait a moment," Barstow whispered back. "It still could be thorough preparation—they may have known that Ford escaped with us."

Ford was continuing. "What was *The Sacred Cow*?"

"*The Sacred*— Chief, you weren't even supposed to know that there was such a publication!"

"Give my intelligence staff credit for some activity, at least," Ford said dryly. "I got my copy every week."

"But what was it?" demanded Lazarus.

Rodney answered, "An office comic and gossip sheet that was passed from hand to hand."

"Devoted to ribbing the bosses," Ford added, "especially me." He put an arm around Rodney's shoulders. "Friends, there is no doubt about it. Miles and I were fellow workers."

"I still want to find out about the new rejuvenation process," insisted Master Hardy some time later.

"I think we all do," agreed King. He reached out and refilled their guest's wine glass. "Will you tell us about it, sir?"

"I'll try," Miles Rodney answered, "though I must ask Master Hardy to bear with me. It's not one process, but several—one basic process and several dozen others, some of them purely cosmetic, especially for women. Nor is the basic process truly a rejuvenation process. You can arrest the progress of old age, but you can't reverse it to any significant degree—you can't turn a senile old man into a boy."

"Yes, yes," agreed Hardy. "Naturally—but what is the basic process?"

"It consists largely in replacing the entire blood tissue in an old person with new, young blood. Old age, so they tell me, is primarily a matter of the progressive accumulation of the waste poisons of metabolism. The blood is supposed to carry them away, but presently the blood gets so clogged with the poisons that the scavenging process doesn't take place properly. Is that right, Doctor Hardy?"

"That's an odd way of putting it, but—"

"I told you I was no biotechnician."

"—essentially correct. It's a matter of diffusion pressure deficit—the d.p.d. on the blood side of a cell wall must be such as to maintain a fairly sharp gradient or there will occur progressive autointoxication of the individual cells. But I must say that I feel somewhat disappointed, Miles Rodney. The basic idea

of holding off death by insuring proper scavenging of
waste products is not new—I have a bit of chicken
heart which has been alive for two and one half
centuries through equivalent techniques. As to the use
of young blood—yes, that will work. I've kept experimental animals alive by such blood donations to about
twice their normal span." He stopped and looked
troubled.

"Yes, Doctor Hardy?"

Hardy chewed his lip. "I gave up that line of research.
I found it necessary to have several young donors in
order to keep one beneficiary from growing any older.
There was a small, but measurable, unfavorable effect
on each of the donors. Racially it was self-defeating;
there would never be enough donors to go around. Am
I to understand, sir that this method is thereby limited
to a small, select part of the population?"

"Oh, no! I did not make myself clear, Master Hardy.
There are no donors."

"Huh?"

"New blood, enough for everybody, grown outside the
body—the Public Health and Longevity Service can provide any amount of it, any type."

Hardy looked startled. "To think we came so close . . .
so that's it." He paused, then went on. "We tried tissue
culture of bone marrow *in vitro*. We should have persisted."

"Don't feel badly about it. Billions of credits and tens
of thousands of technicians engaged in this project
before there were any significant results. I'm told that
the mass of accumulated art in this field represents more
effort than even the techniques of atomic engineering."
Rodney smiled. "You see, they *had* to get some results;
it was politically necessary—so there was an all-out
effort." Rodney turned to Ford. "When the news about
the escape of the Howard Families reached the public, Chief, your precious successor had to be protected
from the mobs."

Hardy persisted with questions about subsidiary techniques—tooth budding, growth inhibiting, hormone therapy, many others—until King came to Rodney's rescue by pointing out that the prime purpose of the visit was to arrange details of the return of the Families to Earth.

Rodney nodded. "I think we should get down to business. As I understand it, Captain, a large proportion of your people are now in reduced-temperature somnolence?"

("Why can't he say 'cold-rest'?" Lazarus said to Libby.)

"Yes, that is so."

"Then it would be no hardship on them to remain in that state for a time."

"Eh? Why do you say that, sir?"

Rodney spread his hands. "The administration finds itself in a somewhat embarrassing position. To put it bluntly, there is a housing shortage. Absorbing one hundred and ten thousand displaced persons can't be done overnight."

Again King had to hush them. He then nodded to Zaccur Barstow, who addressed himself to Rodney. "I fail to see the problem, sir. What is the present population of the North American continent?"

"Around seven hundred million."

"And you can't find room to tuck away one-seventieth of one per cent of that number? It sounds preposterous."

"You don't understand, sir," Rodney protested. "Population pressure has become our major problem. Coincident with it, the right to remain undisturbed in the enjoyment of one's own homestead, or one's apartment, has become the most jealously guarded of all civil rights. Before we can find you adequate living room we must make over some stretch of desert, or make other major arrangements."

"I get it," said Lazarus. "Politics. You don't dast disturb anybody for fear they will squawk."

"That's hardly an adequate statement of the case."

"It's not, eh? Could be you've got a general election coming up, maybe?"

"As a matter of fact we have, but that has nothing to do with the case."

Lazarus snorted.

Justin Foote spoke up. "It seems to me that the administration has looked at this problem in the most superficial light. It is not as if we were homeless immigrants. Most of the Members own their own homes. As you doubtless know, the Families are well-to-do, even wealthy, and for obvious reasons we built our homes to endure. I feel sure that most of these structures are still standing."

"No doubt," Rodney conceded, "but you will find them occupied."

Justin Foote shrugged. "What has that to do with us? That is a problem for the government to settle with the persons it has allowed illegally to occupy our homes. As for myself, I shall land as soon as possible, obtain an eviction order from the nearest court, and repossess my home."

"It's not that easy. You can make omelet from eggs, but not eggs from omelet. You have been legally dead for many years; the present occupant of your house holds a good title."

Justin Foote stood up and glared at the Federation's envoy, looking, as Lazarus thought, "like a cornered mouse." "Legally dead! By whose act, sir, by whose act? Mine? I was a respected solicitor, quietly and honorably pursuing my profession, harming no one, when I was arrested without cause and forced to flee for my life. Now I am blandly told that my property is confiscated and my very legal existence as a person and as a citizen has been taken from me because of that sequence of events. What manner of justice is this? Does the Covenant still stand?"

"You misunderstand me. I—"

"I misunderstood nothing. If justice is measured out only when it is convenient, the Covenant is not worth the parchment it is written on. I shall make of myself a test case, sir, a test case for every Member of the Families. Unless my property is returned to me in full and at once I shall bring personal suit against every obstructing official. I will make of it a *cause célèbre*. For many years I have suffered inconvenience and indignity and peril; I shall not be put off with words. I will shout it from the housetops." He paused for breath.

"He's right, Miles," Slayton Ford put in quietly. "The government had better find some adequate way to handle this—and quickly."

Lazarus caught Libby's eye and silently motioned toward the door. The two slipped outside. "Justin'll keep 'em busy for the next hour," he said. "Let's slide down to the Club and grab some calories."

"Do you really think we ought to leave?"

"Relax. If the skipper wants us, he can holler."

8

Lazarus tucked away three sandwiches, a double order of ice cream, and some cookies while Libby contented himself with somewhat less. Lazarus would have eaten more but he was forced to respond to a barrage of questions from the other habitués of the Club.

"The commissary department ain't really back on its feet," he complained, as he poured his third cup of coffee. "The Little People made life too easy for them. Andy, do you like chili con carne?"

"It's all right."

Lazarus wiped his mouth. "There used to be a restaurant in Tijuana that served the best chili I ever tasted. I wonder if it's still there?"

"Where's Tijuana?" demanded Margaret Weatheral.

"You don't remember Earth, do you, Peggy? Well, darling, it's in Lower California. You know where that is?"

"Don't you think I studied geography? It's in Los Angeles."

"Near enough. Maybe you're right—by now." The ship's announcing system blared out:

"Chief Astrogator—report to the Captain in the Control Room!"

"That's me!" said Libby, and hurriedly got up.

The call was repeated, then was followed by, "All hands—prepare for acceleration! All hands—prepare for acceleration!"

"Here we go again, kids." Lazarus stood up, brushed off his kilt, and followed Libby, whistling as he went:

> *"California, here I come,*
> *Right back where I started from—"*

The ship was underway, the stars had faded out. Captain King had left the control room, taking with him his guest, the Earth's envoy. Miles Rodney had been much impressed; it seemed likely that he would need a drink.

Lazarus and Libby remained in the control room. There was nothing to do; for approximately four hours, ship's time the ship would remain in para-space, before returning to normal space near Earth.

Lazarus struck a cigarette. "What d'you plan to do when you get back, Andy?"

"Hadn't thought about it."

"Better start thinking. Been some changes."

"I'll probably head back home for a while. I can't imagine the Ozarks having changed very much."

"The hills will look the same, I imagine. You may find the people changed."

"How?"

"You remember I told you that I had gotten fed up with the Families and had kinda lost touch with them for a century? By and large, they had gotten so smug and sot in their ways that I couldn't stand them. I'm afraid we'll find most everybody that way, now that they expect to live forever. Long term investments, be sure to wear your rubbers when it rains . . . that sort of thing."

"It didn't affect you that way."

"My approach is different. I never did have any real reason to last forever—after all as Gordon Hardy has pointed out, I'm only a third generation result of the Howard plan. I just did my living as I went along and didn't worry my head about it. But that's not the usual attitude. Take Miles Rodney—scared to death to tackle a new situation with both hands for fear of upsetting precedent and stepping on established privileges."

"I was glad to see Justin stand up to him." Libby chuckled. "I didn't think Justin had it in him."

"Ever see a little dog tell a big dog to get the hell out of the little dog's yard?"

"Do you think Justin will win his point?"

"Sure he will, with your help."

"Mine?"

"Who knows anything about the para-drive, aside from what you've taught me?"

"I've dictated full notes into the records."

"But you haven't turned those records over to Miles Rodney. Earth needs your starship drive, Andy. You heard what Rodney said about population pressure. Ralph was telling me you have to get a government permit now before you can have a baby."

"The hell you say!"

"Fact. You can count on it that there would be tremendous emigration if there were just some decent planets to emigrate to. And that's where your drive comes in. With it, spreading out to the stars becomes really practical. They'll have to dicker."

"It's not really my drive, of course. The Little People worked it out."

"Don't be so modest. You've got it. And you want to back up Justin, don't you?"

"Oh, sure."

"Then we'll use it to bargain with. Maybe I'll do the bargaining, personally. But that's beside the point. Somebody is going to have to do a little exploring before any large-scale emigration starts. Let's go into the real estate business, Andy. We'll stake out this corner of the Galaxy and see what it has to offer."

Libby scratched his nose and thought about it. "Sounds all right, I guess—after I pay a visit home."

"There's no rush. I'll find a nice clean little yacht, about ten thousand tons and we'll refit with your drive."

"What'll we use for money?"

"We'll have money. I'll set up a parent corporation, while I'm about it, with a loose enough charter to let us do anything we want to do. There will be daughter corporations for various purposes and we'll unload the minor interest in each. Then—"

"You make it sound like work, Lazarus. I thought it was going to be fun."

"Shucks, we won't fuss with all that stuff. I'll collar somebody to run the home office and worry about the books and the legal end—somebody about like Justin. Maybe Justin himself."

"Well, all right then."

"You and I will rampage around and see what there is to be seen. It'll be fun, all right."

They were both silent for a long time, with no need to talk. Presently Lazarus said, "Andy—"

"Yeah?"

"Are you going to look into this new-blood-for-old caper?"

"I suppose so, eventually."

"I've been thinking about it. Between ourselves, I'm not as fast with my fists as I was a century back. Maybe my natural span is wearing out. I do know this: I didn't start planning our real estate venture till I heard about this new process. It gave me a new perspective. I find myself thinking about thousands of years—and I never used to worry about anything further ahead than a week from next Wednesday."

Libby chuckled again. "Looks like you're growing up."

"Some would say it was about time. Seriously, Andy, I think that's just what I have been doing. The last two and a half centuries have just been my adolescence, so to speak. Long as I've hung around, I don't know any more about the final answers, the *important* answers, than Peggy Weatheral does. Men—*our* kind of men—Earth men—never have had enough time to tackle the important questions. Lots of capacity and not time enough to use it properly. When it came to the important questions we might as well have still been monkeys."

"How do you propose to tackle the important questions?"

"How should I know? Ask me again in about five hundred years."

"You think that will make a difference?"

"I do. Anyhow it'll give me time to poke around and pick up some interesting facts. Take those Jockaira gods—"

"They weren't gods, Lazarus. You shouldn't call them that."

"Of course they weren't—I think. My guess is that they are creatures who have had time enough to do a little hard thinking. Someday, about a thousand years from now, I intend to march straight into the temple of Kreel, look him in the eye, and say, 'Howdy, bub—what do *you* know that *I* don't know?'"

"It might not be healthy."

"We'll have a showdown, anyway, I've never been satisfied with the outcome there. There ought not to be anything in the whole universe that man can't poke his nose into—that's the way we're built and I assume that there's some reason for it."

"Maybe there aren't any reasons."

"Yes, maybe it's just one colossal big joke, with no point to it." Lazarus stood up and stretched and scratched his ribs. "But I can tell you this, Andy, whatever the answers are, here's one monkey that's going to keep on climbing, and looking around him to see what he can see, as long as the tree holds out."

DAVID WEBER

continued ☞

DAVID WEBER

MORE PRAISE FOR
LOIS MCMASTER BUJOLD

What the readers say:

"My copy of *Shards of Honor* is falling apart I've reread it so often.... I'll read whatever you write. You've certainly proved yourself a grand storyteller."
—Liesl Kolbe, Colorado Springs, CO

"I experience the stories of Miles Vorkosigan as almost viscerally uplifting.... But certainly, even the weightiest theme would have less impact than a cinder on snow were it not for a rousing good story, and good storytelling with it. This is the second thing I want to thank you for.... I suppose if you boiled down all I've said to its simplest expression, it would be that I immensely enjoy and admire your work. I submit that, as literature, your work raises the overall level of the science fiction genre, and spiritually, your work cannot avoid positively influencing all who read it."
—Glen Stonebraker, Gaithersburg, MD

" 'The Mountains of Mourning' [in *Borders of Infinity*] was one of the best-crafted, and simply best, works I'd ever read. When I finished it, I immediately turned back to the beginning and read it again, and I can't remember the last time I did that."   —Betsy Bizot, Lisle, IL

"I can only hope that you will continue to write, so that I can continue to read (and of course buy) your books, for they make me laugh and cry and think ... rare indeed."   —Steven Knott, Major, USAF

What Do You Say?

Send me these books!

Shards of Honor	72087-2 ◆ $5.99	☐
Barrayar	72083-X ◆ $5.99	☐
Cordelia's Honor (trade)	87749-6 ◆ $15.00	☐
The Warrior's Apprentice	72066-X ◆ $5.99	☐
The Vor Game	72014-7 ◆ $5.99	☐
Young Miles (trade)	87782-8 ◆ $15.00	☐
Cetaganda (hardcover)	87701-1 ◆ $21.00	☐
Cetaganda (paperback)	87744-5 ◆ $5.99	☐
Ethan of Athos	65604-X ◆ $5.99	☐
Borders of Infinity	72093-7 ◆ $5.99	☐
Brothers in Arms	69799-4 ◆ $5.99	☐
Mirror Dance (paperback)	87646-5 ◆ $6.99	☐
Memory (paperback)	87845-X ◆ $6.99	☐
The Spirit Ring (paperback)	72188-7 ◆ $5.99	☐

 # LOIS MCMASTER BUJOLD
Only from Baen Books

If not available at your local bookstore, fill out this coupon and send a check or money order for the cover price(s) plus $1.50 s/h to Baen Books, Dept. BA, P.O. Box 1403, Riverdale, NY 10471. Delivery can take up to ten weeks.

NAME:

ADDRESS:

I have enclosed a check or money order in the amount of $